from
Diane
Christmas, '79

MYSELF AS WITNESS

By James Goldman

Fiction
Waldorf
The Man from Greek and Roman
Myself as Witness

Plays
Blood, Sweat, and Stanley Poole
(with William Goldman)
The Lion in Winter
They Might Be Giants

Musicals
A Family Affair
(with John Kander and William Goldman)
Follies
(with Stephen Sondheim)
Evening Primrose
(with Stephen Sondheim)

Screenplays
The Lion in Winter
They Might Be Giants
Nicholas and Alexandra
Robin and Marian

James Goldman

MYSELF
AS
WITNESS

Random House New York

The historical material on which this novel is based is drawn from many sources, and the author wishes to express his particular indebtedness and gratitude to the works of Amy Kelly, W. L. Warren, A. L. Poole, Sir Maurice Powicke, Alan Lloyd, Kate Norgate, Urban Tigner Holmes, Jr., John Appleby, S. Painter, Joseph and Frances Gies, and the countless contributors to the *Dictionary of National Biography*.

Grateful acknowledgment is made to the following for permission to reprint previously published material:

Doubleday & Company, Inc.: Excerpt from *The Maligned Monarch* by Alan Lloyd. Copyright © 1972 by Alan Lloyd. Used by permission of Doubleday & Company, Inc.

Alfred A. Knopf, Inc.: Excerpts from *John, King of England* by John T. Appleby. Copyright © 1958 by John T. Appleby. Reprinted by permission of Alfred A. Knopf, Inc.

Excerpts from *King John* by W. L. Warren. Used by permission of the Public Record Office, London.

Library of Congress Cataloging in Publication Data
Goldman, James.
Myself as witness.
1. John, King of England, 1167?-1216—Fiction.
I. Title.
PZ4.G634My [PS3513.0337] 813'.5'4 78-57121
ISBN 0-394-41923-5

Manufactured in the United States of America

2 4 6 8 9 7 5 3

First Edition

A Note to the Reader

King John, the youngest son of Henry II and Eleanor of Aquitaine, ruled England from 1199 to 1216. His reputation as one of the most sinister, corrupt and vicious kings in Western history has been, for centuries, both a popular belief and an academic tradition.

I have written about King John before; he makes appearances in both *The Lion in Winter* and *Robin and Marian*. Following the mainstream, I conceived him as a violent, unstable person with no principles at all. Not so this time around. Several years ago, this completely villainous King John began to seem increasingly improbable to me. He was too black, too terrible. And so I went back to the history books, and the more I read the more it seemed apparent that tradition had it wrong: a very different John must have existed. What had begun as an emotional conviction gradually seemed to be substantiated by the facts.

What are the facts? Remarkably little survives that was written while John was alive, and the picture of him that emerges from these scattered sources is suprisingly complimentary. The evil monarch we have come to know begins to appear in chronicles written a generation or more after his death. On top of which, the writing of history was a curious procedure in those days, and the chroniclers on whom we have relied give us reports of devils and dragons with the same conviction and seriousness that they accord verifiable political events.

Why these chroniclers made John into a monster is an unanswerable question. Possibly because England had had enough of Henry and his children, possibly because John's reign saw more defeats than victories, possibly in response to political pressures of the moment.

In any case, over the last twenty years a number of historians have begun to make a new assessment of King John. My story rests on their revisionary work. I have put it into the form of a chronicle which I have based, as strictly as I could, on fact. If it is known that John was, on a given day, in Dover, I have put him there. The writs and official letters are, with one exception, quoted from existing documents. The political maneuvering, the battles and campaigns are all drawn from data. There is, I think, no other way to reassess a figure out of history: one must base it on the evidence.

There are, of course, limits to this. Unlike the historian whose interest centers on the facts, my interest centers on the people: who they were and what they felt and why they did the things they did. In short, what I have written, though it deals carefully with history, remains a piece of fiction.

I have put my chronicle into the hands of Giraldus Cambrensis, as distinguished an author as there was in England at this time. He knew John and his family intimately, he was much involved with the Plantagenets. But in the years the novel covers, he was not among those present. He was living in retirement at Lincoln, studying and writing in the quiet of the cloisters there. Even so, I like to think that I have used his eyes and ears, and that what I have written here is what he might have told us.

—J.G.

To Bobby, with my love

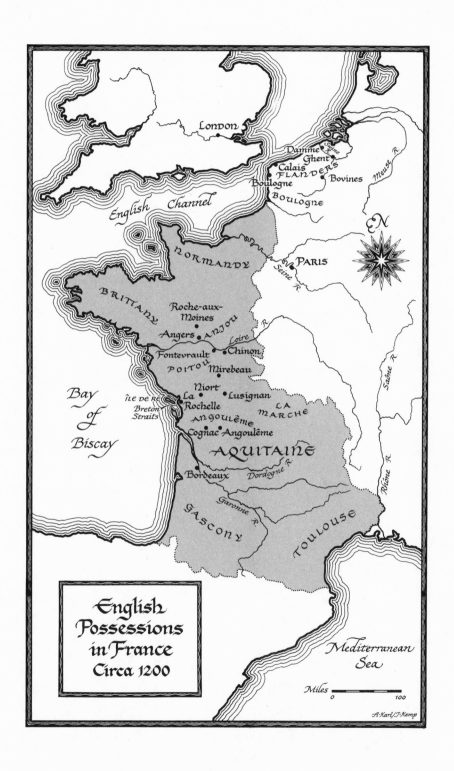

London

Damme
Ghent
Calais
FLANDERS
Boulogne   Bovines
BOULOGNE

English Channel

PARIS

EN

NORMANDY

Seine R.

BRITTANY

Roche-aux-
Moines

Angers • ANJOU

Loire

Fontevrault • Chinon
POITOU
Mirebeau

Niort
La • • Lusignan
Rochelle
ÎLE DE RÉ
Breton
Straits   ANGOULÊME   LA
Cognac • Angoulême   MARCHE

Bay
of
Biscay

AQUITAINE

• Bordeaux   Dordogne R.

Garonne R.

GASCONY   TOULOUSE

Saône R.

Rhône R.

Mediterranean
Sea

English
Possessions
in France
Circa 1200

Miles
0   100

A·Karl/J·Kemp

MYSELF AS WITNESS

At Lincoln
The 11th Day of April, A.D. 1212

It is impossible to think.

The hammering and clatter from the yard is terrible. And in my chambers, they are packing me.

We've had two weeks of rain, the roads to Corfe are fit for frogs. I do not choose to go. My place is here. Someone is screaming in the yard; undoubtedly, we've lost another mason. They are putting up a new west face to our cathedral. Pride and wastefulness. The old face kept the weather out.

I must attempt to be more orderly.

This morning, I was called from prayer. That's never lightly done. I knew at once that something must be very wrong. A clerk, a man of no particular importance; he was waiting in the cloister with, he said, a message from the King.

I have the text in front of me. It reads:

"THE KING to Giraldus Cambrensis: Whatever greeting is due you. We order you to join us here at once. MYSELF AS WITNESS, at Corfe on the 2nd day of April in the 14th year of our reign."

Peremptory. Arrogant. No trace of courtesy. Why am I being summoned? For how long? What clothes am I to take? And does he think that I do nothing here? Across the table from me at this moment are the notes for my *Principia Universalis*. Nothing on this scale has been attempted since Lucretius, who is all right in his way but sadly out of date.

I've never been much loved by these Plantagenets. Perhaps because I write the truth. And truth, as Esdras tells us—I, 3:10— "beareth away the victory." Which is more than it has ever done for me. We did not part on happy terms, King John and I.

They have just come to tell me I am packed. We leave at Lauds, well before the sun is up; this clerk, myself and, of my servants, only Jean, my cook. The King sets an uncertain table; either prodigal or desolate, depending on his mood. I see no reason why, no

[3]

matter what my future holds, I should not go on dining to the end with some consistency.

I must go and bid farewell to Hugh. He's not as great a bishop as I might have been; but never mind all that. He is an honest man and I shall miss him.

Till next time, if God wills it.

G.

At Buckingham
The 14th Day of April, A.D. 1212

How strange it seems, this being on the roads again. We pass through towns I have not seen in years, past churches shuttered by the Interdict. So much has changed. Or has it? Is it me? Tomorrow, Oxford. Will it be as I remember?

I was forty-six years younger when I saw it for the first time. I had been in Paris studying the Trivium; to some acclaim, it must be said. 1167. It was then that Becket and King Henry were at one another's throats and all of us in residence, the masters and the students, were recalled to England.

Oxford in those days was nothing much. One hundred students, possibly, attending lectures on theology delivered by the current deacon or the prior, nameless men of small distinction. Then we came, the refugees from Paris. That was the beginning.

It took time, of course, and labor, none of which was mine. In any case, four years ago, when last I saw it, Oxford was a university of fifteen hundred students with a faculty of scholars led by Map himself. He's gone now, Map is, dead of age at sixty-nine. They buried him with honors. I was there.

Till next time, if God wills it.

At Oxford
The 16th Day of April, A.D. 1212

The university is desolate. The buildings, like so many bones, still stand about, but all the life is gone. It is a shocking thing to see.

We arrived in time for Vespers yesterday. The sun was shining for a change as we came down the High Road from the north, past Beaumont Castle and Saint Frideswide's. Carts and wagons everywhere. The town itself is thriving. The demand for cloth, I'm told, keeps rising; there are weavers opening up on all sides and the marketplace was thick with people.

We survived the crowd, went left on Catte Street, making for Saint Mary's, which has always been the center of the university. I felt the change at once. No students, drunk or sober, silence from the taverns. The bookbinder's shop was closed, and further on, both parchment-makers, too.

Saint Mary's rose ahead of us. A cart went by; then no other sound except our horses walking slowly, crunching on the gravel. On we went, into the church yard. There were people here, a few; some stableboys and several minor clerics, none of whom I recognized. They knew my name if not my face, and after Vespers, as we ate, they told me all.

It started with the murder of the girl. Three years ago, come autumn. She was from the town and made her living in the kitchen of a nearby tavern. Townsfolk never seem to understand the student's need for drink. In fact, they do not seem to understand the need for students altogether. There is constant friction, and though no one saw the murder, they decided to accuse a clerk, a student at the university.

The fellow fled. In rage, the people of the town descended on Saint Mary's and went off with several students. These they held for weeks, and having asked for and received the King's consent, hanged two of them.

There was a quick diaspora. The masters and the students, reading what was written on the wall, dispersed. Some went to Paris, some to Reading, and a large group went to Cambridge, where, it seems, they hope to form another university.

It was late when they had finished and they took me to Map's chambers for the night. I've had no rest. The first bells of the morning should be ringing soon. John prowls, he keeps on prowling through my thoughts. He loves books and destroys a university; he studies law and lets two students hang. He's made of parts that will not fit, like all his family. Damn these Plantagenets. They plague me, I've had forty years of it. King Henry and Queen Eleanor and all their sons, alive and dead: I've served them, every one.

God knows what thing it is John wants me for. Am I to be his envoy to the Pope? I'd make a useful one but I will not be used, not any more. I'm sixty-six and forty is a ripe age. No, my lord, I will not have you use me.

Matins. Time to go. With luck, we'll spend the night in Abingdon.

Till next time, if God wills it.

G.

At Swanage
The 20th Day of April, A.D. 1212

Corfe tomorrow.

Everything is foul. The inn, the weather. Dinner was abominable. There is no brandywine. My horse is lame. That's perfect: I go limping to my fate.

I try to tell myself there may be splendid things in store. Perhaps I'm to be elevated to the See of York. Or possibly Prince Henry, who is five or thereabout, may need a tutor. Or the Queen, for all I know; she's young enough. Or, best of all, the King has changed his mind and has no use for me.

All vain, it's all in vain. No good has ever come to me from John. How brave am I? Not very. I would give five pennies for a butt of wine. No; ten. It's cold. The damp is liquid on the walls.

Till next time, if God wills it.

At Corfe

The 21st Day of April, A.D. 1212

They have given me a room. Which, in itself, is interesting. In fact, the whole day has been filled with implications.

They are all I have to work with. John is elsewhere. Glastonbury, possibly. Nobody here seems sure. Nor are they sure of his return. This week or next. So I must wait. The time thus far has not been wasted; I've been busy peeping, peering, sniffing, nosing out my situation.

We arrived well after lunch. The way from Swanage was horrendous, up and down hill from the coast, mudslides and gullies. To my eye, the Purbeck Hills have always seemed uniquely desolate; wild, bleak and, most of all, depressing.

Corfe fits perfectly into the scene. Of all the castles in the realm, it is John's favorite. It sits—or, more precisely, seems to slump— upon a hillcrest overlooking nothing. Why it should be here at all is mystifying. There is nothing to protect or guard against; no town, no route to anywhere, no river thick with trade. In fact, the only military action in the area occurred some centuries ago at Swanage where King Alfred won a victory, against whom no one seems to know.

The castle loomed above us as we waded up the final hill. We reached the gate. The officer in charge stood forth. I gave my name. He nodded—or was it a bow? A good sign if it was—and led the way across the bailey.

In the yard, life looked no drearier than usual, the masons chipping at the marble and the peasants buying, selling. There was little in the stalls; root vegetables and eggs and chickens and a sheep or two.

We went directly to the Great Hall, up the steps and in, where I was greeted by the Seneschal himself. Another sign? He told me of the King, inquired of my health, my journey, offered food which I declined and drink which I did not, and took me up the stairway to my room.

My room: it has a bed, a stool, a chest, two pegs for clothes, a window and a door that bolts from my side. Not unusual. What gives the room its implications is the having of it. There are few private rooms at Corfe. I have seen earls and barons bedded in the Great Hall on the rushes with the dogs.

The wine arrived, the Seneschal departed and I slipped off to the chapel. I was weary but I felt like praying, and besides, it was a chance to look about.

The chapel here is on the third and highest level of the keep. Small, very plain—austere, in fact—and little used, it is the only thing in Corfe I like. The stairway up is narrow and the light is poor and she was several steps above me when I saw her.

She is ravishing. Pellucid, flaxen, delicate; I cannot put her into words. If I could paint, I'd do her in the margin. For a moment, I felt twenty-three, in Paris with Adèle again. I nearly spoke her name. I stood their blinking in the dimness. Then I bowed and managed a "Your Majesty."

I'm not alone in never having met the Queen. She is much talked about, of course, but little known. Her marriage, the attendant shock and scandal; she was always with the King and, consequently, much in public then. But that was years ago and Isabelle is over twenty now.

She nodded at my greeting as she started down. Which, in view of the dimensions of the stairwell, put me in a difficult position. It is not an easy thing to keep one's dignity while walking downstairs backwards.

Dinner was a strange affair; the Queen alone upon the dais in the Great Hall and the Seneschal and I together at the dormant table. There were knights and officers-in-residence down at the lesser end, as usual. I tried not staring at the Queen, with mixed success. I wonder what her voice is like.

In any case, there being no one of importance, save myself, for talking to, I made do with the Seneschal. The man is either singularly uninformed or secretive or stupid. I suspect the last. I left the table knowing far too much about the problems of his stewardship: collecting rents and keeping poachers off the pastureland. But not one fact of use to me.

So here I sit, door bolted, paper on my lap. The lamp flame guts and sputters in the wind, my eyes are watering. There is no point in closing them: I am too tired to sleep. How late it is I cannot guess. The keep is full of night sounds; creaks and timbers groaning, sudden barking from the dogs.

Tomorrow, if the day is decent, I must do some walking. There are interesting rocks here. Purbeck marble—black; what other color would it be?—is rather handsome, and some churches, Exeter among them, have begun to use it for—

Pounding. Someone pounding on my door. And shouting. I can't understand—

T.n.t., if God

At Corfe
The 22nd Day of April, A.D. 1212

The King was at his table in the Great Hall. Next to him, a nobleman whose face I did not know. We were alone, the three of us. The lamps had not been lit. What light there was came from the fire blazing in the center of the floor. The dogs, as always, lay curled up around it.

I stood waiting by the dogs. The officer who led me down had placed me there. The King chose not to notice me, he went on talking to the man beside him. I have never liked this kind of waiting; ever. Standing there but having no existence till I'm beckoned into life. I waited for what seemed a long time. I could see their faces, bright or dim, depending on the flames. I heard the sound their voices made, but not the words. At last, he looked at me.

"Giraldus?"

"Yes, my lord." I bowed and moved across the floor and up the dais steps. I saw no smile or sign of welcome. He sat back. I stood across the table from him, waiting.

"Map is dead," he said.

I nodded. "Dead and gone, my lord."

An odd way to begin a conversation; odd and most disquieting. I watched him move his dagger, slicing from the lamb bone he was holding.

"All of them are dead." He looked up from his meat. "They're all dead."

"All of whom, my lord?"

"There's Map for one, Roger of Hoveden, Ralph Diceto, what's-his-name of Canterbury—"

"Gervase." I listened as he went on listing every chronicler of note in England. It was true; the last ten years had taken all of them. No one was left; there was no history being written, not by anyone of stature.

"Well?" John looked at me. "Have I forgotten anybody?"

"Only Ralph of Coggeshall."

"He was a fool."

I could not argue that. And if the future cared about the past, it would not find a record of this time. It was a tragedy of sorts, but not my tragedy. I'd done my share. I had been England's best, along with Map; what things we wrote, the two of us. But that was years ago.

The King went on. "I have no chronicler, Giraldus. Nothing of these years is in the book."

"It's history's loss, my lord."

"The loss is mine. Great things are going to happen. Very great. They must be written down. I want a record kept."

"I understand, my lord, but—" Suddenly, my hands felt very cold. "Oh God, John," I believe I said, "not me. You can't want me."

"I am not John to you."

I bowed my head. "Your Majesty."

"Nor have I asked you yet."

What course to take? I only knew I wanted none of it.

He spoke. "It took you long enough to get here."

"Lincoln is a great way off, Your Majesty."

"Not ten days off."

"Your summons came; I left at once."

"You're growing old, Giraldus."

"Who is not, my lord?"

He left it there, as well he might. The King has aged, his beard is gray now, he is forty-five and looks it. There was wine in front of him. A pitcher, goblets; three of them, the empty one for me. He poured more for himself and his guest; then paused, then put the pitcher down. The gesture was not wasted.

"I am honored that you think of me, but you are right, my lord: I'm old. Extremely old, in fact. I'm frail, my health is poor, my memory comes and goes, I have no interest in the great world any more." I sighed and let my shoulders droop. "My days pass by in quiet and seclusion."

Plausible enough, I thought. He seemed to think so, too. He nodded, waited. Some lamb was caught between his teeth; he sucked it loose and then turned to the man beside him. "Tell me what you think."

The man looked up at me. His eyes showed signs of unmistakable intelligence, a rare thing in a nobleman. "I think he treats you like a fool."

John shrugged. "That's possible. Why don't we ask him?" Then, no color in his voice, he said, "What do you think of me, Giraldus?"

What in God's name could I say? The truth is vast; I sliced a part of it. "I see you as you are, I think."

He seemed to ponder; then he frowned. "Why did you think I sent for you?"

I took another slice. "I thought you wanted me to go to Rome."

It made him smile. "As enfeebled as you are?"

I shrugged. "The Pope has some respect for me."

"Would you have gone on my behalf?"

I hesitated.

"Would you? Are you with me or against?"

How could I dodge it? It's a lunatic and dreadful thing, his struggle with the Pope. Six years of Interdict. Dear God, six years without a single Christian burial or baptism in all of England. Sermons in the church yard, bodies in the ditches. And three years of excommunication.

"Well?"

"At some point, you must settle with the Pope, Your Majesty."

"On whose terms? His or mine?"

There was no turning back. If I was going to the dungeons, let it be. "His terms. You won't get yours."

[11]

His knuckles, on the tabletop, went white. "I've fought six years for nothing, have I?"

"Not for nothing. At great cost; as you must know, my lord, since you alone have paid it."

He was on his feet now, leaning on the table toward me, whispering. "You love the truth, old man?"

I met his eyes. "What little I can see of it."

He paused. I watched his face. The King has many sides. Like all his family, he's made of opposites: direct and devious, impetuous and patient. He is driven but he waits. He waited five years to destroy Briouze, the richest of his barons. Would he do as much for me?

He picked the pitcher up and filled my goblet to the rim. His voice was soft. "I've missed you and I want you with me."

"No, my lord; I beg you, no."

"I want you and you'll come. Because you still have scores to settle."

Was it true? Have I not left the world behind? The fire crackled, there was a whimper from a dog. "I have my work, my lord."

"We're leaving Corfe tomorrow."

"We?"

"Myself and Dammartin." He gestured to the man beside him. Renaud Dammartin; so this was he. I'm never wrong about intelligence.

The King went on. "The roads are mud and I must be in Dover quickly. We will sail from Swanage with the tide. It is my wish that you come, too."

"I understand, my lord, and if I come . . ." I hesitated. "If I do, for how long would it be?"

"How long a time?" He took a deep breath. "Till the end, old man. Until you die. Or I do."

No more; I can't. I haven't slept, the dawn is gray, my head aches and the page is swimming on my lap. I am too old for this; I told him so. The quiet of my days, my hopes for my *Principia*, I told him all of it.

He cannot force me into this. History written by command is slavish and corrupt; I told him that as well. I have to choose. Dear

Lord. At Lincoln, all my pens and papers; everything is there. I miss my room.

Till next time, if God wills it.

At Corfe

The 23rd Day of April, A.D. 1212

What is history?

A question for the ages. I have something like an hour to settle it. The sun is high, the King is with the Queen, and outside in the yard the servants load the wagons for today's departure.

History is a record of events. Self-evident. What else is there to say about it? There is much. For in that simple sentence lies a pivotal distinction: on the one hand, the occurrence, the event itself; and on the other, the recording of it.

There is need of definition, too. For instance, what is an event? A tree falls in the forest. An occurrence, yes, but hardly an event. Suppose it falls and kills the king. We have a notable occurrence now; no more than that. It needs a witness, someone to remember or record it. Does it not? If, on this spot five hundred years ago, this king were terminated by this tree and no one saw or knew or ever will know, can we call it an historical event?

To be less theoretical, there is the chronicler at Osney. I have seen this fellow's work. He makes an entry for each year. In general, he writes a single sentence: *"Nihil memoriale accidit."* The year that Henry died, the year that Richard went with half of Europe on Crusade: to mark such things, this man has written, "Nothing memorable happened."

I have spoken to the man. He is not brilliant. Neither is he deaf nor blind nor lunatic. He simply does not see the loss of Normandy as an event. The passing of his abbot or the fire that destroyed the priory, these things he carefully notes down.

He has a point. An irritating point, I grant you, but it comes to this: the witness makes a judgment. The historian selects. It must be so. Suppose the King employed a million clerks and put them in a million towns and cities, charging them to write down everything that happened every day. The war is lost, the barber's pig had piglets; a complete and total record. Is it history?

Obviously not. Why obviously? Because history is a record, not a reproduction. Clearly, something is required of the keeper of the record. Something which involves the use of minimal intelligence.

Historians are much like storytellers, are they not? They take events and put them into order. Facts must be connected, they must shed some light or have some bearing on each other. In a word, there must be form.

And one thing more. The final cause, the function or the use of history. Why does it exist? What is it for? Dogs get along without it. So do many men, both barbarous and civilized. Sometimes whole centuries go by without a book. Aside from the Bede, there is no trace of Alfred's reign, or Aethelred's. They managed very well without their chroniclers because they felt no need to find some meaning in events.

There is a purpose to all things. There is an order in the turmoil, there is sense beneath the chaos, there is something to be learned and this is why Man struggles to remember—

They are calling me. I must unbolt the door. I have no answer for the King. I should go home; what I can do has all been done.

T.n.t., i.G.w.

Two porters, come and gone. They have my things. The King is waiting at the bottom of the stairs.

The proper use of history is the elevation of mankind.

At Sea
The 24th Day of April, A.D. 1212

They tell me nothing, neither John nor Dammartin. Instead, they test me. Little probes, barbed questions. I am like a bit of gold picked up in haste: they wonder, am I genuine?

Exempli gratia: this afternoon. The air was damp and I sat huddled by the brazier near the aftercastle. Dammartin approached. He sat beside me.

Now, there is an art to life at court. Like learning to play the Irish harp, it is extremely difficult and, in the end, not worth the trouble. Still, I do it rather well. I kept on looking at the coals. It was his move. Eventually, he made it.

"Giraldus, you must answer me a question."

"If I can, my lord."

"What does John see in you?"

Which string to pluck? "He sees his youth, I think. I knew him then, when I was wise and he was foolish."

"Does he trust you?"

"No, my lord."

"Then why should I?"

Renaud Dammartin, Count of Boulogne, is a rare variety of nobleman. His court is filled with troubadours and artisans, he writes and paints, plays music; all the graces. And he kills. Sword, dagger, ax. Like Richard Lionheart, a civilized barbarian.

I looked at him. "You must withhold your trust, my lord."

"Till when?"

"Till I trust you."

I rose and bowed and left him to digest it.

John has tested me, as well. There is no point to it. I told him so.

"There are no guarantees of loyalty, my lord."

He shook his head. "I think there are."

"Not all the vows in Christendom mean anything."

He smiled at me. "From you, they would."

He's wrong, of course. I'm as corrupt as any man.

Till next time, if God wills it.

At Sea
The 25th Day of April, A.D. 1212

No wind. The sea is flat, the sail is useless; all the men are on the oars. The mist, as sheer as cambric, colored like the dawn, hangs

[15]

over everything. I sit here on the forecastle alone. I listen, waiting for the sounds to come; the harbor sounds. It should be soon. I feel suspended.

Twenty, I was twenty when I first saw Dover. On my way to Paris on a morning much like this. The cliffs, the little valley and the port, the Western Heights and Dover Castle, beautiful and fearsome. I remember my excitement; everything was possible.

I have been looking at my hands; brown spots and heavy veins. Can life begin again? All things come down to spirit in the end; the will is everything. There is a passage in Corinthians to that effect. Or is it Matthew? I don't know. Does flesh contain the possibility—

I hear them, I can hear the sounds. Faint, muffled by the distance and the mist; the beat of hammering, the cries of men and gulls. We're shifting course; the captain heard them, too. The air is stirring. There is light and more light. I can see the sky. The mist is parting to the left. We're slipping through.

Ah, Dover.

At Dover Castle
The 25th Day of April, A.D. 1212

The King has told me everything. Can it be done? He thinks so, he believes it. I don't know. Can any man redraw the map of Europe? Is it possible? God, what an undertaking, what a chronicle for me to keep: *The Continental Conquest* by Giraldus—

This will never do. These pages are not notes for yet another volume of my *Life*; not any more. I'm history's keeper now. My thoughts and feelings have no place here. A compendium of facts; pure data for the great work I will write once I am back at Lincoln, once the rush of things is past and I can see the meaning of it all. Well, then—

Today. This morning. Thursday. Matins ringing in our ears as we approached the port. We slipped into the harbor, past the Roman jetty to the pier.

We disembarked with little ceremony. Six, or was it seven

knights?—no matter; trivial. In any case, our escort from the castle led the way across the sand, past fishing boats and shipwrights working, smells of pitch and Wednesday's herring—is this too detailed?—up High Street, past the new, distinctly vulgar Maison-Dieu and thence to Castle Hill.

The hill seemed to have steepened since I climbed it last. Three hundred fifty-odd feet it rises. At the top were masons working on the outer battlements; the wooden wall is now half stone.

We crossed the bailey, moving toward the keep. I knew that it must happen soon. There would be letters, papers, secrets on the King's desk, waiting for him. Was I out or was I in? We reached the steps. John paused. To Dammartin, he said good morning. Then, to me: "Well? Aren't you coming?" There it was.

John's chambers here are on the second level of the keep. The room was full of clerks. He sent them off, went quickly to his desk. The letter bore a heavy seal. He broke it open, glanced across the page, then held it out to me.

One single German sentence; that was all. In rough translation: "If the sea is good, I land in Dover on the twenty-sixth." Tomorrow. I looked up. The King was smiling. He began to speak.

The letter was from Henry Hohenstaufen, Otto's brother. Men of limited distinction, both of them. Still, Otto is the King of Germany and holds great power in his hands. Not great enough, perhaps, to crush the French alone; but Otto does not plan to act alone. Nor does John.

Germany and England: think of it. Together, in alliance, massed against the French. What they are planning is a vast invasion. Otto, from the north, will lead his armies down; and John, from England's counties in the south, will rise.

The secret can't be kept, of course; not any more. An army must be raised. And taxes to finance it all: supplies and boats and war machines. When Henry comes tomorrow, we depart for London to announce it to the world.

John sat back in his chair. I stood there blinking, I'm afraid. "You think it can't be done?" he asked.

My mind was full of questions, dozens of them. Who is loyal, who is not? Can Otto be relied on? Or our barons in the south of

France? Or those at home? And what about the Pope? Where would he stand on this? Against us, surely. And King Philip, who rules France with greater skill than any man since Charlemagne. The problems, like the open sea, stretched on to the horizon.

"I am not a military man, my lord." I paused, then said the obvious. "It will be very difficult."

"I know," he said. I wonder if he does.

Till next time, if God wills it.

At Dover
The 26th Day of April, A.D. 1212

The lighthouse is a wondrous thing. The Romans had a gift for building; it is centuries old and perfect. From its summit, on clear days, the view is glorious. The whole earth seems to drop away and one can see the English coast from Ramsgate all the way to Folke-stone and, across the Channel, France.

We stood there shortly after dawn, the King and Dammartin and I. Below us, from the giant brazier, wisps of smoke still rose from last night's signal fire. We had come to catch some sight of Count Henry's ship.

There were no clouds, no mist, and we could actually see Bou-logne on the French coast. There it was: the spires of the upper city like the points of pins on the horizon. It was Philip's city now; the French had taken it from Dammartin. I watched him looking at it and I knew why John put such faith in his loyalty: he would do anything to take his city back.

The King was restless, never still. He has his father's energy; all Henry's boys were blessed with it. Or cursed. He was the first to see the ship. He stopped, stood absolutely still. I felt as if the moment were a point of punctuation, marking off the future from the past.

In any case, Count Henry was received with all due pomp. He is a classic Hohenstaufen. That's to say, as arrogant as he is dense.

Till next time, if God wills it.

At Faversham
The 30th Day of April, A.D. 1212

My instincts as a chronicler are faulty. We are on our way to London, having spent three days refining all the terms of our alliance, and all I can think about is leaving Jean this morning.

I have sent him home to Lincoln. I'm condemned to royal cooking now, and doing nothing made him fretful and morose. He has been with me since my student days in Paris and our parting was not easy.

He was waiting for me in the yard, a bundle in his hands. He has a poet's soul beneath a pirate's face and he was scowling.

"Well," he said, "don't hurry home on my account."

I let him have these liberties of speech; it eases our relationship. I smiled. "I've written Bishop Hugh and if there's anything you need, he'll see to it."

He nodded grudgingly and handed me the bundle. "Here," he said. I opened it. Inside were packets of rare spices: ginger, licorice, cinnamon and clove and many more. "They're wasted on you," Jean said when I thanked him. "You're a man without a palate." That was all. He turned and stomped away across the yard.

We took our midday meal at Canterbury. Becket is the only saint I've ever known. I rather liked him, and I knelt beside his grave and prayed awhile.

I cannot sleep; although the ale at Faversham is only fair, the oysters are magnificent and I have seen too many of them.

Till next time, if God wills it.

And tomorrow, London.

At the Tower, London
The 1st Day of May, A.D. 1212

May Day. In all the towns and villages along the Dover Road, we saw them bringing in the May. Sprigs, branches, boughs of walnut, hawthorn, yew; the streets awash with green. And flowers, berries, clumps of woodruff for the wine bowls.

Clear it was, no clouds, and warm enough to heat these bones. We paused midday in Gravesend. Men and women, boys and girls, all dancing round the birch pole. Music, wine, and on all sides, such fondling. Surely, God made English girls for May and June. They seem a little chalky in the wintertime, it's true. But oh, the look of them on May Day; milky-cream, round arms, sweet swellings and the cleft between.

I watched the King, the glitter in his eyes. A girl approached him. Smiling, dark-red hair, it tumbled down and down. He bent, reached out and touched her breast. She kissed his hand and ran away.

My betters in the Church inveigh against the customs of the day. They do not understand what God intended.

On we went, past Deptford, Greenwich. Many memories. The winding of the Thames, now near the road, now lost beyond the trees. I drifted, as I had on many afternoons so long ago.

I was unprepared for London when it came. The sun was setting, nearly down. Saint Olave's soon, I thought; then Southwark and the Bridge. Instead, we left the road, went through a little wood down to the riverbank. Nearby, a royal galley waited. And, across from us, the City.

I have been away ten years. So much has changed. I sometimes think the world is changing: everywhere I go, new things. We boarded and began to cross. The city wall includes the Tower now; the little vineyard in between is gone. And London Bridge is finished, all complete, with houses on it and what seems to be a chapel in the middle. And Saint Paul's: still rising, not yet done but twice the height it was before.

How vast the Tower is. There are, they tell me, larger keeps, but I have never seen one. There were torchlights. People waiting. In the City, there were scattered flames: no night goes by without some houses burning down.

We glided to the Tower dock in front of Middle Gate. I looked across the faces waiting on the quay. Des Roches was there. We disembarked, he kissed the King and bowed to Dammartin. To me, he did not even speak. I kissed his ring; I had no choice—he is a bishop, after all.

They turned, the three of them, and started up the steps. I saw no sign to follow. I must speak to John and find out what my place is: do I follow uninvited, do I not?

My room is good. It has a narrow window on the river. There are normal river noises, shouts and singing from the ships and wharves; and silence in the Tower. As I sit here, they—whoever John is keeping council with this year—are making plans. The times are labyrinthine; truly. I have seen three Kings maneuver. And two Popes. I know the meaning of complexity but this court is like a hill of ants.

I failed to bolt my door. Des Roches has just appeared.

At the Tower, London
The 2nd Day of May, A.D. 1212

We have three kinds of churchmen: holy men and worldly men and those, like me, who wobble in between. Peter des Roches is of the second class. He can, if need be, say a Mass; I've heard him do it. But the skills that raised him from the clerk he was when I last saw him to the See of Winchester are purely secular. He is a man of politics in bishop's clothes.

He stood there in the doorway to my room. His bearing and his voice are like a soldier's; habits from the days he spent at Richard's side in war. His hair is gray now, like his eyes. He spoke.

"Giraldus." With a smile.

I rose and bowed. "Your Grace."

"Still Peter to my friends." He came across the room. "As rare as unicorns these days, old friends."

He held his arms out: we embraced. He is a hard man, like his name. There is no give to him.

He stepped away. "The King has told me you're to be our chronicler."

"Do you approve?" I watched him closely. He will be John's next Justiciar, I'm told, and his opinion matters.

"Need you ask?"

I thought so. "Peter, I may be too old for this."

"Not you." He shook his head. "You have no equal."

He meant it or he didn't. Either way, the same response was called for. Humbly: "Thank you, Peter."

"We should go," he said. "The King is waiting." Then he paused. There had to be a reason why he'd come to me. It came now, as I thought it would. "Giraldus, to be frank, I am surprised to find you here and not in France."

I knew what that meant. In an effort to add greater power to the Interdict, the Pope had ordered all the higher clergy from the country. Peter is, I think, the only bishop left in England. I looked up. "You're here," I said.

"I'm loyal to the King first; then the Pope."

"I'm here, too, am I not?" I met his gaze, apparently with some success. He touched my arm.

"Come, let's go down," he said.

The royal rooms are on the second level. I have never seen the private chambers: bedrooms for the King and Queen, the children and the household servants. I had been in the solar before, of course.

Nothing had changed. The same white-painted walls and tapestries, the two great chairs where Eleanor and Henry used to sit, the trestle table by the wall, the benches and the stools. The hanging lamps were lit. The room seemed shadowy and cool.

The King was standing at the table by an open chest of jewels. The Queen, all blanketed in furs, sat curled up in the chair that once was Eleanor's. We bowed. John spoke.

"How many will we have tomorrow, Peter?"

"Something like a hundred."

They were speaking of Ascension Day, of course. The baronage assembles every year to celebrate the Feast.

The King went on. "FitzWalter and de Vescy; are they coming?"

Peter nodded. "They're in London."

"Good." John turned to me. "You know them?"

"They are since my time, my lord."

"So much the better. Let me tell you who they are." He closed the jewel chest.

"John?" It was the Queen. "I saw this man at Corfe. Who is he?"

I was introduced. I bowed. She smiled and I began to understand why John had married her. Her voice is light, her eyes are full of life. There is about her something indescribably enchanting. Though she spoke exclusively of children and domestic matters, I suspect her of intelligence. Beyond the beauty, used or not used, is a mind. I wonder if she even knows it. John, I think, does not.

In any case, FitzWalter and de Vescy. Of the two, FitzWalter is the one that matters. He is not a great earl, though he does hold Baynard's Castle, which sits on the Thames directly, well inside the City walls. Apparently, the man is suspect, though they have not told me why. In any case, I am to watch him at the Feast tomorrow when the treaty is announced. A most obscure assignment. This alliance with the Germans will do one of two things: unify the kingdom or the opposite. But what am I to watch for? Signs of treason on FitzWalter's face? Pure foolishness; or so it seems to me.

It was much later when we rose to go. Good nights were said and then the King, as if on impulse, turned to me.

"Stay a little."

Peter left. John filled his goblet, I filled mine. The Queen was dozing—or pretending to, I'm not sure which. We drank.

"What are your thoughts?" John asked.

"On what, my lord?"

"On many things." He paused. "Let's start with being here."

"With being here, my lord?"

"Don't answer me with questions. Were you ever with my father in his private talks with Becket or the Marshal?"

"No, my lord."

"With Richard when he spoke about the State with Mother?"

"No."

"You've just been present for the first time and you ask me what I mean by being here? What will you write about tonight?"

"The facts, my lord."

"What are the facts?"

"What happened, what was said."

He nodded toward the Queen. "Is she a fact? If we had fought or kissed, would you have put it down?"

I did not know. I had to answer something. "Do you want to see my work?"

He nodded. "Yes, I do. Both copies."

"Both?" I did not understand.

"Your version and the one you write for me."

I needed an inspired reply. One came to me. "My lord, what of the copy in my head?"

He nodded and he smiled. "Show me nothing."

"Yes, my lord. Just as you wish."

From the next room came the sudden crying of a child; one of the princes waking from a dream. The Queen's eyes opened. Then she stood and stretched and, as she left the room, she turned to me.

"Good night, old man," she said.

John sat down on a stool. We talked till after Matins rang, well past the middle of the night. He is so filled with hope about the future; and suspicion, too. Not only for FitzWalter or de Vescy. Like the sunlight, his suspicions fall on everyone. He was not this way as a boy; it was not in his nature then, but he was taught mistrust by masters.

I am suspect, too. As well I should be.

Till next time, if God wills it.

At the Tower, London
The 3rd Day of May, A.D. 1212

Ascension Day, midmorning. They have started to arrive. By water, for the most part. I am sitting by my window on my stool; thus I can write and watch at once. The Earl of Chester is below me now. The dock is filled with courtiers and servants.

Shortly, I shall be among them, listening for the meanings underneath the words, my eyes collecting every move and gesture that they make. For it is indirectly that the truth reveals itself. When I was young, I was more skilled at this than most. It made me marvelously useful.

I am even better now, I think. My age is advantageous. If I squint and stumble just a bit or if I cup a hand around an ear, they take me for a harmless relic. I have other methods, too: a certain vagueness to my face and they assume my mind has gone; one nod at dinner and it's safe to talk because I sleep.

My heart is actually thumping; at my age. I am too old and wise to feel like this; I know, I know. These are my contemplative years, and one day, have no doubt of it, I will be back where I belong. But not yet, not just yet.

FitzWalter: is that him below? The King described him as a tall man with a jousting scar across one cheek. He's too far off, I cannot see from here. I'd best go down.

Till etc.

At the Tower, London
The 3rd Day of May, A.D. 1212

The feast began at midday. It has yet to end. The moon is up and most of them are still there in the Great Hall, drunk. I am, myself, not altogether sober and my throat is raw from all the singing and the talk.

The day was not without its interesting passages. To start with, I have met FitzWalter. He was speaking with the King when I went down. The inner yard was thick with earls. I nodded to the ones I knew, evoking, in the main, surprise; I think they thought me to be dead.

FitzWalter is not easy to describe. John's age or nearly, he is put together on a large scale: massive chest, thick neck, large features. On first glance, one takes him to be merely oxlike; nothing like his father, who was Henry's Chief Justiciar, a man of more than moderate intelligence.

John introduced me. Thinking it was best to seem a trifle senile, I inquired how his father was, well knowing he had died some years ago. I doddered on, a few more questions of this kind, establishing my witlessness. I then attached myself to him, watching and listening as he moved about the yard.

His talk is ordinary, even dull. His mind, a small thing for so vast a setting, is a sluggish instrument. He has no wit. But he has something. People listen to him. I was not the only one who followed him about. At one point, someone asked him what he made of Henry Hohenstaufen being here. FitzWalter shrugged. "He's come for dinner, surely, like the rest of us." No man, I thought, can possibly be that obtuse. I was about to press him on it when the trumpets called us to the feast.

The barons took their places first, of course. Once they were settled, we went in, those of us at the dais table. That's to say: the King, Count Henry, Dammartin, des Roches, the Earl of Chester, Hugh de Burgh and I. The Queen did not attend.

John took his place, the Great Hall echoing the cheers and cries of "*Vivat Rex.*" The ewerers came round. We washed our hands and then, the shawms and trumpets sounding off, the feast began. The first course entered bit by bit: boar's head and tusks, cygnets and peacocks in their plumage, minwheel tails, a multitude of snipe and heron pies, roast eels and swan's-neck pudding: all the usual. The panters cut the bread, the butlers poured the wine and tasted. I have never seen a butler poisoned but it has been known to happen. The wine was safe. We drank.

Sext rang: noon came and went before the course was over and the marshals, squires and ushers took the slops away. There was some music for a while which, as always, brought forth barking from the dogs.

The King made his announcement as the second course began. He waited till the subtleties appeared: a pastry unicorn not quite life-size, a castle made of marzipan which took two men to carry and arrays of flowers spun from sugar. All this was paraded up and down and then, as most eyes drifted toward the doors through which more food would come, the King arose to speak.

"My lords." It was inaudible. He signaled for a roll of drums and in the hush that followed, he began again.

"My lords." There followed some remarks of welcome and a toast to Henry, the Count Palatine. Count Henry rose, returned the toast. The wine, surprisingly, had improved his speech and one could understand entire phrases. "Good to be here," for example. Or, "My brother sends you greetings." Not unnaturally, the focus of attention wandered from the dais. They were searching for the second course and signaling for wine. One could not blame them—but I knew what was coming.

Then it came. The King stood up again. Count Henry knelt and in a firm voice, clear and slow, did homage. "I become your man from this day forth," and so on. Heads began to turn. He went on. "I hold faith to you for all the lands I claim to hold of you." The hall was growing still. And by the time the Count had finished with the Oath of Fealty, I have seldom heard such silence.

And why not? The heir to Germany had sworn in public that the King of England was his overlord. Count Henry rose. John spoke. I think I have it right. He said:

"My lords, this solemn moment will be further solemnized tomorrow by the signing of a treaty in the presence of my highest officers and those of you who care to come. This treaty binds our countries, Germany and England, in a pact to make no separate peace with Philip, King of France. This act we do in public so that the friends of England may rejoice and all our enemies be openly confounded."

Adroitly done. There was no threat of war against the French. Quite the reverse; the King had merely vowed to "make no separate peace." The true intent, of course, is just the opposite and I was peering at the baronage to find out who, if anyone, had grasped this when FitzWalter stood up, turned and bolted from the Hall.

I followed instantly. Why had he fled? Could it be outrage at the King's pronouncement? Was he less than loyal? Were his ties with France so deep that he could not contain himself?

I should have known. The garde-robe chambers are too few for feasts and state occasions and, by custom, we restrict their use to problems of the bowel. I found FitzWalter just beyond the entrance to the Great Hall, pissing in the corridor.

I joined him and we faced the wall together, side by side. I let a moment pass and then: "My lord," I said, "what do you make of this agreement with the Germans? Is it good?"

He shook the last drops from his organ, which is legendary, so I'm told; and justly so. This done, he turned to me. "You're not the fool you seem to be, Giraldus. Nor am I."

I met his eyes. "The question stands," I said.

"All things are good for someone; even plague."

"But is it good for England, do you think?"

He paused. "I understand you write."

"From time to time, my lord."

"Can you tell how a story ends from hearing the beginning?"

"No, my lord; not if it be well told."

"Then we must wait and see what happens, mustn't we?" He grinned and clapped me on the back and left me there.

I don't know what to make of it. In fact, I'm not sure what to make of anything. My eyes keep closing. They are singing in the Hall now. I can hear them. Student songs, and half of them have never studied anything. I brought a bottle with me to the room. Red wine. A third of it remains. It seems a shame to leave it. Possibly a little more will clear my mind.

> *Nos vagabunduli,*
> *Laeti, jucunduli—*

Good tune, that's how it went.

At the Tower, London
The 4th Day of May, A.D. 1212

The treaty has been signed. We met at noon. The Great Hall had been swept, there were fresh rushes on the floor; even so, the smells of yesterday were in the air and none of us were feeling very well.

The pens were brought, the ink and wax. No one had much of anything to say. Of moments such as this is history made.

In need of air, I left the Hall and with what speed I could, went down the stairs and out into the yard near Lion's Gate. The lions, four of them, lay dozing in the sun in their enclosure.

Going nowhere in particular, I strolled around the keep, the stables to my left, on past the pigsties and the dairy. Just ahead, there was a wooden fence, a gate. I opened it, no reason why. I stood there for what seemed the longest time.

The Queen was walking in the Tower garden. Down the narrow paths, past daffodils and berry blossoms and the herbs of Spring. Save for a gardener working here or there, she was alone. The sight of her was like an antidote. She saw me in the gateway and she smiled. I have just come from walking with her.

Isabelle is not an easy woman to describe. Though she is seldom seen, the beauty of her person is a well-known fact and there are many tales about it. I have even heard it said that Normandy was lost because the King refused to leave whatever bed the Queen was in. Not true, and Normandy was lost for other reasons; but to see her is to understand why people tell such stories.

She seemed eager for my company. She talked about the day at first; the season of the year. And then the herbs. She knows them— which is cumin, which is coriander. Then she spoke about her sons, Prince Henry and Prince Richard, and her daughter, Joan. She travels with them, they go everywhere together.

As a rule, I do not find much pleasure in domestic conversation, and although she speaks with charm, I had begun to drift a bit. The roses were in bud and we had stopped to look at them. She paused, then asked a question.

"Did you know the Queen?"

It took a moment: I was under the impression I was talking to her.

"Eleanor?" I ventured.

"Yes."

I shrugged. "She never liked me much, I fear."

"What sort of woman was she?"

[29]

"She was like a storm at sea: magnificent to watch from shore but terrible to cross." A little fancy, I admit; it seemed to please her, nonetheless.

She nodded. "So she was."

It was, I thought, her wish to talk about it. "When," I asked her, "did you meet?"

"At Fontevrault. I married John in August and we went directly there. We found her in the cloister, leaning on a cane with jewels. She looked at John and bowed to him—they hadn't met since Richard's death—and said, 'Your Majesty.' And then she turned to me and said, 'So this is England's Queen.' Before we left, she gave me a city."

Isabelle broke off. I stood there, picturing the scene: great Eleanor past eighty, John already flecked with gray at thirty-five and Isabelle a queen of twelve.

She had one final question for me. "Was she ever pretty?"

"Yes." I nodded. "She was beautiful."

We left the garden when the bees began to swarm. The hives are nearby and the Queen is frightened of them. It was time, in any case, she said, for her to see the children bedded for the afternoon.

I left her at her chambers and continued to the chapel. How austere it is, this little place; no decoration, no adornment. And how strangely beautiful. Twelve pillars, one for each apostle. Years ago, I'd named them and I knelt now by Saint Paul's to pray awhile.

No prayers came. What I had instead were memories. One in particular. It was November, forty years ago exactly. I was twenty-six, fresh from my student days in Paris, and I came to London hoping I might meet the King and come away with some position in his service. To that end, I knelt here in this chapel, praying for advancement.

I could not have chosen a more catastrophic moment to appear. For it was then, precisely then, that Eleanor of Aquitaine destroyed her marriage and her family and, for years to come, her very life. She went to war against the King. Her armies, all of Aquitaine at her command, were storming north. She meant to conquer all of Henry's lands in France and she had sent the princes, all her sons but John, to Paris where they would be safe.

John was in England with his father and that day, as I knelt praying here, they came into the chapel. I could hear King Henry from a distance. He was raging. When most men rage, their voices split and crack. Not Henry's. Like a trumpet call on Doomsday; terrifying. And his face, when he appeared: Hell is as real to me as Heaven, and I can't forget the sight of it. I pressed against my pillar while he prayed aloud, if you could call it praying.

And beside him through it all was John. A child; five or six. A small boy, frail; not stocky then. He kept close to his father: motionless, as if by being still he might be somewhere else. His eyes were on his father as the King cried out to God to damn the Queen and visit death upon her. Then he closed his eyes, the boy did, and his hands began to move. As still as stone save for his fingers curling round each other. Wringing. All these years, it has stuck in my memory: this image of a child's wringing hands.

I did not meet either King on this occasion.

I have sent for supper in my room. I do not feel like going down. Till next time, if God wills it.

At Lambeth
The 23rd Day of May, A.D. 1212

We have been sixteen days at Lambeth. The castle-keep is small and sadly out of date and we are living in the manor house. It is a pleasant place. The Queen enjoys the woodlands and the walks; the King is near the City. He can meet in secret and seclusion and, with dry roads, be in London in two hours.

And in secret and seclusion it has been. Each morning, we assemble in the library: the King, des Roches and Hugh de Burgh, myself and Dammartin. We leave the manor house, the mist still heavy in the air, and make our way along the gardens to the library. Des Roches, who keeps the keys, unlocks the door.

The chill inside is dungeonlike. I light the lamp. There is no fireplace, nor are there windows; no way in except the door, which, later when the sun has risen past the trees, I open up for light and air.

The room is small. The walls are oak. There are five chairs around a trestle table, three low chests that hold the books and secret papers; nothing else. I function, for the most part, as a scribe and take down what is said.

The plans for the invasion are exceedingly complex. In part, because John's armies must coordinate with Otto's; secret messages are, as I sit here, speeding back and forth. In part, because the force John plans to raise in England is so vast. In part, because there is so little time. And finally, because of what had happened to the last invasion, seven years ago.

Who can forget the debacle of 1205? The French had taken Normandy the year before and John was in a rage to have it back. An army of great size was raised, a large fleet was assembled. All the steps that we were taking had been taken once before.

The army never sailed. The memory of this hovered in the room unspoken till this afternoon. The King was speaking of that great barbarian, the Earl of Chester, when I blurted out, "He turned against you last time, Sire." There it was, out in the open. John had sailed. The royal galley put to sea in hope that Chester and the rest would follow. No one did.

John looked at me, unblinking. "Am I likely to forget that?"

"No, my lord."

"In fact, I've thought of little else for years."

He sat back in his chair. "I made a terrible mistake. I failed to understand my Normans. After all, I'd lost their province, hadn't I? Their lands in Normandy were gone. I counted on their greed; what baron wouldn't fight to gain back half of what he used to have?" He shook his head. His voice, as he went on, was calm enough. "I know why no one followed me. They thought I couldn't win. I've taught them; they know better now. It's taken seven years, I've scarcely had a month of peace, but no one doubts me any more. There's not a castle left that stands against me.

Scotland, Ireland, Wales, I've crushed them all. My barons won't stay home this time."

He may be right, for all I know.

Till next time, if God wills it.

At Lambeth
The 24th Day of May, A.D. 1212

William Longsword came today. No one had thought to warn me. It was twilight. I was walking in the garden with the King and Queen when, round a corner of the hedges just ahead, a figure bounded. For a moment, I was certain I was looking at King Henry, risen from the dead.

For Longsword is his father to the teeth. I mean the teeth. In all details. The man has Henry's face, his voice, his energy, his gestures. "Oh, my God," I may have said. I watched him kiss the King and then he raised the Queen up, like a child, and held her in the air. His greeting, when John introduced me, was a friendly one. He has, he said, faint memories of me.

They must be very faint indeed. For I had not laid eyes on William Longsword since he was a child of five. The day we put his mother in the ground.

Poor Rosamund. She was so fair and died so young. It was in summertime. 1175. Or was it '76? We were at Woodstock and I watched them evening after evening, Rosamund and Henry, close together in the palace gardens. Henry, in his time, had many mistresses; and many bastards, too. Our kings are meant to fornicate. Henry the First, a hundred years ago, had nineteen bastards, so they say. There is no stigma to it. John's half brother Geoffrey— dead two months ago; I miss him—rose to greatness in the Church and Longsword is our foremost soldier.

Rosamund was beautiful and Rosamund was highly born; the Cliffords are a great and ancient family. But what set her apart from Henry's other mistresses was this: he loved her. He adored her, he was tender, gentle, kind. She was his Queen in everything but name. She sat, at state occasions, by his side; sometimes on the adjacent throne.

Too much? I thought so then; I still do. He was using Rosamund for vengeance. For revenge on Eleanor. The Queen had lost her war. The King had taken everything: not only lands and castles. He had robbed her of her liberty. She was his prisoner until the day he died. Except for Easter and Christmas Courts, when she joined the King wherever he might be, the Queen lived locked up in a suite of rooms for fifteen years. And even this was not enough. He wanted her to know that she had been replaced in every way.

Long after Henry's death, I spent an afternoon with Eleanor. She spoke about the years of her imprisonment. Her lack of bitterness surprised me. Had she won, she told me, she'd have done as much for Henry. She forgave him everything, or so she said, except for Rosamund.

I can still hear the way she said the name, her rage and scorn, and Rosamund, by then, two decades dead. She did not poison Rosamund; the tales one hears are false. She would have liked to, but the wish is not the deed, and Rosamund died of a fever. I was there, I watched it happen day by day.

We buried Rosamund at Godstow, in the chapter house. The King attended briefly, then he left. Without a word to William; nothing for his bastard son. The boy stood mute, no public tears, among the nuns at graveside. What would happen to him? Who would bring him up? To this day, I have no idea.

I spent the evening with the royal family, looking for some trace of that abandoned boy. He's not apparent in the man; at least, I haven't found him yet. I listened while the brothers talked. Longsword was fresh from meetings with the Count of Flanders, who, this year at any rate, is part of our alliance. France, he told us, had begun to raise its armies for the war that is to come. This is, of course, to be expected; after John's announcement on Ascension Day, there is no other logical response.

We drank and ate and drank again. The princes' bed is in the corner near the door. A nurse appeared, removed their clothing, pulled the blankets up and drew the curtains round the bed. The Queen began her needlework; the brothers went on talking.

They are intimate, these two. One feels this not by what they say but how they say it; in the text beneath the text. They spoke at length of Philip, of his weaknesses and strengths. John is our expert on the French King. They go back in time together thirty years or more. John was to marry Philip's sister, and he might have had she not been King Henry's mistress—but those are other stories.

When I left, the Queen had gone to bed. I bowed and went away perplexed, beset by fuzzy questions. Is it odd that John should find the only brother that he cares for in the child of his mother's greatest rival? If so, does it matter? Are emotions part of history? To what extent do great events depend on parents and their children? Are the father's sins not visited? I've no idea.

I have just dropped my pen. My fingers have begun to cramp. Till next time, if God wills it.

At Lambeth
The 1st Day of June, A.D. 1212

Tomorrow, it begins. Our talks are done, the war exists on paper. In the morning, all of us go off in all directions: Dammartin to meetings with the Counts of Flanders and Brabant; des Roches and Hugh de Burgh to London; Longsword to our allies in the south of France; and John goes north to make sure that our Norman earls will come when they are called.

I go with John, of course. The man is in a fever to depart. Till next time, if God wills it.

At Huntingdon
The 4th Day of June, A.D. 1212

North we go. John rides in front, he knows the way. He travels like a man possessed, at speeds no animal was meant for. We keep up as best we can.

By we, I mean the royal government. It always goes where he goes. Only bits and pieces of it, as a rule; we're less than sixty altogether. Scribes and clerks from the Exchequer and Justiciar, some knights and men-at-arms.

And portions of the royal household, too. The Queen has stayed at Lambeth with the children. With us are John's valet, Petit, and his ancient bathman, William. In their wagon are the King's possessions: that's to say, his tub, his chair, his bedding and his books. He goes nowhere without his chest of books.

The Treasury is with us, too. Not all of it, of course; we carry no more than a keg or two of pennies and a portion of the royal jewels. The King has faith, great faith, in precious stones.

I have just seen this for myself. We're stopping at the priory and John had commandeered the prior's cell. Old William came and fetched me in. I found John, finished with his tub, enfolded in a blanket on his chair. In front of him, an iron chest lay open. I had never seen him with his jewels before. His love of them is legendary. Yet he seldom wears them as so many of our barons do, although I think he finds them beautiful. He held a sapphire in his hand as I came in.

I bowed. "You sent for me, my lord?"

"Sit down."

There was no other chair. I sat down on the bed's edge, waiting.

"All of them have stories. Hugh of Lusignan was ransomed with this stone." He paused. "This one and many more; I held him dear. I was a fool to let him go. I should have kept the stones and killed him, don't you think?"

I nodded. John is known for never killing prisoners he can ransom; in this case, a rule he should have broken. Hugh of Lusignan was Henry's enemy. And Richard's, too; and Eleanor's. But most particularly, he is John's. He was to marry Isabelle, the thing was all arranged, when John appeared and took her for his own.

There were two candles in the cell. John moved the jewel so that it caught the light. His voice was low. "The Jews, they understand. A man may own a shire but he cannot move it. Land gets left behind"—he smiled at that—"as I well know."

He put the gem amongst the rest and closed the lid. From then till deep into the night, the two of us played chess.

Till next time, if God wills it.

At Alnwick Castle

The 13th Day of June, A.D. 1212

Our sweep into the north has been a great success. At every fortress on the way—at Nottingham and Pontefract, and York and Richmond, Durham, Warkworth—at each stop, we have been flawlessly received. That is to say, with vows of loyalty and offers of support, of men and money for the war that equaled or exceeded our demands.

The same is true of our reception here; or seems to be. Which is it?

Alnwick Castle has, for centuries, been the seat of much duplicity. Of all the fortresses along the Scottish border, there is none of greater strength. It is a fulcrum in the endless border wars between the Scots and English, and the earls who hold it are forever tilting back and forth from side to side.

The current earl is no exception. Eustace de Vescy: How can I describe him? Feral? He is long-faced, tall and thin. His skin is pale, his hair is yellow and his teeth are perfect. He is always with FitzWalter, they are intimates. On top of which, he has betrayed the King at least once in the past.

He met us in the Great Hall. There was no pretense at friendship and their talk was crisp and brief. De Vescy bowed, then spoke.

"What do you want of me, my lord? How many men?"

John told him.

"And what else?"

John named a sum of money.

"And what more?"

John paused, then made a one-word answer. "You," he said.

De Vescy frowned. "You doubt my loyalty?"

"I want you with me on the battlefield."

"You want more surety? I have several children. Would you like to hold them? Would that put your mind at rest?"

The King holds many children; it is common practice. Henry did it. All kings do.

John paused. "What do you have against me?"

"Nothing, Sire."

"I never touched your wife."

"I know that."

"Keep your children."

There was more, but nothing worth recording.

Loyalty, like love, is an emotion. Greed or fear do not produce it. Or duress. I said so to the King much later, as I left him for the night.

It made him laugh. "If kings relied on loyalty," he said, "we'd have a dead king once a week."

Am I his loyal subject? Yes, I think I am. Is this from greed or fear? I'd like to think not, but I wonder.

We start south soon. First Carlisle, then Penrith; then a visit with the only living Visigoth, the Earl of Chester.

Till next time, if God wills it.

At Wigan
The 15th Day of June, A.D. 1212

The writs went out today. The King addressed them to the reeve of every city in the Kingdom.

The text is brief. They are commanded to assemble men and arms and stand at readiness to cross the Channel with the King when he requires it.

I'm not sure why it stirs me so. The text, the date, all this was planned at Lambeth. It is nothing new, and yet John felt it too, I think. For it is done now, it is fact, a part of history. An entire realm has just been called to arms.

[38]

This evening we were with the rector in his manor house. The King seemed calm and full of confidence. We leave at dawn. By midday, we should be across the Mersey. And by nightfall, Chester.

Till tomorrow, if God wills it.

At Chester
The 16th Day of June, A.D. 1212

I have known the Earl of Chester since 1180. My opinion of the man has never changed. He is a brute. I use the word in both its senses: i) crude of mind; ii) heroic. For not only is he great in size and appetite, his power—after Marshal's—is the greatest in the Kingdom.

He has never been a friend of mine. In fact, God knows how far I might have risen in this world had he not spoken to three kings against me. Henry, Richard, John: he has defamed me to them all. It's not my brilliance he despises, or my wisdom or my wit. These attributes displease him, to be sure, but I am hated for my Welshness. I was born in Pembrokeshire. My great-grandfather, Rhys ap Theodor, was Prince of South Wales.

It is this that Chester can't abide. He is an enemy of all things Welsh. He has invaded Wales more times and killed more of my countrymen than any man alive or dead. Nor are the King's hands altogether clean. Within the last year, he has twice led armies into Wales, the second time with terrible success. It tears at me, I've spent my lifetime serving English kings.

The trouble with the Welsh—dear God, there are so many, but the one I have in mind is this: they will not give up being tribal, they will not unite. They are unconquered and unconquerable. Not only by the English; by themselves. They have no king. Nor have they even now a prince with skill enough to make a country out of them.

Except Llywelyn, possibly.

The King and Chester talked of little else all night. The loyalty of Wales is pivotal, or so the two of them believe. Not only for the men and arms they might contribute to the war, but for the stronghold they might offer France should Philip think to land an army there.

No disagreement as to this. Llywelyn was another matter.

"I'd have killed him," Chester said.

John shook his head. "There was no need. He'll follow me, he'll answer when I call."

"You had him in your hands. You always make the same mistake: you don't know who to kill. You murdered Arthur—"

"I did not."

"He died of something."

"Not of me."

"The point is—" Chester stopped, then turned to me. "What does the King's pet Welshman have to say?"

I cleared my throat. "I'm not sure what the question is, my lord."

"Who would you kill?"

The word "You" trembled on my lips. Instead, I said, "I fight with words, my lord."

"You haven't won much, have you?"

"Not as yet, my lord."

I left them shortly after that.

Till next time, if God wills it.

At Chester
The 17th Day of June, A.D. 1212

No sleep last night, it would not come. I dressed in darkness, left my room and climbed up to the rooftop of the keep. I saw the dawn from there. The castle dominates the town, the view spills out in all directions. To the west, the harbor and the Irish Sea; and southward, just beyond the city walls, the hills of Wales.

The streets, when I went down, were showing signs of life. I moved along them, drifting, scraps of sea mist in the air. So much is new; we build so many things these days.

In time, I found myself at Water Gate. The port was filled with ships: Scotch, Irish, Spanish, Portuguese. There is a cookshop, and I waited with some sailors while the turbot finished boiling and the sea bream fried. When I was five or six, I came here with my father. Can the shop have been the same?

There were no little Welsh boys there this morning. They had all stayed home in Wales, where it was safe. Should I have done the same? Had I stayed home, I might be rector at Saint David's. Nothing much, a life like that. I've known Kings and the Pope esteems me, he has told me so.

I spent the morning bogged in speculation of this kind and when I went back to the castle, Joan was there. I found her on the rooftop of the keep, the King and Chester with her. They were sitting in the sunlight, drinking ale.

Joan is a jolly person, plump and fair. One calls her Joan instinctively, although she is a princess now: Llywelyn's wife. Of all John's bastard children, she's the only one he loves. She must be thirty now, or thereabout. Her mother, Clementina, was a servant girl. John loved her, too, I think.

I bowed, with due respect. "My lady."

"Is that you, Giraldus?"

I assured her that it was. I sat and listened to her talk. She has a son, a boy of four named Davydd. She went on and on about him. John seemed fascinated, full of questions: did he ride yet, could he read? My mind began to wander and I nearly missed it.

"Has he grown much?" John asked.

"Not since Easter."

"Couldn't you have brought him?"

"Not this time."

"Why not?"

She paused. "He's with his father."

"Well then, has Llywelyn grown much?" John was smiling.

"In a way. They've started calling him Llywelyn the Great. I think he likes it."

[41]

"Yes, he would." John frowned. "Who calls him Great? What has he done for such a name?"

Joan looked away. "There mustn't be another war between you. Not another one."

John touched her hand. "Why should there be?"

"He has so many meetings, he is always with his earls."

John shrugged. "That could mean anything." I thought he meant to say more but he left it there.

Until tonight. We were with Joan in her room, John and I. They sat beside each other, smiling. John spoke softly.

"You do love me, don't you?"

"Yes," she said.

"Llywelyn claims to be my friend; but if he's not—"

She interrupted. "Please don't ask me."

John went on. "If you should find out anything, you'd tell me, wouldn't you?"

Eventually, she answered. "Yes, I would."

He touched her cheek. "Don't let it worry you. Llywelyn won't betray me. When I land in France, he'll be there at my side."

They kissed and said good night. I bowed and wished her well and followed John into the corridor. He looked at me in silence for a moment; then he said it.

"Would she tell me, do you think?"

I thought so. "Yes, my lord."

I left him then.

Till next time, if God wills it.

Half a Day from Chester
The 19th Day of June, A.D. 1212

The King is sitting on a tree stump near the roadside, finishing his wine. I have just come from talking with him.

Chester is behind us now. We left this morning early, clattering down quiet streets and through the city wall at East Gate. I had seen enough of Chester, both the city and the Earl, but how the

King felt was impossible to say. He rode in silence, deep in thought. Not sullen. Inaccessible comes closer to it; wrapped inside himself.

At midday, when we stopped to eat, he started out alone across the field. I made no move to follow. Then, to my surprise, he turned and beckoned to me.

When I reached him, he was looking at a field of broom across the road. "The family plant," he said. "My father's father wore it on his helmet, so they say." He smiled wryly, turned, walked on a few steps more and settled on the stump. I sat beside him on the meadow grass. Then Petit came with bread and cheese, two goblets and a wineskin.

Silence. John tore off a piece of bread. He filled his goblet, handed me the skin. When, finally, he spoke, I had to strain to hear.

" 'No prisoner can tell his honest thought
  Unless he speaks as one who suffers wrong;
  But for his comfort, he may make a song.
  My friends are many but their gifts are naught.' "

He paused, then looked to me. "What do you make of that?"

For a moment, I made nothing whatsoever. Then I said, "It seems to be a poem."

"Is it a good one?"

Had he written it himself? I thought not. "No," I said. "Not very."

"Richard wrote it. While in prison; they were holding him for ransom then. He's much admired as a poet. Can you tell me why?"

I shook my head. "He had no talent."

"None at all?" It seemed to please him. "Why is he a legend? Do you know? He never cared for England. Was he here six months in all the ten years he was King? I doubt it. Did he ever win a war that mattered? Did he take Jerusalem? He saw it from a distance at a cost of what? A hundred thousand dead Crusaders. Did he conquer Philip? What did Richard ever win?"

He left it there and cut a piece of cheese. It can't, I thought, be easy having Coeur de Lion for a brother; dead or not. I never liked him much, nor did he me and, on the whole, I think no more of him than John does. What is it that makes a legend? Richard was a handsome man, but so is John. Nor is John less intelligent. Or brave.

Some flies had settled on the bread. The King brushed them away. "The past," he said. "My father's twenty-three years dead and not a day goes by he doesn't talk to me. One-sided, isn't it? I can't talk back. I wish to God I could, I'd make him listen now. I've learned so much. The things kings want are few and simple: very simple. It's the getting of them that is so complex. They say— you hear it said that while Briouze was still alive, I dungeoned up his wife and son at Corfe. And that before she starved to death, she ate the boy. You think it happened?"

"No."

"Why not?"

Though many take the story to be true, I find it much too terrible to be believed. I said so now.

John shook his head. "I do not say I did it but I could have. Kings must learn to do such things." He reached out for the wineskin. "Are you bitter?"

"Me, my lord? Why should I be?"

He filled my glass. "Because you're Welsh."

"I'm proud of that."

"It stopped you, didn't it?" I made no move. "You know it did."

True. Saint David's should have been an independent see—it's twice the size of Canterbury, more than half of Wales. And I, I should have been its first archbishop. But they stood against me: Henry, Richard, Eleanor. And John. They would not let a Welshman rule the Church in Wales. They feared me. I fought back for years, I pled my case in Rome, did everything a man could do. For nothing. There he sat, the youngest member of the family that destroyed me.

"Am I bitter? Yes, my lord."

"The See of York is open. Do you want it?"

What a thing to say. I could not speak.

"What's wrong? Don't you believe me?"

Yes and no. He'd offered me the bishopric of Llandaff twenty years ago exactly. I declined. But still, he made the offer. Did he mean it now?

"My lord . . ." What could I tell him?

"It would have to wait until I've settled with the Pope, of course. An excommunicated King can't go about anointing Princes of the Church; but when the Interdict is over . . ." He was leaning forward on the tree stump. "Well?"

My ears rang. Everything looked faint and drained of color. "Am I not too old, my lord?"

."Too old?" He smiled at that. "You'll probably be dead before I settle with the Pope."

It made me laugh, I don't know why; and then the laughter got mixed up with tears. I thanked him and I told him we should wait and see. The time has passed for me, I think; it comes too late. But then, you never know. The See of York. Dear God.

We talked awhile longer. I have never known the King so giving and serene.

The men are forming up now. We are going back to London, I believe.

Till next time, if God wills it.

At the Tower, London
The 25th Day of June, A.D. 1212

Reports from everywhere were waiting when we came last night. We have no news that is not good.

From Dammartin: we have the full support of Flanders and Brabant. From Hugh de Burgh: our shipwrights work at full speed, and by August we shall have a fleet. From Longsword in the south of France: the barons of Poitou are loyal to our cause.

And more. The inquiry returns exceed our hopes. An inventory of the Kingdom, listing everything from serfs to cows to pewter plate, it makes clear that the base for taxes to finance the war is even richer than we thought. On top of which, the harvest will be plentiful, the Pope has made no new demands and Otto writes that he is ready, when we are, to take the field.

We talked for hours, John, des Roches and I. Was there some problem we had missed, some pitfall overlooked? We could not find it.

We were weary, it was late. Des Roches departed. I stayed on a moment more, for I was puzzled by the King. There was no jubilation in him, none at all.

"My lord," I said.

He cut me off. "Good night." His voice seemed odd.

Perhaps there was some problem. "But my lord—"

This time it came out like a cry. "Good night!" His face contorted and he turned away from me. I hurried from the room and left him weeping at his desk.

I'm at a loss. This evening, for the first time, England seemed to be a single thing: one country. He was King of all the island. Sixth in line since William came and he has done what none of them, not even Henry with his Eleanor, could do. The man has conquered his own kingdom.

I do not understand the King at all.

Till next time, if God wills it.

At Woodstock
The 29th Day of June, A.D. 1212

I see the Queen. I cannot stop myself from seeing her. I close my eyes, I open them: no matter. There she is. Men's boots to mid-thigh; then laced black tights, as smooth as second skin, rise to the tautness of her waist. Above, a scarlet doublet, very short, two little slits on each side, deeply open at the front. And finally, her hair, invisible beneath a man's plumed hunting cap.

Her horse was waiting. The jewels embedded in the saddle pommel glinted in the dawn light. Like a boy, in one bound she was mounted. On her left hand was the metal gauntlet and we waited while the falconer went to the mews and brought for her a white gerfalcon.

The bird sat on her wrist. Her eyes glowed as she looked at it. The soft silk of her doublet touched her breasts and one could watch them rise and fall. I do not covet her. No, truly not. I merely note this image down because to the extent she enters into history—and who can tell what that extent will be?—it is my task to chronicle the Queen.

Well, then. We left the manor yard: the King, the Queen, myself, the falconers, the huntsmen with their dogs on leash, the servants bearing food and other comforts. We went through the gardens, past the pond and out across the meadows to the royal forest. There is something rare about this place. They have been coming here since Aethelred; two hundred years of English kings. For pleasure only; purely that. What draws them here? To ride through Woodstock is to know.

The first kill came midmorning. We were well into the forest, following a stream. It broadened. Far ahead along its banks, two bow shots off at least, were ducks. The huntsmen loosed the dogs. They bounded through the green, the ducks rose up, the Queen released her falcon. With a rush of wings, it went. She sat as still as stone, eyes on the bird. It swooped, it pounced and back it came, its dead prey in its claws. The duck had bled, of course, and when she gave it to the huntsman, there were blood drops on her hand. She brushed her cheek. It left a streak of red. The King, like me, seemed caught; he could not take his eyes away from her.

Much later, when we stopped to eat, they left us. While the servants spread the cloths, they went into the woods. Not far, because I heard them; or I think I did. I've heard the King before. Most evenings, when we travel and our talk is over, John retires to his bed and draws the curtains. I sometimes settle in a distant corner on the floor. Then Petit leaves the room and comes back with a maid or scullery girl. I try hard not to listen. But today I did not try and, God forgive me, I imagined what she might have looked like. Boots and cap still on and nothing else. I could not look at them when they returned.

We ate and sat awhile after. There was talk about the war. From Isabelle. She has, of late, been full of questions, but the King does not respond. He teases her, tells stories, speaks of other things.

She spoke of this as we rode home together in the afternoon. The King had seen a boar and he had gone off with the huntsmen and the dogs. We were alone.

"Giraldus?"

"Yes?" I cleared my throat. There had, till then, been little talk between us. "Yes, my lady?"

"Have you any children?"

"No."

"Do you regret it?"

Did I? "Not remotely."

She glanced down at herself; there is no sign that she has ever carried children. "I have given John two sons and yet he treats me as if I were still a child." She paused, then turned her eyes to me. "What do you think of women?"

I answered without thinking. "I adore them."

"I'm aware of that."

Caught like a schoolboy; what a fool I felt. "My lady—"

"No," she smiled, "that's only as it should be. What I meant— Take Eleanor. When she was young, she gave her King much pleasure and she bore him many children. But she felt—she must have felt—that there was more to her than that."

She looked at me for confirmation and I gave it. "Yes, my lady."

"She was an extraordinary woman and I'm not. I see the two of us quite clearly. She was brilliant, I am merely quick. She truly understood the arts, I only read romances. She could rule a kingdom, lead an army, play at politics; I can't. Nor have I any wish to. She had vast ambitions, mine are small. To gain her ends, she sacrificed her men; two husbands, all her sons. And I would die before I caused John any harm." She hesitated then and seemed to change the subject. "You remember when we met, that evening at the Tower? All your talk about the Germans?"

"Yes, my lady." I could see her; curled up, dozing by the fire in her chair.

"I listened to you; every word. I long to know, I ache to be a part of things. He loves me, but he tells you everything." She smiled ruefully and said no more.

We left the forest and began to cross the meadowland. The sun was low behind us and our shadows, long and dark, preceded us across the green. If she had asked for something that was mine—my horse, my purse, my anything-at-all—I would have given it. But John's affairs are his. I'm like a goblet; I contain the wine, I may not offer it around. I thought I had to tell her so. I started to.

"My lady, if I felt I could—"

She stopped me. "If I felt you could," she said, "I would have asked you."

We dismounted in the yard. I watched her walk away. Exquisite. John returned a while ago. They dined alone, the two of them. I wonder, if I called for Petit, could he find someone for me?

Till next time, if God wills it.

At Woodstock
The 4th Day of July, A.D. 1212

It started quietly enough. In fact, the King seemed more than calm at first.

It was the middle of the morning. We had been in the solar for quite some time, for there were writs to sign and letters to be sent; to Otto, to the Count of Flanders, many more. The clerks were busy and the messengers, as always, came and went with tidings from des Roches and Longsword and the others.

So it was that when the lad appeared, none of us paid him notice. He was weary from his travels, damp with sweat and caked with dust, no different from the rest of them. He waited in a corner for his time to come.

The King, some document before him, signed his name, impressed it with his seal, looked up and saw the lad. "You, there."

"My lord." He bowed from where he stood.

"You may approach." He did. "What have you?"

"May I speak, my lord?"

"Go on."

"But, Sire . . ." He glanced at me and then around the room. "It is for you alone." With a grimy hand, he reached inside his cloak and brought a letter out. It bore a heavy seal. John broke it open, glanced across the page, looked up and spoke.

"I have received it."

"Is that all, my lord?"

John nodded, folded up the paper. "You may go."

The fellow bowed and left the room. We finished with the business of the morning. Then, when all the clerks and scribes were gone, the King stood up and, without speaking, handed me the letter.

I give it, word for word. "The less have joined the Great." No signature, no salutation; nothing.

"It's from Joan," he said. "The Great Llywelyn and his little princes are in league again. I can't think why they'd want another war with me. They always lose." He smiled, we went to eat. Such was the King's position at midday.

But as the afternoon wore on, he darkened. If the Welsh rose up in arms, if they attacked while he and all his forces were in France—it was the thing he dreaded most: a war on two fronts. Was there an alliance between Philip and Llywelyn? And poor Joan; the pain that note had cost her and the danger had the message been discovered.

By nightfall, the King was in a rage. Messengers, just now, have been dispatched. To Chester, to des Roches, to Longsword. The orders, in each case, have been the same: to gather information. Are supplies in movement? Is an army being raised? And to report. To bring the data here with all speed possible.

The King is still in the solar. The night is damp, there is a fire burning and he paces. He said nothing when I said good night.

Till next time, if God wills it.

At Woodstock
The 7th Day of July, A.D. 1212

The Queen has had her wish.

The King, these two days, has been unapproachable. There is, of course, no word; it's still too soon. The atmosphere is bleak. The clerks and scribes work at their papers but the King signs nothing. He goes hunting by himself. I pass the time with Isabelle.

This morning she was bathing in the pond. The locals call it Rosamund's Well, I don't know why. The two of us had gone out early. It was warm and breathless; no air stirred. I settled on the grass. The Queen removed her robe. Beneath, she wore a silken blouse, full-sleeved, which ended where her thighs began.

She slipped into the water, staying near the edge. She cannot swim. Unless one is a child by the sea, as I was, it is not a skill most people learn. We chatted idly as she lolled about; of this and that. The proper tutoring of children, the effect of certain herbs—she is convinced that colewort is an aphrodisiac; but then, the Queen is French. Of such things was our morning made until the King arrived.

He strode across the gardens with a paper in his hand. It was a letter he had written to Llywelyn asking him to come to Woodstock to discuss the war in France. He read it, then looked up at me.

"He can decline, you see, or come at once or offer some excuse for coming later on. No matter what he answers, I'm the wiser for it, don't you think?"

I was about to say I thought so when the Queen spoke. In the water to her chin, she shook her head and softly, as if talking to herself, she said: "No, I don't think that's very clever."

John spun round. "I don't believe I asked for your opinion."

"Did I speak?" She looked dismayed. "I'm sorry, John." She turned away and started drifting off.

"What's wrong with it?" the King demanded. No response. "Come back here."

She turned to face him. "Don't be angry with me; please. If I've offended you—"

"Come here."

She came. He stood above her at the pond's edge, glaring down. She smiled timorously. "Yes, my lord?"

"What don't you like about it?"

"Nothing, John. It's good, it's very good."

He crouched down close to her. "I want to know. I'm not the least bit angry. Is it poorly written?"

"No." She shook her head. He waited.

"Well?"

She cleared her throat. "It's only that . . . it seems to me the thought is wrong."

His voice was low. "The thought is wrong. What does that mean, exactly?"

"Asking him to come to you. If it were me, I'd go to him."

"I can't. I thought of that. What reason could I give?"

"I'd say I missed my grandson."

"That's ridic—" The word died on his lips. He looked at her a long time. "He'd believe that, wouldn't he. He knows I love the boy." She nodded. "I should ask you things more often, shouldn't I?"

At this, she rose. Her silk blouse clung to her. "If I can be of use," she said. And then she looked at me. It was, I thought, a skilled performance. She holds herself too cheap. She's more than quick, is Isabelle.

Till next time, if God wills it.

At Woodstock
The 8th Day of July, A.D. 1212

The letter has been sent. We leave for Wales in two days' time and I am troubled by the strangest thoughts. For I have not been— home, I nearly wrote. Yet, all these years, I've spent more time in Rome than in my native Pembrokeshire.

What is the meaning of a birthplace, anyway? I've always been an alien. At home, I felt like one. Not only as a child; all my life. And here in England, I am one in fact.

What am I really? Sixty-six and do I know? I've served three Kings of England, have I not? I speak my native language with an accent. There is nothing Welsh about me. I have wiped all that away. I'm civilized. I am as French as Abélard, as English as Saint Thomas.

I am half-mad now and then, I think. De Barri is my name. Gerald de Barri I was born. And what is it I choose to call myself? Cambrensis; meaning Wales. I tie it to myself, around my neck, as if it were a burden I was proud of. And a burden it has been. How far might I have gone without it?

In a letter I have left behind at Lincoln, in my rooms, I ask to have my body buried at Saint David's, in the church that should have been the palace of the See I never had. I do not know myself at all.

Till next time, if God wills it.

At Woodstock
The 9th Day of July, A.D. 1212

Everything is changed. We will not leave for Wales tomorrow. Aberconway has been taken by Llywelyn. Longsword brought the news.

He came late afternoon. The King and I were still at work when he strode in, dust-covered, dark with sweat. John looked up, pleased to see him. Wine was poured. Then it began. Longsword was in the midst of news from London, all of which was good, when John broke in, "I'm off to Wales tomorrow. Is there anything I need to know?"

"I was about to tell you." Longsword paused; and then, as if it were of modest consequence, he went on. "They have taken Aberconway."

"Ah." John said it calmly, neither angered nor surprised.

I knew that Aberconway Castle, in the north of Wales, had been enlarged by John last year. To take it meant Llywelyn had an army of considerable size. Or so I thought. I looked at them. "How serious a matter is it?"

"Ah," John said again. "That's what we must determine. It is difficult, and there are many issues to be weighed. The Welsh have always posed a problem. Even Father could not solve it, though he tried. He took his armies in; on more than one occasion, I might add."

He went on in this vein, discussing with considerable clarity the history of a hundred years or more of wars; all victoryless. "No English King," he summed it up, "has ever won a war in Wales. They have not grasped the strategy. One has to fight there in a special way and, to my knowledge, there is only one man who has ever understood how Wales can be destroyed." He turned in my direction. "Only you."

I sat back in dismay. I had not known that John was so familiar with my work. I have, in my *Descriptio Cambriae*, expounded at some length what seems to me to be the only method for subduing my own countrymen. The passage is, of course, mere speculation. Theory, nothing more; an exercise. I said as much.

The King insisted. "Tell us."

What else could I do? I scurried through it. That the war must be a long one. That the progress will be slow because the natives will not fight in open battle; they retreat into the hills, they must be gradually worn down. That their supplies must be cut off. That doing so requires a fleet. And, finally, that the invading soldiers must be light-armed for the fighting in the mountains.

Silence for a moment. Then John turned to Longsword. "Is there any substance to it, do you think?" Longsword was looking at me as if I existed for him for the first time. "Yes." He nodded. "Yes, there is."

"Suppose . . ." John seemed to drift. "Suppose we acted on it?"

Longsword sat up very straight. "What are you thinking?"

"Nothing yet; but we could do it, couldn't we? The men are raised, we have the necessary ships—"

Longsword could barely speak. "The necessary ships? You can't think of abandoning the war in France?"

[54]

De Breauté and three of his associates came in. They carried blankets and whatever else they needed for the night.

The Queen looked up. "Who are these men?"

De Breauté was introduced.

"Why have they come to our solar?"

"To spend the night," John said.

"In here?"

John nodded.

"Why? What for?"

"They keep me safe."

"From whom?"

"My enemies, of course. "

"I see." She paused. "The corridor is near enough, I think."

John shook his head. "They sleep by my bed every night."

"They do?" She smiled, as if in disbelief.

"I fail to see the humor. It's my life I'm speaking of."

"It's my life too. I haven't traveled all this way to be with you in front of witnesses. Ask them to go."

John spoke the words with cold finality. "They stay."

"You are the King." She stood. "By all means, have them guard your bed. God forbid that anything should happen to you there." She smiled, and bending, kissed his cheek. "Good night."

"Good night?" She nodded and began to cross the room. His voice was sharp. "Where are you going, Isabelle?"

Her hand was on the door. "Back to Corfe, of course."

"To Corfe? What for?"

"How can you ask? With enemies round every corner, someone has to guard the children."

Out she went. I nearly broke into applause. John turned to me. My feelings must have shown. "Get out," he said.

I bowed and left the room. The Queen stood waiting in the corridor. I took her arm, we moved on past the guards on duty there. When it was safe to speak, I turned to her.

"You see why it was so important that you came?"

"I do," she answered. "And it's equally important that I go."

It's not the children, she is not afraid on their account. But she is leaving in the morning. "He must come to me," she said, and nothing I could say would shake her.

Till next time, if God wills it.

At Battersea
The 31st Day of October, A.D. 1212

The King has left his room at last; and with a vengeance. Orders came this morning, and by midday we were off to Corfe.

John travels like an army now. We have a hundred men-at-arms or more, a string of wagons filled with weapons, treasure, stores. And then, of course, the royal bodyguard.

De Breauté, as always, sat by John tonight. I watched them, wondering why, of all men, John had chosen this one to protect him. I could understand the fear that lay behind the King's behavior; even Caesar was not safe, the knife can come from anywhere. But why this loathsome creature?

It was late when John stood up. He yawned and stretched and, turning to de Breauté, he said, "Bring me a woman."

"Yes, my lord."

What was so ominous in "Yes, my lord"? It was the tone, the way the words were spoken. John might just as well have told the man to cut out someone's eye and bring it to him. Such a man is capable of any task; from pouring wine and sitting by one's bed to killing children. Anything at all. The King, I have no doubt, would call it loyalty.

Till next time, if God wills it.

At Corfe
The 7th Day of November, A.D. 1212

The Queen avoids the King. She speaks politely when they meet; at table, passing in the corridors. But that is all. Her bed is in the nursery with the children. There is little chronicling for me to do and I am often with her there.

I'm not, I fear, a child-lover. Little minds have little wit, and little hands are sticky. Still, I have been curiously happy in their company. Henry is five, Richard is three and Joan is two. They are themselves, I know; yet all I see is other people in them. Henry makes a gesture with his hands that is so like his grandfather it shakes me.

All this afternoon I sat with Isabelle and watched her watch them play. She seemed so young, a child herself. Her eyes glowed with affection for them and I said the obvious.

"You love them very much."

"Oh yes," she said at once. "I do." And then she paused and looked at Henry. "There he is, our future King. I see his coronation sometimes in my sleep. I feel so proud. And at the same time, I am swept with desolation. John is dead, you see; I've lost my King and I am nothing any more."

The tutor came. She rose and kissed the children. Then we left and as we moved along the corridor, she said, "I think of Eleanor from time to time. At Henry's death, she lost her King, her throne, her crown and yet for fifteen years, until the day she died, she was the Queen. How did she manage that?"

I shook my head. "There's nothing to be learned from Eleanor, my lady. There has never been another woman like her."

"Ah," she said, as if she understood. We had a lovely dinner and played chess into the night. She is, as I have noted, good at games.

Till next time, if God wills it.

At Corfe
The 11th Day of November, A.D. 1212

All too often, history cheats us. Great things seem to happen in the smallest way. This afternoon, the conflict that has split the Kingdom ended with a sigh.

Des Roches arrived today from London. I was pleased to see

[89]

him; anything is better than the stillness here. He found me in the little chapel, knelt beside me, bowed his head a moment and then put a paper in my hand.

It was the Marshal's answer to our plea for his advice. It urged the King to settle on the Pope's terms; terms which only last year John had violently rejected, since consenting to them all would cost the King not only loss of face but loss of power and the restitution to the Church of untold sums of money. Hard advice, and sound enough. But surely not the kind of wisdom which was apt to please the King.

I had expected something easier to swallow from the Marshal and we went to John with little hope. He read the message once and then again. He lowered it, looked up at us.

He sighed; that's when it came. And then he spoke. "I see no other course" was all he said.

The audience was over. Delegates will soon be on their way to Rome. They will be there for weeks negotiating, whittling at the terms; and then, by Spring, God willing, they will be in England with a treaty for the King to sign.

How simple. What a little thing. "I see no other course."

Till next time, if God wills it.

At Corfe
The 1st Day of December, A.D. 1212

The King, ten days ago, went hunting, taking thirty knights and Fawkes de Breauté to keep him company. He had not told us when he would return; he might, for all we knew, be gone for weeks and I, for one, had had enough of Corfe.

The Queen, for all this time, had been the soul of patience. Needlework and children, quiet resignation. So, at least, it seemed. But I was wrong, it wasn't patience, not at all. The Queen was waiting.

I was with her late tonight when we heard shouting from the yard, the skittering of horses' hooves and cart wheels on the ice.

"It's John," she said and rose at once. She moved across the room to where her gowns were hung. She hesitated: which to wear? I thought she looked quite lovely as it was. She chose, at last, a silk pelisse, full-sleeved and lined with sable.

Taking it, she left the room and, minutes later, reappeared. What can I say? Her hair, when loose, falls to her waist like velvet, as it did now, intermingling with the sable at her throat.

The King was surely in his chambers by this time. I stood and started for the door, expecting her to follow.

"No, Giraldus." I turned back. She sat down by the table where the chessboard lay. "I've waited. It's his turn to wait."

I joined her and we played. I may have dozed, it's possible; I cannot say how long we had been playing when the door flew open and the King strode in. De Breauté came just behind.

"I'm back," he said.

She looked up with the gentlest smile. "Evidently. Do come in. And you, too, Fawkes. How good it is to see you both."

"Have you been well?"

She smiled again. "How was the hunt?"

John shrugged. "Enjoyable enough."

"You do look better. Fresh air and the company of men do wonders for you."

"Are the children well?" John asked her.

"When I saw them last. I should be with them now. With all these enemies about, one cannot be too careful." She stood up. "If you'll excuse me—"

"I have more to say."

She bowed her head. "Go on, my lord."

His voice was sharp. "I have decided to return to London."

"With me or without? Am I to join you?"

"No."

She went on instantly, completely unsurprised. "Of course not. You have your needs, I have mine. I understand, John. Everything. I understand it all . . . and I forgive."

He looked at her with narrow eyes. "What is all this? What is it you forgive?"

"My lord . . ." Then, turning to de Breauté, she said, "Don't go;

don't let him send you from the room. I want to say it to your face." She paused. "Fawkes, I forgive you, too."

John's voice was low and dangerous. "For what?"

"My lord," she said, "for doing what you have to do, for being what you must. I'm only glad that you have chosen Fawkes, a man of such nobility and grace, such beauty . . ."

"That's enough!"

"Oh no, my lord, not nearly. I've expected this for years. It's in your family, isn't it? Your brothers, all of them. I've watched you, waiting for it, knowing it would come."

"Get out!" John roared it at de Breauté. The man's lips moved but no words came. He left the room. John's face was white, his hands were clenched.

"Go on," he said.

She shook her head. "I've said it all."

His fist flashed out. She took the blow without a sound.

"Not ever . . ." He began again. "I've never touched a man or boy. Or wanted to. The others did it; Father, Richard, Geoffrey. Only me, I am the only one. How could you say such things?"

A thread of blood ran down her lip. "When did you touch me last? How long ago?"

The King's lips trembled but he made no answer.

She went on. "Your father locked your mother up in Salisbury Tower; Eleanor was Henry's prisoner, wasn't she? But there were reasons. She had raised an army and she fought him in the field. And even then, he let her out for Christmas Court and Easter, didn't he? What have I done that you should keep me here? Am I to be another Eleanor?"

John looked at her. The man seemed shaken literally to his soul. "Oh Jesus, oh Sweet Jesus, no." His head shook back and forth from side to side. "Not that. Not ever that."

Her hands went to the sash of her pelisse. She loosed it and the robe slipped to the floor. Her skin is of such whiteness, as if God had sculpted her from alabaster. She is perfect.

"I do love you, John," was all she said. She took his hand, she kissed it and she placed it on her breast. The King began to weep. His body shook. He bent to where his fist had struck her and he

kissed the blood away. Her arms went round him and she gav\
little cry.

I left the room as silently as possible. They had, I think, forgoċ-
ten I was there.

I retired to my cubicle. There is a little servant girl who comes
to change the rushes on my floor. I sent for her.

Agnus Dei, qui tollis peccata mundi, etc.

Till next time, if God wills it.

At the Palace of Westminster
The 9th Day of December, A.D. 1212

As each day passes by, the King seems better. Changed, I nearly
wrote; although I don't believe in human change. Our souls, I
think, are like a crystal, like a thing with many faces, and what
seems like change is merely shift.

In any case, the King is shifting. Take de Breauté. Although he
still commands the bodyguard, one rarely sees him any more; he
functions from a distance now. And there are other signs. Last
evening, we had minstrels in and there was music for the first time
since the summer. Dancing, too. The King, when he was young,
was wonderful to see. He moves more stiffly now, but all one
watches is the Queen.

Tonight saw further shifting. We were in the royal rooms; John,
Isabelle, Longsword and I. The room was bright and warm, a fire
blazed and torches burned. The brothers had been telling soldier's
tales while Isabelle knelt by the fire, mulling wine. I watched her,
listening to the laughter from the men. Then it subsided and I
heard the King.

"It's over," he began. I turned and watched him rise and move
to Isabelle. He looked at her a moment. "I've been through a dark
time, haven't I?"

She smiled at him and nodded. "Yes."

"Well, we must make amends for that." He turned to me.
"What are the plans for Christmas Court?"

I had no ready answer. We had talked of it, of course, des Roches and I; for there is no occasion more politically important in the year. "No plans as yet, my lord."

John frowned. "Why not? What must my barons think of me? These last six months . . ." He shook his head. "I want them all here, every baron in the kingdom."

Was there time? So much to do. There are three hundred barons roughly: all those letters to be sent and rooms prepared and food and wine enough for twelve days' feasting. "But, my lord—"

"Giraldus, get a pen and paper."

Which I did. We spent the evening making lists, beginning with the gifts. Two treasure chests were brought. We moved a trestle table to the fire and we spilled their contents out: cascades of rubies, emeralds *en cabochon,* as big as knuckles; brooches, buckles, sword-chapes, dagger pommels, cups and plates and ornaments of gold.

It is the custom for the King to give his barons precious things at Christmas time. And they, in turn, give gold and jewels to him and to each other. What the King gives is a matter of some delicacy. If a baron wants to know his standing in the King's esteem, he reads it in his gift.

A massive emerald ring to Chester: he is up. A dagger-chape to Norfolk: he is down. And so it went until we came to old Arundel.

"This," the King said, picking up a goblet.

I began to note it down when Isabelle said, "No, my lord, I don't think you should give him that."

"Why not? It isn't good enough?" She shook her head. "Well, then?"

"You gave it to him once already."

These things happen on occasion. They are not supposed to: what the King gives is not meant to pass from hand to hand, from baron this to baron that. They do it nonetheless; there is some risk but the economy appeals to them.

John scowled. "The old fool gave it back to me?"

The Queen looked up at him, so serious. "What should we do?"

"I think—" He couldn't finish. He was laughing. "Try again," he managed to get out. "Perhaps he'll like it better this time."

There was little we accomplished after that. How good it is to weep from laughter for a change.

Till next time, if God wills it.

At the Palace of Westminster
The 20th Day of December, A.D. 1212

Excuses. Dozens of them, more each day. They vary: some are clumsy and transparent, some bear touches of invention. All in all, it comes to this: a good half of our barons are not coming; they are daring not to come. They are "detained" or "health prevents" and "circumstances unforeseen" arise on every hand.

The King is calm about it; rather pleased, in fact. He finds it most revealing, making careful notes of all who do not come and why. The Queen, unlike him, is a tigress, white with rage as she goes storming up and down the corridors. When spoken to, she spits the words: these pigs, to treat her King like this. She'd put them all in chains, I think.

As for myself, I think the King is right but all my feelings go with Isabelle. How can they treat the Crown with such contempt? It is an outrage.

Chester, Warenne, old Arundel, half a hundred others are already here and many more will come. But even so, my hand shakes as I write of this offense.

This afternoon, I stood with Longsword on the palace parapet. His eyes, the whole time, stayed on the horizon. What, I asked him, was he searching for? Was he afraid the absent barons might attack us? He denied it.

Till next time, if God wills it.

At the Palace of Westminster
The 23rd Day of December, A.D. 1212

Dammartin is here with news that changes everything. The French are on the Flemish border, they have taken St. Omer with forces far too great for such a purpose. He has been in Flanders and had seen the army for himself.

The rest he has not witnessed but he takes it to be true: that men were being raised all over France, that armaments and war machines were even now in transit to the Channel ports, that cargo ships were gathering; and galleys, too. In short, a fleet. And there can be no other purpose for a fleet except to cross the Channel. France was planning to invade.

We heard this during supper, over meat and pudding. John kept silent, listening to it all until the end. His face was thoughtful, nothing more. At last he spoke.

"Is Philip in command at St. Omer?"

"No," Dammartin replied. "The Prince is."

"Louis leads the army?"

"Yes, my lord."

"Then taking St. Omer was his idea?"

"It was."

John smiled. "We should thank him. Louis is a fool, he moved too soon. They don't dare cross the Channel till the spring. If only he had waited, England might have been surprised."

John looked at Longsword then; a long look, hard and bright. "This time," he said.

"This time," his brother answered back.

I understood their meaning. This time there would be a war and this time we would win it. The French were coming to our shores and every man and boy in England would be on the beaches waiting for them.

War is monstrous, I abhor it. Even so, my eyes filled up.

Till etc.

N.B.: the King is forty-six tomorrow. Christmas Eve.

[96]

At the Palace of Westminster
The 24th Day of December, A.D. 1212

Christmas Court. It has begun. I feel—it doesn't matter what I feel. Start with the Hall. The Great Hall.

It is vast, the size of a cathedral. Hung with green, it was; bay, holly, fir. The servants stood in line along the walls, a hundred of them, surely. The musicians sat upon a platform in one corner: trumpets, fiddles, bagpipes, flutes and tabors, cymbals, bells. Beside them stood the maskers, dancers, troubadours and jugglers.

In the center of the floor, a fire blazed. A trestle table of great size stood near it, bearing knights and dragons all of marzipan. And spreading out in all directions were the tables for the barons of the realm. For all of them: for those who came and those who did not come. Two hundred empty places. John insisted on it being so.

We sat and waited for the King and Queen. Time passed; a lot of it and there was shifting in the Hall and murmured voices. Suddenly, the trumpeting began. A fanfare, golden sound, it soared out to the walls and ceiling, tumbling back, cascading down. Then, at the far end of the Hall, the great doors opened and they stood revealed: the King of England and his Queen.

I felt it instantly, like needles in my flesh. For even at this distance, there was something in the two of them. They moved in through the doors and, grandly, as if all the country had just risen to its feet, they started out across the Hall.

The King was dressed in gray; all gray with no adornment save his coronation crown, a thing which I had never seen him wear. The Queen was soft and glowing; ivory silk and rubies. Rubies everywhere.

They moved across the vast space, past the empty tables to their place upon the dais. Then the fanfare ended and John turned to me. I stood and bowed my head and spoke a prayer, and in the silence afterward, the King began to speak.

"Today," he said, "we mark the fourteenth Christmas of my reign. My father marked his fourteenth in the year that I was born and I have spent some time in weighing what I've done against the things that he achieved.

"What have I done? This Hall rings out the answer. I am King of a divided country. I should know; it's my work that divided it. I've been a spendthrift. I have wasted friends and countless soldiers, wealth and territory. Lost: I've lost so much, and yesterday I learned I stand a chance to lose it all."

He paused and looked across the faces and the empty tables. "All of you should know that France is planning an invasion. Troops are moving and a fleet is being formed. They could not choose a better time; or so they think. We've never seemed so weak. But are we? That's the question. Will we let this island fall? Are we to be a part of France? A province? When their ships come into view, who will be there to greet them? I, for one. Who else?"

They stood, they rose up. Every baron in the Hall was on his feet. John looked at them. His eyes were glittery and very bright.

"We may be there alone," he said. "It is a possibility. Fitz-Walter and de Vescy and their friends, whoever and however many they may be, they think I'm done. But I know one thing they do not: I know what I can do and I will do it. I will call this country to its feet and it will rise and follow me. In thousands, tens of thousands, men will come. With rakes and axes in their hands, if nothing else. No Frenchman sits on Henry's throne. His line goes on, it does not stop with me."

His voice rang out, it filled the Hall. "My children and their children will be kings. We will survive!"

The Queen was smiling as she wept. If, at that moment, Hell appeared, he could have led us through the gates.

Till next time, if God wills it.

At the Palace of Westminster
The 31st Day of December, A.D. 1212

The year will end soon. Any minute now, the bells will ring and we will never see 1212 again. It has not been the best of years: two wars aborted, plots, conspiracies, dark days. But Fortune's wheel is turning and the year ahead is filled with hope.

Our meetings here are ended. All our basic plans and strategies are drawn. It now remains to implement them. John, who is convinced our best hopes lie in victory at sea, is off to Portsmouth in the morning. I go with him. Longsword will be leaving for the Midlands, charged with seeing to the building of transport and war machines. Des Roches stays here to raise the necessary taxes. We may not meet again till spring.

Dear Lord, I have so much to thank You for: for bringing me from Lincoln to the heart of things; for giving me the strength to do what little I have done; for the high promise of an ending to the Interdict; for showing John his way again; for—

There they go. The bells. Be kind to us, my Lord; give us a good new year and, if it please You, let me live to see it all.

At Portsmouth
The 13th Day of January, A.D. 1213

Each day, we rise at dawn, put on our furs and instantly go out. The pathway from the King's house to the shipyard is a sheet of frost, the Channel winds come howling in through Spithead to the harbor and the docks are thick with ice. We generally arrive before the carpenters and shipwrights, for the King is in such haste.

Ships and more ships, they are all John thinks about. He sees the Channel as a fortress wall; it's this the enemy must breach, and with a fleet ranged all along our coast we can destroy them at their weakest point. Which is to say, before they land.

The problem that we face is this: our fleet is far too small. In 1205, which is the last time count was taken of our royal galleys, we had fifty-one of them. These vessels are the primal ship of war, the spine, the cutting edge, and we must treble what we have by May. The yards of the Cinque Ports are busy, too; but how in God's name can it all be done in time?

They have, since we arrived, begun four ships. This morning, as the sun came up, we watched them put a fifth keel down. They cannot start a sixth; they lack the artisans, the space. I watched John move among the workmen, confident and sure, a word for everyone.

The sun was well up when we left the yard. The harbor is a splendid one, in use for centuries as a landing place. But Portsmouth—that's to say, the town itself; the yard, the cottages, the King's house and Saint Thomas' church—is not a quarter of a century old. King Richard had it built.

John stood there scowling at it. "Christ, he could have made it larger, couldn't he? It's half a town, it's no damned good to me like this."

He broke off.

By midday, the plans were made. The shipyard will be doubled and the docks expanded and a warehouse built. By afternoon, our men were moving through the countryside enrolling workers.

It is evening and the King is sitting near me, by the fire, on his traveling throne. Each night we write a message for des Roches in London, and the one before me ends as follows: "In the spring, our fleet will mass here and the harbor will be ready."

He believes it.

At Folkestone
The 27th Day of January, A.D. 1213

We have been following the coastline, port to port. The scene in every shipyard is the same: the keels go down, the shipwrights work as if possessed and John is met with cheers.

There is a tide of feeling in the land. It washes over us no matter where we go. The King was right: the common people may not care about a war in France but they will fight and die to keep their country safe.

This afternoon, the King and I went walking near the port. The sea is cruel at Folkestone, churning, eating at the shore. There was a bank of fog some distance out and, for a moment, I imagined

French ships moving through it. I have never been in battle. Would I run?

"My lord?" I said.

"What is it?"

"Is it difficult to kill a man?"

He looked at me. "In what way difficult?"

"The doing of it, taking life; how does it feel?"

"It varies."

"Ah," I said and left it there. How often had he done it? Fifty times? One hundred? More? He'd spent his life in battle; did he see their faces when he slept? All foolish questions; juvenile. A scholar writes, a soldier kills; it must come easy to them.

We move on: tomorrow Dover, then to Sandwich. Our inspection of the Cinque Ports will be finished in a week and after that, I do not know.

Till next time, if God wills it.

At Sandwich
The 2nd Day of February, A.D. 1213

William Marshal is in London. We are meeting him in Canterbury. It is snowing. We shall ride all night, if need be.

At Canterbury Cathedral
The 4th Day of February, A.D. 1213

We watched his coming from the great cathedral steps. The snow had stopped, the day was very bright and we could hear him, hear the music and the cheering, as his equipage moved through the town.

The King, who had not slept, looked pale. We had done nothing all night long but talk of Marshal; even as we rode. No one is certain of his age; some say he is past eighty. John was three when

Marshal entered Henry's service and has always stood in awe of him, which is an easy thing to do.

The sounds were louder, nearer. They were past the Butter Market, moving down Saint Peter's Street and we would see them soon. When had I met the Marshal first? Could it be forty years ago? It is an odd thing, greatness. As a rule, one has it young or not at all. Not so with Marshal; it has come to him as he has aged. The man has grown great.

Down below, the people on the street were shifting, craning: who would be the first to see? Then suddenly, the air was filled with singing, and around the turn the servitors appeared. Two hundred men or more, in uniforms of gold and black, their voices raised in song, strode toward us down the lane. Then the musicians: pipes and drums and portatives.

Then came the huntsmen, thirty of them, surely; some with greyhounds, some with limers, held on double leashes. Next, the carts, each drawn by five matched horses. In the first were kegs of ale. The next held chapel furniture, the third was filled with fittings for a bedchamber. Another carried kitchen things and two more came with tapestries and chests of clothes.

Behind these came the sumpters, heavy-laden; each horse with a rider on its back, each rider with a monkey on his shoulder. In the packs the horses bore were all the finer things: the silver and the gold utensils, roundels, cups, plates, bowls. The final sumpter, carrying the altar ornaments and sacred vessels, passed us by.

There was a pause before the knights appeared. I cannot say how many hundred. Each came mounted on his palfrey, with his war-horse leashed behind, the horses' hot breath misting in the air, their hooves a rumble on the ground.

The squires came on foot, of course, each one behind his knight. Fine-looking boys with falcons on their wrists. Next, riding two by two, there came the household officers: the seneschals and chamberlains, the stewards, butlers, chaplains, doctors, pages, cooks, the grooms and clerks.

And then the Marshal.

Riding all alone, he came. His head was bare. His hair and beard are white, he wears them both close-cropped. He reached the bottom of the stairs, dismounted and began to climb. His back is straight as ever and his step is firm. His face, I saw as he came close, is deeply lined now but his eyes are still bright blue.

He stood before the King. "Your Majesty," he said and bowed.

"My lord." John's voice was soft. "How was your journey?"

"Long."

Then came a moment with no words. The greatest earl of all stood looking at the King who had deprived him of his lands and held his son in hostage.

It stretched on, the moment did, and then I can't say who moved first, but suddenly the King was weeping and the Marshal knelt and they were holding one another.

I have always held a dim view of emotional display before the common people. I, myself, have never wept in public. Nor did I today. My private conduct is another matter; I have loved the Marshal for so long.

There is a feast now in his honor. I must stop this sniveling and go down.

Till next time, if God wills it.

At Canterbury Castle
The 5th Day of February, A.D. 1213

I am not a petty person. I do not remember small affronts or shabby treatment. Yet, the feast last night in honor of the Marshal did disturb me. To be seated at the table's end, to be ignored or largely so by those who clustered round the King, such things did not sit well at all. Nor did I much enjoy it that the Marshal scarcely greeted me. I am an old friend, am I not?

I left the Great Hall early and retired to my room. I prayed, undressed and, freezing, slipped beneath the blankets, curling as a child does until some warmth might come. My face was to the wall, I heard no knocking at the door nor footsteps on the rushes. He can still move like a great cat.

"Giraldus?"

With a gasp, I sat up straight. The Marshal stood there by my bed. "My lord," I said, and moved to rise.

He put a cold hand on my shoulder. "Stay," he told me, sitting down beside me with a sigh. "The old bones ache at night."

"I know; I have some of my own."

"How long is it, Giraldus?"

He had come through Lincoln after Normandy was lost and I had seen him then. "Eight years," I said.

He looked at me; how clear his eyes are. "Have you been well?" he asked.

I nodded. "Yes." Had exile made him bitter? If it had, there was no sign.

He smiled. "The Hall just now was full of strangers. I have many names to learn. They go, they go; the friends drop off. We're all that's left."

I felt it, like a bubble rising. There was nothing I could do to stop it. I apologized, of course, and then I turned my face away. A tear or two, no more; and only for a moment. Self-indulgence; it was weak of me, and maudlin.

There was brandywine, a flagon of it, on my table. And one goblet, which we shared. We drank and talked for hours, deep into the night. His mind is keen as ever and his strength is undiminished. He had many things to ask of me. I answered him as best I could.

Till next time, if God wills it.

At Canterbury Castle
The 7th Day of February, A.D. 1213

All yesterday, the Marshal and the King were closeted together, coming out at mealtimes side by side, displaying such affection for each other. Not today. From morning on, the two had been at quiet odds. For each has suffered at the other's hands, or thinks he has; and I could all but see the feelings wriggling, like so many moles, just underneath the surface.

Late tonight, it all erupted. We were sitting in the oriel, one of those tiny roundish rooms so much in fashion nowadays. A fire burned, the air was hot and close and there was space, just barely, for the three of us to sit.

"I often wonder," John was saying, "how my father might have dealt with what I face from day to day, what strategies or plans he might have made."

The Marshal nodded. "Yes, I'm sure you do."

John went on, just a bit too sharply, "Tell me, did he always follow your advice?"

"By no means . . . but he always listened."

"Ah." John nodded. "What, in your opinion, would have been his course in 1205?"

I stiffened in my chair. That was the year the two of them had fallen out.

"It would be guesswork. Who can say?" The Marshal paused. "But I can tell you for a fact what he would not have done."

There was an edge to John's voice now. "Go on."

"He would not have turned on me."

"I see." John licked his lips. "Would you have openly humiliated him? That's what you did to me, you know."

"I merely stopped you from a war you would have lost."

John nodded. "Yes, of course. I should have thanked you, shouldn't I? You had my interests in your heart."

"I did."

"And what about your interests? What about your castles and estates in France? Did Philip take them from you? He did not. You are the only baron who has holdings on both sides. You must be very close, you two."

"He trusts me and I've fought against him all his life. Why can't you do as much?"

"The man's my greatest enemy and you're his friend: that's all I know."

The Marshal may be great and wise but he is not a saint. His hands were clenched, his voice was low and rasping. "If that's all you know, God help you. Have you any notion what you've done to me? You tore my home away from me, you took my son, you drove me into exile; seven years of it. And when I come to serve you in your time of need, you spit at me."

The King could barely speak. "Then tell me this. Why are you here? Why did you come?"

"I came because—" He stopped. He sighed. "I don't know why. I had to come, I cannot help myself. You and your family, I am tied to you."

"I know." John looked away. "I may forget it now and then but I do know."

No more was said for quite some time. The two of them have come together now, I think.

Till next time, if God wills it.

At Canterbury Castle
The 8th Day of February, A.D. 1213

Des Roches arrived tonight with news from Rome. He found us in the Marshal's chamber, standing by the fire. He looked half frozen from his journey, for the night is bitter cold. He joined us, warmed himself a moment, then began.

A message from John's delegation to the Pope had come to London yesterday. The facts were these: negotiations were extremely difficult. The Pope was adamant, he would not give on any point: the King must make his peace with Stephen Langton and he must make total restitution of all lands and monies taken from the Church. We had expected this, of course. John said so.

"Yes, my lord," des Roches replied, "but there is more. The treaty must be signed and witnessed by the first of June."

John looked up sharply. "Must?" he said. "It must be signed?"

"That is the situation as our people see it; yes, my lord."

"And by the first of June?"

"The first of June."

"Why then? What happens on the first of June?"

"Your deposition, Sire."

John's head snapped back. "My what?"

"The Pope has theatened to depose you."

"Let him threaten."

"There is more, my lord." It came to this: the Pope had given Stephen Langton certain letters. In them, he declared King John deposed and called upon King Philip to replace him. Were the treaty signed in time, the letter would be burned and never published.

There was silence in the room. Why would the Pope take such a stand? What was he thinking? He cannot, of course, depose the King; not really, not in fact. But such a declaration carries dreadful weight. I was about to say so when the Marshal said it for me.

"It's important that we understand the power of these letters. What they do, what they amount to is a call for a Crusade. The Pope has put his blessing on the French and they can march against us with his banner flying in a Holy War."

John's voice was cold. "I know that. Well?" He looked around at all of us. "You're my advisors. How do you advise me? Shall I take this Pope's priest, Stephen Langton, and install him in the See of Canterbury? Shall I strip the kingdom for the money they insist I owe? And having done all this, shall I then kneel down like a coward and accept this ultimatum?"

No one spoke. John raked his eyes across our faces. "Shall I?"

"You may have to," Marshal answered.

John stepped toward him. "Are you telling me to swallow this?"

"I'm telling you it may be necessary."

"May be? Any fool can tell me may be. You're my wise ones. You," he snapped, his angry eyes on mine.

"My lord?" I answered.

"What would you do?"

"In your place, my lord?" I ventured, having no idea what I would do.

"Well said, Giraldus. Christ, what do I keep you for?" He stood there breathing deeply for a moment. Then he spoke. "I have said yes to Langton, I have said yes to the reparations but I cannot live with this. I will not take an ultimatum. I will not submit." He turned to go.

"My lord?" It was des Roches.

[107]

"There is no more to say." John roared it out. "I will not bend."

"My lord, I only meant to ask, what answer shall we send the Pope?"

"No answer. Let him wait."

He turned and left the room.

The Marshal sighed and shook his head. "I hope he's right," he said.

I licked my lips and asked the question. "What would you have done?"

The Marshal had no answer, either.

Till next time, if God wills it.

At Canterbury Castle
The 10th Day of February, A.D. 1213

The King rode off this morning, filled with great enthusiasm and high hope. He will be gone a fortnight, visiting his people; freemen, farmers, peasants, commonfolk. They are to be his army. He is not depending this time on his barons and their knights; nor will he hire mercenaries. When the call to arms goes out, it is to be addressed to all of England; he would visit every village in the kingdom if he could.

It is as if he had a vision. Let the Pope depose him, let the barons play their games; he will survive because his people stand beside him. Will they do it, will they come? He has no doubt of it at all.

He is, I fear, unreasonably optimistic. Why, for instance, should the common people fight at all? They cannot profit, they have no estates to gain, they must know that their enemy is skillful and experienced. And if the people do not come, what then? Or if they see the papal banner in the field against them, mightn't they lay down their arms?

Last night, I talked about it with the Marshal and it troubles him as well. For it confronts us with the very situation which he feared: two enemies at once.

And so, we went to see the King. We found him in his bed, not yet asleep. The Marshal came directly to the point.

"This going to the common people, John. There is some risk in it."

John nodded. "There are many risks, I know that."

"Have you thought," the Marshal asked, "of what might happen if they do not come when they are called?"

"Oh, that." John smiled and shook his head. "There is no possibility of that. My people love me. You will see."

We did not press him further. He believes it to be so.

Till next time, if God wills it.

At the Tower, London
The 26th Day of February, A.D. 1213

We are still waiting for the King to come. Longsword has joined us and the days go by in meetings, planning, the decisions and details that make a war: how many horses, how much fodder, garde-robe pits and drainage, longbow maintenance and mangonel repair. My interest in such things is limited; I tend to drift as Longsword and the Marshal argue out how many carts we need or where the stones will come from for the trebuchets.

Today, when work was done, I went with Longsword for a walk. The sky was clear and bright sun glinted on the snow. We wandered through the City, out the northern wall to Mooresfield. Here, the marsh is smoothly frozen and there must have been a hundred young men skating. They strap horses' shinbones to their feet and push themselves along with poles. They have no skill at all, they fall and tumble constantly. The air was filled with shouts and laughter.

I was laughing, too, and thinking that our jesters ought to come and study here, when Longsword sharply turned away. I looked at him. His face was taut, his lips were pressed together tight.

"What's wrong, my lord?"

"What's wrong?" He raised his massive arm and pointed at the skaters. "Tell me what you see? Is that an army? Are they soldiers? Christ, John puts his faith in peasant boys and turnip farmers. What does he think the French are coming with? Milkmaids, for the love of God? He'll have us on the beach with hoes and hay rakes. And I sit here with the Marshal making battle plans, for Jesus' sake."

"The King believes they'll fight," I said.

He looked at me as cries of laughter rose around us. "What do you believe?" he said and, turning, started off across the snow back to the City wall. I hurried after him.

Till next time, if God wills it.

At the Tower, London
The 28th Day of February, A.D. 1213

The King is back from visiting his people and the Queen is with him. He had gone to Woodstock for her and the two of them had toured the land together. It was good, I thought, for him to use her in this way and I had never seen the two of them more close or pleased with one another.

The King could not stop talking of their travels, of the way that they were greeted and the feeling in the land. The Queen's eyes never left his face; though she had been there with him through it all, she hung on every word.

I could not read the Marshal's thoughts, or Longsword's. They sat smiling and attentive, saying little. For tonight was clearly not the time to give reports or bring John up to date on this or that. Tomorrow would be soon enough.

We left them early in the evening. Marshal walked with me in silence up the stairs. We stopped outside my room. I turned to him. "What do you think?" I asked.

"I think . . ." He paused. "I think the Queen has grown."

An odd remark, I thought. And then I realized that she'd been fourteen at the most when he had seen her last. "She's lovely, isn't she?" I said.

"She's more than that," he answered and then clasped my arm the way he always does when it comes time to say good night.

Till next time, if God wills it.

At the Tower, London
The 1st Day of March, A.D. 1213

The evening started quietly enough. We were exhausted, all of us, from endless meetings. For the King had been away from London nearly sixty days and every clerk and councillor in the government had something to report.

We sat around a table in the royal chamber; John, the Marshal, Longsword and myself. The meal had ended. Isabelle had settled near the fire, intent upon her needlework. There was a pleasant brandywine and I was lost in reverie and listening, I confess, with half an ear.

There was a web of feeling in the room, fine threads connecting them in complex ways. The brothers and the Marshal and the Queen as well, although she sat apart; the four of them were tied into some pattern that became less clear the more I thought about it.

In the main, they talked about the war. I heard the King say he anticipated twenty thousand men to come when they were called to arms. The number, roughly the total populace of London, sounded high to me. The Marshal thought so too, apparently.

"Did you say twenty thousand men?" I heard him say.

John smiled. "I know my people; you will see."

At which point, Longsword spoke. "I don't see that it matters much." He said it softly, almost with indifference.

John turned to him. "You don't?"

"Not really." Longsword shrugged. "I can be wrong, of course; an army full of dairymen and shepherds may be just the thing to terrify the French."

"I see." John paused. "What would you like to have our army made of?"

"Soldiers."

"Mercenaries?"

Longsword nodded. "I keep thinking there is something to be said for fighting wars with fighting men."

John sat up very straight. "You have no grasp of what I'm doing, none at all."

"I know how wars are fought."

"Not this one. If my people stand behind me, I'm invincible."

"Invincible? They'll run around like ants, your people will."

"They'll fight." John snapped it out. "They'll fight because it's home they're fighting for."

"I want no part of it." Longsword was on his feet. He leaned across the table. "You're a fool."

John stood up slowly. "I'm your King."

"God help us." Longsword's voice was choked and thick. "Yes. You're the King who lost us Normandy and Brittany. This time you'll lose it all."

"You bastard!"

"That's right, I'm the bastard, Father's bastard—"

"Stop it!" Marshal's voice rang out. He brought his fist down on the table. "Stop it!" There was a silence in the room.

The next to speak was Isabelle.

Her needlework lay in her lap. Her eyes burned in the paleness of her face. "How dare you? William Longsword, that's your King, how dare you speak to him like this? And John, how dare you tolerate it? And you, sir." She turned to Marshal. "You, how dare you bring your fist down on the table?"

Marshal rose. "My lady, my dear child—"

"You may not call me that. You're not my father and I haven't been a child for years. I am ashamed of all of you. You, too, Giraldus; sitting there without a word. You and the Marshal, how you love to play at being wise men. I was with the King in Normandy. I know what he endured. I know what happened at Mirebeau—and so does each of you."

The brothers looked at one another. Longsword was the first to move. He reached out for John's hand and kissed it.

John could scarcely speak. "I know, I know, I know," he said, as if that answered everything. They sat, and for a while no one spoke.

Then Marshal started talking of the loss of Normandy. For he had fought there; Longsword, too. They shared in what had happened: the decisions wrongly made, the messages that came too late, the blunders and the accidents. I watched their faces, twisted by the anguish of mistakes, lost chances and regret.

The Marshal sighed and summed it up. "The war, I like to think, was lost before it started. It was lost when Henry died and lost again when Richard led us to disaster on Crusade and lost a third time by the tithes that paid his ransom and a fourth by the exhaustion of his endless wars." He shook his head. "It was not possible to win. Time after time, it did not matter, north or south, which way we went. The wheel was turning. No man could have stopped it."

John looked up at him. "Is that the truth?"

The Marshal shrugged. "It's my belief. The truth is always something else."

The Queen had risen and she moved across the room. She stood in front of John and Longsword. Then she knelt and, reaching out, she gave a hand to each of them. She seemed, I thought, to be the wise one; older and more knowing than the brothers. She said nothing, but the words were on her face. From all the fighting and regret, she was absolving them. I've never seen a sadder smile.

Till next time, if God wills it.

At the Tower, London
The 2nd Day of March A.D. 1213

This is John's message to his people. It is being copied now and in the morning messengers will carry it to every sheriff in the country.

Thus it goes:

"Give warning by good agents to the earls, barons, knights and all free and serving men, whoever they may be, that they be at Barham Down at the end of the coming Lent, equipped with horses and arms and all they can provide, to defend our person and themselves and the land of England, and let no one who can carry arms remain behind under penalty of being branded with coward-ice and of being condemned to perpetual slavery; and let each man follow his lord."

Our fleet, by Lent, will be at Portsmouth. Every craft in Eng-land capable of fighting on the water will be there.

As for the issue of the mercenaries, it has been resolved. We are to have them but to hold them in reserve. It is the King's design to have his people win this war.

And as for Philip, may the devil take him.

At Barham
The 18th Day of March, A.D. 1213

Barham is a village of no consequence at all. A dozen cottages, a daub-and-wattle church and literally nothing else, it molders in a little valley off the main road, ten miles south of Canterbury, ten miles north of Dover.

We left at dawn from Canterbury. It has taken us the day to reach here; for the road, dear God, the road is filled with men.

They come and keep on coming, men of every kind. There are some knights, of course, their squires riding just behind. But for the most part, they are ordinary folk: young farmers with an ax or scythe in hand, townspeople, merchants who have never held a blade, old men with bent backs, limping from the journey.

Most of them had never seen their King. Some bowed, some wept, some waved and shouted; many merely looked at him as if he were a figure from some song or story which they knew by heart.

The day was warm and cool at once; a spring day. We rode slowly. John had something for them all: a smile, a word or two, a gesture of some kind. One old man told us he had fought at Véze-lay with Henry: fifty years ago. Another, that he'd been with Rich-ard on Crusade. Some of the men weren't men at all, but boys;

ten, twelve years old. And there were family groups among them; uncles, cousins. Many came with all their sons.

The King, at one point, left the road. To have a better view of it, he said. We rode across a field and then turned back. His eyes were glazed with tears, the corners of his mouth were twisted down with rage; both things at once. "You see?" I heard him say. "I knew they'd come. You see, you see?"

We did not stop at Barham. It was twilight when we reached it and we rode on past the cottages and up into the hills. Before us, stretching out for miles, was Barham Down. Rich meadowland and rolling fields. A broad stream wandered through it all, and camped along the stream were men. Not many yet; three thousand possibly, no more than that. But Lent has only just begun.

Till next time, if God wills it.

At Barham
The 5th Day of April, A.D. 1213

The King returned this afternoon from several days in London. I was working with the Marshal when he came. The two of us are quartered in the cottage nearest to the church and we went out to him at once.

The Queen was with him. He had brought her, out of pride, I think, but who can blame him? All of England knows of Barnham Down by now. She could not wait to see it. We set off at once, the four of us, across the valley toward the hills beyond which lies the Down. It is a walk of twenty minutes.

Sheep were grazing. The beginnings of the evening mist were stirring in the twilight. On we went. Behind us, in the town, a dog barked. Then the hills began; low hills with gentle slopes. Some birds flew past us; gulls, they may have been, for we are not far from the Channel here.

At last we reached the highest hill of all. It rises up more sharply than the rest. We climbed in silence; everything was still. I listened to our breathing and the sound our feet made on the grass. Then,

[115]

as we neared the crest, the noises from the Down swept over us like summer thunder; rumbling, deep, as if the earth were moving. Every time I make this climb, it shakes me. Isabelle drew back. John put an arm around her. There was little left, a few more steps. We reached the top together.

"Oh, my God," she said, and stood there motionless, her eyes wide at the scene below.

One hundred thousand men. Five Londons in a single field. They are like beetles from this height, a mass of moving things. They were in shadow now and fires burned. How many fires? Jesus knows. The air was thick with smoke and smells: meat roasting, fodder, feces, human flesh. The stream that wanders through the field is utterly befouled. They drink it, for there is no other water. They have fevers and the nights are cold and many of them die. We bury those we can: the rest we leave in stacks. They fight between themselves, they rob the living and the dead, there is no discipline or order here. And yet—I've been amongst them and I know this to be true—and yet if John commanded "Die for me!" one hundred thousand men would do it. It is terrible and beautiful, this field; it breaks the heart.

The Queen began to weep. She turned her face to John. Her lips moved. "Oh, my God," she said again. "They're doing this for you."

Till next time, if God wills it.

At Barham
The 7th Day of April, A.D. 1213

The facts are these:

A messenger arrived from France this morning early. I was still at breakfast with the Marshal and the King when he was ushered in. He had, he told us, come from Soissons, where King Philip has been holding council with his noblemen. This much, of course, we knew; we have our agents and informants, as does Philip, I've no doubt. In any case, the council met, deliberated and brought forth a document. He had a copy of it in his purse.

John placed it on the table for the three of us to read. A most extraordinary thing it is. Put simply, it dismembers England, carves it into slices like a roasted joint and serves it to the French nobility as if the war had been already won. And not content with this, it then proceeds to take John from the throne and crown Prince Louis, Philip's son, as King of England. There is even an addendum as to what his rights and powers are to be.

"Incredible," the Marshal murmured. Then he looked up at the messenger. "One further question."

"Yes, my lord?"

"How did this copy come into your hands?"

The fellow shrugged. "I took it from the wall where it was posted."

"Posted?" I have never seen the Marshal more surprised. "You mean to say this document is public knowledge?"

"Yes, my lord. Their scribes are making copies, dozens of them."

"Christ," the Marshal said.

John thanked the fellow and dismissed him. There was silence as he looked first at the Marshal, then at me. "Well? What are we to make of this?"

I thought I knew. "It means that Philip is a fool."

"He's not." The Marshal's voice was sharp. "I wish to God he were a fool. How can he be so sure? What does he know?" He went on in this vein, convinced that Philip had some new ally, some secret that would overwhelm us.

Nonsense, and I told him so. It was a blunder, surely; something done from mindless arrogance and gall, from bloated pride and self-conceit.

John spoke then. "No, you've missed it, both of you. You do not understand the man. He hates me. Philip hates me, he has done so all his life, since we were children; forty years. He hates my family, too; no matter that they're dead. My father made a cuckold of his father: that goes deep. We are a single thing in Philip's

[117]

mind, we live inside his brain, he does mad things because of us." John paused and wiped his hand across his eyes. Then, turning to the Marshal, he went on. "Is he a brilliant soldier? Yes or no?"

"The man is brilliant in the field."

"Then why, I ask you, does he come for England? Why not take the Aquitaine? There's not a province like it on the Continent. It's priceless and it's mine and these five years, while I've been helpless here, did he attack it? Did he touch it, did he send a single man? Could I have stopped him if he had? It's not my lands he wants. It's me. He wants me broken and he wants me dead. And this—" He took the document and crumpled it. "This thing, it isn't public. It's a private message, it's for me. It says 'I'm coming for you, John; I'll have you this time.' "

He stood up and began to pace. To what extent, I wondered, was the King correct? Had he explained a document or a relationship? Or were the two things one? My thoughts were interrupted by the King.

"Giraldus?"

"Yes, my lord?"

He held the crumpled paper out to me. "Have copies made of this."

"Of course, my lord. How many?"

"Dozens."

"What in God's name for?" I blurted out.

"I want it read all over England. Let my people hear the sound of Philip's voice. He's given us a common cause, that's what he's done."

I rose to go. The scribes are quartered in the stable just across the way, and I was moving toward the door when John spoke out again.

"Giraldus. One thing more." I stopped and turned. A smile was spreading on his face. "I think . . ." The smile grew broader. "I believe the time has come to make our peace with Rome."

My mouth fell open. "Peace with Rome?"

"I've kept them waiting long enough. I've made my point. If Innocent had wanted me deposed, he would have done it months ago and they must know I know that now. I think you'll find his people happy to negotiate." He paused. "I want you on your way as soon as possible."

My heart stopped. "Me, my lord?"

"Unless you'd rather not."

"I'll do my best, of course, but . . ." There was ringing in my ears. The size of the responsibility, the magnitude. But is it possible? Can it be done in time? I have no answer, for I do not know.

Till next time, if God wills it.

At Canterbury Castle
The 10th Day of April, A.D. 1213

The time, the time; it is the time that presses in. It leaves no room. The first of June. My back is to the cliff. For God's sake, how can I negotiate when time is on the other side?

I have been saying so all day. Des Roches is down from London and I've sat with him, the King and Marshal working out the limits in which I can move. What tactics can I use? Can I make threats, delay, break off the talks? No, I cannot. Is there a line that I can draw or one demand I can refuse when, on the first of June, John is deposed and Philip has his holy war? The other side has only to sit back and wait. I have no arguments with teeth.

On top of which, I shall be dealing with the papal emissary. Pandulf is his name. Although of little rank, he is an intimate of Innocent's and has the powers of a cardinal. We have not met. His reputation is enormous.

How do I compare? What are my powers? I know brilliance when I see it. Becket, Abélard; these are great men and I am not. I'm clever, I say clever things and tell good stories. I am tempted to suggest they send some other man. But only tempted. I have always lost to Rome. The Pope has robbed me, ruled against me, stolen bishoprics and sees which should, by rights, have come to me. I would not miss this for the world.

Vespers is ringing, there is yet another meeting. I must go.

Till etc.

[119]

At Dover Castle
The 13th Day of April, A.D. 1213

My heart is pounding and I cannot sleep. I sail at sunrise with the tide. My traveling chests are packed; my clothes and robes in one, and in the other, all the letters, papers, documents, the to-and-fro of five full years of Interdict and excommunication.

It is vital that I move in secret. Philip must not know what we are doing till the thing is done. He wants his holy war and he will wait, we think, until the first of June before he sails. Thus we have time to plot and plan.

I go, therefore, without an entourage. I have a squire for protection, nothing more; a pleasant, round-faced youth with muscles like an ox and limited intelligence.

Our boat is small; we enter France on tiptoe. Pandulf is in Paris. He does not know I am coming; it ensures a safer journey and there may be some advantage in surprise.

I shall be sixty-seven next week, if God wills it.

At L'Hospice de Dieu, Abbeville
The 15th Day of April, A.D. 1213

It is possible, I find, to love a country without caring for the people in the least. The look of things, the land, the food and wine, the music; all exquisite. And the people: they have eyes like little stones and souls like raisins. France is much too good for Frenchmen. I have, in one single day, endured more rudeness—never mind.

I crossed the Channel in good form, considering the largeness of the water and the smallness of the boat. It took the full day and the sun was down as we approached Boulogne. The beacon fires of the lighthouse, on its hilltop to the left, showed us the way. We slipped into the river mouth and sailed on to the lower city. There, as Dammartin had promised, by the Roman jetty, was my way ashore; two oarsmen in a fishing boat. They rowed us past the city, up the Liane to open country and a manor house.

We left this morning early, dressed as pilgrims: wallet round the neck, broad hat and hooded cloak. On assback. Pilgrims, as a rule, are poor but there is one thing that they have in plenty: time. They wander, dawdle, inch along. Some actually read from books, so slowly do they walk. The road south is a busy one: the farmers with their carts, the minstrels, shepherds, merchants, monks. The road was never empty and we dared not race. A maddening day.

The hospice, I need hardly say, is unendurable. I have seen better-looking barnyards. Tom, my squire, takes it with a smile. In fact, he smiles at everything. An irritating habit; I must speak to him about it.

What else? French insect life is interesting. Their flies are like the flies in England but the maggots here are fearless.

Till next time, if God wills it.

At Clignancourt
The 18th Day of April, A.D. 1213

Paris. I can see it from my doorway. Open fields and then Montmartre, rising up in tiers of vineyards to the ruins of the temple at the top. To sit there on a summer day with friends and wine and look down on the walls and turrets of the city is a memory no man should be without.

At the last moment, I decided not to stay at Saint-Denis. The sight of it at noon today persuaded me. The abbey dominates the town; nothing but churchmen everywhere and I must not be recognized.

From Saint-Denis, they have two roads to Paris now. I can't think why. The Roman one is beautiful and by it, running parallel, two hundred yards away, a second highroad has been cut and all along it there are cookshops, shabby stores and little modern houses. Blight it is; a blight upon the landscape.

We took the Roman road, of course, and, turning right, we made our way to Clignancourt. Once there, I faced the problem of a place to stay. I solved it brilliantly, I think. Beside the church, there is a small, abandoned dairy house. I made arrangements with the village priest in flawless French and here we are.

I shall send Tom into the city in the morning. I have written down exactly what he is to say to Pandulf. He is sitting by me on the floor now, memorizing. He is frowning and his lips move. I have no reason to believe he'll ever get it, but at least he isn't smiling.

At Clignancourt
The 22nd Day of April, A.D. 1213

I wait, I wait. He keeps me waiting. If, that is, he means to come at all. What if the Pope has no wish to negotiate? What if all this is sham and Innocent wants France to govern England? What if—

No. I must not think these thoughts. He wants me to, this Pandulf does. Four days ago, Tom came back from the city with his note. One sentence: "I will come to you." It traps me here. I cannot go to him; to do so weakens our position, which is weak enough to start with. And I cannot write again, else I sound desperate. There is nothing I can do but wait.

And so I sit and watch the peasants pass my doorway. And I eat because I must. And sleep and count the days. He wants to break me. I will not be broken.

Till next time, if God wills it.

At Clignancourt
The 24th Day of April, A.D. 1213

He came today. He sent no note, he set no time. He merely stepped into my doorway, bowed and introduced himself.

I had been dozing and he caught me, as he meant to, unprepared. My first thought was to bound up, bright and full of energy. I stopped myself in time, I'm glad to say. I shook my head as if to clear it, groaned and let him help me to my feet.

He is a small man, light and quick; one feels he dances well. His face is smooth and young, he can't be thirty. He is Roman, so he tells me; though to my ear even his Italian has an accent.

I allowed him to assist me to a chair. He was effusively apologetic for the days of waiting. I assured him I was grateful for the respite, so depleted was I from my journey. I inquired of the Pope's health; he of John's. I offered wine, which he accepted. Had he eaten? He had not.

I sent Tom off for bread and cheese and we began.

"Giraldus?"

"Yes?"

He looked at me. He has fine eyes, sincere and open; and he looks at you directly at all times, particularly when he lies. "May I be frank?" he asked.

I shook my head. It was, I hoped, a good move. "No," I told him, "to be frank is not enough. We must be statesmanlike. We sit here with the future in our hands. The issues are too great for anything but wisdom, Pandulf, and high-mindedness." It came out with conviction; and why not, for it was true.

He nodded somberly and we began to take the points at issue one by one. The first was Stephen Langton. Did my King, once and for all, consent to his election to the See of Canterbury?

"Yes," I said, "the King consents."

He sat back. "Good; that's a beginning. Next, I think, I need to know the meaning of consent."

"You want a definition of the word?"

He flashed his Roman smile at me. "Wouldn't you?"

I knew, of course, what that meant. John has made no secret of his animosity to Langton. To the point, I fear, of threatening more than once to take his life if ever he set foot in England. I could not win on this one; still, I snapped my answer back. "Am I to understand you want the King to guarantee his safety?"

"Yes."

"In writing?"

"Yes," he said.

"As part of this agreement?"

"Yes," he said again.

"No harm will come to Langton."

"Why should I believe you?"

I stood up. "I speak for John. It's his word that I give you."

"Let him put his word on paper."

"You impugn his honor, do you?"

"Sir," he said, "that is unworthy of you. Why are treaties ever written down? Why were the Ten Commandments cut in stone? So that all men may know."

Well played, I thought. I held out for a bit and then consented. "Done," I said. We both made note of it.

Then Pandulf frowned and shook his head. "It could be clearer, don't you think?"

"In what way?"

"If we added that the guarantee applies to everyone—"

"To everyone?" I asked, as if I did not know.

He looked at me with deep sincerity. "But, surely, it's a general amnesty we're speaking of. It isn't only Langton who has suffered. Your entire clergy is in exile."

"I'm aware of that."

"If Langton comes, they all come. Laymen, clergy; all who have endured the grievous pain of separation from their homeland. Think, my dear Giraldus, what it means to be cut off from everything you know and love."

"They fled, they made their choice."

"They had no choice. And even if they did, are we not here to heal the wounds? To make peace? To forgive? To rise above the rancor? Yes, Giraldus, we must open up our hearts and find a better way to live with one another."

"So we must," I said. His eyes were moist; mine, too. We filled our glasses and we drank to brotherhood. One bottle went; another came. He told me of the great esteem with which the Pope regarded me and how he, in this single afternoon, had come to share it. I told him of the deep respect inspired in John and his advisors by the very name of Pandulf. There was mutual humility, a lot of it, and then we got down to the issues.

There were only two that mattered: money and submission to the Pope. The latter was the nub of everything, the crux, the single thing on which no compromise was possible. There are some countries—Poland, Sweden, Denmark, Portugal among them—that have made the Pope their overlord. Their lands are feudal fiefdoms of the Apostolic See. This gives the Pope, in theory and in fact, great power over secular affairs.

He broached the matter quietly. "As to the question of submission—"

"As to that," I said, "there can be no discussion."

"None?"

I shook my head. "The King will not submit."

He looked at me intently. "There are pressures I could bring to bear."

"They will avail you nothing."

He sat back. "Suppose I were to break off these negotiations?"

"That would be a pity," I replied, "but you must do as you think best."

"I think—" He paused a moment. "Shall we talk about the reparations?"

"By all means."

He took a paper out. "We are prepared to settle for one hundred thousand pounds."

"One hundred thousand?"

"Not one penny less."

"I see," I said. The sum was staggering, of course. When you consider that a mason or a carpenter, skilled labor, can be hired at fourpence a day, which means the fellow earns six pounds a year, the magnitude becomes apparent. On the other hand, the sum was less than John had pocketed. For five years, since the Interdict began, the King had taken all church income for his own. They were entitled to it back. Our difficulty was we didn't have it.

"I'm afraid we have a problem here," I said.

"Perhaps together we can solve it."

Where to start? I cleared my throat. "My country, as you know, is threatened by invasion. We have met this with a massive effort; men and ships and armaments. The drain upon our treasury is terrible."

He nodded sympathetically. "I understand."

"We owe the Pope a debt, a great one; and we feel it keenly. Something must be done to right this wrong. Unhappily, the sum you mention lies beyond—"

"Oh, spare me."

I stopped cold. "I beg your pardon?"

Pandulf's face was white. "Do you expect me to believe the Treasury of England does not have one hundred thousand pounds?"

"What you believe is immaterial. The money is not there."

"Then raise it. You've a King in England, haven't you? Is he so weak he can't impose a tax?"

"Not now, not at this time."

He stood. His voice shook and his eyes were blazing. "You old fool, what do you take me for? Your King will not submit, you say? Your King is penniless, you say? Am I to sit for that? No, I will not! These talks are ended! Do you hear me? We are done!"

I got up from my chair. My heart was pounding. Here it was: the breaking point. I had to chance it, now or never. In one move, I risked it all.

"You think you frighten me? You little ass. Go back to Paris, go to Rome? You won't go out the door."

He pulled his lips back, like a wolf does; it was meant to be a smile. "Won't I?"

"Have you seen the declaration from Soissons? I have a copy if you haven't."

"It has come to my attention."

"Then suppose you tell me, does the Pope want Louis on John's throne? Does he want France to rule in England? Like the plague, he wants it. He plays France and England, one against the other. Our wars make him strong. If Paris wins, Rome loses—and you know it!"

There it was. The game was on the table. Who to move and win? We stood there silently, eyes locked. And then I sat and leaned back in my chair and crossed my legs and picked my pen and paper up. I smiled at him and my voice was calm.

"I'm ready, Pandulf. Any time you say."

He looked at me a moment more—and then he sat. It took the balance of the afternoon and went on well into the night but what I had to win, I won. The reparations were reduced, the payments to be made in modest sums for years. As to submission to the Pope, no mention; not one word was said. The treaty text is drawn and ready for the King to sign.

My eyes burn and my head aches. I must try to sleep. The triumph that I felt is gone and I am overcome by sadness. Map is dead; I have no one to tell.

Till next time, if God wills it.

Near Boulogne
The 2nd Day of May, A.D. 1213

The Channel is uncrossable. A storm has raged for days. I sit here in this Godforsaken manor house, the treaty in my travel chest and Pandulf on my hands. For his instructions are to see the treaty signed and witnessed, after which he must deliver it to Langton.

The hours wobble by. I talk with Pandulf, we play chess, he tells me of his life in Rome. I find this interesting; not his life, but the fact he tells me of it. It's as if the fellow cannot stop negotiating. Everything he says or does is for some end and it is damned unnerving listening to him when you don't know what his end is.

Sitting here is damned unnerving, too. The boatsman has been by to say the weather will be breaking soon. He says so every day, he thinks it pleases me. The rain flies through the open windows. Out across the fields, the trees bend double in the wind. The treaty must reach Langton by the first of June. I make that thirty days.

Till next time.

Near Boulogne
The 10th Day of May, A.D. 1213

Trapped, we are still trapped here and I cannot bear it. Even drinking does no good. The weather will not break. I'd pray to Neptune if I thought he'd pay attention.

T.n.t., i. G. w.

At Dover Castle
The 12th Day of May, A.D. 1213

We reached the harbor late today. The port was devastated from the storm; small boats, upended, lay like turtles on the beach. Thank God our fleet is not assembling here.

The King was waiting for us. We went briefly through the treaty, he assented to the terms, there was some talk of minor matters such as who should stand as witness to the signing, after which the meeting ended.

Copies of the text are being made. And there are letters patent being written, dozens of them to be read throughout the Kingdom so that all may know that peace with Rome has come. Our scribes are busy.

As for me, I sit here feeling curiously empty. Everyone was most polite, they said "Well done, Giraldus," and tonight I sat at John's right hand. What more am I entitled to?

The signing has been set for Sext tomorrow.

Till next time, if God wills it.

At Dover Castle
The 13th Day of May, A.D. 1213

There is a formal chamber on the second level of the keep, and it was here the treaty would be signed. A simple ceremony; only those with a direct involvement would be there.

I was the first to come. I had the copies of the document. A single trestle table with a single stool stood at the center of the floor. I put the papers on it, sent a servant for the pen and ink. The afternoon was gray, no sunset light. I thought it best to have a fire started and the torches lit.

They came in one by one, the Marshal first. We spoke. He seemed as tense as I was; for the thing was not yet signed and treaty rooms are slippery places. Longsword came next, with the Earl of Warenne. Then came Chester, Dammartin, des Roches and Pandulf.

Nods and murmurs; little else. The air felt weighty, there was pressure in the room. The bells of Sext began to ring. We listened, no one moving. There was silence as the last stroke died away. I cleared my throat and someone coughed and John strode in.

He went directly to the stool. A servant pulled it back. He sat, picked up the pen and dipped it in the ink. He bent and touched it to the paper, writing briskly, scraping it across the page. And then the witnesses and it was done. Like that. The King had made his peace with Rome and God.

There were no speeches, no one cheered, no trumpet fanfares; nothing but some servants who came in with little cakes and brandywine. I felt a mix of things. The Church, I thought, asks too much of its churchmen. What has God to do with treaties, why do popes behave like kings?

And thus preoccupied, I missed the start of it. Pandulf was near me, talking to the King. He was to sail at dawn for Calais on his way to Pontigny where Langton was in residence.

"I can," I heard him say, "convey the facts of what we've done to Philip, if you like."

John pondered it. "It might be useful, knowing his reaction. Will he see you? Are you friendly with him?"

Pandulf made a modest shrug. "He finds my company amusing. He's at Gravelines at the moment, I believe. At least, those were his plans."

John cocked his head. "He talks to you about his plans?"

Another modest shrug. "From time to time. He tells me many things."

"Such as?"

"Oh, for example, what his forces are, how many men or ships."

"All that we know," the King said. "We are very well informed. But thank you."

Pandulf sighed in deep relief. "Thank God. That means you know about the letters and I didn't want to be the one to tell you. You, there." This was to a servant who was passing by with wine. Pandulf turned, held out his glass.

"The letters?" John said softly.

Pandulf did not seem to hear. He thanked the servant. "As for Langton," he was saying as he turned back to the King, "I ought to reach him in a week or less."

"What letters?"

Pandulf paused at that. A long pause. I was witnessing a masterful negotiation. "Don't you know?" he murmured.

"Would I ask," the King snapped, "if I did?"

"The letters from your barons, Sire."

"Well? What do these letters say?"

"They promise their support to Philip's army when it comes."

The King said nothing for a moment. Then, as if indifferent to this news, he went on. "Is that all they say?"

"In substance yes, my lord."

"How many letters are there?"

Pandulf shrugged. "I've no idea if Philip showed me all of them."

"How many did you see?"

"How many?" Pandulf frowned, half closed his eyes, as if to see the memory. "I didn't count, my lord. I didn't know it mattered at the time. Perhaps between fifteen and twenty."

"Were they signed?"

"Of course, my lord."

"By whom? What names?"

"Robert FitzWalter."

"Yes."

"Eustace de Vescy."

"Go on."

"Saer de Quenci, Geoffrey de Mandeville . . ." He shook his head. "I should have read more closely."

By this time, the room was still and all of us were listening.

John's next question was the right one. "Why should I believe you?"

Pandulf looked at him straight on. "Because you'd kill me if I lied."

John weighed it. "You intend to serve me, do you?"

Pandulf's answer was to kneel. "I am your man, my lord."

John turned and walked in silence to the open window. Dusk was coming and he stood there, looking out across the Channel toward the French coast. It was then it happened. Calmly, with no sense of urgency at all, he called my name.

"Giraldus?"

"Yes, my lord?" I joined him by the window.

"Would you and—" He broke off and beckoned for the Marshal and des Roches. When the three of us were there in front of him, he said, "I've reached a grave decision. May I ask you, with all speed, to draw a charter of submission to the Pope."

The silence was tremendous. Had he lost his mind? Submit to Rome? The very thing we'd fought against? What could we do? My mind spun; nothing came.

The Marshal spoke. "For Christ's sake, John, do you know what you're saying?"

"If I didn't, would I say it?"

"Have you any notion what this means?"

"I know exactly what it means. You don't, you've missed it. So have it." He paused. His eyes were clear and very bright. "What does it cost me to submit? A little pride, a bending of the knee; that's all. I grant you it's a price that no king likes to pay but look you what it brings me: Rome. I buy the Pope. I hold my lands of him, and any man who strikes me, from my barons to the King of France, that man becomes his enemy. Let Philip or FitzWalter face it for a change. Let France be under Interdict, let all my enemies be excommunicated. Draw the charter."

Saying which, he turned to Longsword, Pandulf and the others. "Come," he said. "It's time for dinner and there's much to celebrate."

[131]

I watched them leave the room. Then, turning to the Marshal, still not sure, I said, "You think it's possible he's right?"

The Marshal nodded. "It was there, in front of us; for all this time."

We spent the evening working on the text. It needs revision, copies must be made, but we should have it ready for the King to sign by late tomorrow. All in all, the more I think, the more it seems a brilliant move. For it inverts the situation: Philip has not only lost his holy war, he is an enemy of Rome if he attacks. The price we pay for having God on our side for a change seems very small indeed.

A while ago, when Marshal left me for the night, I saw a sad look on his face. I asked him what the matter was. "I'm sorry Henry's dead," he said. "How proud he would have been."

Till next time, if God wills it.

At Dover Castle
The 15th Day of May, A.D. 1213

The Holy Sepulchre, the Templars' church, is seldom used. It stands in isolation on the barren stretches of the Western Heights. A strange and ancient structure, it is round, not cruciform, and there is something pagan and disturbing in the spirit of the place. It was the King's wish that he sign the Charter of Submission there.

We left the castle after dusk, the same small group that stood as witness to the treaty yesterday. Each of us held a torch. John led the way across the bailey, down the steps and into town. There were some people on the streets, not many, and I watched them draw back as we passed and whisper to each other.

On we went. The town behind us now, we crossed a meadow to the path that winds up to the Western Heights. The land on top is wild; rocks and hillocks, clumps of weeds and brambles. Light clouds scudded past the moon; my torch blew out.

[132]

The church door, when we tried it, would not open. It was warped and rusted into place. Des Roches and Longsword put their shoulders to it and it opened sharply, with a cracking sound.

The air inside was dank. We placed our torches in the brackets on the walls and formed a circle round the altar. Pandulf stood before it. John knelt down.

"I, John," he said, "by God's grace King of England, Lord of Ireland, Poitou and Aquitaine, do swear from this time forth to be a faithful servant of Saint Peter, of the Church of Rome, of my liege lord the Pope. And God; His servant, too."

He rose. I moved to him with pen and ink. He signed the charter. "*Jubilate Deo*," someone said.

Tomorrow is Ascension Day. No one has spoken Peter of Wakefield's name but his prediction is remembered. What he saw, what he foretold is not to be. The King is still the King.

Till next time, if God wills it.

At Dover Castle
The 16th Day of May, A.D. 1213

Pandulf sailed for France this morning early. He will land at Gravelines where, according to our information, Philip's camp is made. Once having shown our documents to Philip, he will ride to Pontigny and Stephen Langton.

Spirits here are very high. There is, we think, some likelihood that Philip, suddenly without the Pope, may well abandon all his plans and send his soldiers home. In that event, what should we do? We have a fleet, we have supplies and war machines, we have the men at Barham Down. Longsword is all for making war in France. The King is not so sure.

In any case, I leave with John tomorrow. We shall tour the Cinque Ports once again and count our ships.

Till next time, if God wills it.

The French have not disbanded. Philip did not send his armies home. By no means. He has sent them into Flanders, hurling them across the border with great force.

Des Roches and Longsword left the Tower this morning with this news and found us here on our way back to London. We have spent the evening in John's tent debating what to do. The meaning of the French attack is clear. Philip has not abandoned his designs. It is to make his northern flank secure that he has mounted this assault. Without the Pope, he could not count on Flanders when his armies come for us.

What should we do? Des Roches was all for sending aid to Flanders. Longsword argued for invasion, for attacking France directly from Poitou while all her armies were engaged three hundred miles to the north.

The King, through all the argument, said nothing. Not till Longsword, who was pacing, sat and looked at him. "You've heard us out. Which is it?"

"There are other courses open."

"Such as?"

"Philip cannot walk on water. He must sail to get here."

Longsword, out of patience, closed his eyes. "Now there's a brilliant observation."

"It is not without some merit," John snapped back. "He has to cross the Channel and he has the ships to do it. And to spare. His fleet is twice the size of ours."

"I know that. Everybody knows it. What about it?"

"If you mean what can we do about a fleet that size, I'll tell you. There is one thing we can do." John leaned across the table toward him. "We can sink it!"

In the morning, we are off to Portsmouth where our fleet is anchored. We are going to destroy the French at sea.

Till next time, if God wills it.

At Portsmouth
The 27th Day of May, A.D. 1213

We sail tomorrow and the King is furious. He has, from time to
time, a weakness in the stomach and the bowel and he is bedded at
the moment, doubled up in pain. A surgeon has been leeching him
since sunset and he may be too unwell to take command.

It struck him suddenly. He seemed all right this morning as we
moved about the port. The clamor and confusion were enormous.
Food, supplies and weapons, all this must be loaded. To say nothing of the horses and the knights; for we must be prepared for
skirmishing on land. No less than fourteen hundred horses to be
prodded into open boats. There are not wharves enough, and
many ships are loaded on the shore and hauled across the mud and
sand. Some break before they ever reach the water. It is chaos.

I had never seen Greek fire made before, and we had stopped to
watch it when John first complained of feeling ill. I thought, of
course, it was the stench, for it is made by boiling sulphur, pitch,
petroleum and niter all together in great iron kettles. It is terrifying
stuff, a dreadful weapon. Once lit, water cannot put it out; nor can
its flame be smothered save by sand or vinegar or urine in great
quantity.

We moved on to the wharf. The air was better. They were
bearding fishing boats. They fasten metal bands around the hulls
to strengthen them for ramming. It was here that John bent suddenly in pain.

"My lord—"

"It's nothing."

But it was; and by the middle of the day, the King was pale and
fevered. He is in no way afraid; this ague, if that be what it is, has
come and gone before. But whether he is fit to lead us at this
moment is another question. We must see him soon.

The Marshal led the way: then Longsword, Dammartin and I.
The King lay on his bed, still clothed. He looked at us with hot
eyes.

"I am well enough," he said, as if expecting someone to deny it. "I have waited seven years for this and I will not be cheated."

"Can you stand?" the Marshal asked.

"You doubt it?"

"No, my lord."

"It's settled, then."

"It is, my lord; and if you'd come into the next room, there are charts and maps that you should see."

John nodded, sat up, stood—and fell.

The fleet will sail as planned tomorrow, under joint command: Longsword and Dammartin.

Till next time.

In Portsmouth Harbor
The 28th Day of May, A.D. 1213

The wind is in our favor and the tide is turning. I sit huddled near the bow of Longsword's galley. Spread before me in the harbor are five hundred ships. Or so they tell me, for there is no way of counting. They are jammed together, bumping, bobbing, filled with horses, fodder, armaments, supplies and men; vessels of every kind.

There must be fifty galleys, fully half of all the Kingdom has. These ships of war are long, low, sleek and very powerful, with castles fore and aft and platforms at the center where our soldiers stand to fight, throw rocks and hurl Greek fire. Longsword's galley, in the modern manner, has its rudder at the stern, not at the side; and at full speed, propelled by forty oarsmen, its mobility is startling.

There are busses, too—great transport ships on which are packed one hundred men or more. And cogs, their huge sails flapping in the wind. But mostly there are small craft, fishing boats and shore and river vessels. Everyone is shouting.

We are turning, moving toward the harbor mouth and open sea.

The sky is gray: why do I feel as if the sun were shining? We should sight the coast of France, I'm told, tomorrow morning.

What a day for England.

Somewhere Off the Coast of France
The 29th Day of May, A.D. 1213

Fog. The fleet is fogbound. There is nothing to be seen. Our ships collide, they bump and crunch into each other; this in spite of all the calls the sailors cry.

I have just been with Longsword and the captain. They seemed calm enough. They have a new device they call a compass. I stood watching while they made one. It requires a lodestone and a saucer filled with water and an iron needle and a piece of straw. They touch the needle to the stone, then thrust it through the center of the straw and float it. As if moved by unseen hands, the needle turns. It points north. Why it does so, no one knows.

We are, they think, not far from France, roughly between Boulogne and Calais. Our course is north and east and we are moving very slowly. This will take us past Gravelines, Ostend, Dunkirk and Damme and all the other ports along the Flemish coast. The French fleet may be scattered in amongst these ports or anchored in a single harbor. All we can be reasonably sure of is that Philip will have placed his ships along this shore so that, as soon as Flanders falls, he can set sail for England.

It is early evening and we will be eating in a while. I sit here by the hearth fire on the deck. Around me, men are pissing into jugs; we may be under fire soon.

Till next time, if God wills it.

Upon the Swine
The 30th Day of May, A.D. 1213

I must be very quick. Not long ago, there was a crevice in the fog. It came a little after dawn, and through it we could see the coast: low pastureland and scattered cows.

The oarsmen raised the pace and as the fog began to lift the contours of the shore came clear, and round us, for the first time in two days or nearly, we could see our fleet.

I went with Longsword to the bow. He had no notion where we were. The sea was calm. A flight of gulls flew past. Then someone called his name. We turned and there was Dammartin, his galley next to ours. He raised an arm and pointed to the light mist just ahead.

"It's Damme," he cried. "We've come to Damme."

He must know every feature of this coast; for Damme sits somewhat inland on the River Swine, or Zwyn as the natives insist on spelling it, and there was nothing here to see save for some lowlands and a river's mouth.

What's happening is this: our fleet will stay at anchor here until reconnaissance is made. Longsword and Dammartin themselves are going in. They've commandeered a fishing boat, the thing is filled with hay and they have dressed themselves as common seamen. I am going with them, though they do not know this yet. It is an hour's sail upriver, and if Philip's fleet is there at Damme I want to see it. As the King said, "I will not be cheated."

I dressed in seamen's clothes and when their boat was ready, I went down. I was prepared to make a dreadful scene but Longsword seemed content to have me there. He has begun, I think, to think about his place in history.

Two sailors worked the oars. We sat in silence on the hay. Our speed, once on the river, was quite good. The Swine has little current; it grows narrower each year, I'm told, and will silt up one day.

The land we passed looks much like Brittany; bleak beauty if one cares for bleak. The clouds were lifting and the day would be a fair one. There was little river traffic, little movement on the shore; some sheep, a shepherd, not much else.

The Swine is full of bends and turns, it's never straight for long, and so one comes on Damme quite suddenly. We had no preparation for it, none at all. We simply moved around yet one more bend and there it was.

The port of Damme stands where it is because the river all at once becomes extremely broad, as if it meant to be a lake. A splendid harbor, still and wide. The town lies low along the shore, a busy place and prosperous. But there is no port in existence great enough for what lies anchored there today.

I gasped. We all did. None of us could speak. The oarsmen's hands dropped from the oars. We drifted silently.

Then Longsword spoke. "Almighty Christ" was all he said. There has never in all history been such a fleet. It dwarfs our own. It is three times, four times our size. The masts rise up as dense as wheat stalks in a field. Two thousand ships? Is such a number possible?

"Dear God," I said, "what can we do?"

They had no answer. We could not engage them here; they would engulf us. Nor could we lie waiting for them on the open sea; without surprise or some advantage, we would not survive. Perhaps our only course was sailing home and waiting there for Philip to invade. I was about to say as much when Longsword spoke.

His eyes were on the harbor. "Take us in," he said. The oarsmen looked at him. "Go on," he said. "Get on with it."

"What for?" asked Dammartin. "We've seen enough."

"There's something wrong. I know it, I can't tell you what it is but something's wrong here."

We went on, across the water. Closer, closer. There was little movement, little noise. Could the French navy be asleep? We passed some small boats; they were empty. Just ahead, there lay a galley. On it, sailors moved about, engaged in early morning chores.

"Keep going," Longsword said.

The ships were packed about us now on every side. On each, it was the same: no soldiers. Only seamen, just the ship's crew, not a warrior in sight.

"Where are they?" Longsword muttered. "Where for Christ's sake are their men?"

"Why don't I ask?" said Dammartin. He stood. A cog rose next to us. He shouted up. In Flemish. In a moment, there were several faces peering down at us. I could not understand a word. It was all over in a minute.

"Well? What is it?" Longsword snapped. "What did they tell you?"

Dammartin sat down.

"What did they say?"

"The soldiers . . ." He began again. "There's not a soldier in the port."

"Impossible."

"They've gone to Ghent with Philip. Philip's laying siege to Ghent."

"With all his men? He took them all?"

We rowed back faster than we came.

Our fleet is forming as I sit here. Warships first, and then the cogs, filled full with knights and men-at-arms. And after them, the fishing boats and smaller craft. We strike with everything we have. The day is fair. We're moving. We are moving, starting for the river mouth. My heart pounds. I can barely put the words down.

On the Swine
The 31st Day of May, A.D. 1213

In we went, to Damme. Our galley led the way. Behind us, lost to sight, our fleet stretched out for miles. Clear sky, high sun, not noon yet; nothing but the sound of oars. The time stretched like a bowstring; then it broke. Before us lay the harbor.

I stood next to Longsword in the bow. He turned and roared out a command. The oarsmen bent, the galley skidded forward. There were soldiers all around me now, some armored, some with pots of

Greek fire, some with crossbows. I was pummeled, shoved about, but I would not give way. I was about to see the greatest naval battle in the history of man; I was its chronicler.

We were halfway across the harbor. Nothing yet, no movement on the French ships. I held on with both hands to the forecastle rail. Behind us, speeding in our wake, came Dammartin and then more galleys. Three, four, five, six, pouring from the Swine into the harbor.

There were barges just ahead, and fishing boats; small craft. The sailors turned, they saw us now. We kept our speed. Straight at them; we were going to ram them, splinter them. I saw the sailors diving, leaping for the water. Then we hit. I turned my face away. Our galley shuddered, that was all. We kept our speed.

Ahead of us, not thirty yards ahead, there lay a galley. Just as great as ours, it was. Its sailors watched us from its castles, fore and aft. Just stood there, helpless, watching as our prow made for the center of their ship. The men around me braced themselves.

Just moments left before we struck. Longsword was shouting; words I could not understand. There was, I thought, a look of rapture on his face. I closed my eyes. The crash came.

They were severed, cut in two. Our soldiers lit their pots of fire, flaming arrows arched off from our crossbows. I saw men in flames, like torches; screaming, choking from the smoke of their own flesh. I saw two sailors crushed to pulp. I saw a man without a head, still walking, two steps, three, before he fell. I vomited.

We went on to the next ship and the next. Smoke everywhere: and flames, the smell of burning wood and cloth and skin and hair. Some of their sailors fought as best they could but most of them took to the water; men and rats all swimming for the shore.

How long did this go on? An hour possibly. And then—Sweet Jesus, please forgive us—then a strange and dreadful thing began to happen to us all. We wanted more. More men to die, more ships to burn. Like lusting, like a thirst, like fever; out of all control. It gripped us and we did dark things. *Kyrie eleison, Christe eleison, Kyrie eleison.*

At last the fever left us. We were spent. Around us, there was nothing to be seen but broken ships and drifting smoke. We started drawing back across the harbor. We had no idea, till then, of what our other ships had done.

They had done just as we had done. Flames, wreckage, sunken ships; the carnage stretched from shore to shore. Black smoke filled up the windless air, so thick and vast it blotted out the sun. In half an afternoon, the French fleet had been disemboweled: a third of it, six hundred ships or more.

But Longsword was not finished yet. He knew exactly what to do, he saw it crystal-clear. On land, the French outnumbered us and Ghent was only twenty miles away. Philip would know of our attack, he would be gathering his forces, charging back to Damme. Thus we had much to do and very little time. I listened to him snap the orders out.

It is now after midnight. We are nearly done. Our ships, with half their crews, are moving down the Swine. The other half, the balance of our mariners, are manning French craft. Every vessel worth the taking has been taken. They are loaded, filled with weapons, goods, supplies; God only knows what plunder.

All that now remains is closing up the harbor mouth. A line of French boats has been strung across it and our men are sinking them with rocks. Those ships we've had to leave behind will not be sailing, not this year.

There has not ever been, on land or sea, a victory so total and complete. We have lost nothing and the enemy has been annihilated.

Surely, the 30th of May will be remembered. Songs and stories will be written glorifying what we've done. And yet, and yet . . .

Till next time, if God wills it.

At Dover Castle
The 3rd Day of June, A.D. 1213

"Longsword—Longsword—Longsword—"
We could hear the chanting long before we reached the harbor. It was deep, a rumbling sound, mere noise at first. Uncertain what

it was, I moved with Longsword to the bow. We could not see the people yet.

We had sent word ahead, of course. A fast boat had, that morning, been dispatched with details of the victory; yet neither of us was prepared for what we saw as we moved into port.

It was a perfect day; bright, clear. The chalk cliffs blazed back at the sun. Our galley led the fleet. Above us, on the castle wall, as dense as starlings in the spring, were soldiers. As we passed, they raised their swords, the metal flashing in the light.

The jetty and the port were massed with people, and the chanting, as we glided closer, swelled into a roar. Yet there was even greater cause for cheering than they knew. For all about us on the deck lay treasure, chests of treasure such as I had never seen. The greatest noblemen of France had been with Philip, and their ships had held the ransom of a dozen kings.

A wooden shipwright's platform had been moved out to the jetty. On it stood the King and Queen. Around them, countless flags and pennons snapped and fluttered in the wind. I stepped back, leaving Longsword in the bow alone. He looked magnificent, his great mane of dark hair, his crimson cloak. He raised his right arm in salute. The sun was in my eyes, I know, but for a moment he looked so much like his father that it shook me and I nearly knelt as if he were the King.

Steps led up to the platform. Longsword started toward them, then turned back and beckoned me to follow. I was deafened by the cheers, I could not hear the words the brothers spoke. I saw them kiss. Then Longsword knelt. The Queen held out her hand and Longsword put it to his lips.

The people, when we left the platform, could not be contained and I was seized, hurled up on someone's shoulders, carried through the throng. I have been pinched and pummeled, hugged and squeezed and nearly dropped on more than one occasion. I am bruised and welted, top to bottom; but the brandywine, I'm glad to say, is helping.

We are meeting soon for supper. Nothing they can serve us has a taste as sweet as victory.

T.n.t.

"What then? What happened then?" The Queen, eyes bright, sat leaning forward on the chair's edge, caught up in the tale. As were we all.

For Longsword is a natural storyteller. Having reached the moment just before the battle, as we led the fleet into the harbor, he had stopped to fill his goblet. We were in a private chamber in the higher reaches of the keep. The walls are hung with tapestries and in the fire's light, the figures on them seemed to move. Our chairs were clustered by the hearth: the King, the Queen, the Marshal, Longsword and myself; the five of us.

"What then, my lady? We attacked. The oarsmen bent, their oar blades slashing through the water. Stroke and stroke again. We flew across the harbor at a speed so great no arrow could have caught us." On he went, in this vein. It is not my style, of course; too rich by far, too overfleshed. And yet, it came out sounding like a legend; like some bard's tale, wondrous and heroic.

Who could speak? The images came faster now: the carnage that we saw when we withdrew across the harbor. Flames and wreckage, men and rats. And Dammartin, demanding that we land, press on to Ghent, find Philip and destroy him.

It was then John spoke. "Why didn't you?" was what he said.

His voice was low and William, like the rest of us, was taken unprepared. "I'm sorry, John. What's that again?"

"Why didn't you?"

There was no missing it this time; yet William seemed to. "Are you asking why we didn't go ashore?"

"I am."

"It seemed unwise."

"In whose opinion?"

"Mine."

"You were in joint command with Dammartin."

"The fleet was English; surely that makes mine the larger joint." He said it smiling.

[144]

"Fair enough," the King said, smiling back. "But why, in your opinion, was it so unwise?"

"You know as well as I do, John."

"I don't at all; I wasn't there."

"Their fleet was thrice the size of ours; three times as many soldiers is the way I read that. We'd have been outnumbered three to one at Ghent."

The King sat back and shrugged, as if it were an idle talk, mere gossiping. "I read it that you lost your nerve," he said. "I would have gone ashore."

There was a pause. When Longsword spoke, his tone was just as casual as John's. "You would have made a grave mistake, I think."

"Would I?" John frowned, as if debating it. "The fleet was my idea, the naval war was my idea. The strategy, the timing, everything was mine. Your victory won itself, it seems to me. You could not lose; they had no soldiers."

"True enough; but still, we did destroy their fleet and there's some treasure in the harbor."

"Oh, indeed there is. You brought the plunder home, no doubt of it; but not the victory. It was there: at Ghent. You could have taken Philip."

Longsword's hands were clenched tight but his voice stayed calm. Dead calm. "I don't see how."

"There is a tide," John said. "That's what you missed. You could have swept on, nothing could have stopped you."

"Possibly." He paused. "You know, that may be why you've lost so many wars. These tides of yours, they haven't won us very much."

The danger in the room was heavy, like midsummer heat. Where would it end? Could no one stop them?

"I was there," I said. "You might ask me."

John turned. His eyes bored in. "What would you know?"

"I know what history is, my lord. It's true, there is an ebb and flow to things. There are those times when one can strike against all odds and win the day. But you weren't there at Damme; the bodies and the smoke and flames. You would have done as William did, for you could not have seen what you see now."

[145]

He looked at me in silence for what seemed at least a lifetime. Then he nodded. "Possibly," he said. "It's possible." He turned to William. "Had I been there . . . Who can say?" He smiled and raised his goblet. "Brothers: we can fight and love each other through it all. I love you, William."

"Yes, I know."

Much later, as we left the room, the Marshal turned to me. "You should have been the Pope," he said.

Till next time, if God wills it.

At Dover Castle
The 5th Day of June, A.D. 1213

We leave this afternoon and I was packing when the Queen came in. She seemed subdued and thoughtful, sitting still and saying little as I put my things away.

Then, slowly, she began. Her mind turns more and more to politics and she was full of questions: what would happen next, how dangerous a man was Stephen Langton, how much power could he wield at Canterbury, matters of this kind. She grasps things quickly and she was, I thought, about to ask another question when she turned away.

"What's wrong, my lady?"

"Nothing." Then she raised her eyes to mine. "Our victory at Damme, it was a great one, wasn't it?"

"A triumph; yes, my lady."

"It was wrong of John to say it won itself." She shook her head. "I love the two of them beyond all other men. I hate it when they fight; it makes them small."

And then, as if she hadn't said it, on she went to other questions. I was sorry when she rose to go. I told her so. She kissed my cheek.

"I love you, too, Giraldus." She was smiling. "In a different way, of course."

Till next time, if God wills it.

At Barham

The 6th Day of June, A.D. 1213

A sharp wind swept across the Down. The King stood on a hillock in the center of the field. Around him, spreading out across the ruined meadlowland, were all the thousands who had come when he had called.

He cupped his hands around his mouth and shouted out the news: the French had been defeated, England's shores were safe. He thanked them for their sacrifice, he put his blessing on them all.

What with the wind, how many of them heard his words? How many, next year or the next, would answer if he called a second time? For they had suffered much these weeks, and to no purpose in the end.

John felt it, too, I think. He turned to me when he was done. "Remember this," was all he said. I wiped my eyes; the wind had made them tear.

Till next time, if God wills it.

At Battle

The 11th Day of June, A.D. 1213

The news is good. We have, these last days, moved along the coast, distributing the French ships Longsword took as bounty to the Cinque Ports for their contributions to the fleet. This being done, we started north to London, stopping here to pass the night.

St. Mary's is, I can't resist the rhyme, a shabby abbey; small and graceless, poor and in a state of deep decline. We were at dinner, wedged together in what passes for the Great Hall, choking down the food, when Pandulf found us.

In he came, all smiles.

"My lords, I bring you news from Damme."

And gorgeous news it was. We had no sooner left the Swine when Philip had come charging back from Ghent with all his men.

His rage was uncontrollable. It lasted through the night. At dawn, he went down to the harbor and surveyed his fleet. Full half of it lay ruined, sunk or burned. But we had struck in haste and many ships remained afloat; five hundred of them, maybe more. King Philip stood there on a jetty, looking left and right. He said no word. And then he turned to Eustace the Monk, in whose command the fleet had been.

"Burn them," he ordered. "Burn them all."

John's face, on hearing this, was blank with disbelief. "Impossible; it can't have happened."

"But it did, my lord."

"He put his own ships to the torch?"

"He thought your navy would return and take what it had left behind."

John closed his eyes, as if to see the moment better. "Christ," he said, and then the laughter started. On and on it went. I was the one who brought it to an end.

"Pandulf?"

"Yes, Giraldus?"

Had he told the good news first to soften us for something bitter? "Have you been with Stephen Langton?"

"That I have. My lords, I bring you greetings from our venerable father, the Lord Stephen, Archbishop of Canterbury."

He had everyone's attention.

"Yes, of course," John said. "You spoke with him?"

"At length, my lord."

"Where is he now?"

"At Pontigny."

Of course, at Pontigny. The holy place where Thomas Becket lived in exile. As if by sleeping in his bedclothes, he could cloak himself in Becket's greatness.

"How did he receive you?"

"Graciously, my lord. He asked for news of you. He bears no rancor, none at all; or so he says."

"You gave our Charter of Submission to him?"

"Yes, my lord."

"And then?"

[148]

"He read it through, he wept, he prayed . . ." For just a moment, Pandulf seemed uncertain. Not his style at all; he always knows the next move and the next. "My lord," he went on, "I must tell you this: Lord Stephen is a most extraordinary man."

This well may be. His reputation as a scholar is enormous and his Paris lectures, some of which I've read, are not untouched by brilliance. My own opposition to him is in no way like the King's. I stand on principle.

In 1205, the year the last archbishop died, the monks of Canterbury met and they elected his successor. John, who did not like their choice, brought force to bear and, in a second vote, they named the man he wanted. Innocent, opposed to both, insisted on a third election, that of Langton. Thus, depending on one's point of view, we have had three archbishops in the See or none.

I say the first election should have stood. It is the monks who have the right, not kings or popes. The fact that I was once elected by Saint David's monks only to have the bishopric torn from me by the Pope does not affect my feelings in this matter. Not one whit. There is a true way and a false way in all things and Langton, till the day he dies, is an impostor in the eyes of God. I longed to say so but I kept my peace.

"He is extraordinary," Pandulf said again.

John cocked his head. "In what way?"

"You must meet the man," was Pandulf's only answer.

Which we will, at some point soon.

Till next time, if God wills it.

At the Tower, London
The 30th Day of June, A.D. 1213

Midmorning, I was summoned by des Roches. I found him in his council chamber on the second level. He enjoys austerity and there is nothing in the chamber save the table where he works and two stools opposite.

The Marshal sat in one of them, a letter in his hand. Des Roches looked up and nodded to the empty stool. We sat in silence till the Marshal finished reading; then he handed it to me.

It was, of course, from Stephen Langton to the King. A graceful piece of work, it said in substance, always with the King's permission and approval, that he planned to land at Dover on the 16th of July. That his first wish was to embrace the King. That he would lift the ban of excommunication then and there. And having done so, he would celebrate the first Mass heard in England since the Interdict had started nearly seven years ago.

I put the letter down. No one, as yet, had said a word. And what was there to say? The man was coming, as we knew he would. We had a date now, that was all; but nothing else had changed. I wondered why des Roches had wanted us.

The Marshal wondered too. "Well, Peter?"

"Clearly, we have many things to do. I've made a list, if you'll bear with me." Mainly, there were ceremonial details. A proper welcome, someone had to go to Dover to receive him. Not the King; some man of lesser rank. And after that, where should he meet the King and where should Mass be held and who should be invited? Minor matters, yet of real importance; for it was a new beginning, and the man whose office brings him wealth and power second only to the King's was coming home to England after thirty years abroad.

So long away; it troubles all of us. Does it imply that Langton is no Englishman, not any more? Like me, he went to Paris as a youth of less than twenty, reaching there, I think, the year I left. My roots, the things I loved and cared about, were here. I came home. He did not.

I was adrift in all of this when someone spoke my name.

"Giraldus?"

"Yes?"

It was des Roches. He looked at me, impersonal and brisk, as is his way. "You go," he said.

"Go where, my lord?"

"To Dover."

"You want me to greet him?"

"Someone has to."

"No, my lord."

"Why not?"

What reason could I give? My feelings, my objections to the man, had no place here. "The honor is too great."

He shook his head. "You've earned it. I can think of no one better suited."

"It would be the proudest moment of my life; that I, a humble clergyman, should greet a prince." I sighed. "But no, it is not right. How would you feel, my lord, were you to go to Paris and be greeted by a clerk? I beg you, send a man of stature. Someone," I said, turning toward him, "like the Marshal."

"Me?" the Marshal said.

I nodded. "If it please you."

"But of course it pleases me. How could it not?"

Des Roches sat back. "You'll go?"

"I'd leave this afternoon if need be. Only, Peter, is it politic? I am an earl, and every baron in the Kingdom would be outraged if I went. Why him, why Marshal and not me? No, Peter, we must send our ranking churchman. He must go, whoever he may be." He turned to me. "Giraldus, who is first in rank?" As if he did not know.

What could I do? I nodded across the desk at the Bishop of Winchester, Peter des Roches.

He nodded briskly back. "I take your point. It is, of course, my place to go. No question of it; absolutely. And I would, except that I myself am excommunicated and I cannot give this honor to a churchman in disgrace." He sighed. "You see my problem."

"Yes, my lord," I told him, though the only problem in the room was mine.

I leave for Dover in a week.

Till next time, if God wills it.

At Dover Castle

The 15th Day of July, A.D. 1213

Everything is done, I think. I have my list in front of me, I have
gone over it and over it—the ceremonies on the jetty, the reception, quarters in the castle, food—all in minute detail. I do not
know the size of Langton's entourage but surely it will be at least
as great as Marshal's when he came: a half-dozen ships or more
with treasure, holy relics, vast possessions, clerks and clergy, servants, guards and men-at-arms. Et cetera.

This morning I went down into the town. There is an entry well
up on my list that reads: "Provide a cheering throng." There's
nothing like a mass of screaming commonfolk to warm the hearts
of princes, be they secular or sacred. It would take some organizing, certainly, and I was on my way to see the reeve and put the
matter in his hands.

I never saw him. I had scarcely reached the streets when it began. An old man hurried up to me: "Oh, Father, is it true he's
coming home?" He knew. We had not told the people, but they
knew. I nodded yes, he kissed my hand and started weeping. Others came, in twos and threes, old, young, all full of tears and questions. Could I open up their church now, would I hold
Communion? One of them, a young girl, had a baby at home and
it was dying and please, Father, could she bury it in holy ground?
And Mass; and all the things they'd starved for all these years.
Today? Could it begin again today?

I told them no, not yet but soon. They asked me why. What
could I say? That there were documents that needed signing, acts
of politics to be performed? That there were money questions,
reparations, gold to change hands and their dead would have to
wait? I did the best I could before I turned and fled.

I feel such shame. The only issue here is God. They knew it on
the street, the people did. I knew it once myself, but I have been
too long with kings and princes. God is coming back to England.
This is all that matters. Langton is ambitious, granted. So am I. It
makes no sense to hate a man I've never met. His reputation is so
great. They tell me he has written lives of all the saints and poetry

[152]

and history, too; a book on Richard Lionheart, no less. Can I be jealous of the man? Is it myself I hate? No matter, foolish questions, and I have no answers for them, anyway.

Till next time, if God wills it.

At Dover Castle
The 16th Day of July, A.D. 1213

No sign of him no message, nothing. It is twilight and Lord Stephen has not come.

I have sent the people home. Below me in the town, the streets are quiet. In the port, a fishing boat, the last arrival of the day, is moving toward the jetty. We shall have to do it all again tomorrow; and the next day and the next until it suits him to appear.

Why do this? If it be a game, why bother playing it? Call it small-minded if you will, but I have sent word to the kitchen not to throw the food out: let him have it stale. And as for—

This is senseless. Possibly the man is ill; or there are storms along the French coast. Who can say? In any case, I'm going out. The air will do me good.

Till etc.

At Dover Castle
The 17th Day of July, A.D. 1213

I left the keep and went across the bailey, through the gate and down the long stairs to the town. I wanted company. I thought perhaps of visiting Saint Martin's; it's a handsome abbey and the drink is good. Instead, I turned down High Street, wandering past the shops and houses to the port.

It was a perfect night. The air was warm and soft, the moon was full, the sky was bright with stars. The jetty lay before me. I had left the flags and canopies in place and in the moonlight they

[153]

looked black. There was just breeze enough to move them. Death, I thought. Was it a sign, was someone going to die? Ridiculous.

The fishing boat I'd seen was moored now and its crew, a half a dozen men or so, were moving slowly toward me down the jetty. They passed by me, bowing as they went. I turned to watch them go and all but walked into another man.

"Good evening, Father."

I stepped back. He was a pilgrim from the look of him, the cut and roughness of his cloak. He wore his hood; I could not see his face or tell his age. His voice was deep and sounded English.

"Lovely night," I said. He nodded. "Have you been on pilgrimage, my son?"

"I have," he answered quietly.

"Where did you go?"

"To many places; and for much too long. I've been away too long."

He paused. I thought he meant to say more. It can be a hard thing, coming home from pilgrimage; as if one's native land were foreign and one has no place.

"My son?"

He looked up.

"I can take you to Saint Martin's, they'll be glad to keep you there."

He shook his head.

My hand went to my purse. "Perhaps . . ."

"No, Father; I have everything I need." He turned then to the canopies and flags. "What is all this?"

I shrugged. "A show of earthly pomp," I said.

"For me?"

For him? I nearly laughed, but there was something in the way he said it.

He went on. "Has John come here to meet me?"

"John?" I could not seem to think.

"The King."

"The King, of course, of course." I'd called him son, I hadn't bowed, I hadn't knelt, I hadn't anything. "The King's at Winchester. I am to take you there."

[154]

"May I ask who you are?"

"I'm called Giraldus."

"Giraldus?" I could scarcely nod. "I'm an admirer of your *De Instructione Principum.* It is a splendid piece of work."

My book, he knew my book. "My lord . . ." I had composed a speech of welcome that deserted me completely.

"Come," he said, and took my arm. We started down the jetty. When we reached the beach, he bent and took a pinch of sand and rolled it back and forth between his fingertips. His lips moved. It was difficult to hear.

"I'm home," I think he said.

Till next time, if God wills it.

At Petersfield
The 18th Day of July, A.D. 1213

We ride as fast as possible, yet somehow word precedes us and the people know. They know Lord Stephen has returned, they line the streets of every village we pass through. There is no cheering. They stand waiting silently and when we come, they kneel, they bow their heads.

Lord Stephen will not pass them by. He stops, he blesses them, he speaks. Each time, a few rise up and come to kiss his hand. The King and half our barons are at Winchester awaiting him but he refuses to be pressed. It moves him deeply, all of this, although he tries to keep it hidden. He is not, I think, a man who likes emotions, least of all his own.

He is outside the abbey now. Though it is late, the villagers are there, all pressed around him. Some of them are weeping, I can hear it through the open door.

A messenger from Winchester has found us. We will meet the King tomorrow on Morn Hill.

Till etc.

At Winchester
The 19th Day of July, A.D. 1213

The King, the Marshal and des Roches stood waiting for us on the hill crest. Up we climbed, Lord Stephen first and I a bit behind. Winchester lay below us, we could see it all: straight Roman streets and the cathedral with its roof of red and pinnacles of burnished gold.

We reached the top. The King stepped forward and Lord Stephen opened up his arms, forgetting for a moment that there could be no embrace. For John, until tomorrow's ceremonies, is still excommunicated. There could be no Kiss of Peace today. Instead, they bowed; first one and then the other.

They are much alike in size; strong, stocky men. And similar in manner, too, both born to be obeyed. John's hair and beard are flecked with gray. Lord Stephen is cleanshaven and his hair, what little there is of it, rings his head in close-cropped white.

Their talk was commonplace. How was Lord Stephen's journey, was he pleased to be in England once again? And on Lord Stephen's part, how was the Queen and were the children well? Such things. And then a few remarks about the hopes they shared for friendship and for peace, an invitation from the King to dine tonight and that was all.

Lord Stephen bowed and turned and started down the hillside toward the town. We watched him go in silence for a little. Then the questions started; first the King, then Marshal, then des Roches. What did I know, what had he said? What plans, if any, did he have? Where was his entourage, why had he come alone? What questions had he asked of me?

I told them what I knew, which did not come to much; for in the three days I had known the man, Lord Stephen had not said a single word about himself.

Till next time, if God wills it.

At Winchester
The 20th Day of July, A.D. 1213

There was no sound in the cathedral; none. Though every place
was taken, no one moved or spoke. We sat down at the front: the
Queen, now many months with child, all pearls and ivory silk; the
Marshal in his heavy robes of office; Longsword and myself.

At last, they came; Lord Stephen and the King. They stood
before the altar for a moment. Then the King knelt down and
made his oath. He swore upon the Gospel to uphold the Church,
to make full restitution of all property, to honor and observe the
ancient laws of Henry I and Edward the Confessor and to grant
full amnesty to all the bishops and the barons who have lived, for
all this time, in exile.

When this was done, Lord Stephen, in a ringing voice, absolved
him from the weight of excommunication and declared the Interdict to be, as of that moment, at an end. This said, he bent and
gave the King the Kiss of Peace.

And then bells, the ringing of the bells. They have not rung for
all these years. The air shook from the sound. In every town in
England, shore to shore, there would be bells today. Our grief is
over, God has come again, we are at peace. I wept.

At Winchester
The 21st Day of July, A.D. 1213

Lord Stephen neither eats nor sleeps. He tries to do so much so
quickly. Day and night, he labors in the bishop's office, papers
everywhere, as clerks and scribes race in and out like squirrels. The
Church, for seven years, has had no life, and he would resurrect it
overnight.

The King is busy, too. For in the press of things, such matters as
our grand alliance and the war with France have been neglected.
Longsword is, as always, in a fever to attack, to follow up the
victory at Damme. The taxes have been raised, we have the fleet

and war machines and he is all for using them at once. The King resists. He wants, as always, to be certain he is safe at home. So much has happened in these weeks and he is all for waiting till the pieces fall in place.

And as for me, I shuttle back and forth between Lord Stephen's office and the King's. I carry messages and papers. The two of them, at least thus far, are working openly with one another. *Deo gratias.*

Till etc.

At Winchester
The 22nd Day of July, A.D. 1213

I was in transit from one office to the other when I came across the King and Queen. There is a modest garden near the castle-keep and they were sitting underneath an elm tree in the shade.

"My lord," I said and handed him the papers I was carrying. He took them and began to read as Isabelle looked up at me. Her eyes were red, she had been weeping. What had happened? She would tell me, if she chose. I sat beside her.

"Lovely day," I ventured.

"Yes," she said and looked away across the garden, seeing none of it, I think.

I waited, then I tried again. "How beautiful the roses are. Like Woodstock."

"Yes." Another silence. I sat back and waited for the King to finish. It was pleasant in the shade, birds called to one another, insects buzzed about. And then the Queen spoke.

"John?" she said. He did not seem to hear her. Louder this time: "John?"

He looked up from the papers. "I've already told you no."

"I want to go."

"I can't allow it. There is nothing more to say."

"I'm going home." She moved to rise, as if she meant to do so then and there.

"It is impossible."

"I haven't seen him since I was a child. I was twelve, that's all I was. He needs me. If your father needed you—"

"He never did."

She paused. I saw the tears well in her eyes. I have not met her father, Aymer, Count of Angoulême, but he is said to be a civilized and thoughtful man. She misses him from time to time, and when she does, she tells me stories, things they did when she was young.

She shook her head, as if to shake the tears away. "It's grave. The letter said it's grave. If he should die—"

"How can I let you go? With Philip's troops in Poitiers, it's too great a risk." The King was right of course; for Angoulême lies half surrounded by our enemies.

The Queen's eyes seemed to flash. "It's my life, I can risk it if I choose."

"There's more than that at risk. I would remind the Lady Queen that she is carrying an heir."

"I've borne you three. How many does the King require?"

"Mother had eleven."

"Wasn't that excessive?"

"I came last."

"I know."

Her hand rose to her lips as if to catch the words and take them back. I know repentance when I see it and the King had only to be gentle for a moment.

Instead, he stood. "The Lady Queen," he said, "will have as many children as I want. And should she act against my wishes, I shall place her under lock and key." With which, he turned and strode away across the garden.

What was I to say? I understood her feelings but he could not let her go. I reached out for her hand. She drew it back.

"My lady, if there's anything that I can do . . ."

"What can you do?" Her voice was sharp. I waited, hoping she would let her anger out on me, but all she said was, "Shouldn't you go after him? He's walked off with your papers."

There was nothing I could do but leave her there.

Till next time, if God wills it.

At Winchester
The 23rd Day of July, A.D. 1213

I am everybody's go-between. I go between the King and Isabelle, who stays inside her room and will not speak to him. Between the King and Longsword, who goes skulking up and down the corridors because John has decided there will be no war with France this year. And, as before, between Lord Stephen and the King with papers in my hands.

I am entitled to my temper, too. I said so to the Marshal after supper and he told me to behave myself. There's no one I can rail against.

Till etc.

N.B. I should make note that the Great Council is to meet in two weeks at Saint Alban's. It has not met for years, of course, since half its membership, the higher clergy, has been unavailable. But they are trickling back from exile now, old friends and enemies, and I'm to go there with Lord Stephen and the Marshal.

I should also note that free men, four from every shire, have been invited to attend. It was Lord Stephen's notion. He put it this way to the King: "It was your common folk who came to Barham Down. Your free men may be pawns but they are still your strongest pieces." Reasonable enough. John thought so, too.

At Saint Alban's
The 3rd Day of August, A.D. 1213

I must one day do a book about the Nature of Emotion. It is terra incognita in the main, though Aristotle has some splendid things to say. I was reflecting on the subject just this afternoon: on the impermanence of what we feel. Emotions grow or wither, live or die. Except for one: one feeling which, regardless of events or circumstance, endures unchanged. I have in mind sheer loathing.

It's astonishing. One can have neither seen nor thought of certain men for years and then, on meeting them again, on merely being near, be swept away by detestation. God may not forgive me but I have in mind a number of the bishops here. Eustace of Ely, William of London, Jocelyn of Bath. The list is endless: avaricious, flatulent, small-minded men.

And as if this were not enough, we have the exiled barons, too. John's amnesty included them as well, for many of them fled the country when the clergy left. The odious FitzWalter is among those present, as is his putrescent friend, de Vescy. They seem somewhat pallid from their months of exile, a condition caused, no doubt, by all the rocks they have been living under.

Bishops, barons, we must have a hundred of these creatures here. They represent all shades of loyalty, opinion and belief. On one point only do they feel the same: they are incensed about the free men. That a merchant and an earl should sit together makes them rage.

We meet tomorrow for the first time. I have hopes for very little. Not Lord Stephen. He believes that great things can be done, that peace and trust and better lives for everyone are possible. A new beginning is within our reach, he is convinced of it.

I have been asked by Jocelyn of Bath to join him for some brandy. I would rather lose a tooth.

Till next time, if God wills it.

At Saint Alban's Abbey
The 5th Day of August, A.D. 1213

Saint Alban's church, in which the Council meets each morning, is as vast a place of worship as we have in England. All around it, in magnificent design, stand all the other abbey buildings: lesser chapels, cloisters, dormitories, guest house, school, the novice quarters, the infirmary, the kitchens, barns and workshops. Everything, in short, is civilized and exquisite; except, of course, for our deliberations which—

I must be fair. The Council first met yesterday. The members took their places quietly enough. The Marshal said a few words, then Lord Stephen spoke. His text was beautifully composed, a brilliant and uplifting sermon on the possibilities that lay before us. Then, since few of them had been at Winchester, he gave them an account of what had happened there. He took them through the oaths that John had sworn, he even read the laws of Henry I aloud.

This done, he said, "My lords and brothers in the Church, the time has come to cope constructively with those specific issues which confront us."

We've had chaos ever since; no end of it in sight. Some barons love the Church, some loathe it. Some long for peace and some for vengeance on the King. Some bishops are true men of spirit, some are merely earls with mitres on. Some are as hostile to the barons as the barons are to them, some go about embracing all the free men, some are threatening not to meet again if there are trades-men in the hall.

And yet, there is one interest that they share, one passion which unites them: greed. They lust for money. Reparations, restitution, claims and more claims. Half the baronage has suffered losses at John's hands, or so they say. And every church in England has its case for missing revenue and confiscations caused by seven years of Interdict.

Some claims are fair, but many are outrageous and absurd. This afternoon, two Sussex churches claimed the loss of the same gold reliquary; a situation complicated by the fact that neither of them ever owned it.

Through all this, Lord Stephen perseveres. I sat with him to-night and marveled at his faith. Why bother with the Council anyway? It has so little power or authority. I told him so.

"I know," he said, "but when it meets, it is the only time that all of England comes together. There's a chance to reason here."

He's wrong, of course. Outside my room, a group of earls are shouting at each other. And we have another week of this.

Till next time, if God wills it.

At St. Alban's
The 12th Day of August, A.D. 1213

The Council, having come to one decision, has disbanded. In a
fine display of mindless unanimity, it has decided it should meet
again. We are to reconvene in London at Saint Paul's in two
weeks' time.

We leave here for the Tower in the morning.

T.n.t.

At the Tower, London
The 16th Day of August, A.D. 1213

The King arrived midmorning on his galley, having been at Lambeth visiting the Queen. We met him on the dock, the Marshal
and Lord Stephen and des Roches and I, and spent the day in
conference on the Thames.

The royal galley is an awesome ship; both fleet and vast, it has a
crew of sixty men and every comfort one can think of. On the
aftercastle, underneath a canopy, there was a trestle table and a
group of chairs with arms. The day was clear and hot, but there
was cool wine on the shaded table and a soft, light river breeze.

The Thames, in recent years, is not as lovely as it was. So much
is being built these days; new docks and sheds, more shops and
houses, everything all crowded in. More people, too, and they mis-
use the river, filling it with refuse, rotting vegetables and offal. Still,
on days like this it can be beautiful, and there were shouts and
cheers for John from seamen on the boats we passed.

The King had much to ask about Saint Alban's: Who was there
and what was said? We told him in detail. He asked about Fitz-
Walter and de Vescy: How had they behaved? No worse or better
than the rest, we said. He asked us why the Council was so quick to
meet again: Was all the haste for money and no other reason? Yes,
we said. By this time we had glided under London Bridge, past
Billingsgate—and then it happened.

Baynard's Castle. There it stood; or, rather, what was left of it, the broken walls and shattered towers on which John had spent his rage. The castle has a dock and on it was a man. A huge man, tall and thick and unmistakable. FitzWalter. Looking at the ruins of his fortress.

It was John who saw him first. He signaled for the galley captain, murmured orders. In a moment we were turning, easing toward the shore. FitzWalter's back was to us and he neither saw nor heard the ship till we were near the dock.

He turned. His features, which are strong and curiously fine considering the soul that lurks within, showed nothing. Neither pleasure nor surprise.

"Your Majesty." He said it with a bow.

The King was equally polite. He stood, moved to the ship's rail. "It's been far too long. How are you, Robert?"

"Very well, all things considered."

"Are Matilda and the children with you?"

"Not as yet."

Well-mannered words and pleasant smiles; yet underneath, like metal buried in the earth, there lay rich veins of loathing. How this hatred started, no one knows. It's possible there are no reasons. One hears stories; that the King despoiled FitzWalter's eldest daughter, for example. To be fair, she is a jolly girl, her good eye twinkles and her legs, though of unequal length, are shapely. There are other stories, too, all equally as dubious.

There was some further talk and then the King said, "Robert, I should like us to be friends."

"I, too, my lord, and I would offer you my hospitality but, as you see"—he gestured toward the ruined walls behind him—"as you see, I cannot ask you in."

John nodded. "It was wanton of me, Robert, but I thought you meant to have me murdered."

"I, my lord?"

"In battle on the fields of Wales. And when you fled the country, what was I to think?"

FitzWalter shook his head. "You take me to be capable of that?"

"I'm sure you are," John answered calmly, "and you know I'd do as much for you. In fact, I've been advised to have you killed. You have some friends who might object; but not enough to keep me from it. It's a tempting possibility."

FitzWalter's face was ashen but he stood his ground. "I have more friends than you may think."

John grinned. "I've never murdered anyone. I have no wish to start with you."

They looked at one another. Then FitzWalter bowed. "I'll see you at Saint Paul's, my lord."

John turned and nodded to the captain. We began to glide away. The Marshal was the first to speak. He looked at John.

"I'd have him killed if I were in your place. He lost us Normandy. He did it at Vaudreuil, he gave our fortress to the French. There was no battle, not one sword was drawn, he simply opened up the gates. I met with Philip not long after. He refused to meet FitzWalter, he would not receive him. Why? I asked. And Philip said, 'A man like that is like a torch; you use him if you must and then you toss him in the cesspool.' "

"It may come to that," John answered, "but not yet."

More wine was poured and everybody drank. Save me. I could not join them, I could not, for there was something which I had to ask.

"Lord Stephen?"

"Yes, Giraldus?"

"Is it true FitzWalter came to you at Pontigny?"

He nodded. "Yes. I saw him several times."

"You actually received him?"

"Certainly."

I paused. "You can't have known his reputation; surely not."

"Of course I knew." His glance included all of us. "You underestimate the man. He's everything you say; and more. But there is one thing that I fear you overlook. Men listen to him. I have seen it. When he acts, they follow. He is someone to contend with. Certainly, I saw him. I'd have been a damned fool not to."

Nothing else was said about it. John sat back, his eyes half closed. I knew what he was thinking: What side did Lord Stephen stand on? All those feelings of mistrust were stirring in his mind. I know because I felt them, too.

Till next time, if God wills it.

At the Tower, London
The 24th Day of August, A.D. 1213

The King expects to make a brief address tomorrow when the Council meets. I have been writing it all afternoon. Below me now, the Hall is full of barons. I must go and be polite.

Till etc.

At Saint Paul's Cathedral
The 25th Day of August, A.D. 1213

I am in someone's office; whose, I cannot say. The deacon's or the sexton's, does it matter? I am in this room and through the walls I hear them shouting and their feet are stamping on the floor. Des Roches has sent me here to write their names down. It is pointless; there are far too many. I must try to put events in order.

It was late morning when we came; the King, des Roches, Lord Stephen and I. We went directly to the bishop's chamber. From its doorway, we could see the nave, the empty choir benches. There we stood.

The Council was to meet at noon. We watched the members come. No freemen this time, only barons and the clergy. They arrived, some singly, some in little groups; some sat directly on the choir benches, some moved here and there in quiet conversation. There was nothing, I am certain of it, nothing to betray what was to come.

The bells of the cathedral rang. The Council settled into place. Des Roches, who was to greet them, strode out to the choir floor.

He waited. Then, when there was something close to silence in the church, he spoke. He welcomed them and told them how the meetings would proceed: that talk would be confined to reparations and that each claim, one by one, would be examined, openly discussed and settled in some manner mutually agreed upon. It was a time to put past grievances aside, he said, and called on them to exercise their wisdom and good will. This done, he left the nave.

Lord Stephen took his place. He was to lead them all in prayer, after which the King would speak. All heads were bowed. Lord Stephen, starting with a passage from Corinthians, spoke movingly about the need for peace and trust. The church was silent at the start. And then I heard some muttering; or so I thought. Faint noises, whispers. Where, from what part of the floor? I could not say.

Lord Stephen heard it, too. He looked up sharply, with a frown. The whispers died. And then, a moment later, there it was again; more widely spread now, louder, clearer. "Laws . . ." Was that what they were whispering?

Lord Stephen broke off sharply. "What is this?" I heard him say. And then, from all sides, it began. "King Henry's laws . . . now . . . read the Charter . . ." Someone stood. One baron, then another. They were shouting. Cries of "Henry's charter, Henry's laws" rang out and echoed off the walls.

We were at the bishop's doorway still and I could barely hear the King, the shouting rose so high. "The bastards." That was all he said. "The bastards," and he turned away in rage and left us, left St. Paul's.

Des Roches was close to me. His eyes were on the choir and he started naming names. Great names. Geoffrey de Mandeville, Earl of Essex. Henry Bohun, Earl of Hereford. Roger Bigod, Earl of Norfolk. There were more, more barons shouting for the Charter. Clare, de Vere; were they among them, have I got it right?

A messenger was sent, there was a copy at the Tower, it was brought. Lord Stephen has it, he is out there now. He reads a sentence and they shout and bang their swords. The floor shakes. Pandemonium.

[167]

Lord Stephen was magnificent. He read the Charter to the end and
then he called for silence. He demanded it and got it and, his voice
like ice, like frozen scorn, he laid them low. They were in a cathedral, not a jousting field. They were the leaders of the Kingdom,
not barbarians. No further meetings on this level would be toler-
ated: he would deal with statesmen or he would not deal at all.

He raked them with his eyes and left the floor. The only sound
in the cathedral was the noise his boots made on the stones.

Once out of public view, his pace increased. We joined him. We
were all but running when we left Saint Paul's. It was imperative to
reach the King; for were he, that moment, organizing an attack on
the cathedral, I would not have been surprised. Nor, in my heart,
could I have altogether disapproved.

We found him in his chambers at the Tower. He was standing
by a window looking out across his City. When he turned, his face
was pensive; not a sign of rage or outrage.

"What are we to make of this?" he said.

The argument that followed started slowly. I, myself, was much
confused. Why all this sudden interest in King Henry's laws? Each
monarch for a hundred years has sworn to follow them and none
has done so. There are few surviving copies of the text, so little
interest has there been. Beyond some vaguely written passages on
debts and monies owed the Crown, there's nothing worth remem-
bering. And yet Saint Paul's had shaken with cheers.

Des Roches is certain that FitzWalter stands behind it all; that
we are dealing with an act of vengeance, a conspiracy born out of
one man's hatred for another. I am not so sure. Nor is Lord Stephen.

"Sire," he said, "there may be other forces working here; the
movement of the times, the pressure of events—"

John cut him off. "For Jesus' sake, this isn't metaphysics."

"May I speak?" I asked.

John glared at me. "You always do."

I paused, then plunged ahead. "My lord, these laws were read three weeks ago and no one noticed. What has happened in the time between? I fear that we may never know the truth. And lacking that, how can we possibly be wise?"

"What are you saying, man? That I should sit here and do nothing?"

"For the moment, yes. How can we deal with something when we don't know what it is?"

"That's your advice?"

I nodded. "Yes."

"Then think again. I want some action taken. Bring me a consensus, find a line for me to follow. If you can't—"

He left it hanging, turned and stalked out of the room. We've talked for hours and none of us is certain what to do. Perhaps by morning, we shall see more clearly.

Till next time, if—

With all the stress, I quite forgot. There is one glad thing to report. The Queen, who is at Corfe, has given birth. A daughter. They have called the child Isabelle.

At Saint Mary's, Luton
The 26th Day of August, A.D. 1213

How many miles have we done since morning? Forty? Are we forty miles from London? It is not enough.

We met this morning early. Still uncertain what to do, what course to take, we went to see the King. His chambers were deserted. He was gone. We called for Petit. He knew nothing; only that the King was up at dawn.

The captain of the guard knew more. He'd seen the King ride off with forty men, he'd heard him cry, "To Nottingham!" Lord Stephen caught the meaning of it instantly. Reprisals. He was off to take his vengeance on the barons of the north; while they were all in London, he would bring their castles down.

We had to stop him, surely. With a hundred barons shouting for King Henry's laws, it was no time to rush about the Kingdom breaking most of them. Lord Stephen called for men and horses. We were ready in an hour. The Marshal and des Roches remained behind. We had the Council on our hands, it had to be suspended, there were certain to be repercussions.

We are three long days from Nottingham. Lord Stephen hopes to overtake John on the way. He does not know the King as I do: no man travels with his speed.

Till next time.

At Nottingham Castle
The 30th Day of August, A.D. 1213

The sun was down when we arrived. We crossed the Trent and made our way through quiet streets. The castle walls loomed dark and high. The captain of the guard stepped forth as we drew up.

Lord Stephen spoke. "Is the King here?"

"Yes, my lord."

He bowed and passed us through. We crossed the bailey to the keep. More guards; they flanked the door. Behind them, torches burned. Lord Stephen introduced himself.

One of the guards, an officer, bowed low. "My Lord Archbishop."

"I have come to see the King."

"Tonight, my lord?"

"At once."

The fellow frowned. "The King has gone to bed, my lord."

"It's on my head," Lord Stephen snapped. "Announce me."

In we went and up the narrow stairs. The rushes underfoot were soiled, dogs whimpered in the darkness. On the second level was a door. The officer moved toward it, hesitant. Lord Stephen thanked him with a nod and knocked.

We waited. There was noise within, the bolt slid back, a face appeared. Old William's face; John's bathman, peering at me.

"Is that you, Giraldus?"

"Yes,"I said. His eyes are poor. "May we come in?"

The King was in his tub. He stiffened instantly. "What's wrong in London? Is there trouble?"

"No, Your Majesty," Lord Stephen said.

"What brings you, then? Why have you come?"

"Because the trouble's here, my lord."

John frowned. "In Nottingham? Am I in danger of some kind?"

Lord Stephen sighed. "My lord, I'm not accustomed to the chase and I've been four days chasing you. May we stop playing games?"

"I'm playing several," John said. "Which one do you have in mind?"

I watched Lord Stephen closely. How would he approach it? Recklessly. "My lord, this expedition is a grave mistake."

"Is that a fact or an opinion?"

"It is fact. You saw what happened at Saint Paul's."

"I did."

"And having seen it, you come north to take revenge?"

"I do."

"They will not sit for it, your barons; they will not."

John's eyes were very hard and bright. "They always have, they always will. How old, you tell me, how old are King Henry's laws? One hundred thirteen years. Has any king obeyed them ever? No. Nor will I be the first. FitzWalter thinks he'll bring me down. He thinks—"

"My lord, if you'll permit—"

John's voice rang, as his father's had. "I'm speaking, sir! The King is speaking!" It echoed. In the silence after, John went on. "I will not leave the Crown a smaller thing than when I found it."

Lord Stephen shook his head. "You must not take me for an enemy, my lord."

"Why not? There was no talk of charters till you came."

"I meant it only for your good. I have some grasp of what you face here. I've received more barons than FitzWalter. All my years in France, your exiles came to me. I listened and I learned but I am not against you; I'm not one of them. I read the Charter at Saint Alban's to appease them, that was all."

[171]

They looked at one another. Could Lord Stephen be believed? If Innocent could sit upon Saint Peter's throne and lie, if Langton was his friend, his choice, his man . . .

John spoke. "This talk of laws and charters, can you stop it?"

"I can try."

"If I turn round and come to London quietly, if I keep my part of the peace, will you keep yours?"

"I will, my lord."

"You'll swear to that?"

Lord Stephen nodded. John stood, rising naked in the tub. His chest, his legs, all scars; old battle scars; so many of them. "Swear it, then."

Lord Stephen knelt, he bowed his head and swore to God. When this was done, he rose, went to the King and gave to him the Kiss of Peace.

"Good night, my lord."

"Good night."

Lord Stephen turned and left the room. I stayed. John waited till old William closed the door and slipped the bolt in place. "He's damned convincing, isn't he?"

I nodded.

John sat slowly in the tub again. "I knew he'd come. He had no choice, he had to follow me." And then he smiled. "You raced for nothing. I'd have waited here a week."

Till next time, if God wills it.

At Nottingham Castle
The 1st Day of September, A.D. 1213

I am to be a spy, a carrier of secrets back and forth. My orders are to be Lord Stephen's confidant, to make myself a part of all he does and bring what gleanings I can gather to the King. It is unquestionably dirty work and I, as all the world knows, am a man of probity and principle. Duplicity is not among my skills; but I must learn.

I leave for London shortly with Lord Stephen and the King. I long to say I feel dishonored by the role that I must play, but part of me, a small part to be sure, can't wait to see what happens.

Till next time, if God wills it.

At the Tower, London
The 6th Day of September, A.D. 1213

Conspire. From the Latin, *conspirare*; literally, to breathe together. This is exactly what I have been doing with Lord Stephen, calculating every breath I take. For we have come to a decision. It is this: to enter a conspiracy against which we conspire.

Lord Stephen sees no other way of dealing with FitzWalter and his followers, whoever they may be. These people, we feel certain, have no interest in the law. The betterment of jurisprudence is no part of their design. There is a contradiction, a disparity between the movement—if it be a movement—and the leaders of it. Like the child at night who calls for water not because he's thirsty, we are dealing with a call for laws that is a guise for something else. Or so Lord Stephen thinks. In fine, he sees a gap between the surface and the substance into which, if we are clever, we can drive a wedge.

The reasoning is neat and clear. The doing of it, though, is quite another matter. For FitzWalter has to think that we are with him, for him, traitors to the King. Which, in Lord Stephen's case, may be the truth, for all we know.

It is so intricate. Like the rings around an onion, circles of duplicity. How many? Are there some I cannot see? FitzWalter's people might be anywhere. So might the King's. Those guards, this clerk, that scribe, these servants; any of them might be listening, watching us, observing everything.

In any case, we must arrange a secret meeting with FitzWalter. Possibly tomorrow. As to where, that still remains.

Till next time, if God wills it.

At the Tower, London
The 8th Day of September, A.D. 1213

We needed a safe place to meet and settled on Saint Dunstan's. Standing, as it does, midway between the Tower and Baynard's Castle, it was perfect for our purposes. If we had business in the city, we would naturally pass near it. And FitzWalter, on the dim chance that he ever felt the need to pray, might wander in without attracting notice.

We then composed a note. It read: "You have more friends than you might think. Tomorrow, Terce, Saint Dunstan's." Taking it, I went out for a stroll and, nearing Baynard's, found an urchin who delivered it.

This morning, quite as if by accident, I found Lord Stephen having breakfast in the Great Hall. Naturally, I joined him. Turning to me, in a voice distinctly audible, he said, "I've just remembered, I have business in the city."

"What a shame. I'd hoped to spend the morning with you. There's a passage in Saint Mark that troubles me."

"Why don't you come along? We can discuss it on the way."

Which is precisely what we did. No doubt we're being overcareful; still, you never know. In any case, we met by Lion's Gate an hour later and set forth on foot down Tower Street. The morning was autumnal, brisk and clear, and we were early at the church. We meant to be.

The deacon, not unnaturally, was overwhelmed. What could he do for us? Lord Stephen smiled. "Yes," he said, "there is a small thing you might do," and sent him on an errand that would take him half the day.

We had his office to ourselves. We sat. Parishioners, a few of them, moved by our open door. Time passed, Terce rang, we waited. No FitzWalter. Then we heard a clinking noise, the sound of light chain mail. Lord Stephen looked at me. We rose, moved to the door and out, as if to go. FitzWalter stood there, scowling in the dimness at the figures kneeling in the nave. He is, as I have said, heroical in size; magnificent, in fact.

Lord Stephen spoke as if surprised. "FitzWalter? Is that you?"

He turned. His face showed no surprise, of course; our being here was natural enough. He bowed. "My Lord Archbishop."

"There's a matter I've been meaning to take up with you." Lord Stephen hesitated. "Have you time?"

FitzWalter cast one final look around. "Apparently," he said.

We went back to the deacon's room. There were two chairs; I took the stool. Lord Stephen spoke of little things. How was Fitz-Walter's wife, poor woman; and his children, were they well? Then, in a more official voice, Lord Stephen said, "I have been deeply puzzled by what happened at Saint Paul's."

FitzWalter nodded. "You have been abroad, my lord; of course you find it puzzling."

"Can you help me understand it?"

"I'm not sure." FitzWalter frowned. "I've been abroad myself, you know."

"I'd no idea there was such interest in King Henry's laws." Lord Stephen paused. "Did you?"

"No, not at all."

"When did it start?"

"I think," FitzWalter said, "I think it started when you read them at Saint Alban's."

"I'm responsible?" Lord Stephen smiled wryly. "Is it spreading of itself, I wonder, or is it a movement? Do you know?"

"A movement?"

"Does it have a leader? Is it organized?"

FitzWalter seemed to ponder. "Yes," he said at last, "or so I'm told."

"Who leads it? Have they told you that?" No answer. "Can you ask them?"

"They would ask me why you want to know."

"Because I have a message for him. I would tell him—" He broke off and looked at me. I nodded, got up, closed the door. "I'd tell him this: he has more friends than he might think."

FitzWalter looked up sharply. "You?"

Lord Stephen nodded.

I sat ready with my speech. Lord Stephen, too. Our reasons, motives, why we could be trusted, all of that. For surely he would want to know.

At last, he spoke. "I see" was all he said. He stood and crossed the room in silence, drew the latch back on the door and opened it. I wondered, Had we lost him? He was in the doorway when he turned to us and said, "Tomorrow."

Out he went. I waited till the clinking died away. "What do you think?" I asked.

Lord Stephen shrugged. "I think that, in the end, Giraldus, you and I are like the apple in the Garden: irresistible."

He smiled. I might have pointed out the apple was devoured. Instead, I smiled back.

Till next time, if God wills it.

At the Tower, London
The 9th Day of September, A.D. 1213

FitzWalter came with company this time: his lifelong friend and fellow lout, Eustace de Vescy, and a dim-eyed brute of somewhat lesser stature, Saer de Quenci, Earl of Winchester. They came into the deacon's office, dripping from the heavy rain outside. The water on their chain mail glistened in the candlelight.

They stood. We sat. No greetings were exchanged; nor did we speak. It was FitzWalter's meeting; let him open it.

He did. In no uncertain terms. "You say you are my friends," he snapped. "You're not. We neither like nor trust each other. Yet you come to me."

Lord Stephen nodded. "And you want to know the reasons why." He launched into the speech he had prepared for yesterday. He spoke it movingly: the anguish he had suffered at John's hands, the years of exile, the deceits, the persecution. Anything, he would do anything to wound the King and make his power less.

FitzWalter's face stayed blank, which is, I think, its natural condition. Did he believe Lord Stephen's tale? I could not say. In any case, my turn was next and I was going through my story in my mind. In essence, it was like Lord Stephen's: hatred of the King and all his family, how they had blighted my career, destroyed my life. I had to keep it simple, little words for little minds, and I was tinkering with my vocabulary when FitzWalter spoke.

"Why is the Welshman here?" he said.

Lord Stephen's voice still trembled with emotion. "Ask him. He has reasons even deeper than my own."

FitzWalter turned to me. "You do?"

I nodded. "Yes."

His lips drew back. It was a smile. "You lie," he said. "You are the King's man. And the Queen's. I know; I know your secrets."

"Tell me one."

He laughed. "You take me for that great a fool?"

Inside me, something snapped. It was the laugh that did it. "Yes, I do. And further, I'm as proud to be their friend as I am sickened by the sight of you." I simply could not stop myself; it all poured out. There were some good things in King Henry's laws, and other laws were needed, too, or else I feared the King might fall. And this was why I'd work with him. Nor for his reasons, not to harm the King. To save him.

I stopped at last. My heart was pounding, I could scarcely hear. FitzWalter and his colleagues looked at one another. I was sure I'd ruined everything. But they were nodding. We were in.

They left us shortly after that, with promises to meet again at some point in the future. I felt spent, exhausted by it all. "I don't know what came over me," I said.

Lord Stephen looked at me, eyes wide. "You mean that wasn't what you meant to say?"

I shook my head.

It may be weeks before we hear from them. They know we're useful to their plans but at the rate their minds move, it will take some time for them to see exactly what those uses are.

Till next time, if God wills it.

At Lambeth
The 15th Day of September, A.D. 1213

The Queen is here. She came from Corfe just yesterday, her infant in her arms. Another Isabelle. The King arrived in time to greet her and they spent the night together.

I have always liked it here. The palace is a modest thing. It sits upon a rise, with smooth lawns sloping to the Thames. Life is so peaceful and so still. Yet just across the river is Westminster, one can see it from the terrace; and beyond the river's bend, just out of view, is London. Thus, the King can come and go with ease.

The days, at summer's end, are beautiful. I spent the afternoon with Isabelle. She is, to my eyes, lovelier than ever; smoother, softer, more enchanting. She was full of questions and I told her much of what I know. Not all, of course; there is no need to worry her.

She let me hold the child. I said how pretty but all babies look alike to me.

Till next time, if God wills it.

At Lambeth
The 17th Day of September, A.D. 1213

The sun was low, the afternoon was turning chill and we were just about to go inside when we heard shouting from the river. Looking out, we saw a galley crossing from Westminster. In the prow, arms waving, calling to the Queen, was Longsword.

It has been two months since we have seen him. He has been away since Winchester when John was given absolution by Lord Stephen and— Oh, come; no need for secrets here. He has been leading raids across the Channel: Cherbourg, Dieppe, Fécamp, Calais. Small actions, probing Philip's forces, testing, seeking information.

We were at the riverbank when he leapt out and splashed across the water to us. He was gentle with the Queen, no tossing in the air. He could not wait, he said, to see the child.

Afterwards, we settled by the fire and bombarded him with questions. Isabelle, who not so long ago would have retired to her needlework, has broader interests now. She hung on Longsword's every word, she asked keen questions, she is quick to see the meaning. Which is clear enough.

The news from France all points to war. Not till next summer, naturally; they have a navy to rebuild. Their shipyards are at work, Longsword has seen them.

"There's no doubt of it," he said. "They mean to try invading us again."

The Queen sat very straight. "I know what I would do," she said, "if I were King."

He looked at her. "Which is?"

Her voice was crisp, her eyes intense. "Strike first; that's what I'd do."

She said it with such certainty. He smiled. And I did, too, I fear.

"You men." She glared at us. "You think the armor makes the general? Eleanor fought wars as well as any man." And then she grinned. "Except the one she lost to Henry."

We apologized for smiling.

"So you should," she said.

She left us after supper, for the child is still at breast. I went with Longsword to his room. He asked me what had happened at St. Paul's. Before he came this afternoon, he'd seen the King; but what was my opinion?

"It's a complicated question."

"Do you take FitzWalter seriously?"

"Put it this way: he is like a clumsy rider on a splendid horse."

"I see." He nodded, then he frowned. "How many are they?"

"We don't know as yet."

"Ten barons? Twenty? We could crush them."

"Not with Philip on our hands."

He stood. "I tell you, I can do it."

[179]

There is great fierceness in him; Longsword has the family rage. I put it carefully. "The feeling here is one war at a time. How can we fight in France come Spring if we have torn ourselves apart all winter? Don't you see? FitzWalter and his friends must wait."

"I know, I know . . ." He took a deep breath, then bent down and whispered in my ear, "You think it's Henry's laws they want? It's John. They want his head."

I nodded. It was true, at least to some extent, but now was not the time to make distinctions. Not with those eyes looking at me. "Yes," I said.

"I'll have them. If not now, I'll have them later. Every God-damned one."

He loves his brother, William does. He means it.

Till next time, if God wills it.

At the Palace of Westminster
The 2nd Day of October, A.D. 1213

Old FitzPeter died tonight. I wish his soul good fortune. It will need it, I suspect; a dour, hard man he was, and for my part I never cared for him. Yet I am saddened by it nonetheless.

The country might have missed him had he died with more dispatch. Ten years as Richard's Chief Justiciar, thirteen as John's; those palsied hands had held their share of power in their time. A mighty man who, at the end, was trotted out for ceremonial occasions, like a flag. A lifeless symbol. He was at Saint Alban's, he was there at Dover when the King submitted to the Pope and did I even note his name? There seemed no point.

I should have put him down. It wasn't right. These figures stand for something, surely. He'd served Henry twenty years before I came; I was a clerk, he was a marshal. Always distant to me, always cold; but always there.

Is that what saddens me? The breaking off? I have had moments, looking at the Marshal who is eighty-God-knows-what, and thinking that I could not bear it if he died. *Pater omnipotens*: who does not want one?

I have no idea what time is made of. Nor did Aristotle. And it is Augustine, isn't it, who wrote: "What then is time? If no one asks me, I know; if I want to explain it to a questioner, I do not know."

Time, I sometimes think, is like the ocean, like a wave. We drift, we float upon it. When it crests, it takes us with it and we rise. Up, up we go; so high. And sometimes we can roll with it, ride on and on. But always, at the end, there is that sudden trough.

Ah, poor Giraldus; who will weep for you? Self-pity is a maudlin and revolting trait. I lack it and, in any case, I don't expect to die.

Till next time, if God wills it.

At the Palace of Westminster
The 5th Day of October, A.D. 1213

We have buried old FitzPeter with considerable ceremony, and the King, to the surprise of no one, has replaced him with des Roches. A natural choice, or so it seems to me. Though there are many men about with greater charm or wit, des Roches is able, hard, clearheaded and unswerving in his loyalty. On top of which he has, in fact if not in name, been acting as Justiciar for eighteen months or more.

There is resentment in some circles at the choice. Des Roches is from Poitou, a Frenchman born, and many of our barons do not trust him—as if being born in Dorset were a guarantee of honor.

All in all, these have been weighty days and there is much I must record. The secret meetings with Lord Stephen and FitzWalter have resumed, the basic strategy for our campaign in France is coming clear and—

I cannot; for there is something on my mind. Or nothing. Possibly it's nothing, I had after all been drinking, it was dark and there were shadows, it was late. For all I know, I dreamed it. Even so . . .

[181]

The night before last; it was then that we had gathered in the Great Hall, John and Isabelle and Longsword and the Marshal and some others. We were there in Peter's honor and there was extensive drinking to his health. The wine was fresh and excellent, it seemed a shame to waste it and I was among the last to leave.

The corridor was dimly lit; the torches, most of them, had gutted out. Eventually, I found the stairs. They seemed extremely steep and I was tempted to postpone them till the morning. Had it not been for the chill, I might have.

Up I went, and in the darkness at the top I paused to orient myself. Then, leaning lightly on the wall, I made my way along without mishap until, apparently, I stumbled on a dog. I fell.

This made, of course, some noise. I was about to swear when from nearby, a little farther down the corridor, there was the sound of sudden movement. I had startled someone. I looked up and saw, or thought I saw, the Queen. Her arms had been around a man, embracing him, and she was drawing back. I looked away at once because the man, or so I thought, was taller than the King.

How ludicrous. I sit here now, dear Lord, and see the scene: an old man blurred by wine lies sprawling in the darkness and he looks up from that vantage, from the floor, and thinks a man that he can scarcely see is tall.

On top of which, there are the words I heard her whisper. "No, John; let me see to him. He'll be embarrassed if it's you." And come she did and asked me if I'd hurt myself and helped me to my room.

Nothing: it was nothing, after all.

At the Palace of Westminster
The 17th Day of October, A.D. 1213

We meet tomorrow with FitzWalter. He has finally agreed to talk specifics. No more threats or rhetoric; the man is coming with proposals. So are we.

There are such possibilities. Lord Stephen is well read in Roman

Law and I know quite enough to follow after him. What we have written down is, in the main, addressed to basic principles. Our notes are crude and unrefined, I know, but what we have is nothing less than the beginnings of a Code. My eyes tear when I think of it.

Till etc.

At the Palace of Westminster
The 18th Day of October, A.D. 1213

We held our meeting at my vintner's on the Vintners' Quay. Fitz-Walter and de Vescy were already there. The two of them were perched on wine casks by a table. Candles burned. We crossed the sagging warehouse floor. They stood, we bowed; we were all being very formal with each other. Then we sat and placed our papers on the table.

"Well, my lord," FitzWalter said, "how shall we do this? Do you care to start?"

Lord Stephen nodded. "If you like." He picked our paper up and read the first proposal of our Code. " 'King John concedes that he will not take men without judgment, nor accept anything for doing justice, nor perform injustice.' "

This was met by silence. Not resistance. Merely no response, as if Lord Stephen had been speaking Arabic. Finally, FitzWalter spoke.

"That's very interesting," he said.

Lord Stephen nodded. "Good. You've no objection to it?"

"No. Do you?"

This last was to de Vescy, whose intelligence can cleave through knotty problems like a spoon. He shrugged. "It does no harm that I can see."

"No harm?" I blurted out. "Good God, sir, it's a fundamental, it's—"

Lord Stephen interrupted. "What Giraldus means to say is possibly we haven't understood each other. What proposals do you have in mind?"

FitzWalter held a page of notes. "You want to hear them now?"

"I do indeed."

He glanced down at the page. " 'No baron can be made to serve in foreign wars; or taxed for them against his will; or forced to offer men or arms or tribute or support of any kind.' " He raised his eyes.

Lord Stephen paused. As well he might; for if this single article were law, the King would lose all power to conduct affairs abroad. "Go on," he said at last. "What next?"

FitzWalter's face was hard. "There is no point in going on if John will not agree to this."

Lord Stephen kept his temper. "We are here to listen, nothing more. Go on."

"We will not yield on this proposal."

"We?" Lord Stephen's face was wry. "Who are you, anyway? How many barons do you speak for? Say a number, name the names." FitzWalter shook his head. "Why not? Are there so few?"

"You'll find out when the time comes."

"When there's war, you mean?" Lord Stephen sighed. "We're here to keep the peace; that's what these talks are for. Now do go on."

There followed roughly ten proposals— No, I cannot call them that. They had no basic substance, not a principle among them. They were all concerned with wealth, with property, inheritance. Such things as: "If a man shall die owing money to the Jews, the debt shall not gain interest while the heir is underage."

But why go on? We heard them out, arranged to meet again and left them there.

Outside, Lord Stephen turned to me. "Not bad," he said.

"Not bad?" I looked at him. "But they don't care at all. They'll stand for anything that cuts away the powers of the King. They're interested in that and nothing else."

"Exactly." He was grinning at me. "Stretch your mind, Giraldus. We can be as fine and fair as we know how. They won't object."

He is a wiser man than I, Lord Stephen is.

Till next time, if God wills it.

[184]

We went today to the Exchequer. It has only recently become an institution with a permanent address, for in the past it traveled with the King like all the other arms of government. But life keeps growing more complex, I'm not sure why, and it is situated here now at the palace.

We were there, the Marshal and the King and I, because we needed money. We are funding our allies for next year's war in France. Sums of the most appalling size are flowing from our treasuries to Germany and Holland, Flanders and Brabant. Knights, arms, supplies and war machines come dear.

The current treasurer, William of Ely, an aging cleric of invisible distinction, has an office in a tower with a window on the Thames. We sat there half the morning listening to him fret.

The gist of what he had to say was simple: we are running short. There is no way to fund an effort of the size John contemplates without the imposition of new taxes.

Now, such taxes, in the past, have not been dangerous to raise: the King demands, the barons give. Reluctantly, perhaps, and sometimes threats and force have been employed, but never has the baronage refused. This time, some of them might. The question was, How many? I had told the King about our latest meeting with FitzWalter. He had listened with his full attention; so, at least, I thought. Yet, his last words to Ely were that he would raise more taxes.

What was I to say? FitzWalter had refused to tell how many barons stood behind him. Less than twenty is a reasonable estimate, but even so, we faced a risk. I was about to point this out when Marshal did it for me. We had left the little tower and were moving silently across the palace gardens when he stopped and spoke.

"We must be careful, John," he said. "However small their number, there's a danger taxing them without first having their consent."

John shrugged. "Then we must ask them for it."

"If we do, we face an even greater risk."

"Which is?"

"The possibility that they'll refuse."

John stood a long time silently before he spoke.

"I take your point," he said.

Till next time, if God wills it.

At the Palace of Westminster
The 1st Day of November, A.D. 1213

I sat across the table from the King, my pen in hand. He looked at me.

"Are you ready?"

"Yes, my lord."

The sun was barely up. I had been summoned from the chapel, from my morning prayers. There was, it seems, a writ he wanted me to draft.

He cleared his throat. "The King to all his barons, greetings and whatever, all the usual." I nodded. He went on. The gist of it was this: the Great Council was to meet at Oxford on the 15th of November. The barons were to come unarmed and were to be accompanied by four honest knights from every shire.

I glanced at him. Could he be serious? "These knights, my lord, are they to sit as members of the Council?"

"Absolutely. Yes. Be sure to make that very clear. I'll witness it myself; and one thing more." He paused. "The writ is to be dated for the seventh of November."

"But, my lord . . ." The whole thing was absurd. The barons would not come unarmed, no question of it. Worse, they would not tolerate the knights. But most of all, the writ would never reach them, not in time to be in Oxford on the 15th of the month.

"Go on," he said. "Whatever's on your mind."

"I only meant, my lord, the purpose of the meeting. Is it taxes? Are you asking their consent?"

"That's obvious, I would have thought. Of course I am."

"But, Sire, none of them will be there."

"None of them?"

I nodded. "It's impossible."

"Yes, isn't it," he answered, with the most enchanting smile.

Till next time, if God wills

At Oxford Castle
The 15th Day of November, A.D. 1213

It was a fine performance. John was never better. No one knew the truth, of course, except the Marshal and des Roches and I. We sat there in the Great Hall, notes and papers for the meeting neatly laid out on the table. All the customary clerks and scribes sat at their places, looking out with consternation at the sea of empty places. Not one baron anywhere. They whispered anxiously to one another.

Then the King strode in. He ran the gamut: rage, suspicion, doubt, dismay, all the appropriate emotions. We joined in from time to time. It was important that our entourage be witness to this outrage. They would spread the word that John had come in good faith to consult his barons and solicit their support.

The King is free now, free to act as he sees fit. For he can say to any man, "I called, I came and I was scorned."

We have been drinking since midafternoon.

Tomorrow, John is off to Chester; for the earl is one of us and they have plans to make for France. The rest of us return to London.

T.n.t.

At the Palace of Westminster
The 28th Day of November, A.D. 1213

I have, for three days now, been following a tutor. Hiding in the shadows, sneaking after him. His name is Lucien, he is young and French and gentle-faced. His field is mathematics, which he teaches to Prince Henry; and I simply cannot stop myself, I follow him. To meals, on walks. Last night, I stood for hours outside his door but he did not appear.

It is, I think, a little mad of me and I must put a stop to it, this prowling after Lucien. It is foolish and demeaning, but suspicion is a worm; a dog's worm, pale and thin, it fastens to one's insides and it wriggles there.

Let me go back. Three days ago, a sunlit afternoon. The Queen had summoned me to her solar. I found her with the children. They were dozing. As a mother, Isabelle is like the seasons; changeable, now bored with it, now fond. That day, it pleased her to be loving and I sat and listened while she talked. Prince Henry, who is six now, has begun his education: mathematics, languages and rhetoric. As for his religious training, nothing had as yet been done, and turning to me with those eyes of hers, she said, "Giraldus, may I put him in your hands?"

I was speechless for a moment. I felt deeply touched. And flattered, too, for generally such things are left to men of greater rank. My vast distaste for wee folk seemed to disappear. I nodded. Yes, of course. It was an honor.

Later, when they woke, she called the boy. He came and sat by me. We talked. He was, I think, a little bored; a feeling which we shared but we were both polite. It was at this point that Lucien came into the room.

The Queen was standing in a shaft of sunlight by the window. Lucien bowed. She smiled and beckoned to him. He had papers, Henry's lesson, in his hand. He gave them to her and she turned to put them in the light and then I saw it. They were standing just as I had seen them in the corridor that night. How many weeks ago, and I had put it from my mind, I swear it, but the picture was so clear. It was Lucien she had embraced.

And then she turned and came to me. "See what a clever boy he is," she said. I took the papers, glanced at them. He is a clever boy; I told her so and fled the room as soon as possible. But not before I saw his eyes, the way he looked at her. I marked it, I'm no fool.

Except I am. It's not enough, a look, a moment's image of two figures in the sunlight. It proves nothing. There are many men of

[188]

Lucien's stature here: clerks, stewards, barons, soldiers, guards; young men and handsome, dozens of them. I lack evidence of any kind.

What do I want it for? Suppose I knew the truth. What then? What kept me outside Lucien's doorway half the night? It's not from moral outrage at adultery; it can't be, I've committed it my-self. Am I afraid of what might happen? Do I want to warn the Queen, to stop her? Is it envy, jealousy that I am not the man? I have no answer.

I awoke this morning from a dream of Eleanor and Henry. I have lost the details, they are gone, but it was of the two of them. They loved each other once so very much, and yet he locked her up in Salisbury Tower at the end. It came to that.

The bells toll Vespers. Where is Lucien? In the chapel, praying. I've begun to learn his habits, God forgive me. I must go.

At the Palace of Westminster
The 4th Day of December, A.D. 1213

Clever. He's too clever for me. He must see her when I sleep, that's how he does it. I must give up sleeping. Possibly it is the Queen whom I should follow. Isabelle the Innocent. The darkest things can seem like innocence. Today, the Marshal asked me if I felt unwell. I looked so thin, he said. I must go down to dinner. She will be there. Isabelle.

At the Palace of Westminster
The 9th Day of December, A.D. 1213

Or is it possibly the 10th? I hesitate to ask; it worries them, they take me to be worse and I am not. My fever, so they tell me, has been high, and I have not been altogether rational, but that is past and I am much, much better now.

night or two ago, they found me on the Strand near Charing
ss. I had been prowling after Lucien, there's a little inn he
frequents and I waited outside in the cold. Apparently, I fell
asleep. Some pilgrims came across me just before the dawn, I'm
told. I have no memory of it, nothing clear.

On looking back, I think I must have had this fever all along.
The tutor and the Queen? How did I think such thoughts? Exhausted; I was overburdened, stretched too far. I see that now.

My head hurts. Should I mention it?

Till etc.

At the Palace of Westminster
The 15th Day of December, A.D. 1213

They call themselves physicians. In they come, their faces grave,
and look at me with mindless eyes. I ask them have they read their
Galen and Hippocrates? Oh yes, they say. And they have studied
at Montpellier, too, they say. I nod and bite my tongue.

Three days ago, a new one came. He held a glass bowl in one
hand. He gave it to me.

"Piss," he said.

I filled the vessel, which he took, and moving to the window,
held it to the light. He bent close, peered at it with great intensity
for quite some time. This done, he tossed the contents out the
window, turned to me and said, "Your head aches, I believe."

I answered that it did, a fact he might have divined in view of
the bandage I was wearing round it.

"Good," he murmured, as if my discomfort pleased him. "Mus-
tard seed and rue." These he proceeded to compound, mixed with
the white of one hen's egg, and thereupon applied the stuff with a
feather—nothing else would do, it had to be a feather—to the side
of my head which did *not* ache.

But why go on? These doctors clearly do no good. This fellow
did no outright harm; his balsam made my bedclothes sticky, noth-

ing more. He left me as he found me, which is all that one can hope for.

Death is often on my mind. I shall be sixty-eight this coming year and most men never see the farther side of forty. What, I sometimes wonder, is it that decides our span? The Marshal roars along at over eighty, Rosamund was dead at thirty-five, John's oldest brother, William, died at three.

All deaths are natural, so it seems to me. For accident is part of life. And fate and fortune have their place in Nature, too. Some men are dead from wounds that others never even go to bed for. There are coughs that kill and plagues that mend. It is a mystery.

Is it God's time that we go in? Is it He who beckons us? "Till next time, if God wills it." Is that truly my belief or do I write it just in case? God is omniscient, He knows all; I am convinced of that. But is it part of His design to give us numbers, eighty-three to Eleanor, to Arthur seventeen? And if so, when does He decide? Does He allot our time when we are born or does He give and take away? And if the latter, on what grounds? So many ghastly people live to great old age.

I have no answer, none at all. Perhaps there is no scheme; perhaps there is, but it lies far beyond our understanding. I sometimes like to think that once He gives us life, He turns away; that it is somehow up to me to keep alive.

In any case, I am distinctly better. I shall live. In fact, for the first time in weeks, I am about to put my two feet on the floor and weave across the room to where my cask of brandy waits for me.

So much for my mortality. Except for this:

Till next time, if God wills it.

At the Palace of Westminster
The 22nd Day of December, A.D. 1213

The King and Queen are off this afternoon to Windsor for the Holy Days. The Christmas Court is large and lavish this year and it irks me not to be there. I am up and dressed all day now, I am well enough; these idiot physicians have no reason to confine me to my room.

An hour ago, I said as much to John and Isabelle. Of course, they would not hear of it. They had come by to give their gifts and wish me well. John gave me, of all things, a quillon dagger with a golden handle and a ruby at the tip.

"For the campaign in France," he said, "though God forbid our fortunes sink so low you have to use it."

He embraced me when he left. The Queen stayed on a moment longer. She has been to see me often in these weeks, to read to me and pass the time. She, too, was in high spirits, very gay. How well I looked, she said, and she would miss me these twelve days. And then she put a package in my hands; her gift to me. I opened it and saw a tiny portrait of herself on ivory. It was perfect.

"Do you like it?"

I could only nod. She smiled and then she said, "Giraldus?"

"Yes, my lady?"

"I just thought, I've never asked you, have I?"

"Asked me what?"

"The night you fell asleep near Charing Cross; what took you there?"

"Delirium," I said. For just an instant, I was tempted to confess it all but it seems so absurd now and I felt ashamed. "It was the fever," I went on, "and far too much to drink."

She scolded me, she touched my cheek, she kissed me lightly. Then she went.

I shall be all alone for Christmas. Damn.

Till next time, if God wills it.

At the Palace of Westminster
The 1st Day of January, A.D. 1214

Although I cannot say for certain, I believe the new year has arrived. In any case, the bells are ringing in my ears; and have, for quite some time. I am, as Map was fond of saying, a Homeric drinker. Polly, on the other hand, is not. She lies here by me on the bed half dozing, half awake. She smiles, she sighs, her eyelids lift a moment and her gray eyes look at me. I bend and kiss them closed.

She is a wet nurse, one of many, for the infant Isabelle. Her breasts are flawlessly white and full, so very full. She likes her life, she tells me. Fed and cared for, clean and warm. A sweet girl, twenty from the look of her; she doesn't know her age. She comes from Devon. Cream, one thinks of naturally. Her milk is even richer. I have tasted it tonight. A child again.

She stirs. She wants me.

Here I am.

At the Palace of Westminster
The 5th Day of January, A.D. 1214

Everyone returned from Windsor late this morning. I was with Prince Henry, I've been using him to pass the time. The boy has little grasp of Latin, which is not surprising in a child of six, and so I tell him Bible stories: Cain and Abel, Noah and the Flood. He seems to have inherited the family interest in things biblical. In short, he falls asleep, and he was dozing in my arms when I was summoned by the King.

So much has happened. Where to start? We sail for France next month. The fleet is nearly ready, men and armaments are moviing even now toward Portsmouth. We shall go there soon ourselves.

But first, we go to Canterbury for the talks. I had not known about them and my thoughts are spinning at the magnitude of the event. Thank God I am myself again, and just in time. What lies ahead will be momentous.

At Canterbury Castle

The 9th Day of January, A.D. 1214

The talks are in their second day. Historic is the only word, for there has rarely been such power in a single room. Four heads of state are here: the King, of course, Ferrand of Flanders, William of Holland, Renaud Dammartin of Boulogne. Add to this officials of high standing from the Dukes of Limbourg and Brabant and from Otto, King of Germany.

They have come quietly, no public pomp or ceremony; none at all. We meet in secret; no one knows. Let Philip learn about the Great Alliance when the time comes: on the field.

The room we gather in is large and bare. Broad trestle tables in the center for the mighty; lesser tables for advisors and the scribes who note the data down. I have been placed at one of these.

I sit there now. They are at supper and will soon return, for we must work into the night. The generalities have all been said and they are dealing with specifics now. How many men, how much equipment, when and where the troops should move, which castles must be taken. All the strategy; for what they plan is at the same time simple and complex, and once this meeting ends, they cannot meet again.

In essence, if I understand it right, the King will strike at Philip from the south. He will be in command alone while all the others, under Longsword, close on Paris from the north and east. A simple scheme, two armies pressing toward each other with the enemy between them.

The complexity is time, for north and south must move together. Philip must be forced to fight on two fronts at the same time; everything depends on this. But how can it be planned? How long, for instance, will a given siege take? Two weeks? Three? Suppose you plan for two and it runs four. What happens to the timing then? And if the timing goes wrong in the south, how is the north to know? A messenger can travel at great speed, as much as thirty miles a day or more; but if he has five hundred miles to go, what then?

Such questions baffle me. They give the King no pause, however.

He and Longsword dominate the talks. They have a gift for this, they make allowances, contingent plans, they see alternatives, they take into account—

No more. I hear them coming. Have there ever been such days as these?

Till etc.

At Dover Castle
The 18th Day of January, A.D. 1214

I spent the afternoon with Longsword in the harbor, watching everything. The wind was bitter but I did not care. He sails tomorrow for the north. His force is small, no more than thirty ships or so. They carry men and arms and horses, clerks and scribes but, in the main, his ships are packed with treasure.

Why so much? A mounted man-at-arms receives fourpence a day, foot soldiers fight for two. Small pay to put your life at risk. It is the mercenaries who are costly and the bulk of Longsword's forces would, I knew, be mercenary. Some of these, like Richard's famous captain Mercadier, are skilled professionals. But many of these foreigners are *routiers*. These—one cannot call them men, they have no souls—these animals are murderous. They kill for pleasure, rob and rape, they slaughter anything.

I turned to him. "My lord?"

Longsword, his mane of dark hair flying in the wind, was kneeling by a casket of treasure. "Yes?"

"Will you be using *routiers*?"

"On the whole."

"You mean to say your army will be mostly *routiers*?"

"Certainly. Of course."

"But why?"

He shrugged; it seemed that obvious to him. "Because they kill so well."

The wind grew brisker and I felt the chill of it. I cupped my hands and blew on them.

ou should go in, Giraldus."

"I'm all right."

I sit here by the fire waiting for the warmth to come. The Church prohibits *routiers*, but it uses them. The slaughterhouse Rome likes to call the Albigensian Crusade is using them this minute. Innocent has many things to answer for. And I? Each time I pray for Longsword and for victory, what of me?

Till next time, if God wills it.

At Dover Castle
The 19th Day of January, A.D. 1214

Longsword is gone. I stood out on the jetty with the King and Queen and watched him sail.

Their parting was a quiet thing. No ceremony, nothing much; and yet, the three may never meet again. I stood a little to the side, of course. I saw the brothers hold each other. Then they kissed. Then Longsword turned to Isabelle and kissed her, too. And after that, a word or two for me and that was all.

At the Tower, London
The 22nd Day of January, A.D. 1214

No time to stop for breath. I race with John from council room to council room. Details and issues overlooked, new problems, questions unforeseen: there is no way to think of everything and there will be no King in England, not for months.

Until the war is over, we shall have three governments. The chief of these, of course, is always with the King, wherever he may be. A second is with Longsword in the north. The third, with Marshal and des Roches in charge, is here at home. There is, I think, no precedent for such division of authority. All will resolve itself, no doubt, but at the moment I am drowning in the trivia.

[196]

I disappeared at midday with Lord Stephen for a meeting with FitzWalter. It was empty and eventless; no demands, no new complaints, not even a request for further meetings. They will wait until the war is over, so we think. If John wins, we shall never hear of Henry's laws again; not from FitzWalter and the barons of the north, in any case.

This done, I hurried back for further talks. I've yet to pack and in an hour we are leaving here for Portsmouth.

T.n.t.

At Portsmouth
The 31st Day of January, A.D. 1214

The Marshal came this afternoon with knights and men-at-arms for the campaign. It was a joy to see him; riding at the front, as always, with a back as straight as any boy's, bareheaded in the cold, his beard as pure white as the frost which clung to it.

The King went out to greet him, followed by the Earls of Chester and Derby; and myself, of course. They are the only earls of note among us. As for all the other barons of importance, we elected not to ask for their support. Our forces are quite large enough and we are better off without the company of those whose hearts we can't be sure of.

We spent the evening clustered by the fire, deep in military talk. The wind came seeping through the walls; I huddled in my furs and wondered how the soldiers camped outside survived such nights. The Marshal, being weary, was the first to leave the room. I left a while later, climbed the stairway to my cubicle and found him sitting on my bed.

He had his brandy flagon, I had mine. We spoke of many things: the problems he would face at home, the difficulties of the war ahead of us. The barons who remain in England are no problem; like FitzWalter, they will wait and see. So he believes. But if the war goes poorly, if it takes too long, if John should ask for further taxes or more men . . . his voice was low and, for a moment, sounded old.

"God help us then, Giraldus."

There was more talk, some of it about the Queen, who will be coming with us. He is not as fond of her as I; in fact, he is not fond of her at all. He fears she may become a burden to the King.

"I think . . ." He paused. "I sometimes think she longs to be another Eleanor."

It made me smile. "No chance of that," I told him. "There can never be another one."

That launched us, we were off on waves of memory and brandy-wine. Those were great days that we had lived through. We did them all again. My eyes were heavy at the end; the Marshal's, too. I felt such love for him.

"William." I used his Christian name, a thing I rarely do. "For Jesus' sake, stay well."

He promised and we wept awhile, like two old fools.

Till next time, if God wills it.

At Portsmouth
The 2nd Day of February, A.D. 1214

The wind is wild, it hurls itself across the harbor. On the beach, the small boats, like dead fish, are lying on their sides. I've seen such storms in boyhood at Saint David's, when the gales came howling down the Irish Sea. It is insane to sail in this. I said so.

Candlemas was done. I stood outside the little church beside the King, the Queen, Lord Stephen and the Marshal. We were crouched against the power of the air, our eyes teared and our cheeks were wet.

John thanked Lord Stephen for his blessing, clasped his hand. "God keep you while I'm gone," he said and he was turning to the Marshal when I spoke.

The King, from time to time, puts faith in omens, a belief I hoped to use. "My lord," I said, "the weather is a sign. We are not meant to sail in this."

His eyes burned into mine. "The storm is meant for me," he said. "God tests me and, by Jesus Christ, I'll sail into the teeth of it."

I write this in the King's house. Isabelle sits by the fire, wrapped in furs. We may be called at any moment. She seems calm. I wonder how I seem to her.

Off Yarmouth
The 7th Day of February, A.D. 1214

The storm still rages. We are twenty miles from Portsmouth, pitching on the Solent in the shelter of the Isle of Wight. The mainland is a mile or less away and will John put ashore? Or better still, sail back to Portsmouth? He will not. The storm, he still believes, is meant for him.

Beyond the shelter of the Isle, the sea is mountainous. We've had five days of this. The Queen, like most of us, looks vernal, lightly touched with green.

Onc cannot argue with the King. I've tried.

"My lord, do you believe the will of God is knowable?"

He thought a moment. "No," he said.

"Yet you believe He tests you with this storm?"

He nodded. "Absolutely."

"If that be, why does He test so many of us? Why not you alone?"

"To answer that, Giraldus, we should have to know His will."

Till next time, if He wills it.

On the Breton Straits
The 14th Day of February, A.D. 1214

We left the storm three days ago and pitched our way across the Channel. Then, once past the tip of Brittany, near Brest, we

[199]

started south along the coastline into better weather. Since then, all the talk has been of Poitou and what may or may not lie ahead.

Poitou means many things to John. It is the key to our campaign and much depends upon the barons there. But it has even deeper meanings for the King. It forms the northern part of Aquitaine, which he inherited from Eleanor intact. A vast possession, it includes La Marche, the county of his enemies the Lusignans, and Angoulême and much, much more. It is, today, a little less intact than formerly. In fact, it teeters like a great weight on a fulcrum, now toward Philip, now toward John.

This afternoon, we sat together on the castle in the bow, the Île de Ré on one side and the mainland on the other. It was calm; slack sails, no wind at all. The oarsmen kept a steady stroke. We should, at this rate, land at La Rochelle tomorrow.

John expects no trouble at the port. "It lives on English trade," he said. "It needs me. Greed is on my side." He paused a moment. "Greed and fear; you mix them in the right amounts and what comes out is loyalty."

I frowned. "There's more to loyalty than that."

"Such as?"

"There's always love, my lord."

He smiled and shook his head. "Not when the world's at stake. It is the world, you know."

I looked at him. I think he understands. Most wars don't matter very much. Some acreage changes hands; now theirs, now ours again. How many wars did Richard fight? One has to reckon them in dozens and when he was done, the world was left the way he found it; nothing altered save the dead. But there are Rubicons; some wars change everything and should we lose, our world won't ever be the same again.

And so I looked at him and nodded. "Yes, I know."

He turned away then, looking at the sea ahead. "I must not lose, Giraldus; not this time. It's final. I shan't have another chance."

Tonight, when dinner came, it was a different John. He sat by Isabelle, a roasted lamb joint in his hands. Hunched over it, he squinted up at her. "It's been a long time since you've been to Paris, hasn't it."

She smiled. "We'd only just been married; it was beautiful."

"I'll take you there this summer, if you like."

Her smile grew. "Won't Philip mind?"

He reached out with his hand and touched her cheek. "Not when I'm done with him."

She took his hand and kissed the juices from his fingertips.

Till next time, if God wills it.

At La Rochelle

The 15th Day of February, A.D. 1214

The day dawned clear and very cold. The sea was flat. The oarsmen stroked us past the last cliffs of the Île de Ré and toward the harbor mouth. The fleet, behind us, seemed to stretch from shore to shore.

The harbor is magnificent, protected by two spits of land. The port itself sits at the inlet's end. The King strode to the bow as we approached. I stayed below him with the Queen.

The wharves along the port were dense with people. Everything seemed very still. Our oars dipped in the water, I could hear that; and the breathing of the Queen. She took my hand. We swept on toward an open dock. On it were soldiers, dignitaries and a bishop with his mitre on.

The King raised up his right arm in salute, the crowd responded with a roar, trumpets from somewhere rent the air. They welcomed us with everything but laurel wreaths.

At La Rochelle

The 19th Day of February, A.D. 1214

There has been literally no time. The rush of things is overwhelming, for we have been doing nothing less than reconstructing La Rochelle. Everything is to be centered here: supplies and treasure,

[201]

reinforcements, writs and orders, all communication will be passing though the port.

It is a great port, to be sure; a city of two thousand souls at least. But we have twice that many men to house and feed and more to come. The building starts at dawn: rough shelters, kitchens, structures for supplies and stores. Our troops are camped on higher ground above the port. Already there are drainage problems and today a hundred men were out with shovels digging garde-robe pits. The King is constantly in motion, watching everything; I totter on behind as best I can.

Each day some local count or other comes to swear his fealty to the King. This is a matter of no small importance; much depends on the security of the surrounding countryside. John knows these men by name; he has spent years here, don't forget.

One came this afternoon as we were moving through the port. The Count of Something, elderly, one twisted leg. John seemed to like him better than the rest. They spoke, in French of course, about such things as wives and children. Then the King, his tone more serious, began to ask about the counts who have not come to him as yet.

"The Counts of Niort and Milécu," he said. "You know them well?"

"I do, my lord."

"They've yet to swear their loyalty. You think they will?"

The old man shook his head. "I begged them to, but they will not."

"In that case, I must go to them." He turned to me. "Two hundred men and siege machines. Tomorrow."

"Yes, my lord."

The game begins.

Till next time, if God wills it.

At Milécu
The 20th Day of February, A

Four castles in as many days. We circle them, the mangoi
set in place, some stones and arrows fly, there is a modicum of
blood and then surrender. It is very strange, this war.

There is, in fact, a sense in which it is not war at all. Absurd as it
may sound, it is a kind of rhetoric: persuasion by the sword. These
Poitevins are not our enemies. Nor are they friends. They simply
serve whichever king they think is stronger, John or Philip.

Thus the castles fall, the lords come out, they kneel to John and
swear their loyalty. John picks a soldier from our ranks, some officer that he can trust, leaves him in charge and we move on. The
peasants working in the fields pay no attention to us; nothing in
their lives has changed. Their master serves a different master, that
is all. Nor are we interested in them. The lands they till have no
importance. Only castles matter.

We have many more to take.

Till next time, if God wills it.

At Niort
The 2nd Day of March, A.D. 1214

Niort has fallen like the rest and La Rochelle is now secure.

I stood with John this evening on the battlements. It is a splendid fortress, which should come as no surprise, since Henry built it.
Great square donjons, two of them, and splendid turrets rising high
above the Sèvre Niortaise.

John had stood here many times before. The last time was in
1206 when, with the remnants of his army, nothing left but rage to
fight with, he had savaged Philip to a halt and won the truce which
closed that dismal war.

He was looking north toward Anjou, far away, a hundred miles
or more. "He's there, you know," he murmured. "Philip's up there
with an army; camped near Angers, so they tell me."

"Does he know we're here, you think?"

He grinned. "Four thousand men at La Rochelle can hardly be a secret."

I was calculating; fifteen miles a day, the French could be here in a week. "My lord . . ."

He guessed what I was thinking. "It's all right, old man." He put an arm around my shoulders. "Nothing's going to happen. He's not coming to attack us."

"But, my lord . . ." It made no sense. "If we grow stronger every day, why would he wait?"

"Because he knows the way I fight. He likes great battles and I don't. He's at his best when armies meet head-on; I like to strike and move away. If he comes marching down, I won't stand still. He knows it. There will be no battle in this war until I say so. I will name the time and choose the place. That's when he'll come—and not before."

John seems so certain of it all; so sure. He's either wise or foolish. Who can say? I only know that he believes it.

Till next time

At La Rochelle
The 6th Day of March, A.D. 1214

We returned this afternoon to face a mass of papers and reports. From Longsword in the north; from various commanders here; and from Lord Stephen and the Marshal back at home. In general, the news is good; no problems worth recording. John is in a splendid mood; exuberant, in fact. As for myself—

Can John not see? Has he no eyes? Or have I Lucien on the brain again?

The Queen has found a friend. A poet, if you please. A troubadour. His name is Cardenal. He plays the lute and sings his verses in a soft and silken voice. We met this evening. He was sitting near the fire by the Queen, in mid-song when I came.

What can I say? Not only is he blond and thirty, he is talented, already famous for the lofty, moral tone of his sirventes. When he finished, we were introduced. His hand is firm, his features clear, his glance direct. He'd heard of me, of course, and he was full of praise, but never mind.

He had just fled from Toulouse and the horrors of the Albigensian Crusade and he was full of bitterness against the Pope, an attitude with which I cannot disagree. In fact, I cannot think of anything he said that was not touched with dignity and moral rectitude.

I sat with Isabelle when he had gone and listened to her talk about him. Of the beauty of his verses and his bravery, and the suffering which, apparently, he has endured. That Isabelle is fond of poetry is true. And yet all I could think about was Eleanor; her court of love at Poitiers, summer nights beneath the pear trees in the palace gardens, poets' voices, *pastourelles* and love songs. *Lancan vei la folha Jos dels albres chazer*. I heard my name and looked up, half expecting Eleanor.

The Queen was smiling. "It's late. You're half asleep."

I rose. "Good night, my lady."

"Did you like him?"

"Cardenal?" She nodded. "Very much indeed," I told her. "It's a shame we leave so soon, it would be nice to know him better."

"So you shall."

I felt my heart sink. "Is he coming with us?"

"Aren't you pleased?" She peered at me. "Is something wrong?"

I shook my head and reassured her; nothing in the world was wrong.

She seemed relieved. "I'm glad," she said. "I've never had a poet of my own before."

Till next time, if God wills it.

At La Rochelle
The 8th Day of March, A.D. 1214

We have written to the Marshal to report the following:

That as of this day, no less than twenty-six castles and fortified places have been restored to us.

[205]

That all barons, thus far, do us homage.

That we meet with minimal resistance.

That all goes to schedule and to plan.

That we set out tomorrow on the second phase of our campaign. Namely, securing all of Aquitaine so that when we move north we face no problems from our rear.

That we take with us roughly two-thirds of our force, the balance to remain here under Chester's hand and Derby's to assure the safety of the port.

That we are well and God is with us.

Vivat Rex.

At Saintes

The 13th Day of March, A.D. 1214

The streets are filled with pilgrims on their way to Compostela. They are worse than sheep: they clog the road, they will not clear the way, the more one prods at them the less they move. They look at us as if we were irrelevant. The fact that they are witness to an army come to change the face of Europe has less meaning for them than the whereabouts of supper.

Isabelle, it seems, feels much the same. She scarcely notices when castles fall; her thoughts are all on Angoulême and nothing else. She is a Countess now, remember. Since her father's death some months ago, the Queen has been the ruler of a county thrice the size of Dorset. This is no small thing and she has wealth and power in her own right.

John is equally as single-minded; all he thinks of is his war and Isabelle has only Cardenal for company. Or me. We are sleeping at l'Abbaye aux Dames tonight and I was resting after supper in the Great Hall when she came to me. The hall is beautiful but very old, and rain was drifting through the roof. I stood and bowed.

"My lady."

"What a dreadful place this is." She looked forlorn, so sad.

"Is something wrong?" I asked.

[206]

"It's going home again, I think." She made a tiny smile. "One moment, it's a joy to think of; I imagine seeing friends or being in my room again. Then I remember Father's dead and I'm a woman, I have children of my own. And Hugh of Lusignan, what if he's there? You think I have to see him?"

I could understand her feelings. She had been about to marry Hugh when John had swept into her life. The Lusignans are rich and powerful, the County of La Marche is theirs, and Hugh is not a gentle man. Or so I'm told; we've yet to meet.

I tried to raise her spirits. "Hugh will mind his manners if he comes. You are a Countess and a Queen, remember, and your King is with you."

"So he is." She said it in the oddest way and turned and left me there.

Till next time, if God wills it.

At Cognac
The 15th Day of March, A.D. 1214

We have been following the Charente valley, moving with what speed we can. There is no proper road to Angoulême; two rutted cart paths flank the river as it writhes its way along, and we are marching with an army.

Cognac is a wretched place. The town exists on river trade in chalk and salt, the local wine tastes evenly of each, and there was only bread and cheese for supper. Saint Lazare, the local church, is minuscule. The kitchen is the only room of any size and there we sat, the three of us: myself, the Queen and Cardenal. The King was outside with his men. I sipped my wine and watched the two of them, engrossed in working on the speech that she would make in Angoulême. They did not touch, she held the pen. They worried over words; was *"magnifique"* le mot juste or *"superbe"*? We did not hear the King come in.

"I'm not intruding, am I?"

He spoke softly, with a quizzical half smile. I knew at once there would be trouble.

Isabelle was on her feet, all welcome and concern: she knew that tone as well as I. "Oh John, poor lamb, come sit in my place by the fire."

"That's kind of you." He nodded. "Yes, I will." He moved around the little table, took her chair.

She bent and kissed his cheek, then straightened. "There's not much," she said. "What can I get you?"

"Wine." She brought the pitcher. "Isabelle?" His eyes were on the paper now. "What's this?"

She shrugged. "It's nothing, really."

"Ah." He nodded as she poured, his eyes still on the paper. Then he frowned. "But how can it be nothing?"

"I meant nothing that would interest you."

"Of course. A letter to the children, is that it?"

"It's an address."

"You're giving an address?"

"I am."

"To whom?"

"My people."

"I'm a fool." He struck his forehead with his palm. "I keep forgetting; you have people now." He picked the paper up and and moved his eyes across the page. "That's nicely put . . . well turned . . . yes, that should bring them cheering to their feet."

The Queen looked down at him. "Oh, stop it, John."

He raised his eyes. "Have I offended you?"

Her face was white. "What do you mock me for?"

"I don't, at all." His eyes went to the page again and he began to read aloud.

She waited till he paused for breath. "You like that last?" she asked. "It's Cardenal's. He's helped me more than I can tell you."

There was silence. Why, for God's sake, had she brought the poet into this? Where would it end?

John turned to Cardenal. "I take you for exactly what you are, my friend." He paused. I held my breath. "A wise and gifted man of principle. I'm glad you're here. She needs attention, which I cannot give her at the moment. Guidance, too; for she is still too young to know her place."

"My place?" Her eyes were blazing. "What of you? Your place is at my side. I'm going home. Why do you ruin it for me? I am a figure in the world now. I have Angoulême."

John reached out for the paper, for her speech, and slowly, very slowly, crumpled it between his hands.

Her voice shook, she could barely speak. "How dare you? I'm a Countess, I'm as rich as Chester, I have—"

"You have nothing. Only what I give you. Angoulême belongs to me. It's mine."

They were like Eleanor and Henry, battling over Aquitaine. I had to speak. "My lord," I said, "there is no argument; the laws are clear."

John spun on me. "What laws? You have the gall to tell me what the laws are?"

"Someone must. She holds her lands of you but they are hers; exactly as you hold your kingdom of the Pope. She is your Queen but she is also Isabelle of Angoulême."

"I am," she said and, moving like a queen, she left the room. John watched her go in silence. Then he drained his glass and picked the pitcher up. My heart was pounding. What would come?

He looked at me. "You spoke against me."

"No, my lord."

"You took her side."

I shook my head. "I love you both."

He was, I think, about to say more but he changed his mind and hurled the pitcher at the wall. The wine splashed back at us. He wiped his cheek and turned to Cardenal.

"You ever speak of this," he said, "I'll kill you."

Angoulême is still three days away.

Till next time, if God wills it.

At Saint Michel
The 18th Day of March, A.D. 1214

I was riding with the Queen this afternoon when Angoulême came into sight. The Charente makes a sharp twist near the church of Saint Michel and suddenly the way is clear, one sees it all. The city sits on limestone cliffs that rise up sheer above the valley.

We dismounted. She said nothing, not a word. Her eyes were on the fortress walls above us and the great square tower of Saint Peter's. Then she turned to me. I saw no tears, no signs of joy or grief. I simply knew she needed to be held and there was only me to do it.

We moved on to Saint Michel, where we are quartered in the rectory. At supper, we were three: the King, the Queen and I. No Cardenal; the man keeps to himself now and is rarely seen. The meal was silent, for they barely speak. They say good morning and such things, they nod, their public face is seemly and polite. But that is all.

The supper ended. John went out into the night. I sat with Isabelle awhile. She talked of many things but not of John and not of coming home.

Above us, on the fortress walls, the banners are already flying. We shall enter Angoulême in triumph in the morning.

At Angoulême
The 20th Day of March, A.D. 1214

We entered from the west. The great gate in the fortress wall stood open. Side by side, the King and Queen moved through in robes of state, the bright sun glinting on the gold.

Inside the city, there was scarcely space to move. Her people, thousands of them, filled the promenade along the ramparts. There were cheers and cries, like Babel, when she passed. Our soldiers opened up the way for us.

At last, the square before Saint Peter's. It was clear, the crowds held back by armored soldiers of the palace guard. The morning sun was in my eyes, I could see shapes, the mass of the cathedral; nothing more.

The portals opened. John and Isabelle stepped through. There was a moment's hush and then the singing, like cascading water, washed around us. At the nave's end, in the distance, stood Girard, Bishop of Angoulême. The benches, row on row of them, were filled with notables. All eyes were on the King and Queen as they passed by.

The singing stopped, the King and I stepped to one side and Isabelle moved to the altar all alone. The air around her was of many colors, sunlight through the stained-glass windows high above. I could not take my eyes from her. I can't recall the ceremony: only Isabelle surrounded by the light.

It ended and the swearing of the oaths began. They came before her, one by one, the lords of Angoulême: Jarnac, Ruffec, La Rochefoucauld; Villebois and Barbezieux; Chassenon, Plassac and Confolens and many more. They stretched across the transept, major lords and minor ones.

The ritual is brief. They kneel, they place a hand upon the Gospel book and swear their fealty: that they hold their lands of her, she is their overlord in all things and they do her homage.

When the last had sworn, the King stepped forward. He moved slowly to the Queen. They stood a long time looking at each other; then she knelt. Her lips moved and her voice came pure and clear, and in the very place where, fourteen years before, the two of them had made their marriage vows, she swore her fealty to her King.

There was more singing, then; more shouts and cheering, too, as we paraded back along the ramparts to the palace where the feast began. The Great Hall in the castle was filled with figures from her childhood. They all remembered her, of course, and were so happy for her and so proud. And she received them all with smiles of pleasure, introducing them to John. "My lord, may I present Philippe of Saint-Whatever," and the King would glance and nod.

Midafternoon, she slipped away; to find a moment's peace, she said. I watched her go. I have myself come home from years away, more famous than I left. It is not easy and, on impulse, I arose and followed her.

[211]

I found her in the palace gardens. There were traces, here and there, of Spring: fresh color to the grass, a bed of crocus, blue and white. The fountains, drained for winter, were still empty, and she sat upon the rim of one, her fingers trailing through the nonexistent water. I made sure to scuff my boots across the stones as I approached.

She looked up at the sound. "Giraldus." She was pleased to see me, full of talk of how things used to be. The summer days, the games and daydreams, lessons with her tutor by the fountains. And that arbor by the pear trees, she had done much reading there.

She smiled. "Romances for the most part; foolish things. And sometimes Father came and read to me. One day, it was an afternoon in August, very hot, he came there with a man I'd never seen before. A handsome man, or so I thought. I looked at him, he looked at me. His name was John, he told me . . ." She bit her lip and turned away. "I loved him." That was all she said about it.

At Angoulême
The 21st Day of March, A.D. 1214

The festivities had ended. It was late, the guests had gone, the dogs were feasting on the leavings on the Great Hall floor, a servant passed by here or there. It is the saddest time. I wandered with the Queen through the debris, down empty corridors and up the stairs.

The King had left us earlier. She paused outside his room, then moved on to her father's chambers. Everything was as it used to be, she told me. Nothing had been moved or changed: the table where he worked, his bed, his chair, the books he liked. She picked a book up, ran her fingertips across the cover of it, put it down again.

"He liked to read to me," she said. "Philosophy and law. He had no son, you see. I never understood a word of it."

She settled in her father's chair. "I loved him but I didn't know him very well. I was so young and vain. I know how beautiful men find me, I have read it in their eyes my whole life, for as long as I remember. Vanity. I wish to God I had a different face. It isn't me." She turned away. "What have I done to John? He looks at me with such disdain. So cold; as if he hated me."

"He thinks about his war," I told her. "It consumes him."

"But, Giraldus, why so cruel, why does it make him cruel?"

I brought a chair and sat beside her. There was little I could say. I felt ashamed of my suspicions; Cardenal meant nothing to her. No man did except the King. I listened as she talked about the day: how she had dreamed of it for months, how different the reality had been from all the dreaming. "Hollow" was the word she used.

I took her hand. "I know how hard it is, my lady, but you must be patient with him. You must—" I broke off. Someone was knocking at the door. She nodded to me and I crossed the room and opened it.

The King came in.

She stood. "My lord."

"It's late, I know . . ." He paused. "I thought, perhaps, we ought to talk."

She nodded. "If you like."

He seemed uncertain where to start. He looked about the room, he asked if he might have some wine.

"It's yours as much as mine," she said.

He went to where it was and poured. This done, he turned to her. It started quietly enough. "I know we've only just arrived," he said, "but at some point I must be moving on. I've many things to see to, Hugh of Lusignan among them."

"Yes, of course," she said, "I understand. When do you plan to go?"

"Within the week, I think."

"So soon? I'd hoped to stay here longer."

"That can be arranged."

She stiffened slightly. "I don't understand."

"I'll deal with Hugh and come back for you. You can sit here for a month or more, if that's enough."

Her voice was ice. "Is that your wish, my lord?"

"It's yours. I know that much." He turned to go. "That's all, I think."

"That's all you came to tell me? Is that all you have to say? For Jesus' sake, John, what's the matter?" He turned back. "We haven't spoken in a week, you come here in the middle of the night and what I hear from you is Hugh of Lusignan."

"What would you have me talk about?"

"All right," she snapped, "let's talk about him. You can't think I care for him. I never did. I won't be left behind."

"Then come. I can't see that it matters."

"You're a fool."

John's face went white.

"On two counts."

"Isabelle, I warn you."

"One, for treating me this way; and two, for going after Hugh."

"I have to and you know it."

"There's a better way to do it. Why not have him for a friend?"

John stood in front of her. "Your friend, but never mine."

"He has a son, you have a daughter. Give him Joan."

I looked at Isabelle and scarcely knew her. Taut and pale, hands clenched, eyes burning with intensity. It was a brilliant stroke and well she knew it.

"Give him Joan?" John's voice was soft with wonder. "Give your daughter to the Lusignans?"

She whispered, "Yes."

"For my sake? You would do that much for me?"

"And more. I'd die for you."

It was past time for me to slip away. I left them weeping in each other's arms.

Till next time, if God wills it.

At Angoulême
The 22nd Day of March, A.D. 1214

A letter has been sent to Hugh inviting him to Angoulême and promising safe-conduct. He is in Chalus, or so we're told. If so, he'll be here shortly. If he comes.

[214]

The King and Queen, I'm glad to say, are constantly together.
T.n.t.

We have had word from Hugh of Lusignan. An equerry arrived
this morning with a letter in his hand. In brief, Hugh writes that he
is at Soyaux, some ten miles to the east of here, and would arrive
tomorrow, if it please the King. John penned his answer at the
bottom of the message. "Come," he wrote. And signed it "John."

We spent the balance of the day preparing for the talks. The
House of Lusignan is both distinguished and illustrious. Hugh's
uncle Geoffrey was a friend of Richard's, a crusader whose exploits
are legendary. His uncle Aumary is nothing less than King of Jerusalem. His brother Ralph is Count of Eu. Hugh towers over all of
them.

To deal with such a man is worrying enough. But one must add
to this the past he shares with John, a maze of thirty years or more
of friendship and betrayal. John stole Isabelle away from Hugh,
John has both ransomed Hugh and held him prisoner. Hugh, on
his part, captured Eleanor on one occasion, captured Marshal on
another and has joined with Philip countless times. Then, it was
John who raised Hugh to his title, made him Count of La Marche
only to betray the man to Philip shortly after. And then, too—

But why go on? I do not understand our rulers. When I make an
enemy, I keep him. Yet these kings and counts change sides as
easily as I change stockings. How in God's name can they trust
each other? Ever. Under any circumstances. Why sit down and
talk? Why make agreements no one means to keep?

At one point late tonight, I raised this question with the King.
Our work was done, our plans and strategies were neatly on the
page. "My lord," I said, "if history and experience mean anything,
this man will knife you in your back."

"Of course he will. What else do you expect?"

I must have looked dumfounded. "But, my lord . . ."

He smiled at me. "The trick is knowing when. He may not come at me for years. And in the meantime, he can be of use." He stood and stretched. "Or I may knife him first; who knows."

Till next time, if God wills it.

At Angoulême
The 28th Day of March, A.D. 1214

He came alone. The King and Queen received him in the garden. I was with them and I watched him striding toward us down the path. He is a tall man, lean and stiff, big-boned. His hair is white, his face is lined and weathered, its expression stern and dour. His cloak was gray, he wore no weapons and no jewels.

He stopped before the King and bowed. "Your Majesty."

"How are you, Hugh?"

He grinned. "Not dead yet." When he smiles, it changes him completely. Suddenly, his face is wry, his pale eyes sparkle slyly. Then, to Isabelle: "My dear." She offered him her cheek. He kissed it. I came next. "And you must be Giraldus."

"Yes, my lord." He took my hand. His fingers pressed like thumbscrews, he is made of steel.

There is an arbor by the central fountain: budding vines, a marble table underneath and benches. Food and wine had been laid out.

John gestured toward it. "Come," he said, "let's sit and talk." He turned and started off. Hugh moved to Isabelle. "May I?" She nodded and he slipped his arm through hers. I followed after, giving them my full attention.

He spoke first. "They tell me that you've had another child."

"Yes. Her name is Isabelle."

He made his wry face. "Not another one like you, I hope." She smiled at that and asked about his son. "Young Hugh?" he said. "He's not like me at all."

"How so?"

[216]

"He's handsome, to begin with. And . . ." He paused. "The time; where has it gone? They call me Hugh the Brown—and look at me."

The King was in the arbor, waiting. Hugh sat slowly. Was he playing old or did his bones ache? What was in those pale eyes when he looked at Isabelle? I nibbled at my food and listened to their talk. The King and Hugh began to speak about the past. They laughed, they actually laughed as they told stories of the beastly things they'd done to one another. Isabelle joined in from time to time.

Then John sat back and wiped his eyes. "Well, Hugh, my friend, what are we going to do?"

Hugh sighed. "I'm in a difficult position."

"Yes, I know," John answered. "Difficult but hardly new. It happens every time I fight with Philip. Whose side are you on this time?"

Hugh shrugged. "If I knew that . . ." His face grew grave. "May I be honest with you?"

No one laughed. In fact, the King, with gravity exceeding Hugh's, said, "Nothing less will do. There is too much at stake."

Hugh took a deep breath. "I must tell you, then, that I have been with Philip. He is camped in Anjou with an army of great size."

"How great?" John asked.

"Tremendous. Naturally, he asked me where I stood. On whose side would I fight? I told him neither one."

"How did he like that?"

"Not too well."

"I understand," John said. "I don't much like it, either. Frankly, Hugh, I'm puzzled. What's so difficult for you? You've always chosen sides before."

Hugh straightened and leaned toward the King. His face was heavy with foreboding. "I hear voices in the night. They tell me it is final this time. You and Philip will not fight again. The outcome is forever."

John, whose love of omens is no secret, took this gravely in. "These voices, they don't say who's going to win?"

"I ask but they refuse to tell me."

"Ah." John nodded somberly. "I understand. If you choose me and Philip wins, you lose as much as I; and if you choose him and I win, your loss is just as great."

"Exactly so."

There was a pause. The fountains had been filled, I heard the water splashing. What would happen now? How would the King maneuver it?

John stood. "I want you with me, Hugh; you and the members of your house."

"I know, I know. I cannot answer for the rest but as for me—"

"I want you by my side with arms and men. I know more than your voices do. I know my plans, I know the strength I have. And one thing more." He moved around the table to the Queen. He stood behind her. "Tell him, Isabelle."

She looked at Hugh straight on. "I offer you my daughter for your son."

"Your child?"

"My daughter Joan."

Hugh's eyes went soft, I saw it happen. "Oh," he said. "I see." He turned away.

There was a moment's silence. Then the King's voice, low but firm: "I want to know you're with me, Hugh."

Hugh's head turned slowly back. He raised his eyes to John. "I'm yours," he said.

There were embraces after that; more wine, much talk. It was late afternoon before Hugh left us. We went with him to the castle yard and watched him ride away.

There was a question which I had to ask. "My lord, does anything he said have any meaning?"

John grinned at me. "I doubt it." Then he laughed. "I loved his voices."

"Is he with you or against you?"

"Even God can't answer that."

He seemed so unconcerned. "If you don't know, how can you let him ride away?"

"Because it doesn't matter where he stands, he'll join me either way."

It made no sense. "But if he thinks the French are going to win . . ."

"You haven't got a touch for this at all, Giraldus. He will join me even so. He can't betray me if he isn't with me first."

He's right, I have no touch for it. Nor do I want one. How, I wonder, do kings sleep at night?

Till next time, if God wills it.

At La Réole
The 18th Day of April, A.D. 1214

Three weeks and we have been to Montbron, Massignac, Roche-chouart, Limoges, Saint-Léonard-de-Noblat, Bourganeuf, Aubusson, Felletin, Treignac, Uzerche, Sarlat-la-Caneda, Cadouin, Lauzun, Barbaste, Marmande and La Réole. We are received with open arms and oaths of loyalty at every point. Tomorrow, we start north through Bordeaux, back to La Rochelle.

I cannot wait.

At La Rochelle
The 27th Day of April, A.D. 1214

We reached the port this afternoon and went to work at once. John's office was a sea of paper: letters, writs, reports, accounts, notes, secret messages, communications of all kinds from field commanders here, from Longsword in the north, from home.

In sum, it all goes smoothly. Longsword, as we planned, has been conducting raids with modest forces here and there throughout the Lowlands, thus attracting all attention to himself while we assemble. Only Otto runs behind; he cannot keep to schedule but we made allowances for that.

[219]

From home, des Roches, the Marshal and Lord Stephen have the same thing to report: no trouble, no disturbances of any kind. There seems to be a stillness in the Kingdom. One can almost hear it here: a hush that waits upon the outcome of the war.

And one more letter not worth noting but I note it anyway. To me from Lincoln. From old friends who say they think of me from time to time and wish me well on being sixty-eight.

Till next time, if God wills it.

At La Rochelle
The 2nd Day of May, A.D. 1214

May Day has come and gone. It brought us sun and warmth, a perfect holiday. The one thing it failed to bring was any word from Hugh of Lusignan. He knows we plan to start north in the early part of May; we told him so in Angoulême.

The King seems unconcerned about it. "Hugh? He wants to see me sit and sweat awhile. I'd do as much for him."

The days are more than full. Our force has grown, new men arrive from home and there are thousands here. They must be housed and fed and organized and disciplined.

The King is often with them, leaving me behind to bicker with the scribes. They're lazy, careless, always whispering among themselves or going off to piss. I must do everything myself.

I have a letter to des Roches to write, instructing him to send the Princess Joan to us as soon as possible. The King intends to keep his word. I wonder what young Hugh is like.

Till etc.

At La Rochelle
The 12th Day of May, A.D. 1214

We march. We leave tomorrow in the morning. Everything stands ready for the war. Our troops are fresh, our carts and wagons stand by loaded with supplies and arms, our war machines stretch out in line along the road.

There is a sense of calm here, as if this were just one more campaign. The Queen remains at La Rochelle to wait for Joan. The King is with her now. He seems completely unperturbed that nothing has been heard from Hugh. In fact, it almost seems to please him. When I mentioned it tonight, he smiled. "He'll come," was all he said.

As for the Queen, she seems as calm as all the rest. Am I the only person with a sense of history here? Tomorrow, Fortune's wheel begin to turn. My heart pounds at the thought of it.

Benedictus qui venit in nomine Domine. We come in Thy name, Lord. Amen.

Before Vouvant
The 19th Day of May, A.D. 1214

The King is sending messages to Hugh. He sent the first two days ago: he took the fortress at Mervent, a castle which belongs to Geoffrey of Lusignan. The castle here is Geoffrey's, too, as well as many others in the area. If need be, we shall take them all. We may not have to, for inside the castle, at this moment, fighting for their lives, are Geoffrey himself and his two sons.

Our siege is in its second day. The fortress looms up high above the abbey gardens where I sit. Its tallest tower has been named for Mélusine. The Lusignans claim their descent from her. She was, or so the legend goes, the daughter of the King of Albania and a fairy princess named Pressine. She married Count Raymond of Poitiers and built many castles for him; Lusignan itself and Vouvant, too, among them.

There are many people who believe such things. The Lusignans themselves believe; they make no secret of it. As for me, I've never seen a gorgon or a manticore; I cannot prove they don't exist. But fairy princesses? I draw the line. And yet, if such things be, then Geoffrey had best look to her, for nothing else can save him.

Till next time.

[221]

At Vouvant

The 20th Day of May, A.D. 1214

We were awakened in the middle of the night with stunning news.
The French have moved. Their army is divided. Philip, as we
hoped, has taken half of it and leads it to the north, toward Longsword. Louis, with the balance, has come south to close with us
and is encamped at Moncontour, two days or less away from here.

John roused our men at once and, in the dark, our siege resumed. He longed to capture Geoffrey first, before we faced the
French. All through the balance of the night, our trebuchets
hurled stones against the castle walls, our archers sent up arrows
tipped with fire.

The castle held. At dawn, its walls were still intact. The King
and I stood on the field intently watching the assult when, to the
east a mile or more across the valley, knights appeared. A score of
them in armor racing toward us. Were they French? Had Louis
moved so rapidly? Was this a vanguard come to parley?

So we thought. We quickly formed a group of men around the
King and started toward them, out across the field. We watched
them come. One knight rode at the front, well in the lead. The
others dropped behind as he rode up to us, reined in and spoke.

"Sweet Jesus Christ," he said. The voice was unmistakable.

John looked up with a smile of welcome. "Hugh, I've been expecting you."

Hugh raised his visor. "My uncle's in there, for the love of
God."

"I know."

"I have to see him."

"Soon enough. I'll have his body out by dinner time."

"For God's sake, John—"

John's voice soared out. "Too late, that's what you are. You've
been with Louis, making plots."

"I swear not. God Almighty, I have an army half a day behind
me. It's for you. I've brought my son, he's with them. What else
do you want of me?"

"The truth. You were to come to La Rochelle."

"There wasn't time. I have three thousand men. How quickly can you raise three thousand?"

"There are messengers. You might have sent a message."

"Why? What for? You'd never have believed it." It was possible, I thought. John shrugged. Hugh's words came faster. "Let me see Geoffrey, let me talk to him. I tell you, I can move him to our side."

"What would you say to him?"

"The same thing that I've said to half the barons in Poitou. They're with me, John, I've brought them. They believe in you."

John pondered it, or seemed to. Then he turned. "I'll stop the siege. You have till midday."

Shortly after noon, the castle gates swung open. Hugh appeared; and after him came Geoffrey and his sons. They knelt, they swore the necessary oaths, the King embraced them all.

We are about to move to Moncontour. Hugh's men will join us there. There is some talk of marching through the night. Dear God, how fast it goes. A victory over Louis means the war.

Till next time, if God wills it.

Near Moncontour
The 21st Day of May, A.D. 1214

It is twilight. I am resting on a hillside listening to the workings of the military mind. They sit here in a circle: John and Hugh, young Hugh and Geoffrey and his sons, and half a dozen barons from Poitou. They look out, now and then, across a mile or so of meadowland to where the French are camped. How many thousands of them? Five, perhaps. I am not expert in these matters; John has given me the number.

They are talking of tomorrow's strategy: Can they outflank the French or not; and if so, from the east or west or both; and if so, with what loss of life? How many bodies would there be, what toll could they afford?

[223]

They sound the way a miller does: How many bushels can he grind today and will it profit him or not? The fact that every soldier has a soul is not a thing they weigh, not on their scales. How do they do it? Have they learned how not to feel? Is inhumanity a skill? Or are they men with no imagination?

Not far off, by John's tent, a lamb is roasting on the fire. I have no appetite.

Till next time, if God wills it.

At Moncontour
The 22nd Day of May, A.D. 1214

We assembled on the hillside shortly after dawn; John's troops and Hugh's. In all, six thousand men or more. The mist was heavy on the meadowland between us and the French; we could not see them at the start. Then as the sun rose higher, it began to lift and there, across from us, was Louis' army. They were breaking camp.

It seemed incredible. The enemy was moving from the field. Calmly, in good order, with no haste. We stood and watched them take their tents down, load their wagons, mount their horses, turn and march away.

There was some talk about pursuit but there was little to be gained from that, it seems. The French had surely learned of Hugh's arrival; we were nearly double what we were before and they would not give battle on these terms. Our way is clear now to the north and we can cross the Loire and enter Anjou. This is all John thinks of, for the Loire serves as a border. To the south of it, John's part of France. And to the north, King Philip's.

T.n.t.

At Parthenay
The 24th Day of May, A.D. 1214

For the moment, we have set the war aside. The Loire will have to wait a little.

We are here for the betrothal.

Isabelle arrived this afternoon with Princess Joan, the bride-to-be. A pale but rather pretty child with eyes like Eleanor's, she is at once the most and least important element in what goes on.

I had been racing back and forth all day with drafts of the betrothal papers: rights and obligations, details of the dowry, legal matters. None of this comes into force until the marriage, which is years away, assuming that it ever happens. Still, the time for bargaining is now, and I was on my way to John with what I hoped was something final when I saw them: Isabelle and Joan.

I hurried over. They were sitting in a sunlit corner of the cloister, talking softly. Joan remembered me from all our nursery afternoons. I bowed to her, she gravely took my hand. How was her journey? Good, she said.

The Queen was full of questions: Where had Hugh appeared and when and how large was his army and what barons of Poitou were part of it? She knew them all, they were her father's enemies and friends.

"And young Hugh. Have you come to know him?"

"Some, my lady."

"Joan?"

The child looked up. Our bench was by a bed of violets, and she was on her hands and knees, a bunch of them already picked beside her on the grass.

"Yes, *Maman?*"

"Pay close attention. This concerns you." Then, to me: "Describe him to us. What's he like?"

"Young Hugh?" I turned to Joan. "What would you like to know?"

She frowned a moment, deep in thought. And then she smiled and handed me the violets.

I left them shortly after that.

Till next time, if God wills it.

At Parthenay
The 25th Day of May, A.D. 1214

At midday today, before the altar of Notre-Dame-de-la-Couldre, in presence of the King, the Queen and half the barons of Poitou, they were betrothed. Young Hugh knelt on the floor; the Princess Joan stood on a prie-dieu. They were then of roughly equal height.

At Parthenay
The 26th Day of May, A.D. 1214

The Queen and Princess Joan have gone. They left us not an hour ago for La Rochelle. John kissed them both; the child first, then Isabelle. She whispered something I could not hear, he held her very close. Then someone called him.

"Pray for me," he said and left her there.

We shall not see the Queen again until this war is over and I said some sentimental things, I fear. No matter.

In the interest of completeness, I should note that yesterday we wrote to London, giving an account of our activities since leaving La Rochelle. The letter ends:

"Now, thank God, we are ready to attack our chief enemy, the King of France, beyond Poitou. We tell you this so that you may rejoice at our success. Given at Parthenay in the sixteenth year of our reign. MYSELF AS WITNESS."

I must pack these papers. We are moving north again. We should be on the road by noon.

Till next time, if God wills it.

At Mirebeau
The 28th Day of May, A.D. 1214

The Loire still lies ahead of us and there was daylight left when we made camp. We might have pressed on farther but the King would not. He called us to a halt, he beckoned me and I rode with him through the gates into the town. We wandered slowly through the narrow streets. He waved, he smiled, he had a word for everyone as we moved upward to the castle. Why, of all the castles in the Kingdom, why Mirebeau?

We dined, the two of us alone, in the solar. He talked of everything but what it was that brought him here. I found it hard to pay attention, for my mind kept slipping to the past.

The year was 1202. The war that lost us Normandy had just begun. Queen Eleanor was then at Fontevrault, the abbey where she now lies buried. She was eighty-one and frail, but keen as ever. There were hostile forces moving south; she knew at once she was not safe. With skill and caution, she assembled a small escort, nothing to attract attention, and set out. She got as far as Mirebeau, where she stopped to rest.

Word of her presence reached the enemy. Their force was led by Arthur, Count of Brittany, John's nephew and his rival for the throne. We have no laws, as yet, about succession, and King Philip wanted John deposed and Arthur in his place.

Young Arthur brought his forces down at once. If he could take the Queen and hold her hostage, he might end the fighting then and there. He knew that John, to save his mother, would concede him anything. So Arthur raced to Mirebeau with, some say, a thousand knights. They battered down the city gates, the town was theirs but not the Queen. She and her men were safely in the castle keep and she would not give in.

He hesitated: what to do? If he attacked, if Eleanor were wounded in the fighting, it was all for nothing: she was useless to him dead. And so young Arthur, who was fifteen and a fool, decided to negotiate.

Now, I have seen Queen Eleanor at the negotiating table. Like a starved man at a feast, she eats up everything in sight. She is magnificent. For each demand that Arthur made, she had to think, withdraw and ponder. She was dragging out the time. For somehow, through his lines, she sent a message off. To John.

There was no hurry, Arthur thought. The nearest English force was at Le Mans with John, a hundred miles away or more. He had a week to dicker with the Queen.

What John did when the message came has always seemed incredible to me. He left upon the instant with a band of men. He drove them all that day and all that night; no rest, no respite, at full gallop, recklessly. It is not possible to come so great a distance in so short a time. Yet it was done; they did it.

It was still dark when they reached Mirebeau. In silence, they dismounted and crept slowly round the city wall. Gate after gate had been bricked up. Young Arthur, thinking he would make the town secure, had closed them all but one. The city was a cul-de-sac; what he had done was build a crypt.

They found the free gate. In they slipped. The enemy was sleeping in the houses of the town and in the streets. It was the last night of July and very hot; not one of them had any armor on. They were as good as dead.

It was a slaughter. John, they say, fought like a demon, swinging his great battle sword. Limbs fell away in front of him; arms, legs. God knows how many died but not one enemy escaped. He found young Arthur clinging to, of all men, Hugh of Lusignan. He took them both and held them prisoner. It was done, the whole affair was over by the time the sun came up.

It was a dazzling victory. In one battle, he had spun the war around. Not only had he saved his mother, he held Arthur in his hands; and Arthur was the crux, the key. Without him, Philip had no cause, no goal to fight for. In the person of this adolescent lay the raison d'être of the war.

The import of this moment cannot be exaggerated. Philip, when he heard of it, collapsed, abandoned his campaign and fell back in dismay to Paris. John held victory in his hands. How had it slipped away? What happened? How, when everything was his, could he have lost it all?

I longed to ask him. I have wanted to for years. But did I dare? I looked at him across the table. He had paused for wine and he was smiling at some thought or other. There would never be a better time.

"My lord?"

He finished pouring. "Yes, my friend?"

"What happened when you took Mirebeau?"

He didn't even blink. "You mean, how did I lose the war? I

sometimes think . . ." He paused. "You want an honest answer? I don't know. I thought I had it won that morning. Mother, she was waiting for me in this room. I came in, blood all over me and she was there." He pointed. "She was looking out the window at the town. 'Thank God you're safe,' I said. She turned. I can't recall her words exactly. Brutal, I believe she called me. Why so many dead, why so much blood?"

He smiled. "It used to trouble me. I'd saved her life, she might have said so, don't you think?" He stood and wandered to the window. "After that, I started north, I moved to the attack. I kept Hugh in a dungeon until Philip paid his ransom. As for Arthur—" Here he stopped and turned to me. "You think I killed him?"

Half the world believes he did it. John was drunk, they say, and strangled Arthur with his own hands, took the corpse and threw it in the sea. As for myself, I've always doubted it. John sells his captives; that's his way. He holds them all for ransom. Had he wanted Arthur dead, how easily he might have killed him in the fighting here. And blamelessly; for Arthur meant to take his mother and his throne. I said as much.

He nodded. Then he looked around the room and smiled. "It used to trouble me. How I've been haunted by this place. Not any more. It's all behind me now. Mirebeau is just a castle, this is just a room. It's nothing. I can come here, I can eat and sleep. You see?"

I answered, "Yes, my lord."

Till next time, if God wills it.

Near Saumur
The 2nd Day of June, A.D. 1214

We have crossed the Loire. It is behind us. We are moving with great speed. The King keeps all decisions to himself, he will not say which way he plans to strike. Hugh wonders if he knows. I think he does. It's all inside his head, I say; some grand design, some master strategy.

Till etc.

[229]

Near Angers
The 17th Day of June, A.D. 1214

The King has been magnificent. His tactics are his own: original,
deceptive, swift. The French keep at a distance, utterly bewildered,
as we slice across their kingdom. City after city falls. Last week, the
port of Nantes, our greatest prize thus far, bowed down to us. And
with it, Philip's cousin Peter of Dreux, the Count of Brittany himself, fell into John's quick hands.

The Lusignans look at the King with wonder. Feints, false
moves, deceptive marches; then we pivot unexpectedly to the attack. They stand in awe of him.

Tomorrow, we shall enter Angers. What a triumph. The surrender is arranged. The most important fortress-city south of
Chartres, I'm told, and it is ours.

Its meaning for the King is very great. For Angers is no less than
his ancestral home, birthplace of the Plantagenets, the seat and
source of Henry's power. It was here it all began.

Till next time, if God wills it.

At Roche-aux-Moines
The 19th Day of June, A.D. 1214

We left Angers this morning to the sound of cheers. A day of
feasting lay behind us. We moved rapidly, as always, to the north.
Just past the middle of the day, we came to Roche-aux-Moines.

There is a fortress here, a strange one, for it guards no city, road
or waterway. The land around is poor and flat, some scattered
farms and nothing more. The castle simply sits here, isolated, as if
someone dropped it by mistake.

John called us to a halt and waited for the Lusignans to reach us.
They and their Poitevins keep to themselves and always ride a bit
apart.

Hugh came alone. The day was hot and dry. He wiped his face.
"What are we stopping for?"

John nodded toward the fort. "We're laying siege to Roche-aux-Moines."

I looked at John with some surprise. There was no need to take it. Castles of this kind are generally ignored, for they have no strategic value and one merely goes around them.

Hugh was frowning. "Why? Why bother with it?"

"Look around, " John said. "I like the land. It's good land for a battle, don't you think?"

He went on quickly then. The time had come, he said, to take the field, to meet with Louis's army face to face. Our moves thus far had been so fast and their effect so devastating; everything was with us, we would never have a better opportunity.

Hugh pondered it a moment, then he nodded. "Yes," he said, "I take your point."

John peered at him. "There must be no mistake. If there's a flaw in giving battle, we must find it."

They could not.

Our men are making camp. We shall be here at Roche-aux-Moines till Louis catches up to us, however long it takes.

Till next time, if God wills it.

At Roche-aux-Moines
The 27th Day of June, A.D. 1214

The King was resting when the messenger arrived. The days are dry and blazing hot and there is very little shade. A row of dying poplars stands behind John's tent and it was there he found us.

"Sit," John said and gave the fellow water from his flask. Between the gulps, he told us what he'd seen. The French were on the move. Louis had left his base at Chinon and was moving toward us at full strength along the Loire.

"How many men?" John asked.

The fellow's eyes grew wide. "So many, Sire; far beyond what I could count."

"Five thousand? More?"

The man had no idea. I doubt that he can count to twenty-five. John thanked him anyway and sent him off.

We have been talking tactics ever since, with Hugh and all the rest of them. Their voices have a ring, their eyes shine. They are ready for the test, they cannot wait.

Till next time, if God wills it.

At Roche-aux-Moines
The 1st Day of July, A.D. 1214

The French are here. Their vanguard came in sight a little after dawn. There is a hillcrest to the south of us, two miles or more beyond our camp, and it was there they first appeared.

The day was airless, very hot. I sat with John and all the Lusignans beneath the poplars, watching as the first arrivals raised their tents and started making camp. More men appeared; and more. It took the morning for them all to come. Nine thousand men was Hugh's guess. John said ten.

However many, they are more than we expected. Louis, since he ran from us at Moncontour, has all but doubled his command. We are, at most, six thousand, almost half of which belong to Hugh and his allies. The numbers worry me, God knows, but neither John nor Hugh seem troubled in the least. It is the skill, the quality and training of the men that matters. So they tell me.

There is much to do before a battle. War machines must be inspected, knives and daggers sharpened, arrows checked and counted. Maces, lances, chains—all must be ready. To say nothing of the horses and the armor and the flags and the tambours and trumpets. I was with the King all afternoon as, drenched with sweat, we moved from place to place.

Tonight, he walked among his men. They sat around their fires eating, singing soldier's songs. They seem to have no fear at all. I cannot say the same. I have no doubts about the outcome: we shall win. But many of these fellows will be dead tomorrow night; and many more will lose their arms or legs.

Dear Lord, preserve the King and bring us victory.

At Angers
The 2nd Day of July, A.D. 1214

This must be written, I must find a way to put it down.

I never slept. Thus, I was up before the dawn. I watched the cooks, they bent and blew on last night's coals. Across the darkness, in the French camp, I could see their cook fires, too.

The sky grew brighter. Men began to stir. The King appeared. He wears light chain mail when he fights; pale gray. It looked like silver in the dawn.

There was no rush to take the field. There never is. The men must eat, the knights must strap their armor on, the horses must be brought, hand weapons must be given out. The sun was well up when the troops began to form.

Each nobleman commands his own. Hugh's men assembled where he stood, and Geoffrey's men by Geoffrey. Next came Ralph of Eu, Hugh's brother; then the balance of the nobles from Poitou.

We lined up to the east of them. I was to make a benediction and I rode with John as we passed slowly, one last time, along our ranks. Good English faces; they were ready.

All the Lusignans were waiting for us at the center: Hugh, young Hugh, Ralph, Geoffrey and his sons. We joined them. Wordlessly, we turned and looked off toward the distant hillside. Louis's men were lined up in good order, stretching on and on.

I cleared my throat. The time had come for me to lead us all in prayer and I was just about to clasp my hands when Hugh spoke out.

"Your Majesty?" he said.

John turned to him. "What is it?"

"There is something you should know before the battle starts."

"Go on."

"My lord . . ." Hugh paused, as if debating how to put it. Then he blew the King a kiss. "Au 'voir," was what he said.

John stiffened in his saddle. "What?"

" 'Au 'voir' is an expression of farewell. We're leaving now."

"You can't do that."

"We will not fight today."

John's hand went to his sword. "You bastard."

"Go on. Draw it." Hugh was grinning. "Come for me. If I don't kill you, Louis will. I'd rather have you live and lose. You'll see this moment till you die, you'll see see my face, you'll—"

Trumpets. We heard trumpets faintly from across the field. The French were coming, they were moving toward us.

"Christ," John said.

It was madness after that. Hugh spun his horse around and galloped to his men. The others followed, shouting orders as three thousand Poitevins broke ranks and started running from the field. By then the King had turned and galloped to our lines. What could we do? Outnumbered three to one, what hope? It would be slaughter. We could run or we could die.

Our men began to panic and we ran. There was some order to it and we took what things we could. But all the war machines and siege equipment and our stores and wagons—all of this was lost. The French, for reasons which I fail to understand, did not pursue us and by twilight we were back in Angers, safe behind the city walls.

We may be under siege here. No one knows. The King has issued orders for defense, our men are on the ramparts. As for—

I have just been summoned by the King.

At Angers
The 3rd Day of July, A.D. 1214

I found him in the throne room, sitting where his father sat. There was a fire burning, never mind the heat.

"My lord?"

"Who sent for you?"

"I thought you did, my lord."

He shrugged. There was a stool beside him, near his feet. He pointed to it.

"Thank you, Sire." I sat and waited, watching him. His eyes

were bright and full of life; they darted round the room. At last, I spoke.

"My lord, what is it that you want of me?"

"Of you?" he snapped. "What could I want of you?"

I bowed my head and waited.

When he spoke again, his voice was low. "Giraldus?"

"Yes, my lord?" I raised my eyes. His features were askew, all twisted up.

"I am a fool. Oh Jesus, what a fool I am." He started rocking back and forth. "Joan, Joan. I gave one Joan away. I gave her to Llywelyn. Did it help? Is he my friend?" He shook his head. "How could I give away a second Joan? What was I thinking? To the son of Hugh of Lusignan." The rocking stopped, his voice grew calmer. "All along," he said. "They planned it all along, you know. From the beginning. Hugh appearing when he did, persuading Geoffrey to surrender; all of it was planned. And Louis, turning tail at Moncontour; that was to lead me on." He smiled bitterly. "I was so smart."

I made no argument. It might be so and we shall never know, in any case. I stood. "It's late, my lord," I told him.

"So it is."

He rose, I joined him and we started from the room. "I'll kill them all one day," he said. "I'll start with Hugh; and then his son." He nodded briskly. "All the Lusignans."

We went together to his chamber and he settled on the bed. He lay there quietly, eyes on the ceiling.

"Shall I put the candle out, my lord?"

"No. Leave it burning."

"Can I get you anything? Some water? Wine?" He shook his head. I turned and started to the door. "Good night, my lord." There was no answering good night, and I was in the doorway when I heard his voice. The words he spoke were not to me.

"I'm sorry . . . I'm so sorry . . ."

I fled the room and if he wept, I do not know.

Till next time, if God wills it.

[235]

Near Saint Lambert
The 5th Day of July, A.D. 1214

We have crossed the Loire and, with all speed, are falling back to
La Rochelle. We have no other course, for Louis and his hordes
are certain to pursue us, and our weaponry, so much of it, is lost.

Our men seem much dispirited. The King is not. He moves
among them constantly and talks of reinforcements, future battles,
great campaigns that lie ahead. His tone with me is just the same.
I answer him in kind.

One battle does not mean the war, I tell myself. We shall be
back. And in the meantime, all our hopes rest in the north with
Longsword. Victory there means everything.

Till next time, if God wills it.

At La Rochelle
The 8th Day of July, A.D. 1214

The Queen was waiting in the yard when we arrived. We had sent
messengers ahead, of course; she knew the gist of what had happened. She seemed drawn and very pale.

The King dismounted. All she did was take his hand. They
turned and went inside.

The sun is down. It is no cooler. I must join the King now in his
office, we have much to do.

Till etc.

At La Rochelle
The 9th Day of July, A.D. 1214

I have a letter to transcribe and John is waiting. Briefly, then:

We found a least a dozen messages from Longsword, all of them
the same save for his rising anger and impatience. He is ready,

Dammartin is ready. Holland, Flanders, they stand ready, too. It only waits for Otto. And where is the leader of the Holy Roman Empire? In the Rhineland, gathering his forces, as he has for months. They cannot wait for him much longer, for the French are in the Lowlands now and each day Philip's army grows more strong.

At home, they are on tenterhooks, as well they might be. They have had no word from us since Parthenay and Joan's betrothal, and their messages are filled with hope. "We wait," the Marshal writes, "to learn of your great victories which we know will come."

John read it to me with a rueful smile. "How shall we answer that?" he asked.

I shrugged. The truth would never do. We left the matter there and went on working well into the night.

We have the answer now. The letter is in front of me. I give its text in part.

"The King to the earls, barons, knights and all his lieges in England, greetings.

"Know that we are safe and well and everything, by the grace of God, is prosperous and happy with us. We return manifold thanks to those of you who have sent us your knights to serve in the preservation and recovery of our rights and property. And we earnestly entreat those who have not crossed with us to come to us without delay to help in the recovery of our territory.

"Assuredly, if any of you should have understood that we bore him ill will, he can have it rectified by his coming."

The letter makes no mention of our progress in the war; or lack of it. We've written to the Marshal privately, of course; he knows the truth. But there are many barons who might not respond were they to know. They must respond, they must support us. We need more, more men. We cannot challenge Louis as we are.

The King is sanguine. As for me . . . ?

Till next time, if God wills it.

At La Rochelle
The 22nd Day of July, A.D. 1214

Time passes like the pulling of a tooth. Ships come. Each day another one arrives, but none with arms or men and none with messages. We sit suspended here.

The King puts in long hours making plans, devising tactics for the new campaign. The Queen embroiders bits of silk. At night we drink too much, it helps us through the evenings. There is nothing else to do.

The lack of word from England, that I understand. It is too soon, or so I tell myself. But why do we hear nothing from the north? Have they been swept by plague? Is Longsword dead? Mad questions; yet the mind comes up with them.

Perhaps another brandy. It will do no harm that I can see.

Till etc.

At La Rochelle
The 29th Day of July, A.D. 1214

Still nothing.

Twenty days have passed since writing home to England. Twenty days and nothing comes. And what is worse, no word from Longsword.

This evening Isabelle burst into tears. I asked her why.

"No reason; there's no reason."

Waiting is the hardest part.

Till next time, if God wills it.

At La Rochelle
The 2nd Day of August, A.D. 1214

I have composed myself, I think. I've had the afternoon to do so.
I must see the King soon, and the following is, more or less, what
I shall tell him.

I was in my room this morning drafting yet another set of angry
letters home to London. Why was no one coming? Where was our
support? What possible excuse was there for this intolerable silence? In the midst of this, there was a knocking on my door. I rose
and answered.

"Yes?" I did not recognize the face at first; unwashed, exhausted, red-eyed, caked with dust and dirt.

He cleared his throat. "Giraldus."

"Pandulf? Is that you?"

It was, of course. I helped him to a chair, I gave him wine, I
brought a cloth and wiped his face. What was he doing here? I
knew that we had used him as a courier last winter, sending him on
countless trips across the Channel as our coalition formed. Since
then, I'd heard no word of him.

"Where have you been?" I asked him as he filled his goblet up
again.

"Bovines."

The name meant nothing to me. "Where is that?"

"Near Valenciennes."

My heart stopped: Flanders. He'd been in the north. "What's
happened? Why no messengers? We've had no news here, none at
all."

"Since when?"

"Since early in July."

"Not one of them got through? You don't know anything?"

I shook my head. He turned his face away. "Oh God, oh
God . . ."

I knew it then: disaster. Something catastrophic. What? I asked
the worst. "Is William dead?"

"Oh God . . ."

I shook him. "Is he dead?"

"No . . . he's alive."

"What then? Did Otto never come? Was there a battle? Did we lose a battle?"

"I don't want to tell the King. You tell him, would you? I don't want to be the one."

"What is it? Pull yourself together, man."

"Giraldus, it's the end."

I waited. He is given to exaggeration. Certainly no enterprise as great as ours could hang upon a single battle: one withdraws and fights again. He drank. I brought the cask and put it by him. "There," I said. "Now tell me what it is that I'm to tell the King."

He told it poorly, stumbling back and forth in time, repeating things, forgetting, dwelling on small horrors, breaking down. In brief, it came to this:

Otto had arrived at last. Our armies, all of them, were finally in place. We were a force of fifty thousand men. No farmers armed with rakes this time, like Barham Down. All soldiers.

The French, we knew, had formed their army at Péronne, far to the south, halfway to Paris. Longsword decided to march south and meet them there. We broke camp on the morning of the 27th of July.

What we did not know was this: that Philip had already marched; that somehow he had missed our army, passed on by it. He was to the north of us. If we had known, we could have taken Paris. There was nothing in our way, the road was open. Christ— no matter; done is done.

At this point, Philip evidently realized his mistake. His country was in peril, he was cut off by an enemy that had no notion he was there. He turned around and he was racing back toward Paris when the armies stumbled on each other at Bovines.

It is a village, nothing more. A church, some houses by the River Marque, flat, open pastureland. The day was blazing hot and there had been no rain for weeks. The armies were of roughly equal size. One hundred thousand men in battle dress, they lined up on the field.

I have never seen armies in full battle; nor had Pandulf, and what horrified him most was the disorder. Chaos. Everything disintegrates. Like ants, like giant ants, they lunge and stagger mind-lessly. It was, he kept on saying, like a scene from Hell. They have no faces with their helmets on; just beaks and points and flattened tops. The dust, great choking clouds of it, swept over everything. The heat was unimaginable; men fell from that alone.

The French struck first. Then Otto charged. Straight at the center, straight for Philip, in a solid mass. A cry went up, the King of France was struck, thrown from his horse. They saved him somehow, dragged him back. The field, that moment, was so packed with men that they could scarcely swing their swords. Then Otto was unhorsed, then he was saved. And then he turned and ran. The Germans bolted. Thousands of them, cowards, rushing from the field.

The rest of us held firm. Outnumbered now, we could not draw away. We were in peril, only Longsword and Dammartin could save us. They were glorious, the two of them. Time after time they swept across the pastureland in slashing, unpredictable attacks. The French began to waver in the face of it. Then Longsword risked it all. He marshaled every man he could and, riding in the lead, he sliced at Philip left to right. A brilliant move; like Hector at the fall of Troy. Too late but beautiful.

Their numbers told; they were too many for us. We drew back. Of all our leaders, only Longsword and the gallant Dammartin had yet to leave the field. A hush fell. After all the cries and shouting, there was quiet. It was cooler, twilight, shadows on the bodies, thousands of them in the dust. Along the river, Philip and his army stood.

Longsword and Dammartin sat mounted side by side. They had perhaps two dozen men between them. What they did was madness. They attacked. They raced across the meadow, swords held high. Their men were butchered. Dammartin fought on until his horse was killed. It fell on him. Longsword was clubbed, struck by a cudgel from behind.

They were, when Pandulf saw them last, alive. What am I going to say to John? How can I tell him this?

At La Rochelle
The 3rd Day of August, A.D. 1214

I told him.
It was difficult for both of us.
I don't much want to write about it.

At La Rochelle
The 6th Day of August, A.D. 1214

"Balance," I keep saying to the King. One must, above all else, retain one's balance. Everything has not been lost. To be the Lord of England, Ireland, Scotland, Wales is no small thing. And portions of Poitou and most of Aquitaine; all this is English still.

I say these things, the King does not deny them; they are true enough. But I have trouble with my balance, too, and I have suffered nothing. What dominions have I lost? I am no poorer now than when the war began, I have no one to answer to for these defeats, my brother is not at the mercy of my greatest enemy.

Yet with all this, the King still manages to carry on. He works. We have enough to do, God knows. A truce must somehow be arranged and we have written to the Pope for his good offices in this regard. And letters have gone home, of course; brave letters full of calm and resolution. And then, too, we have an army here whose spirit and morale must be maintained, for they may have to face the French if Philip comes for us.

The worst times are the evenings when the work is done. I sit with John and Isabelle; their chairs are close together, yet they seem so far apart. Tonight, we walked along the ramparts. No one spoke. The harbor lay below us. There is no point, any more, in looking toward the sea for ships and men to come from home. We do so anyway.

Till next time, if God wills it.

At La Rochelle
The 10th Day of August, A.D. 1214

Dammartin and Longsword are alive. We have this from a messenger who saw them. He was there, in Paris, when King Philip led his men in triumph through the streets. Behind the King there came a wagon piled high with corpses, and the two of them, on foot, came after. They were tied to it with chains. At least they're well enough to walk.

What happens to them now? Will Phillip sell them back to us? John thinks he will. The Queen is not so sure.

"What if he never lets them go?" she asked tonight.

"I know the man," John said. "The ransom terms will come. He'll make me wait, of course—"

"How long?"

John took her hand. "A month, perhaps."

She turned away. "A month of this?"

Till next time, if God wills it.

At La Rochelle
The 21st Day of August, A.D. 1214

Innocent has sent a cardinal. Curzon is his name. He leaves for Paris in the morning with our terms for peace.

What happens in the north, of course, is not for us to say; the Flemish must make peace for Flanders and so forth. But as for England, John is adamant: he will not yield a single acre more than those already lost. And since our losses all occurred on land already held by France, our terms could hardly be much stiffer if we'd won.

All day, as I sat working on the text with John, he seemed so sure the French would take these terms. It baffled me. For why would Philip, who could have it all, content himself with this? Why has he not attacked us here? With fifty thousand men against our three, why hasn't he destroyed us? At the end, when we were done, I put the question to the King.

He answered with the saddest smile. "He wants the game to last, I think. He has me on the rack and he can turn the wheel as slowly as he likes. He doesn't have to fight me, all he has to do is wait. I can't come back to France again, you see."

Till next time, if God wills it.

At La Rochelle
The 5th Day of September, A.D. 1214

The King is often by himself, he seems to want to be alone. As for the Queen, she drifts in lassitude and quiet melancholy which I try to lift in foolish ways. I read to her, play chess and other games, tell stories, go for walks.

This afternoon began like many others. We were in her room. She lay there on her bed, eyes blank with inattention as I read to her from something I had written long ago. I paused. She asked me to read on.

"Of course, my lady."

I was just about to start again when John came in. He held a crumpled piece of parchment in one hand.

His voice was oddly flat. "I have the ransom terms," he said.

"You do? They've come?" The Queen sat up. "Thank God. John, I've been so afraid . . ." Her voice trailed off. "Something's wrong. What is it?" She was peering at his face. I saw it, too.

"The terms are these," John said. "A clean exchange. I give him Robert, Count of Dreux; he lets us have our brother back. There is, however, one condition."

"Yes?" The Queen was standing now. "Go on."

"It has to do with Dammartin. He is to stay in prison till he dies. I must consent to that, you see. I must . . . unless some way exists to save them both." He turned to me. "Is there a way?"

I had no answer. Possibly des Roches does; or the Marshal. We have written to them, asking.

There is only one thing that seems certain. John was right about the rack; Philip has turned the wheel.

Till next time, if God wills it.

At La Rochelle
The 26th Day of September, A.D. 1214

It is over. Everything is finished here. A treaty has been signed; our terms were met. The Count of Dreux has been released and Longsword, only Longsword, will go free. There was no way to save them both.

As soon as John is better, we will go. He has come down with gout. It grows worse daily and he cannot walk at all. We give him lemon balm to help the pain and houseleek to reduce the swelling. Neither does him any good.

Our army goes home bit by bit. Each day, a few more boats sail out to sea. I watch them go and think my thoughts.

God knows what we shall find at home. The letters we receive seem curiously empty: there is space between the lines.

Till next time, if God wills it.

On the Breton Straits
The 10th Day of October, A.D. 1214

We left this morning early. Through the harbor, out the narrow channel to the Breton Straits, the Île de Ré. There was some mist, the air was chill. I wore a cloak.

Eight months. It was mid-February when we came. The harbor had been filled with people and the air had rung with cheers. I fancied I could hear them now as I stood on the aftercastle watching La Rochelle become a dot, then disappear. A gust of wind brought water to my eyes and I was wiping it away when I heard

[245]

John approach. His fancy has been taken by a shepherd's staff. He leans upon it heavily, but he can walk.

"How does it go with you, Giraldus?"

"Very well indeed, my lord."

He nodded, "Good," and put an arm around my shoulder. That was all. We stood like that for quite some time.

On the Channel
The 14th Day of October, A.D. 1214

I am sitting by the brazier near the aftercastle with the King and Queen. The coast of England is in sight now, lit by sunset. We can see the green of it. And autumn colors; yellow, gold. There is no wind. Our oarsmen move us north, toward Dover.

They are silent for the most part, John and Isabelle. I cannot read their faces. As for me, I feel suspended, caught between the future and the past. Old memories float by me; I am twenty and in Paris, I am forty and in Rome.

The Queen has just remarked about the cold. The King has put his cloak around her. On the shore, the evening mist is forming. We are coming home.

Till next time, if God wills it.

At Dover Castle
The 15th Day of October, A.D. 1214

We entered England quietly, on tiptoe, creeping into Dover after dark. A royal galley and two escort ships, that's all we were.

A circumspect return. No crowd, no guards of honor on the jetty; only several children and a scattering of fishermen who cowered back and bowed as we moved past. We had not sent ahead, no one expected us. There was, I think, no other way of coming home, for we could hardly land in triumph and it begs the question of defeat. Then, too, it gives the King a little time to sniff the air in peace.

What will we find at home? We'll know that soon enough. We've written to des Roches, Lord Stephen, Longsword and the Marshal asking them to come to us, at once and quietly, at Canterbury. Longsword would, we thought, be home at Salisbury Castle. Hopefully, the others are in London or in easy reach. There is so much we need to know.

Till next time, if God wills it.

At Barham
The 17th Day of October, A.D. 1214

Barham: all day long, the memory of it echoed in my thoughts. The road to Canterbury passes near it. There was daylight left when we approached, we might have traveled farther but the King would not. Instead, he stopped and took the Queen and led her through the village, up the hills to Barham Down.

I followed after them, as I had done that day—when was it? Sixteen months ago? We walked in silence through the meadow toward that final hill beyond which all our men had camped. Sheep, little flocks of them, grazed here and there. Behind us, in the town, dogs barked just as they had before. Were they the same or different dogs, I wondered.

Up we climbed. The hill seemed steeper than it was. Some birds flew past, I stumbled on a hillock, then we reached the crest and looked out at the Down.

Nothing. There was not a mark or trace to show that once one hundred thousand men had gathered there. It shook me for a moment: had it ever happened? I have dreams that seem as real. The King and Queen stood near me, side by side. They neither touched nor spoke nor looked at one another. What was there to say, in any case? We turned and came back to the town.

Till next time, if God wills it.

The morning was a clear one, crisp as apples; which is probably what drew me to the orchards. They are lovely here, neat rows of full stout trees all walled about by ancient stones, and I was stretching for an apple that had caught my eye when someone called my name.

I turned. The Marshal. He was striding briskly toward me, hands outstretched. I felt a surge of joy on seeing him. We stood there, smiling at each other like two schoolboys after months apart. Then we embraced. His body is still hard and firm, all bones and sinew, like a rock. I told him so. He laughed and then his questions started: what has happened with the Lusignans, had I been there at Roche-aux-Moines, how had John taken the betrayal? And Boviens, how was he after that?

I told him briefly and we turned and started toward the castle. I was full of questions, too, I said. I had my answers moments later, for the Marshal had come down from London with Lord Stephen and des Roches.

They were already with the King when we arrived. I had missed nothing but the greetings and embraces. It was good to see them both. Some wine was poured and then we settled at the table by the hearth and John said, "Well, then. In a word, how are we?"

This was directed to des Roches. He cleared his throat. "My lord," he said, "we seem to have some problems. To begin with, there's the question of the scutage tax."

The tax, as every child knows, is paid in time of war. A baron either joins the King with men and arms or stays at home and pays the King so many pounds for every knight he should have sent. This summer, neither happened; we had written home demanding aid and neither men nor money came. Nor was it coming now. The northern barons most particularly would not pay, and since de Vescy was emerging as their chief, des Roches had ordered him distrained.

John smiled at that. "You confiscated everything he has?"
"I did."

"With what result?"

"There has been nothing yet."

"Go on," John said. "What do you think will happen?"

"Who can say, my lord?"

"I asked you what you thought," John snapped. He looked around the table. "Do not bend the facts to please me, any of you. Am I clear?"

Des Roches looked up. "There is some talk of raising men and arms against you."

"Some?" The King seemed unsurprised. "No more than some? I know how much was lost in France." He paused. "As for the tax, I think it must be raised. Don't you?"

This last was to Lord Stephen. "I, my lord? I'm not the one to ask."

"I think you are." John leaned across the table toward him. "It's a legal question, isn't it? The tax has always been the law. A king can't rule without it; it's the custom and the law."

Lord Stephen met his eyes, he did not look away. "The only laws that never change are God's."

"Have you been meeting with FitzWalter? Have you?"

"Yes, my lord."

"What does he ask for now?"

Lord Stephen answered him at length. The agitation for King Henry's laws was tied, as we had thought, to our success or lack of it in France. There had been nothing till the news of our disaster at Bovines reached home. At once, FitzWalter and his people came to him. There was no change in their demands: the King must grant them all the rights and privileges that Henry I had granted in his Charter of 1100. What had changed, however, was their tone.

"They fancy that they give me orders now," Lord Stephen said. "They tell me: Tell John thus-and-so and bring his answer back."

"They do?" John's eyes blazed but his voice was even. "What do you say?"

"Nothing. I'm an intermediary, I go back and forth. I have no power, I can't speak for you."

"What would you tell them if you could?"

[249]

Lord Stephen shook his head. "I'm not the King."

"Then tell them I do not take orders, any more than you do. They can wait. As for the tax, the law is clear. No baron is above it."

There was more, some talk about the harvest and such things. When we were done, I had some questions for Lord Stephen of my own. All this insistence on King Henry's laws seemed odd to me, since John had sworn already to uphold them. Surely there was something else these people wanted. Something more.

"Lord Stephen?" He was moving down the corridor ahead of me. He stopped and turned. I put it to him bluntly. "There was something that you didn't tell the King, I think."

He seemed surprised. "There was?"

"You failed to tell him where you stand."

His answer came straight back at me. "I don't think any man should be all-powerful. And that includes the Pope. He schemes to be a worldly king; our bodies and our souls, he wants them both. It is too much, there must be limits to it. As for John . . . " He paused. "John has too many powers. He is far too great."

I looked at him. I had to say it. "What of you, my Lord Archbishop?"

"I? I need my limits, too." And then he smiled at me and added, "But not yet."

Till next time, if God wills it.

At Canterbury
The 21st Day of October, A.D. 1214

This afternoon, the Queen expressed a wish to ride to Harbledown. She has kept so much to herself these days and I was pleased she asked for company.

We left the castle, riding westward on the London road. Not far; the village sits upon the first high hill. The day was dark; low, heavy clouds and trails of mist. It seemed to suit her mood. She scarcely spoke. We left the road before the leper hospital, dismounted, walked a little through the tall, damp grass. Below us the cathedral spires rose, as gray and leaden as the sky beyond.

She looked at this a moment, then she turned. "Are you my friend, Giraldus?"

What a question. I'd have smiled but it was said with such intensity. "What's wrong, my lady?"

"I have no one else to ask. I need to know the truth. What is it we've come home to? You were there with Marshal and the rest of them. What did they say? John tells me nothing. It's my kingdom, too; I have some stake in it. My children: what will happen to them if—" She stopped. I reached for her. She backed away. Her eyes grew very large. "I know what France meant. France was a disaster. All our enemies will come together now."

I tried to reassure her. Let them come together all they choose, whoever they might be; there was no danger, she and all her family were safe and one day she would be the mother of a king. She started in on Longsword then. Where was he, why no word of any kind? I told her it was still too soon to have a message back from Salisbury. It did no good; she had these dreams, we were in peril, all of us.

And then, as suddenly as she began, she stopped. She let me hold her then and told me how ashamed she felt for what she'd said.

"It's only that John cuts me off from time to time. I don't know why. Some nights, before we sleep, he looks at me so strangely; then the look is gone so quickly that I wonder, was it there?" She stepped away. "I need to know the truth, Giraldus. You will tell me, won't you? Nothing secret, nothing that I should not hear; but it is terrifying, not to know."

I promised her I would. She took my hand and held it in her own.

Till next time, if God wills it.

At Silchester
The 26th Day of October, A.D. 1214

Longsword may be dying. All we know is that he has a fever and it will not break.

We were in London at the Tower when the message came. From Isabella, Longsword's wife. He had, she wrote, come home from France so gaunt and weakened he could scarcely walk. And then the fever struck him and he has been wasting ever since.

We left at once. Had not the horses faltered, we would still be on the road. The King and Queen are resting now. The ride has been a silent one. No one has spoken of the possibility of Longsword's death and there is nothing else to talk about.

Till next time, if God wills it.

At Salisbury Castle
The 28th Day of October, A.D. 1214

He is out of danger. Thin and frail, God knows, but there is no more fever. It has left him ravaged and as white as Dover chalk, but Longsword will be with us for a while yet.

He wept to see us. Illness does that, loosing our emotions, and his tears came like a boy's. He kissed the King, he kissed the Queen, he even had a kiss for me; but he was quickly wearied and his wife, the Countess Isabella, led us from the room.

I had not met the Countess till tonight. I knew of her, of course. She was old Salisbury's daughter; Longsword's earldom and his fortune came through her. But what I did not know and was completely unprepared for was her likeness to the Queen.

Isabella, Isabelle. Both heiresses, both young, both comely—though I find the Queen more beautiful. They both were married at the age of twelve. To brothers. Countess Isabella first; then, two years later, Isabelle.

I watched them fascinated as they sat, both sewing, both apparently immersed in where their needles went. They spoke briefly now and then of such things as their children. They have sons the same age, and quite suddenly I understood the lack of friendliness between them. For one son will be a king and one will not.

They talked of other things; the harvest and the coming Christmas Court and then, at last, about the war and, in particular, the horrors Longsword had been through. It was the Queen who broached it.

"Does he talk about what happened at Bovines?"

The Countess nodded. "Yes, of course."

"And prison? Has he said what that was like?"

"A little."

Isabelle leaned forward. "Tell me."

"It's his story. Let him tell you."

"As you wish." The Queen put down her sewing.

"It is his wish, too, I'm sure," the Countess murmured. Then she stood. "You must be very tired, my lady."

"So must you."

They left. I stayed awhile longer by the fire, thinking. How alike they are. Not just the Countess and the Queen but John and Longsword, too. The brothers seem so different, there is little they appear to share; but this is on the surface only, is it not? It must be—for their women are so much the same.

Till next time, if God wills it.

At Salisbury Castle
The 29th Day of October, A.D. 1214

Bovines. It was Longsword's wish to talk about it. John and Isabelle sat by his bed and listened as he took them through the day. He seemed to feel no pride for what he'd done. He lay there filled with anguish and regret; if this, if that. What glory there was he gave to Dammartin.

And afterwards—the march to Paris, walking through the streets in chains, the weeks in prison—this he gave to Dammartin as well. His courage and his wit, his endless gallantry. Their parting was apparently unbearable, for Longsword would not tell of it. He was free while Dammartin would spend his life below the ground in one small cell; it was too much, he turned his face away from us.

The Queen stayed with him when we left. She sat there by his bedside, waiting, should he want for anything. Her face was drained. So was the King's. He stood beside me in the corridor as if he were uncertain, for the moment, where he was.

Then, turning, he began to walk. I fell in step behind him. We went up a flight of stairs and then another flight, up to the highest level of the keep. He paused outside a heavy door, then opened it and wandered in.

I stiffened when I realized where we were. This was her room. Queen Eleanor's. Her prison. It was here that Henry kept her, under guard, for fifteen years. I often wonder what it meant to her, this woman who was Queen of France, then Queen of England, who had held such power in her hands, to see the years pass in this little space.

The room itself is not unpleasant. Lovely views; northward to Salisbury Plain and, to the south, the river valley where New Salisbury is being built. No chains or shackles here; but still a dungeon, nonetheless. Yet she came out at sixty-seven to rule the world again. Where had she found the strength to do it? Was there ever such a woman? I was lost in thought when the King began to speak.

His voice was soft. "I feel no pity, standing here. She hated me, you know. I never understood her reasons for it, but she did. She mocked me; even at the end, when I was King, she took me for a fool. And yet . . ."

He paused and looked around the room. "She hated Father, too. She loved him once, I think, but that was long before I can remember. If I listen, I can hear them vilifying one another. And it's true she raised an army and she fought against him but, Sweet Jesus, how could he have put her here? She was his Queen. There is no crime so great, he had no right, how could he face himself and keep her in this room?"

He started for the door as if a force were pressing him. Then, at

[254]

the threshold, he turned back. His eyes met mine. "How could my father do the things he did?"

I had no answer. I have never had one.

Till next time, if God wills it.

At the Tower, London
The 15th Day of November, A.D. 1214

There is to be a meeting of FitzWalter and the barons in his camp. It comes, I think, as a response to our insistence that they pay their scutage tax. In any case, they meet in five days' time at Bury Saint Edmund's.

Lord Stephen brought this news to us tonight. The King and I were playing chess when he was ushered in. He gave the information tersely, adding, at the end, that he had come at once on hearing of it.

John seemed unperturbed. He thanked Lord Stephen for his courtesy and then, as if it were an afterthought, he asked, "Will you be there?"

"I must go. All my meetings with FitzWalter are for nothing if I don't appear. It's in your interest, surely; I can speak for you, if need be."

There was silence for a moment. Then John nodded. "Yes, by all means, you should go." He paused, then turned to me. "And you, Giraldus, you go, too."

I am, of course, to be John's eyes and ears. My things are packed, we leave here in the morning. I am not, I know, in any danger; not with Lord Stephen by my side. And yet they did cut Thomas Becket down inside his own cathedral and we shall be meeting in the abbey.

Till next time.

At Bury Saint Edmund's
The 19th Day of November, A.D. 1214

Most of us are sleeping in the Great Hall on the abbey floor. The place is packed with barons and their sons and servants, minor clergy, hangers-on.

Who are they, who is here? De Vescy and his fellow barons of the north, of course. But they are modest figures in this company. They have a broader movement now, and far more powerful. The thing has spread.

FitzWalter is a London man; his strength is mainly there, and he has brought in barons, great ones, from the eastern counties close to London. Men such as the Earls of Essex, Hereford, Oxford, and the leaders of the mighty houses of Bigod and Clare.

What do they talk about? King Henry's charter, as before. And something new: the threat of war. The King, they say, will either grant them Henry's laws or they will call their men to arms and strike him from the throne.

I think—no, I cannot think. We are sleeping on the rushes with the dogs, and all around me men have started singing. War songs. It is vital to remember that these men are but one quarter of the baronage. For every earl who came, three earls did not. Proportion. That's the word I could not think of. One must keep this in proportion.

They will meet tomorrow, on Saint Edmund's feast day, in the abbey church before his shrine. There is, except for Becket's grave, no place of pilgrimage so holy and revered in all of England. What will happen when they meet? I stare around me at these faces. Like all devils, they are fallen angels, are they not? In any case, it looks like Hell.

Till next time, if God wills it.

At Bury Saint Edmund's
The 19th Day of November, A.D. 1214

We gathered early in the church. I sat in front, beside Lord Stephen. Behind us, many earls had yet to take their places and the noise was great. These men, if nothing else, have voices. In the midst of this, FitzWalter came. He stood before Saint Edmund's shrine, raised both his arms and called for silence. It was given to him instantly.

I cannot write an accurate account of what he said. There is a sense in which he speaks without the use of words; much as in music, where the meaning comes to us some other way. It's his intensity, I think. He seems to burn with what he feels. In any case, his message was a simple one: the King would sign a charter granting them what Henry had or it was war and—stunned: I sat there stunned at this—and they would march to London and demand his answer now.

It was a call to arms. Would they respond? War songs are one thing; putting armor on is something else. It was a Rubicon and who would follow him across? The only sound was breathing, no one moved or spoke. I watched FitzWalter watching us. I thought of everything that he might do except for what he did.

He turned and knelt before the shrine. Head bowed, voice hushed, he swore upon the body of Saint Edmund to oppose the King till he restore those liberties which Henry had, before God, given them a century ago.

This done, he rose and, looking out at all the silent faces, spoke two words. "Who next?"

They stood. No shouts or cheers. They simply stood and started edging forward toward the shrine. They never reached it. Lord Stephen stopped them. Striding to the altar, rising up, he cried out, "Not in God's house!"

He was glorious. They had good cause, he told them. There was much injustice in the land; cruel laws or, all too often, none at all. But was not war the highest lack of law? How could they cure the illness by invoking the disease?

[257]

And having spoken to their higher principles, if any, he addressed their realer ones. The fear of loss: the King was powerful and if they doubted it, he would be happy to reel off a list of earls who had not come. The fear of punishment: the King, in victory, was unlikely to be kind. The fear of excommunication: he himself would see to that.

He had them. They were in his hands. FitzWalter knew it. Stepping forward, looking up, he said, "My lord, I made my vow because I saw no other way. If I have missed it, show it to me. Tell us what to do."

Lord Stephen answered with great force, "Sit down and reason with the King. It can be done, I know it. I will lead you, if you'll let me. John will listen, he will hear us out and we shall find an answer. There will be a peaceful way. I promise it. You have my word."

It ended quickly after that. He got the barons to agree to meet with John in London in the first week of the new year. Then he bowed his head and blessed the gathering and that was all.

I joined him at the altar as the barons moved away. His eyes were shining; as they should, for he had done a great thing. He had kept his land from violence. I told him so.

He shook his head. "Just for the moment; nothing more. If only John will listen, I can do so much."

It struck me then, the other thing Lord Stephen had just done. He was the leader of these barons now. How had he managed that? I even wondered if he knew it, but I did not ask.

Till next time, if God wills it.

At the Palace of Westminster
The 28th Day of November, A.D. 1214

The King, the Marshal and des Roches: I have been with them half the night. I told them everything, I think; from who was at the meeting to the speech Lord Stephen made. There followed hours of discussion, some of it intelligent.

The end result is this. We are to plan for all eventualities: for war, for peace, for something in between. The King wants all his choices open. We shall write to Innocent in case we need his intervention. We shall meet with Chester and those other barons who are with us. We shall count our funds and see to the availability of mercenaries. We shall husband our supplies and fortify our strongholds.

And when all of this is seen to, we shall wait. The King will make no move until FitzWalter does. As for the meeting with the barons here in January, John has no objection. He consents. He sees it all, I think, as if it were a game of chess, and what would please him more than anything is taking one archbishop off the board.

Till next time.

At the Palace of Westminster
The 16th Day of December, A.D. 1214

We leave for Worcester soon, and Christmas Court. My head aches and I have a fever. I am keeping it a secret; I will not be left behind again this year. Longsword arrived today. His face is grayish; he is far too thin. He looks the way I feel.

Till etc.

At Worcester Castle
The 26th Day of December, A.D. 1214

Not noon and I am drunk again. Or is it still? I can't see that it matters; no one here will notice. We are few this year but we are friends. The Marshal, Longsword and des Roches; and of the earls of England, only five. The five most powerful and most respected: Chester, Derby, Warwick, Surrey, Devon.

We arrived two days ago, in time to watch the King turn forty-eight. We celebrated with a Mass, which I conducted, since Lord Stephen was, make note, among the uninvited. The cathedral,

[259]

which was built by Wulfstan, seems to have some special meaning for the King, and Wulfstan is his favorite saint.

When this was done, we feasted and we drank. There was no end to it, and one by one we fell asleep or went to bed till only John and Isabelle were left. My head was resting on the table, they may not have noticed me. I heard them murmur to each other, words I could not catch.

And then a silence fell. I opened up an eye to see him kiss her; first her lips and then her breasts. He moved an arm; it disappeared between her thighs. I closed my eye, it was the least that I could do.

Till next time, if God wills it.

At Worcester Castle
The 1st Day of January, A.D. 1215

I am writing from the yard as we prepare to leave for London. The portcullis winch has frozen, and we face a brief delay.

These days have been a time-between, a respite. Not one single weighty conversation, no accomplishments to show. I've spent long hours with the Marshal, hearing how it was when he was young. I spent a night with Longsword, who is still not quite himself and tends to melancholy; sighs and wistful smiles. Even Isabelle can't seem to raise his spirits: I have watched her try.

As for the King, he showed no signs of strain or weariness at all; as if this year, which has brought nothing but betrayal and defeat, had been a summer month at Woodstock. He is either moving toward some kind of inner peace or putting up a wall between himself and what is real.

I offer last night as a case in point. I had successfully outdrunk the Earl of Chester and was moving with some caution to my room. The corridor was dark. I saw a light ahead. A torch was burning and beneath it on a stool sat John, an open jewel chest in his lap.

"Are you all right, my lord?"

"I am. And you?"

I leaned against the wall and brought him into sharper focus. "You should be in bed," I told him.

"So should we all." He stood and closed the chest, and as he took my arm he said, "Giraldus, I've been sitting here and thinking what the differences to England might have been had Father lived to eighty-two instead of Eleanor."

I nodded wisely. "Many differences, my lord."

"The chief of which is that he'd still be on the throne." He grinned, then started chuckling softly as we—

They have fixed the winch. And so begins the new year.

Till etc.

At the Tower, London
The 5th Day of January, A.D. 1215

Tomorrow is Epiphany, the day Lord Stephen is to lead Fitz-Walter to the conference table, there to sit and reason with the King.

There will, I fear, be little reasoning. This moment, as I put these words down, men are making camp across the Thames: Fitz-Walter and his people. I can see them from my window; barons, knights and men-at-arms. They are too small a force to do us harm, yet we are clearly meant to notice them.

It seems to me a foolish move; unless, of course, FitzWalter means the talks to fail. In any case, it makes a poor beginning.

T.n.t.

At the Tower, London
The 6th Day of January, A.D. 1215

There was a long, bare table in the center of the room. Lord Stephen sat on one side with FitzWalter and de Vescy. On the other side: the King, the Marshal, Longsword and des Roches. I watched them from a corner where I sat amongst the scribes.

The King did all the talking at the start. He placed a copy of King Henry's charter on the table and proposed to go through its provisions one by one. "So that," he said, "we are agreed upon the meaning."

This he did. He read each article aloud and then, in common language, gave the purport of it. He was very clear. Lord Stephen and FitzWalter and de Vescy listened silently; there was no argument. When this was done, he looked across at them and said, "What is it that you want of me?"

FitzWalter answered him. "We want the Charter reaffirmed."

"I see." John paused. "No further terms or new provisions?"

I sat forward on my stool. Of course there were; we all knew that. The question was how many and what kind.

FitzWalter brought a paper out and started reading from it. What we heard was nothing new: demands that limited the powers of the Crown where baronial finances were concerned. Such things as taxes, levies, duties, forest laws, et cetera.

The King heard all of this in silence. At the end he asked FitzWalter for his paper, told him he would study it. Then, turning to Lord Stephen, he said, "Have you anything to add? If so—" He got no further.

"Study it?" FitzWalter's voice was sharp.

John nodded. "Yes, of course.

"You've known for weeks what I was going to ask. And now you tell me you need time to think about it?"

"Certainly I do." John picked the paper up. "This thing is full of implications. It's important. Don't you understand, don't you know anything?"

"I know you. How much time? How long am I to wait?"

"Till Easter. You will have my answer then."

FitzWalter shook his head. "You know what your position is. You damned well know it now."

John stiffened but his voice stayed calm. "Till Easter. Not one day before."

"No doubt I have your word on that."

"You do."

FitzWalter leaned across the table toward him. "And when Easter comes, you'll need more time. Your word, my lord, means just as much to me as this." He spat upon the tabletop.

John's face went white. "FitzWalter, you're a fool."

FitzWalter stood. "You've seen my men across the river. I have more. More than you think."

"You threaten us?" It was the Marshal speaking. I have never seen him so enraged. "If I were King, FitzWalter, you would never leave the room. Since I am not, I tell you this: the King will answer you on Easter, by my soul, and not one day before."

"By my soul, too," Lord Stephen said.

FitzWalter spun on him. "Is this the way you lead us?"

"It's the only way." Lord Stephen's voice rang out. "I want a charter, not a war."

It hung suspended. No one spoke. FitzWalter's eyes went back and forth between Lord Stephen and the Marshal and the King. He swallowed, as if choking down his rage. "Till Easter then," he snapped and left the room. De Vescy followed just behind.

We went on with the meeting, for Lord Stephen had a paper, too. We heard him out and then, when he had gone, John turned to Marshal with a smile. "I'd say they were divided. Wouldn't you?" The Marshal nodded. John sat back. "Well, then, what do we have?" He paused. "There are one hundred ninety-seven baronies in England. Forty of them, at a guess, are in FitzWalter's camp. Another forty stand with me. The balance, the remainder, is the key to everything, I think."

The King was right. We told him so.

Till next time, if God wills it.

At the Palace of Westminster
The 7th Day of February, A.D. 1215

I have been traveling with the King through Kent and Surrey, paying court to neutral barons. There is growing interest in a charter; they are not so dense or brutish that its benefits escape them. At the same time, they will not be budged or shifted from the middle, they will not take sides. They will, in short, do nothing which might lead to war.

The King is very careful with them. He accommodates, he never presses. There are good things in a charter, true; and war must be avoided, true again. He is in all things careful lately; even delicate. Our mercenaries are a case in point. We've raised them, they stand ready in Poitou, but John believes we dare not land them here. Instead, he orders them to Ireland, where they can be, at the same time, close at hand and out of sight. Whatever steps FitzWalter takes, we must be ready to respond.

Although we have not moved the barons we have visited, the King seems confident. "They'll turn to us," he tells me, "when the time comes." Thus, he was in splendid spirits when we came to London, unannounced and unexpected, late this afternoon through heavy rain. There would be many papers waiting for him, but our traveling clothes were drenched. We went to change.

I spent a while doing it. I had a chill and took a brandy for it, and a second. Then, sufficiently restored, I left my room and started down the hall. To reach the stairs, I had to pass the children's nursery.

I paused outside their door. It would be nice to see them for a moment, to surprise them. Carefully, I moved the latch and only then remembered that the children were at Corfe. Or so I thought; but wasn't that a voice I heard? I listened. It was Isabelle: the children must be here.

I smiled, and wanting to surprise her, I began, as soundlessly as possible, to open up the door. The nursery is a large room. There are four beds, each with curtains, lined along one wall. I heard the Queen again. "Be patient," were the words she said.

The door was nearly halfway open. I could see a bed. Its curtains were closed and by it, on the floor, all jumbled up in haste, there was a pile of clothes. Men's clothes. Then Isabelle came into view. She had removed her bodice, she was naked to the waist. My heart stopped at the sight of her. I watched her slip between the curtains. I heard her say, "I love you."

With a smile, I withdrew. It was the King, of course. His carnal appetites are legendary, I had been so long in changing, he had gone to find his Queen. I moved on, down the stairs. I could prepare his papers for him, organize them, have them ready when he came.

I reached his chamber door and opened it. He looked up from his desk impatiently.

"Where have you been?" he said.

I have been praying half the night to no avail. I ask for guidance; nothing comes. Why was this knowledge given me? What am I meant to do? I feel such anger. But at whom? Who is at fault?

Tomorrow: I can think no more tonight.

At the Palace of Westminster
The 11th Day of February, A.D. 1215

I cannot bring myself to act. Each thought is followed by a second thought and I am stranded, caught between them.

I sit working by the King, decisions of importance lie there on the table. Just today, a message from FitzWalter asking for a meeting. Should the King consent? If so, who should attend? I cannot focus on the question. All I do is look at him and think he is the one responsible. He drove the Queen to this, he treats her as a brood mare, he refused to let her join her dying father and his infidelities and bastards, all the fornicating when we travel and my rage wells up at him.

And then I see the Queen. I watch her sewing by the fire, so exquisite and pure, the King comes in, she kisses him and strokes his hand and I think: Harlot. Whore. He trusts her, he adores her and she cost him France: it was for her that Hugh of Lusignan betrayed him and he loves her still and she requites it with adultery. And has for years: the tutor, Cardenal, God knows how many others and I tremble so from anger that I leave the room lest it be seen.

But most of all, I hate the man: this nameless, shameless, foul and wretched animal whose lust is ravaging the lives of those two whom, in all the world, I hold most dear. I dream of finding his identity and coming at him in some darkened hallway with a knife. I bring it down; again, again. I see the blood.

I dare not tell the King, I am afraid of what he might do. It is the Queen I must confront. She must be made to see the danger of her passions. And the evil of them. It must stop or she will bring us all to ruin.

How am I to do it? I have prayed for guidance endlessly, my knees are swollen from the kneeling and no answer comes.

At the Palace of Westminster
The 12th Day of February, A.D. 1215

It was not yet dawn and I was in the chapel praying. There was silence in the palace, everyone still slept. I did not hear her coming, I was startled when I heard my name.

"Giraldus?"

I turned round. She stood behind me all in white, enveloped in white silk, her face as pallid as the cloth. I felt God guiding me; this was my time to speak.

I rose. "Are you all right, my lady? Can't you sleep?"

She sighed. "I am so troubled and your room was empty, you weren't there."

I took her hand. It felt so cold. "What is it? You can tell me."

"Something's come between us. I have felt it now for days. The way you look at me, Giraldus; with such scorn and rage. What have I done?"

I put it all in just two words. "I know," I said.

Her eyes looked into mine. "You do?" she whispered.

"Yes."

I watched those perfect eyes well up, I saw two perfect tears. "Thank God," she said. "Thank God you know." She seemed about to fall. I put an arm around her. "I've been so afraid to tell you, I've been longing to confess." She fought the tears back. "May I? Will you hear me?"

[266]

"Yes, of course I will."

She knelt before me, clasped her hands and bowed her head. "Forgive me, Father, for I have sinned." She told me how it all began, the longings she had felt, how she had tried to master them, how she had failed from time to time, and to her bitter shame. With Lucien the tutor, and with Cardenal. And with her lover now.

I asked her who he was.

She shook her head. "Oh no. Please, no, Giraldus."

"I must have his name."

She told me. Everything, I know it all. When she was done, I told her she had sinned. "Most grievously," I said.

"I know that, Father. *Mea culpa, mea culpa.*" She was weeping.

"You must swear to never sin again."

"I swear it, Father. On my soul. I have deceived my lord, the King, whom I do love. Dear Jesus, please forgive me."

I absolved her. What else could I do?

It is my burden now. And more than that, for I am gnawed by doubt. Have I been used? Did she suspect I knew? If so, it was a cruel and clever thing, for she has silenced me. I cannot speak her lover's name, nor write it down. I wish to God that I could strike it from my mind.

Till next time, if God wills it.

At the Palace of Westminster
The 14th Day of February, A.D. 1215

My thoughts will not obey me. Papers travel through my hands, the words float past; I think of nothing but the Queen.

She seems untouched by what she's done, as if my absolution lifted everything. Perhaps it has; for after all, it does bring God's forgiveness for her sins. But not for his. Not for the man. I see him, he is one of us. He looks at me with ease and candor, I respond in kind. She has not told him she confessed, I think; but even so, there ought to be some sign in him. How can he live without repentance, does he feel no shame? Is he—

Enough. I will not think of this, not any more. The Queen is cleansed, the episode is terminated. Henceforth, all this is banished from my thoughts.

Till next time, if God wills it.

At the Palace of Westminster
The 16th Day of February, A.D. 1215

Work engulfs me, I am with the King all day. He has sent letters and an envoy off to Rome so that the Pope may know our situation and respond with his support. And he has given his permission to FitzWalter and his people to assemble. They will meet at Oxford next week, and the Marshal will be there on our behalf.

I am myself again. My appetite is fresh, my sleep is peaceful and I never think about the Queen.

Till etc.

At the Palace of Westminster
The 27th Day of February, A.D. 1215

The night was desolate, high wind and bitter cold. I lay in bed, about to put my candle out, when there was knocking at my door.

It was the Marshal. He had just returned from Oxford, riding all day through this dreadful weather, and the chill of it still clung to him. He sat down on my bed. I offered him some brandy, which he took.

He looked so old. There was a tremor in his hand, his eyes still watered from the wind. I waited, filled with questions, while he drank. He asked for more, I poured and then I heard it all.

He is convinced that war is coming. It is war FitzWalter wants. The charter talk, he said, is a device. FitzWalter uses it like bait, he means it to provoke the King, to move him to attack. I nodded, for I thought so, too. And then I asked about Lord Stephen.

"Was he there?"

The Marshal nodded. "He's a fool, you know. A learned fool. He believes he leads them. He is using them, he thinks, to get a charter from the King; and all the while, they're using him." He smiled for a moment. "You should hear the way he talks to them. Philosophy: he might as well speak Portuguese."

The smile left his face as he went on. More men are joining them, it seems. Young men, the sons of barons. "Chester's boy was there," he said.

I shook my head. "Impossible."

But it is not. The sons of many barons loyal to our side are with FitzWalter now. It's greed that moves them, nothing more nor less than that. For when a baron dies, his property reverts back to the Crown. All heirs must buy their titles back. The price is often very high; so high, in fact, that many of them spend their lives in debt. It is the King's chief way to unity, it keeps the baronage in check. Without it, there is chaos; which is what FitzWalter wants, of course.

If war should come, it means that fathers will be fighting sons. Not only Chester; many more.

The Marshal looked at me. "My son was there, as well. My eldest; William. He is with them now, Giraldus."

"Oh," I said.

Till next time, if God wills it.

At the Tower, London
The 1st Day of March, A.D. 1215

The mood has changed. The grimness that descended with the Marshal's news is gone. The King has lifted it.

We were at breakfast. In he came, fresh-faced and rested, took his place and said, "My friends, I've come to a decision. I am going to take the Cross."

I looked at him. "Your Cross as a Crusader, Sire?"

"Yes, of course."

I may have gasped. It was a masterstroke. For once he vows to lead his country on Crusade, his person and his property are sacrosanct. Let anything of his be touched in any way, the power of the Church in full, its condemnation and its prosecution, would come down on the offender.

I digested it before I spoke. "My lord? I can't help asking, do you really mean to go?"

He smiled at me. "I might. But all that matters now is this: the vow protects me for three years. That's more than long enough to stop FitzWalter."

Will it? Does the threat of excommunication carry weight with him? Or with his followers? I think it may.

The Marshal thought so, too. He looked across the table, at the King. "Thank you" was what he said.

Till next time, if God wills it.

At the Palace of Westminster
The 4th Day of April, A.D. 1215

Say what you will about the Pope, he is an honest merchant, he delivers when he's paid. *Damna et interesse*: with interest.

Letters from him came today in answer to our message of two months ago. In forceful terms, he tells the barons to abandon all conspiracies, to give up any thought of war, to be conciliatory and respectful to the King. And more. He reprimands Lord Stephen for his sympathies, for favoring a charter, and he orders him to exommunicate all barons who continue to conspire. And still more. Should the barons disobey, he orders them to Rome to have the issue settled in his court.

As I write, the scribes are making copies for FitzWalter and his brethren to digest. It will not be an easy thing to swallow. For myself, I hope it chokes them.

At the Palace of Westminster
The 13th Day of April, A.D. 1215

Easter week is drawing near and we will leave soon for Northampton, neutral ground, to hold our meeting with FitzWalter. For the King intends to keep his word. He vowed to make an answer to the charter terms FitzWalter gave him—and he will.

Exactly what that answer is to be is still unclear. We spend our days evolving it. This much is certain: he will reaffirm King Henry's laws. It does not seem to trouble him at all. As for the papers which FitzWalter and Lord Stephen gave us, there is much debate. No king is ever eager to relinquish powers, and we move about the clauses with much care. Some are acceptable and some are not and some, with changes and amendments, can be made to serve. In short, we shall go to the conference table ready to negotiate.

This is the King's intention. What is in his heart is something else again. I cannot read him, I cannot be sure. Perhaps he sees a need to bend, perhaps he may believe in change. And then again, King Henry's charter went unheeded for a hundred years; perhaps he thinks the new one will mean no more than the old.

Till next time, if God wills it.

At the Palace of Westminster
The 16th Day of April, A.D. 1215

Good faith, we meant to sit and reason in good faith and we were on the point of leaving for Northampton when a messenger arrived to tell us this: FitzWalter and his people have made camp outside Northampton Castle with an army.

Nothing less, no token force this time. Two thousand knights. Which means, if we assume the normal complement of men-at-arms and archers and the rest, that they have brought ten thousand soldiers to the conference table. Ten: we had no more than that in France at Roche-aux-Moines.

There is no way to reason with these people. Yet the King insists we try. "They want a war," he said, "and they will start one if they can. I understand FitzWalter. I can read his mind, what there is of it. I will not strike first. I have the right on my side and the Pope. If they attack, God help them, for they will destroy themselves."

There was no shaking him in this. He may be right, for all I know. In any case, I leave tomorrow for Northampton with the Marshal and des Roches. We will present the King's position. What will happen if they spit on us again?

Till next time, if God wills it.

At Northampton Castle
The 20th Day of April, A.D. 1215

We reached here late this afternoon. The castle is in loyal hands and we are in no danger. So, at least, the Marshal tells me.

We were standing, when he said so, on the top of the keep. Below us, out beyond the castle walls, were tents and men and kitchen fires, horses, fodder, stacks of arms. The noise welled up around us and I felt afraid. Not for myself; I did not doubt the Marshal, we would leave as we had come, untouched. But what is worse than civil war?

I'd seen enough. I touched the Marshal's arm, he nodded. It was then, as we were turning, that we saw Lord Stephen moving through the troops below. The man is here of course; for they are his terms, too, that we are answering. How could he be a party to this thing? How could he lead these people?

I shall be with him later. What am I to say?

Till next time, if God wills it.

At Northampton Castle
The 21st Day of April, A.D. 1215

We sat on our side of the table waiting, listening to the noises rising from the camp outside the walls. The room was cool and dim. There were no scribes.

Time passed, how much I cannot say, and then Lord Stephen entered briskly, papers in his hands. He nodded, sat, and started glancing through them, bending close to see the words. His face was gray, he looked as if he'd had no sleep.

At last they came, FitzWalter and de Vescy. Side by side, they all but marched across the room. They sat, the Marshal nodded to them gravely and began.

We had, he told them, come to reach a settlement, to find some area where all of us were comfortable. We had proposals to that end and, if it please them, we had copies they might read. He turned to me.

"Giraldus?"

"Yes, my lord." I had the papers, naturally, and I was reaching for them when FitzWalter spoke.

"Read this," he said and tossed a piece of parchment on the table. On it, he had scrawled a list of new demands. I read them, stunned. They were absurd, unmeetable; the King might just as well give up his crown.

The Marshal looked up calmly, as if nothing had occurred. "All right, if you prefer, we'll start with yours."

FitzWalter shook his head. "There's nothing to discuss. The King will sign them as they stand."

The Marshal cleared his throat. "Is that an ultimatum? When I tell the King, he'll want to know."

"He signs them or we force him to. It's in his hands."

The Marshal stood. His voice was filled with scorn. "That's all," he said. "You're free to go."

"Not yet." Lord Stephen's voice soared up. "By Christ, not yet!" He stood, his chair fell back. He started toward FitzWalter, swept with rage. If he had worn a knife, he might have used it. What he said was shattering. He brought the curse of God down on Fitz-Walter's head. He seized the piece of parchment from the table and he called it blasphemous. He told him there would be a char-ter, something to be proud of, not a weapon to destroy the King.

FitzWalter laughed.

Lord Stephen wiped the spittle from his lips and in a voice I will remember till the day I die, he damned FitzWalter's soul to Hell.

So ended our Northampton talks.
Till next time, if God wills it.

It has happened. As it had to, as we knew it would. Three days ago, FitzWalter and his lords renounced their fealty to the King and moved to take Northampton Castle. It is treason. Worse than that, it brings us to the brink of civil war.

The King, I think, will fight if need be; but not now. He wants the barons of the center on his side and he will move against FitzWalter when he has them, not before. The neutrals are the key, as they have been from the beginning.

At the same time, we must not seem weak or passive. Thus, the King has sent off troops in all directions. They are merely on parade, a show of force. For every baron in FitzWalter's camp has castles. They are scattered, like so many pox, across the country and they need to be reminded of the might the King commands. And so the Marshal and his men are marching to the western counties, Longsword and his troops are moving east and Hugh de Burgh will prowl about the north. Our mercenaries, all this time in Ireland, have been summoned; they will be among us soon.

As for Lord Stephen, he is visiting the neutral barons, so we're told. He understands their power, just as John does. They can bring his charter into being if they choose to. If they rally to him, he becomes a third force in the situation.

John has moved against Lord Stephen most adroitly, so I think. Some days ago he asked to see my notes about the charter. He examined them, he chose the single clause most basic to Lord Stephen's case and he has put it in a writ. It reads: "Know that we have granted to our barons who are against us that we shall not take them or their men, nor go against them by force or by arms except by the law of our realm or by the judgment of their peers in court."

[274]

A copy is to go to every baron in the Kingdom. What it does is cut the ground away from underneath Lord Stephen. At the same time, it should bring the neutral barons closer to us. It's a daring move; and dangerous. John will not find it easy to rescind.

Till next time, if God wills it.

At the Tower, London
The 12th Day of May, A.D. 1215

The rebels cannot last long at this rate. They have already stumbled on Northampton Castle. FitzWalter, who has given himself the hilarious title of "Marshal of the Army of God and the Holy Church," has raised his siege and backed away.

Our basic plan remains unchanged: to isolate the rebels, cut them off from all support, and then, if need be, strike them. We are leaving in the morning for the northeast, going first to Cambridgeshire.

Peace, I think, is near at hand. The rebels have nowhere to turn and we shall have them on their knees without a single battle fought before the month is out. A bloodless victory, God willing.

T.n.t.

At Wisbech
The 16th Day of May, A.D. 1215

Each day, John makes some new decision tightening the ring. Invoking ancient laws, he issues orders that the rebels' land be seized, that their estates be confiscated; he appoints new sheriffs, in particular for Devon, where unrest has been reported.

Late today, he placed his brother in command of London. We were sitting in a meadow when a messenger arrived. The rebels had, he told us, broken camp outside Northampton and were marching south.

We went at once to write the order. Longsword is to move his troops to London instantly. I wondered at the urgency. FitzWalter failed to take Northampton; how in God's name could he take our greatest city? When I asked, the King looked up.

"You see, Giraldus, there's a risk to what we've done." He paused. "The Marshal's in the west, de Burgh is north, Longsword is east and we are here. Who does that leave in London?"

"Oh," I said. "But why send Longsword? Why not go ourselves?"

"His men are half our distance from the city, they'll be there in half the time."

He signed the order. It has gone, a messenger went off with it at once and we returned to work.

Till next time, if God wills it.

At Ely
The 20th Day of May, A.D. 1215

They have taken London. Oh, my God. How could it happen? Our reports are senseless and confused. The King says nothing; he is silent, he is cold. We race at full speed toward the City.

T.n.t.

Near Westminster
The 22nd Day of May, A.D. 1215

We reached here after dark. The men in Longsword's camp sat silently around their fires. In the distance, faintly, we could see the light of London.

We found Longsword in his tent. He sat there on a stool beside a table. It was dim, a single candle, that was all. He stood when John strode in. The brothers looked at one another, saying nothing. Then John spoke. His voice was like a whip.

"What happened?"

"How much do you know?"

"They have my City; that I know. How was it done?"

"I came too late, your message came too late." He told us everything. FitzWalter reached here on the morning of the 17th. A Sunday. Half of London was asleep, the other half in church. The City walls, at many points, are in some disrepair. On top of which, FitzWalter's fortress, Baynard's Castle, sits inside the walls directly on the Thames. It was an open door. Once in the City, they were joined by mobs; three days of plunder and destruction. Homes were sacked, the houses of the City's Jews were battered to the ground, the rubble used to patch the outer walls. The Tower and the Palace of Westminster, both outside the City, were untouched, but neither fort had troops enough to make a move.

A silence then. The night was hot, the tent was airless. Longsword wiped his face. "That's all, I think."

John shook his head. "It can't be all." His face was taut, his eyes were red from dust and rage. "You said three days, the City was a mob for three days. Where were you? For Jesus' sake, why didn't you go in?"

"I wasn't sure."

"Of what? You're not alone here, you have men; and more men at the Tower. Christ, what were you waiting for?"

"Your orders."

"Orders?" John's whole body shook. "What orders? If your tent's on fire, do you need an order to move out? Almighty Christ."

"Don't swear at me."

"Don't swear? I'll hang you if I like."

Their fists were clenched, as if they meant to knock each other down. Then Longsword turned away. "I'm sorry, John. I haven't understood this war. I would have killed FitzWalter half a dozen times. In London, when he spat upon the table; at Northampton, at Saint Alban's, Oxford, I'd have cut him down. If I had my way, he'd be dead and we'd be in the City now." He paused, his head moved slowly back and forth. "How can I tell what's in your mind?

[277]

For all I know, you won't lay siege to London. Orders? Yes, I need your orders."

Another silence. Then John shrugged. "It's done," was all he said. I took a deep breath. It was over and we sat and talked for hours: what to do, what steps to take. Aside from summoning de Burgh, the Marshal and des Roches, the brothers came to no decisions. Just as well, I think. The pieces on the board have moved and we need time to ponder it.

Till etc.

At Maidenhead
The 30th Day of May, A.D. 1215

How strange these days have been; so filled and yet so inconclusive. We may not lay siege to London—or we may. The King continues to arrange his forces, moving them from Winchester and elsewhere closer to the city. He spends hours with his brother talking tactics. Taking London would require all our forces and the siege could last for months, thus leaving every rebel fort across the country free to act. Is this too great a risk? Or is it wiser if we take these forts in hope that London, like the last fruit on a dead tree, will simply drop into our hands?

FitzWalter has been busy, too. Not only does he fortify his walls, he sends out messages to all our barons urging them to join him in his fight for liberty and peace; and threatening them with war and death if they do not. As if he had the power to do anything but sit and wait.

Lord Stephen has been busiest of all, I think. According to reports, he was in London with FitzWalter yesterday; the day before in Canterbury with his bishops. He appears to see the fall of London as his chance to move the country to a charter.

Where is Giraldus in all this? Where do I stand? There is so much that's right and good which might be in a charter. What

Lord Stephen told me once is true: no man should be all-powerful. And yet, I feel so torn.

Till next time, if God wills it.

At Windsor Castle
The 31st Day of May, A.D. 1215

We are all together once again: the King, the Marshal, Longsword, Hugh de Burgh, des Roches. We spent the day around the council table, weighing possibilities.

The end result is this: we are divided. Longsword and des Roches are all for striking out in all directions; and at once. They would lay siege to London, at the same time moving out across the country. They can see no other course.

The King opposes this. The Marshal, too. They would attack if need be; but not yet. The barons of the center are still pivotal, they think, and there is nothing to be lost in talking to Lord Stephen, who, it seems, has many of them on his side.

John put it this way. "Let him come and talk his charter to me. Where's the harm? For all we know, what I've already offered is enough. And if it's not . . ." He shrugged and left it hanging there.

De Burgh said very little; he is junior here, he sits and listens. As for me, I think the King is right. The war can still be won without a battle, can it not?

In any case, a message to Lord Stephen has been sent.

Till next time, if God wills it.

At Windsor Castle
The 1st Day of June, A.D. 1215

It was twilight. Feeling restless, I had gone up to the parapets to prowl about. The air was pleasant, cool and clear. The village is

[279]

some distance off. I watched it for a while; peasants, tiny figures moving slowly from one hovel to another.

Then I saw them; riding from the south, a group of knights at gallop. Could it be Lord Stephen, here so soon? I hurried to the yard to greet whoever it might be.

"Giraldus?"

It was Isabelle, all dressed in leather like a boy, her hair pulled up beneath a cap. I bowed.

"My lady."

Breathless from the ride, she dropped down lightly to the ground. "How is the King?"

"He's well," I said.

She closed her eyes and breathed a sigh. "Thank God. The things I've heard at Corfe, the stories . . ."

I could easily imagine. She had been at Corfe for many weeks, we had not taken time to write her. "Come inside and rest," I said.

"Not yet." She took my hand. "I heard today that they have taken London. Is it possible?" I told her yes. "Oh God," she said, "what is the truth of things?"

I took her briefly through it all. Her hand grew tighter. "Oh," she said at one point; and then later, "Oh," again. I ended with the news that came today; that they have laid siege to the Tower now.

"That's everything?" she asked when I was done. I told her that it was and then we went to see the King.

We found him working at the desk in his solar. Longsword was with him. There were cries of welcome, kisses and embraces, questions, happy tears from Isabelle. I hovered near the doorway, sharing in their pleasure. Then the brandy came; I shared in that, as well.

When Vespers rang, I stood. We had a meeting with the Marshal, John and I. I glanced at him, he nodded, downed his brandy.

Isabelle seemed disappointed. "Must you go?"

"I have to talk about the charter with the Marshal."

"Why?" She frowned. "What's there to talk about?"

He smiled. "I won't be long."

"But I don't understand." Her frown was deeper. "You're not going to sign a charter, are you?"

"Possibly. It all depends."

"On what?"

"On what is in it, I should think." He turned to go.

Her voice was sharp. "I want to know. What are you giving to them?"

"Nothing yet."

"What would you give away? How much?" She stood up slowly. "It affects me; I'm Queen of something, after all. And I have sons. I left a boy of eight at Corfe: Henry the Third. He'll have to live with what you're doing; it affects him, too."

"I know that."

"Why sign anything? How can you even contemplate it? How?"

"Because I must."

"You must? Who tells the King he must? What would your father do now? Look at you. You're almost fifty. Henry died at fifty-six and it took all of you to kill him. That's what kings are, Henry was a king!"

"I've heard enough."

"He would have taken London back already. He'd have had it now. A charter? He'd have had the country on its knees, he'd—"

"Stop it!" He was livid. "I am John," he snapped. "I am not Henry, Eleanor or Richard. What they did I cannot do." He started toward her; two steps, three. They stood there, face to face. His voice was low, he all but hissed the words out. "If you can't support me, I don't want you here. Go home."

He turned and left the room. I followed. At the door, I paused for one last look. The Queen had turned away, her face was covered by her hands. Longsword stood near her. He looked up at me, but there were shadows and I could not see his eyes.

Till next time, if God wills it.

Lord Stephen wore his full regalia. John wore gray; no rings or chains or medals to betray his rank. The room was small and bare: two stools, a table. Sun came through a single window, lighting up a corner of the room where no one stood.

Lord Stephen stopped inside the door. They looked at one another for a long time. Then they bowed.

"My lord."

"My lord."

They seemed so calm and cold. The King, I knew, was not. I had been with him through the night, I'd followed him through every tortured turn of thought and even now I was not sure what he proposed to do.

Lord Stephen crossed the room. Each sat down on his stool. Each put his papers on the table. Somewhere in the dimness was a mouse, I heard it scratch across the floor.

Lord Stephen coughed. "You sent for me."

"I did." John pursed his lips. "We have to talk about a charter."

"More than talk," Lord Stephen said. "We have to act."

"What would you say . . ." John paused. "What would you say if I agreed?"

"Agreed to what, Your Majesty?"

"To sign a charter of some kind."

Lord Stephen blinked. "I'd have to ask what your intentions were."

"I can't see that they matter."

"But they do. What is a charter but a piece of paper? All our laws are paper, without force or meaning in themselves. It is in the observance of them, the enforcement of their terms that they have life. In short, my lord, it's the intention of the men who sign which—"

"Is my word at issue here?"

Lord Stephen glanced away. "If I said anything that might imply a lack of candor on your part—"

"Oh, spare me," John broke in. "You sit down with FitzWalter every day, the man's a butcher and damned well you know it; you can talk the law with him and come to me and question my intentions? Christ. Your rebels want a war—"

"They're not my rebels."

"No? You use them and that makes them yours. They want to kill me, it's no secret, and you use these people. You'd use anything, you have no principles at all. Your own pope orders you to excommunicate them. Here: I have his order here." He took a paper from the table, held it up. "His Holiness commands you: go and do it."

"No." Lord Stephen's voice rang clear. "The Pope is wrong."

John grinned at him. "You are as arrogant as you are pompous. You are bloated from your pride. But what you stink of is mendacity. You reek of it. Your only interest in the charter is the power of the Church. There's nothing wrong in loving power; Innocent has sold his soul to get it, but he makes no secret of it and you do."

Lord Stephen's face was very white. "I came to reason with you."

"Reason?" Was the sound John made a laugh? "Are you the only man in England with a mind? You float above the rest of us. I tell you, sir, the earls of England may be nothing more than brutes with property; they may not, for the most part, read or write; they may lead lives in which ideas or principles do not exist. But they are not pretending. They do not put mitres on with one hand while the other hand goes gouging for—"

"No more!" Lord Stephen stood. "I trust you're done."

"Not yet. We haven't settled what you came for. Or has that escaped you? Aren't you interested in my position? Don't you want a charter?"

Silence for a moment, while Lord Stephen seemed to choke. "Go on," he said then. "Tell me. What is your position?"

John got slowly to his feet. His words were simple and his voice was clear. "I want a charter drawn as soon as possible. I will direct my people to sit down with you and with FitzWalter. What emerges from these talks, I'll sign. It may be just a piece of paper;

it may not." He paused. "That's all, sir. I have nothing more to say to you."

He left without another word.

We shall meet at Staines tomorrow. It's a poor place, but convenient.

Till next time, if God wills it.

At Staines
The 7th Day of June, A.D. 1215

There are twenty, sometimes thirty of us, round the table. People mill about, they come and go, they leave to eat or line up for the garde-robe pits, of which there are too few and, losing patience, piss against the walls. There is much shouting, voices roar in argument, the clerks whose task it is to take down what is said can often make no sense of it at all, and at the day's end we are left with nonsense on the page.

We are divided into three. FitzWalter and his rebels, they are one camp. Lord Stephen and his bishops—London, Lincoln, Worcester, Bath and many more—they are another. And the King's men, those of us who speak for John, we are the third.

Each day, the schism widens, pulling us apart. There are, of course, some things on which it's easy to agree. Provisions regulating fishing weirs and river traffic; articles that limit or eliminate most debts to Jews; such things. The Forest Laws, involving as they do the King's prerogative to seize and keep whatever land he chooses without payment to the prior owner, are too vast and too complex to deal with now. They will be dealt with at some other conference in the future.

This leaves us with such matters as the tax laws, the inheritance abuses, tenant rights if any, courts and trials. Plus, I have to add, a concept which Lord Stephen tried repeatedly to put into the language of our clauses: namely, the extension of all rights and privileges to "free men." Mention any of these things and there is instant chaos at the table. In particular, between Lord Stephen and

FitzWalter. To the point that nothing save the Marshal's strength has kept us here.

And still and yet and even so, the little list of things on which we are agreed grows longer. What will come of it? I put that question, not an hour ago, to Pandulf, who arrived here yesterday. The man is papal legate now, a post of great importance which was given to him God knows why; he is the first to say so.

We were sitting underneath an elm tree with our wine. The sun was nearly down. Pandulf had been drinking since midday, which, he maintains, does nothing but increase his brilliance. Thus it was that when I asked him what would come of it, he had an instant answer.

"Nothing. It's a nugatory exercise."

I peered at him. "You sound so sure."

"The King is vassal to the Pope. It doesn't matter what John signs, the Pope will tear it up."

"How do you know?"

"He told me so."

I frowned. "I don't believe it."

Pandulf grinned. "I know; his word has never been his bond, but one thing he has never failed to do is serve his own self-interest. His authority depends on John's. Each power yielded by the King diminishes the Pope. Believe me, he will tear your charter into shreds."

I wonder if it's true. I wonder if John knows it. Or Lord Stephen. There are many things I wonder.

T.n.t.

At Staines
The 10th Day of June, A.D. 1215

The canon's house sits by the roadside at some distance from the church. It is a small place, made of stone. At noon today, the Marshal met there with the King. For, late last night, we had

[285]

achieved a piece of paper which, for lack of something better, has been called "The Articles of the Barons."

It was now the King's turn: to approve what we had done, or not. The Articles lay on a table in a little room. I stood there as the Marshal took John through them, point by point.

Beginning with the clauses on inheritance and property. I don't myself much care about the taxes our nobility must pay but they do, and the changes they demand about such matters as death taxes, wards and wardship, guardians, the rights of widows to re-marry and the settling of debts are, on the one hand, only fair, and on the other, crippling to the King.

Yet he said nothing, not a word. The day was hot, the room was close; no air at all. The Marshal wiped his forehead, turned the page.

The next were easy clauses. Easy in that they do nothing but affirm rights no one challenges: the privileges of cities, merchants, foreign tradesmen. Or, as with the Articles on our judicial system, easy in that they are largely confirmations of the way things are already done. Except for those restricting John's ability to levy fines. He is much given to the laying of colossal fines for slight offenses when his enemies commit them. His reaction was a rueful smile but nothing more. The Marshal nodded and went on.

The clauses on the bailiffs and the sheriffs he was quick to under-stand, for there is much abuse here. It is common for these men, so far removed from London or the government wherever it may be, to break the very laws they should uphold, thereby amassing fortunes for themselves.

The Forest Laws are barely touched on in the Articles. They are, as I have noted, far too difficult and sensitive. The King must disafforest only those lands he has taken. All the rest, the territories confiscated in the past by Henry and by Richard, will be dealt with in some other charter at some other time.

"When we are calmer and at peace," the Marshal said.

John nodded. "Yes. Go on."

The Marshal bent and squinted at the page. The writing, at some points, is far from clear and many of the Articles are merely notes: make weights and measures standard, or no scutage but by common counsel, or no hostages.

"No hostages?" John said.

"You must release the ones you hold, nor may you take them in the future. You must send all foreign mercenaries home, and you may not arrest or exile any baron save by judgment of his peers."

"I gave them that a month ago. What else?"

The Marshal glanced at me. The final clause was coming now. We'd fought against it bitterly and lost. The Marshal pursed his lips. "How can I put this?"

"Bluntly" was the King's reply.

"They want security; some way of making sure the Articles will be enforced."

John grinned. "And how do they propose to make me keep my word?"

"They want a council. All sides are to choose a group of barons, twenty-five of them, to sit in judgment over you."

"Above the King? For Jesus' sake—" He stopped and slowly shook his head. "They think to limit one king by creating twenty-five?" He chuckled. "Can you hear the meetings? Let them try, God help them. Is that all?"

"There are some things we're still debating."

"Anything about the Church?" The Marshal shook his head. "That's odd. Why not?"

"FitzWalter will not stand for it."

"That's hardly fair. Lord Stephen should have something for his time. What does he ask for?"

"Many things."

"Such as?"

"The Articles refer to barons only. He would like to add the words 'free men.'"

"'Free men'?" John frowned. "How many free men have we? One of every four? And most of them are knight or nobles, anyway. You see much harm in it?" The Marshal shrugged. John paused. "Then put it in . . . and tell Lord Stephen it is there because I say so. Let him know I gave the thing he could not get."

The Marshal smiled. "My pleasure."

"One thing more." John straightened. "These are not the Barons' Articles: they're mine. I sign them, they exist because of me and we will damned well call them something else."

So saying, he approved the text in principle. It goes back to the conference table now, to be completed and refined.

We left the canon's house then, and rode back to Windsor with the King. It was a quiet ride.

Till next time, if God wills it.

At Staines
The 14th Day of June, A.D. 1215

The sun has risen; there is daylight now, and for the first time since we came you cannot hear a single argument at Staines. No shouting. What we have instead is grumble. No one here is altogether pleased. Lord Stephen has his Article about the Church which he insisted, with his customary modesty, be written first, ahead of all the rest. The words "free men" appear, like specks of pepper, scattered through the text to the delight of no one save, of course, Lord Stephen. Many clauses have been added since we read them to the King; the Chancery clerks are bickering about the language even now.

As for the scribes, they sit around their tables working frantically. They rub their parchment smooth with goat's teeth so the ink won't run. They write in haste, they make mistakes which they must cut away with knives and then rub smooth again. I fear that we shall have no proper documents for anyone to sign tomorrow.

Pandulf finds this fact amusing. As for me, I feel the strangest melancholy. Weariness, that's all it is. I've had no sleep, I must lie down.

My sleep was restless, full of dreams. The Marshal woke me from it. It was late afternoon, he wanted company and we decided to go riding down the road to Runnymede.

The meadow is a broad and sloping one. The sun had nearly set and all around us was the glow of open kitchen fires. The cooks were busy. It's to be a festive day tomorrow. All our barons, every one of them, will swear their fealty to the King and we shall be at peace again.

The Marshal took great pride in that. As we walked slowly on the grass down to the Thames, he turned to me. "Whatever else we've done," he said, "a dreadful war has been avoided."

"Yes." I nodded, though my mind was wandering. We settled on the ground, the river just in front of us and, for some reason, I began to fret aloud. About the scribes, of all things. "What is happening to them?" I said. "They've changed the way they write, the very shape our letters have. All cramped and sharp, like old men's fingers, twisted up. They use new words, abbreviations, everything in short. I tell you, half the time I cannot read the documents they put before me. Why take all the grace away?"

The Marshal shrugged. "Don't all things change?"

"No. They do not. It isn't written anywhere, it's not a law. I've been to villages where nothing's changed for centuries. Most things never change: they way we plant, the tools we use, the things we make. A wagon: can you tell what century a wagon's from? A plainsong from the time of Gregory could have been written yesterday.

"Why, suddenly, today, must everything be different? Listen to the music now from Paris. Not one voice: two voices. Different notes at once. How can one hear it? Or our churches. Gothic: what a perfect name. It is barbaric, one would have to be a Goth to like it. Spikes and angles; cruel and mean, like knives. It cuts the eye to look at it. They are so proud of what they make, the builders. 'See our vaults and flying buttresses,' they say; as if they had invented something new and wondrous. I can show you churches in the north a century old with such things. We could do it then but we discarded it. We found it ugly."

I went on, I could not seem to stop myself. "The ugliness is everywhere. The way they carve our statues now. You want to show me how a man looks, send me out to walk the streets, they're full of them. What is a sculptor for but to create what is not there,

[289]

to make a new thing out of his imagining? You think the *Book of Kells* looks as it does because they could not paint a man? Oh God, it's all so ugly now. Don't tell me all things have to change."

"Some do." The Marshal paused and looked at me. "In any case, we have a Charter. It exists."

I picked a piece of clover up, I don't know why. "Will we be better for it, do you think? Or will our lives be merely different?"

"I don't know, Giraldus. There's some good in it for some of us. Take me. I've served John and his family all my life. Whatever they have asked of me, I've done. At one time or another, I have stolen, cheated, lied, deceived and killed men for their sake with my own hands. I'll spend my afterlife in Hell for it, no doubt. I don't repent, I'm not ashamed and yet I thank God for this Charter. For the King, you see, the King can never ask such things of me again."

I nodded and we lay back on the grass and watched the stars come out.

Till next time, if God wills it.

At Runnymede
The 15th Day of June, A.D. 1215

I arrived here with the Marshal shortly after dawn. The servants, hundreds of them, sped like ants in all directions through the mist. On every side, there were wagons piled high with trestle tables, benches, pennons, banners, folded tents. Others were filled with platters, goblets, food and tuns of wine. The sheep, whose home the meadow is, strolled calmly through it all.

An hour passed. The tents were up, the tables were in place, the retinues began to come. The rabble that our barons travel with streamed toward us down the road. Knights, squires, stewards, hangers-on; all dressed, as I was, in their fanciest. The mist had lifted, streaks of sunlight played across the field.

It was midmorning when the mighty started to arrive. Lord Stephen was among the first. We nodded gravely to each other. Half the higher clergy of the Kingdom milled around him. Servants scurried about with ale and wine.

The rebels came together, in a clump. FitzWalter and de Vescy and de Quenci and Bigod and Clare and other earls of lesser rank. Their tents stood well apart from all the rest. They marched to them, swords rattling. They alone came armed.

The royal party was the last. I moved across the field to join them. There they stood, the men that filled my life these last three years: the King, the Marshal, Longsword, Hugh de Burgh, des Roches, the Earl of Chester. What a time; and I had been part of it.

The King looked well and rested, at his ease. I moved with him among the throng, through servants, sheep and horses, barons, clergy. Smoke rose from the kitchen fires. John greeted everyone, now serious, now bright and friendly. Then, at last, the time arrived. John gave a signal, someone struck a drum and there was silence on the field.

The meadow rises slightly near a row of trees. Lord Stephen and his bishops stood upon this hillock and we took positions, three groups to the end: the rebels to Lord Stephen's left, the balance of us on his right.

There was, of course, no document to sign. It will, I should make note, be called the Charter of Liberties and copies will be ready later in the week. In any case, Lord Stephen spoke a somewhat lengthy prayer. When he was done, the King and all his barons knelt and swore before God to obey the Charter in good faith. Then John arose, stepped forward and demanded fealty from his barons. One by one, still on their knees, they swore.

I listened to their voices. It was not a sound I will forget: the earls of England vowing to be loyal to their King. We were at peace. A silence. Then a cheer. Then we descended from the hillock toward the food.

The royal table was the longest. At it stood our most important earls, both friend and foe. The King moved down one side and up the other, with a word and an embrace for each of them. And then, it was FitzWalter's turn.

John reached out to embrace him.

"No, my lord; not yet." FitzWalter shook his head. "You have not signed the Charter yet."

John stiffened. "I have sworn to."

"Even so, we will remain in London till you sign." With which he turned and strode away. Had I been King, I would have struck him down.

No matter. It is cooler now, the sun is low and almost everyone has left the meadow. Knights, a little group of them, no more than five or six, are sitting by the river singing soldier's songs. The tents are coming down, the kitchen fires are out, the wagons are half loaded and two servants want the table I am writing on.

Till next time, if God wills it.

At Windsor Castle
The 19th Day of June, A.D. 1215

The copies of the Charter came today. The King has put his sign and seal upon them. There was little ceremony.

Afterwards, we went to work at once. I must have twenty writs to send, each to a different rebel earl: FitzWalter, Clare, de Vescy, Hungtingdon. Each rights some wrong they claim the King has done, each remedies some grievance.

I, for one, am full of hope. It is a brave beginning.

T.n.t.

At Winchester
The 28th Day of June, A.D. 1215

Peace. We have, since Runnymede, had thirteen days of peace and look what they have brought.

The King, this figure of alleged wickedness and guile, what has he done? Not only did he sign the Charter, he insists upon upholding it. He has commanded all his men to cease hostilities, he has instructed that the Charter should be read in public places, he has ordered groups of knights in every shire to inquire into evil customs and abuse, he has restored much land and many castles, he has ordered all his mercenary troops to leave the country. All this he has done.

The rebels, what of them? The men whose movement brought the Charter into being have refused to put their arms down. They have yet to yield the City as they promised: they remain in London and its gates are barred to us. Nor have their castles all across the country opened up their doors. They act, in short, as if we were at war.

The King, aside from writing to the Pope, does nothing to protect himself from what may come. "My lord," I said to him tonight, "peace is like fornication; there is no way one can manage it alone."

He grinned. "As I well know," he said.

Till etc.

At Winchester
The 11th Day of July, A.D. 1215

Until today, the King continued granting one concession after another. More hostages had been released, all rebel property had been returned. He even went so far as to permit des Roches, whose loyalty has made him hated by the rebels, to resign.

Today, it stopped. Today, we learned that they control the Council of the Twenty-five. Those barons who, according to the Charter, sit above the King, have fourteen of FitzWalter's men among them. We have two. The balance, for what good they do, are moderates.

How this was done, we do not know. Nor does it matter much, I think. What matters is that even John must see now that the rebels have no wish to keep the peace. He is reluctant to admit it. He insists we meet with them once more, which we will do at Oxford in a week.

But in his heart, he knows what's coming. He sent Isabelle away today. He wants her safe at Corfe. I stood beside him in the castle yard and watched her go.

When she was gone, he turned to me. He has his gout again. I took his arm and we walked slowly to the keep.

Till next time, if God wills it.

At Oxford
The 17th Day of July, A.D. 1215

Everything is clear. It was from the beginning. From the moment John, this morning, made his entry through the Great Hall doors and not one single rebel baron stood; from then till now, tonight, we have been treated to a rare display of clarity.

We asked FitzWalter why had had not moved his troops from London. He replied that he would do so when the Charter terms were met.

"Which terms?" asked Hugh de Burgh, our new Justiciar.

FitzWalter smiled. "They're in the document, my lord. It calls for all free men to swear their fealty to the Twenty-five."

"I see."

"And further, it requires that all demands that lands and castles be restored are satisfied."

"And you will leave the City then?"

"At once."

He might as well have said he'd stay forever. There are endless claims for restitution, it would take a decade to decide them all. And as for swearing fealty to the Twenty-five, a good half of the free men never will; their loyalty is to the Crown and not to a committee.

And so it went. We took it quietly. Lord Stephen, who was present, spoke out frequently for moderation. There are many here who follow him and he may get it for a while. But not for long.

He came to us tonight to plead his case. He wants to compromise and would the King be willing to leave London in Fitz-Walter's hands till the Feast of the Assumption, the 15th day of August?

"Why?" John asked him. "Is there any hope for peace?"

Lord Stephen argued urgently, and in the end the King consented. "Let him stay."

"Thank God." Lord Stephen sighed in deep relief. "And thank you, too, my lord."

John watched him leave the room. "Poor fool," he said, and then we sat around the table and made plans for war. We will, of course, observe the bargain John just made; for we can make no moves till after Michaelmas in any case. Our plans need time. For in the morning, Pandulf, who is with us, leaves for Rome to bring new weapons from the Pope. And Longsword leaves for France to bring us weapons of another kind; a host of mercenaries.

The feelings of the King are mixed, I think. The Charter lived for thirty days, a brief existence. It is only paper now, and part of him is deeply sorry. It is not a part that we are apt to see again: not till the war is fought and won.

"They've driven me to this," he said. "My hands are clean." He held them out for us to see.

Till next time, if God wills it.

At Colchester
The 22nd Day of August, A.D. 1215

These are maddening days; for it is harvest time and nothing can be done until the crops are in. The war, once it begins, may last the winter and our armies have to eat. First plowshares, then the swords.

We have, today, a message from Lord Stephen. The Feast of the Assumption has come and gone, London is still in rebel hands and would we come to him to make one last attempt at compromise? The man has never understood the situation.

T.n.t.

At Dover
The 3rd Day of September, A.D. 1215

Pandulf has returned, and he was right about the Pope. The letter which he brought from Innocent is shattering in its intensity. The King has been betrayed by evil barons, feckless clergy, by the very Devil who infected those against him and, through force and fear, coerced him to—

But let me give it in the Pope's own words:

"... to enter into an agreement which was not only vile and base but unlawful and unjust. We will not overlook this shameless evil which dishonors the Apostolic See, diminishes the King's rights and disgraces the English nation, endangering a great prince who has taken the Crusader's Cross.

"Such evils would certainly thrive unless the agreement extorted from the prince, our well-beloved son in Christ, the illustrious King of England, were not revoked by our authority, even if he were prepared to stand by it. Accordingly, on behalf of Almighty God, the Father, Son and Holy Ghost, by the authority of the apostles Peter and Paul, and in our own name, with the guidance of our brothers, we utterly reject and condemn the Charter, forbidding, under pain of excommunication, the King to observe it or the barons and their associates to demand its observance.

"We annul and quash the Charter unequivocally, with all securities and undertakings stemming from it and declare it to be null and void of all validity forever."

I have never seen a missive like it.

It is with me now, in my possession. It was given to me by the King with these instructions:

"Go and read it to Lord Stephen."

Till next time, if God wills it.

At Canterbury
The 4th Day of September, A.D. 1215

He read it to himself, of course. His chambers here are glorious, his chair is something like a throne, and there he sat and read the letter twice, as if once weren't enough.

I watched him closely while he read. I'm so divided by this man. His mind puts mine to shame, it is so quick and pure; and at the same time, so afflicted by the sins of pride and arrogance. He sees one side to things: his side. I see them all. I felt John's pleasure in this letter and Lord Stephen's pain. And then, I thought, I am more arrogant than he.

In any case, he finished and looked up at me. "What have I done?" I waited, thinking that the question was rhetorical. "Giraldus, do you know?"

"It's not for me to say, my lord."

"It seemed so clear. The evils were so evident, the means were all at hand; I used them with such skill, I thought. I was so sure." He smiled. "What's to my credit? I have lost a charter, made a war and, in the process, I've destroyed myself. I'm ruined; which is not, I know, an issue of importance. Oh, my God . . ."

He stood and walked away from me across the room. The windows are magnificent. The sun, all blues and greens and reds, came streaming through an allegory down on him. I thought I understood what he had done; his crime, the reason for his punishment. He had become what he deplored so in the Pope: a man with longings to be king of temporal things. John's world is John's and he had lusted for it. He had turned his eyes from God. And then I thought of what he had so nearly given us, the beauties of his Charter, and I felt I might have done as he had done. Except, of course, I lacked his size.

Much later, over supper, he began to talk about resigning and becoming a Carthusian monk. I begged him not to, for his gifts are much too great, and wasting them would be the cruelest crime of all.

His bishops, some of whom are here, will in the morning issue writs suspending him from office.

[297]

"You must go to Rome," I said, "and plead your case."

"I know," he answered. Then he smiled. "Poor Innocent. His words mean nothing to FitzWalter. He can only punish me."

He held my hand a long time when we said good night.

Till next time, if God wills it.

At Dover
The 6th Day of October, A.D. 1215

The King is finally uncaged. We have been waiting for our mercenaries, and today we stood out on the jetty cheering as the first of them arrived. A troop of knights from Flanders; fifty of them. Not an army yet, but added to the troops we have, it means we are a force at last. We leave here in the morning to attack. We haven't far to go.

Rochester, as great as any castle in the kingdom, sits upon the Dover Road and bars our way to London. It belongs to Canterbury, to the Holy See, and it's a good thing for Lord Stephen that he's on his way to Rome.

The rebels have the castle. It was given to them by the castellan. Eight days ago, he simply opened up its gates. Not on Lord Stephen's orders, to be sure; but even so, the King, I think, would strangle his archbishop if he could.

My throat aches from the cheering. War is a disease and, God forgive me, I have caught it.

At Rochester
The 10th Day of October, A.D. 1215

The castle is so great. It sits on chalk cliffs high above the river Medway. I was there with John this afternoon.

We walked, well out of crossbow range, around its outer walls. To me they looked impregnable, like mountains. And above them soared the vast, square tower of the keep, the highest in all England. In the twilight we could make out soldiers at the top of it, along the parapet one hundred twenty feet above us, looking down.

What could we do with such a fort? We had no siege machines, to starve it out might take us half a year. It must, I knew, be taken; it controls the Dover Road, it is the one success the rebels have achieved and taking it is vital to our cause. But how?

The afternoon was growing chill. I looked at John. He has, in recent months, become quite gray. Not young, he's not a young man any more.

"John?" I have begun to call him that. "What can we do with it?"

He grinned and rubbed his hands together. "Come with me," he said.

Till next time, if God wills it.

At Canterbury
The 19th Day of October, A.D. 1215

At last, the first machine was ready. Every ironmonger, cooper, cartwright, wheelwright, carpenter in Canterbury has been put to work, and late today the first of five great trebuchets was done.

It is enormous, with a hurling arm of fifty feet or more in length. The towers that support the arm rise up five times my height at least, the platform upon which it stands is longer than the arm and wider than the road.

I stood beside it with the King as sixty soldiers strained to lift the platform to its wheels. When this was done, four horses were attached. Whips cracked. It moved, but only just, and John himself joined with the soldiers pushing from behind.

By sunset, we had got it to the City gates, through which it barely went.

Five such machines. Can any walls stand up to this?

Till next time, if God wills it.

At Rochester
The 1st Day of November, A.D. 1215

The taking of a fort involves two stages. First, the outer walls must fall. And after that, the castle-keep.

We breached the outer walls today, and Isabelle was there to witness. Longsword and the Marshal, too. We stood along the wood's edge, out of danger. John moved up and down the field, our stones flew at the wall, dust rising from each impact. Nothing, nothing, then a crack. The walls began to crumble and our men poured through. The rebels fell back to the keep, where they are safe until those walls come down. There were few dead, the thing was quickly over; once a wall is opened, it is like a wound.

The afternoon was true November, chilling to the bone. We hurried past the woods to where the abbey stands. An ancient place and lovely, it was founded by Saint Augustine and we are quartered there.

We went directly to the Great Hall, to the fire and the wine. We drank to John, to God, to England, to a host of things I can't recall. Food came and went, we talked, we sang, the Queen went off to bed, a while later Longsword left us. I stayed on, half listening to the Marshal and the King.

They talked about FitzWalter, who, except for rare forays outside the City walls, remains in London where he's safe. He has, it seems, sent envoys off to Paris asking Philip for support. Prince Louis, fancying himself the future King of England, I suppose, was all for coming here at once with arms and men. But Philip ruled against it. He believes that John will win; on top of which, he knows FitzWalter for the traitor that he is.

I may have dozed. In any case, there was the softest humming in my ears, and when my goblet fell I sensed that it was time for me to make my way to bed. I rose, I said good night and left the Hall.

I climbed the stairs and, resting for a moment at the top, I heard a sudden sound. I looked. A door had opened down the corridor ahead of me. I saw the Queen emerge. And then the man whose name I may not write. She stretched up, kissed him quickly, turned and hurried off. He watched her go, then stepping back into his chamber, closed the door.

The harlot. She had promised me. She lied. And what if I had been the King? Was she insane? I started down the hall. I meant to go to her. Instead, I stopped outside his door and knocked upon it.

Smiling; he was smiling at me. "Is that you, Giraldus?"

"Yes."

"Come in, come in. I'm glad for company." He stepped away, I moved into the room. "Some wine?"

I matched him, smile for smile. "Would I say no to that?"

He poured. I watched him closely as we sat and talked; at first, of what to do once Rochester had fallen.

"John," he said, "will take it quickly. He's extraordinary at these things, he's brilliant on the field. Uneven; that's his tragedy. But brilliant." It was true enough. I nodded. He went on. "In any case, the critical decision once we're finished here is do we go for London straight away or at the end?"

I frowned. "The end of what?"

"The country's full of Rochesters; there must be fifty castles armed against us. If the rebels were a spider, would you take the body first or chop the legs off one by one?"

It seemed insane. There I was talking tactics with this pure embodiment of treachery, this foul cuckolder of the King. And the pretense of it. As if he cared, as if he valued my opinion, he leaned forward on his stool and said, "Tell me, Giraldus, what would you do?"

"I?"

"What do you think?"

"I think—" My throat went dry and suddenly my hands were wet. I could not bear it any longer. Not another moment. No. I looked at him as hard as I knew how and said, "I do not think. I know."

He looked as if I'd puzzled him. "What do you know?"

"All. I know everything."

He seemed concerned for me. "Are you all right?"

[301]

"She told me. Isabelle confessed."

He sat back. "Oh. I see." His eyes seemed sad—or was it more pretense and not a sign of shame. His lips moved. "Well?" he said.

"That's all you have to say? You do this shameful thing and you say 'well?'"

"You want to hear contrition?"

"Yes."

"I haven't any."

"You're a devil, then."

"Why so? Because I love the Queen? You do yourself. You long for her, I've seen it in your eyes." I looked away. "And John; he'd fuck a dog if it wore skirts. Do you approve the way he treats her? Where was she to turn?"

"To me," I said.

"What kind of love could you give?"

"There is more than one kind."

"Not for Isabelle, and well you know it."

"But why you? Of all men in the world, why you?"

"Put John beside me. See us both. Which would you choose?"

"Almighty Christ, how can you ask?"

He smiled. "It's hard for you, I know; you love all three of us."

My eyes, it must have been the drink, filled up. "Oh God," I said, "what am I going to do?"

"What can you do?" he said and poured more wine. "Why did you come tonight? What did you want?"

I shook my head, I rocked it back and forth. I did not know. There was a silence. Then he spoke.

"How long ago did Isabelle confess?" he asked.

"A year, perhaps."

"You lived with it a year?" He sighed. "Why couldn't you have gone on living with it?"

I looked up. "She swore to me that it was over. Would you swear? Would you give me your oath?"

"I could," he said, "but it would be a false one. I can't stop." He took my hands, he held them both. "And Isabelle; we can't stop, either of us."

[302]

There was no pretense in him; none left. It was his soul that I was looking at. I took my hands away. I knew what I must do.

"I have to tell the King," I said. " I have no choice at all."

"You'll never tell him."

"Won't I? Why?" He seemed so sure.

"You can't, it isn't in you."

"What's not in me?"

"Cruelty. It would kill him."

He is right, of course. It would destroy the King. A word from me and it would be the end of everything. I must keep silent, must I not? I sit here feeling broken. Is there nothing I can do? I am a chronicler, I keep the record. I can put his name down.

Longsword.

There. Do I feel any better? Oh, my God . . .

Till next time.

At Rochester
The 25th Day of November, A.D. 1215

A decision has been made to sap the walls. In principal, it is a primitive maneuver. What one does is dig a tunnel underneath and then, when it is broad and deep enough, the walls collapse.

The doing of it is not easy. It is night work, sapping, for it must be secret. After dark, our sappers slip out on the field. The shaft which they are digging starts a long way from the keep, for if the enemy suspects, they dig a counter-tunnel and the fighting when the tunnels meet, I'm told, is barbarous. In any case, the tunnel, as it grows, must be propped up with timbers. These are set on fire when the time comes, bringing down the walls above.

Today, we sent for forty bacon pigs, the fattest kind. We will render them and use the grease to fire the timbers, for the tunnel will be ready soon.

I have been watching this with all my interest and attention, for there are so many things I cannot bear to think about.

Till next time, if God wills it.

[303]

At Rochester
The 30th Day of November, A.D. 1215

We fired the timbers shortly after dawn. There was a flash of flame, then smoke. Our men were hidden in the woods. We stood there watching, waiting. It seemed endless; nothing but a trail of smoke that twisted from the tunnel's mouth. In wondered if the fire had gone out too soon, and then it happened with a suddenness that made me gasp. As if the keep were made of sand licked by a wave, a corner of it fell. It simply fell away.

The fighting, while it lasted, was intense. By noon, they had surrendered and, according to the Marshal, there has never been a castle of this strength, this well defended, which was taken in so short a time.

The King was very brisk about it all. As is his custom, he made no reprisals. He is far too practical to kill the men he takes when he can ransom them instead. He saw to this, and then we left the field to finish polishing our strategy.

The main decisions have been made. We will not go for London now. Instead, we shall divide our forces and the King will lead an army north to take the rebel castles, one by one. I go with him, of course. The balance of our men will circle London, under Longsword, keeping watch and cutting off supplies. The Marshal will remain with Hugh de Burgh, for through all this, whatever happens, we must have a government that functions.

There has been no argument about the strategy. Besieging London is a tempting thing but far too dangerous. God knows how long FitzWalter might hold out, and in that time the rebels in the provinces might mass themselves and move against us or the French, for all we know, might come.

Only details remain: how many wagons, how much hay.

Till next . . .

At Rochester
The 6th Day of December, A.D. 1215

I have never liked farewells but these were terrible. The Queen, who cannot bring herself to look at me directly, kissed my cheek and quickly turned away. Longsword met my gaze, at least. I hope he dies in battle; I have never wished for Death to visit any man before, but I can see no other way. I wondered if he read it in my eyes. As for the Marshal, leaving him brought forth a different kind of pain. "God keep you well," he said when we embraced.

No matter. It is snowing lightly and our soldiers in the yard are touched with white. For sanctity and goodness, like Crusaders. They are mercenaries, nearly every one, from Flanders and the Aquitaine, and they could use a little goodness from the look of them.

I sit here in a corner of the Great Hall, dressed and ready in my furs. Not far from me, the Queen is, at this moment, in John's arms. She leaves here later in the day for Corfe, where all her children are. I have just heard her say, "I love you."

I have prayed for understanding. Will it never come?

Till next time, if God wills it.

At Nottingham
The 24th Day of December, A.D. 1215

God's birthday and the King's and we have spent it plotting war. He would not come with me to pray. "Another time," he said.

The map before him on the table made our situation very clear. It is as if a line existed running north to south straight through the heart of England. To the west of it, except for Wales, the land is loyal to us. All our enemies lie to the east. Their castles stretch from Scotland to the Channel Coast: York, Newark, Doncaster and Pontefract; Newcastle, Berwick, Durham, Warkworth, Scarborough, Lincoln, Sleaford, Hertford, Ipswich, Colchester. And more. So many more.

I had not, till that moment, truly seen the size of it. "Sweet Jesus, John," I said, "all that?" He looked at me as if he did not understand. "You mean we have to take them all?"

He nodded. "Every one."

He plans to start tomorrow. It will be a bitter Christmas.

He was forty-nine tonight.

Till next time, if God wills it.

At Hedingham
The 29th Day of March, A.D. 1216

Ninety days of English history gone forever. Lost. Some imbecile has lost my papers. Somewhere between Framlingham and here, the chest in which this precious data lay was dumped, misplaced, forgotten, left to molder in the rain.

I've been to see the wagoners and servants, every cretin through whose mindless hands it might have passed. The very people, I might add, who lost my furs at Berwick and my books at York. Good God, they'd lose the King if he were smaller.

All the rest, the balance of my chronicle, is with me; that I have. I placed it in a separate chest when we left Nottingham at Christmas. It will never leave my sight again. If this, too, had been lost—

I can't go on. I am berserk.

At Hedingham
The 30th Day of March, A.D. 1216

A week ago, we were in Suffolk taking Framlingham. Today we are in Essex with another castle at our feet. So many things go by so fast, so much of what we've done refuses to come back to me. Did we reach Berwick on the 14th day of January or the 17th? Did John fine York a thousand pounds or was it Lincoln? It is tempting to believe such things don't matter.

What does matter is the victory. It is vast; for there is nothing in the north or east which stands against us now. The winter was a string of triumphs, brilliant and horrific.

I have read about destruction on this scale but I had never hoped to see it; and particularly not in England. Castles razed, whole villages put to the torch, fields ravaged, theft and looting, needless slaughter. Savagery.

Who is to blame? In part the rebels, who, time and again, destroyed the land as they retreated, leaving ashes for the King. In part the villagers themselves, who, using war's confusion, brutalized and plundered their own kind. In part our mercenaries, who are vicious and degraded.

And in part the King, who uses such an army. He has done his best to keep his beasts in check; butchery is not his way. Then, too, he has made order out of chaos when he could: appointing new officials, issuing new city charters.

Even so, I cannot cleanse his hands for him. He could have sent this army home. He could have called them mad dogs, which they are, and shipped them back to France. He might have lost his Kingdom if he had. Is that excuse enough?

We seem to have some need to idolize our conquerors. Our Alexanders, Hannibals and Caesars are much loved. If we had seen their slaughters, had we heard the whimpering and smelled the blood, would they seem less heroic? I would like to think so, but I wonder. We find pleasure in destruction, do we not? There is a touch of Saturn in us all: we eat our children.

Till next time, if God wills it.

At Maldon
The 3rd Day of April, A.D. 1216

We are frequently completely out of contact with Westminster. Weeks will pass without a message from the Marshal or de Burgh, and then a cluster of them comes. We move so quickly and the messengers must find us, after all.

A number of them came today, informing us of many things, the chief of which was this: FitzWalter and his people have offered the crown of England to Prince Louis of France. In fact, the rumor is that they have actually proclaimed him King. They might as well proclaim the sun the moon for all the force it has.

It is, of course, an act of desperation, a reaction to the victories John has won. The rebels now have nothing left but London, they have spent the winter never venturing beyond its walls. A French invasion is their last and only hope.

Will Louis come? That is the question. Will he cross the Channel and attempt to take the crown they offer him? It's possible, and so we must prepare. Yet, at the same time, we negotiate. This evening John sent Pandulf off to Paris with conciliatory offers. We have had enough of war, God knows, and we would rather talk our way to peace.

We are so near to it. If Louis stays at home, if only that, Fitz-Walter will surrender and, God willing, we will ring the bells of Easter from Saint Paul's.

Till etc.

At Canterbury
The 28th Day of April, A.D. 1216

Easter week. The streets are filled with pilgrims, there are flowers everywhere and we are going to be invaded. France is coming. Louis has begun to raise an army. Pandulf brought the news this morning.

John seems torn. He is so weary of this war. And yet, a part of him is eager for it. Vengeance is the word. The man from whom he fled at Roche-aux-Moines is on his way here. There will be a different winner this time.

Orders have already gone off to the Cinque Ports. John, as ever, puts his faith in victory at sea. Our fleet will mass in Dover, we shall meet them on the Channel. We have sunk the French before. Damme will be nothing in comparison to this.

Till next time, if God wills it.

At Dover Castle
The 18th Day of May, A.D. 1216

Our fleet is here. There are too many ships to count, the harbor
cannot hold them all, and vessels, dozen upon dozen, lie strung out
along the shore. The arming of them and the loading has gone on
for days. It has been done.

They sail tomorrow for Calais, where Louis's fleet is massed. His
ships, we understand, are small and ours are great. The French did
not rebuild their forces after Damme. God willing, not a ship of
theirs will ever leave the Calais harbor.

All of us are gathered here; the King, the Queen, the Marshal,
Longsword, des Roches, Hugh de Burgh. The day today was somewhat bleak; low clouds, light rain and gusts of wind. I went with
John about the port. The seamen huddled round their fires, sparks
flew, John had a word for everyone.

And then tonight, as darkness came and we were at the supper
table, he stood up abruptly and announced that we must go with
him and pray. Not at Saint Mary's, near the castle: at the round
church on the Western Heights, where, almost to the day four
years ago, he had submitted to the Pope.

We must have made a strange procession. Wrapped against the
weather, torches in our hands, the seven of us left the castle,
crossed the yard, went slowly down the endless stairs, then through
the town already half asleep.

My torch blew out, I walked beside the Marshal, sharing his, and
we were chilled and breathless when we reached the Western
Heights. We moved on, bent against the wind. The church door,
as it had before, refused to open and it took the King and Longsword, pressing at it side by side, to move it back.

There were some candles and we lit them, after which we placed
our torches in the wall mounts. They were rusted. Longsword's
fell; we put it back.

I took my place before the altar, standing where Pandulf had
stood. They grouped around me and I looked out at those faces
that I knew so well. The torches were behind them and I could not
see their eyes. No need to, I suppose. I know their hearts, their
secrets, all their flaws and failings, which are great and many; true,

all true. I closed my eyes and bowed my head and thanked God for the opportunity that He had given me to move among them.

Then, aloud, I prayed for them and victory.

It is late now and the wind is rising. Let me sleep.

Till next time, if God wills it.

At Dover Castle
The 19th Day of May, A.D. 1216

God is good, is good, is good, is good, is good. I say it and I say it and it has no meaning. What has He brought down on us? Sweet Jesus, why this dreadful stroke?

The wind continued rising through the night. The castle seemed to shake from its intensity. I could not sleep. At dawn, I dressed. Where was the King? I found him on the lighthouse tower, braced against the air. Below us, everything was visible; the port, the harbor, all the coast. Our ships were being blown about like shavings, chips of wood. So many of them, beached for days in order to be loaded, were already splintered, shattered by the waves agains the shore. And in the harbor, where they lay so close together, they were grinding, tearing into one another. Some capsized. Crates, barrels, chests were bobbing madly on the water. Men were shouting, horses screamed.

John did not see me, not at first. He had no notion I was there; his eyes were on the holocaust. Then suddenly, he turned to me. His face was terrible.

"My lord—" I reached to comfort him.

He screamed at me, "God must have heard your prayers!" He struck me twice. I fell. I don't recall it hurting but I could not seem to move. And then I felt his arms as they came close around me, holding me. His lips moved, he was talking; incoherently, I think, but there was ringing in my ears and I cannot be certain. I do know that we stayed like this a long time and his tears, against my cheek, were cold.

We have some ships left, to be sure. But not enough to be of use.

At Dover Castle
The 22nd Day of May, A.D. 1216

Three days. We have done what we could, assembling men and arms to meet them on the beaches when they come. We did not know, till dawn today, when that would be.

A fishing boat has sighted them. Their fleet is well at sea still, heading for the Isle of Thanet. With the winds against them as they are, we have a half day till they land. That's if they land at Pegwell Bay by Ramsgate, as we think they will.

The confusion in the castle yard is near to chaos. We are packing weapons and supplies. Our men will march by midday and, with thirty miles or more to go, they may be on the road all night.

The King is leaving now with Longsword and the Marshal. I go, too, of course; and Isabelle. How pale she looks. So do we all, for none of us has slept well since the storm.

Till next.

At Ramsgate
The 22nd Day of May, A.D. 1216

Pegwell Bay is not, as natural harbors go, a great one. Modest is the word; a modest stretch of water, modest hills surrounding it. We rode up one of these, the five of us. The Channel, bit by bit, came into view. The sea was choppy and their vessels, most of them still well away, were wobbling through it toward the shelter of the bay. There must have been five hundred of them; fishing boats and river craft. No ships of war to speak of.

"Christ," John said as we rode toward the cliff's edge. "Christ, we could have sunk them all."

Below us in the bay, a dozen ships or more had beached and, for the first time since the Norman Conquest, England was invaded. Soldiers, little figures at this distance, scurried on the sand. It would be night before the last of them had come ashore.

We dismounted. There was nothing we could do but watch. Our forces would be here by dawn; we would have our revenge tomorrow. John began to talk of where to strike at them, how best the battle might be fought.

"We'll take them on the beach," he said.

"I wouldn't," Longsword murmured.

"No?" John's voice was bland. "You know a better way?"

"I'd put my men along the hills and fight them on the rise."

John shrugged and put it to the Marshal. "Which would you do?"

"Neither one," the Marshal said. "They have more men than we do. Ours are weary, theirs are fresh . . ." He paused. "And many of our mercenaries, don't forget, are French."

John's words came quickly. "You think they'd turn on me?"

"I think they might. If it were my decision, I'd withdraw. I'd wait till we were stronger."

Longsword's eyes flashed. "Old man's talk. Why listen to the Marshal? What makes him so wise?"

"Your father listened," Marshal answered.

"So he did. And Richard, too, and they're both dead and we're up here and those are Frenchmen on the beach." He turned to John. "I tell you, fight tomorrow. I'm a better soldier than the Marshal and you know it."

"Philip took you at Bovines." John paused. "Unless, of course, you meant to lose."

"You can't mean that."

John smiled. "Of course I don't. I treasure your advice. You are the better soldier, as you say." He stopped. I prayed that was the end of it but Longsword could not let it rest.

"If I were King," he said, "we'd be in London now, we'd have FitzWalter on a pike."

That tore it open. John's voice shook. "You had your chance at London. Christ, why didn't you go in? Don't tell me that my orders came too late. There were still riots in the streets, you could have taken him, you could have had FitzWalter. Why, for God's sake, didn't you?"

"You don't think I betrayed you?"

"Should I?"

Longsword shook his head. "You're half mad half the time. There's always someone in the woods betraying you."

"There often is."

"I've served you all my life. How dare you fling this in my face?"

"The day you came from Damme and everybody shouting 'Longsword, Longsword.' Don't tell me; I saw the way you looked. My brother."

"Only half. Christ, if I'd had the other half. I should have been the King. Not you. You lost us France, you made this war, it's you the barons hate." He paused, his breath came short. "They've offered me the Crown, you know."

"They have?" John laughed; it sounded like a dog's bark. "What of them?" He pointed toward the bay. "That's Louis's army. Who else is to have my Crown? How many of you are there? If there's madness in the family, you have it. You the King? A bastard on the throne? The son of Rosamund, the well-known whore, the bitch of Woodstock?"

"Father loved her." There were tears in Longsword's eyes. Of rage or grief or both, for all I know. "He loved her, he'd have married her except for Eleanor. I hated Eleanor; if I'd been old enough, I would have killed her."

"Stop it," Isabelle cried out. She stepped between them, eyes wide, face like chalk. She knew how this might end, and so did I. "For God's sake, stop it."

Longsword pushed her to the side and grinned at John. "I'm not a fool, I know what I can hope for. There's a chance you won't survive this war. Each time you take the field, you know the risk? You know how many men would like to shoot you in the back?"

"I do."

"It only takes one arrow, John, and then who's King? How old is little Henry? Nine? He'll need a regent, won't he; someone has to rule until he comes of age. Unless, like Arthur, he should have an accident. These things can happen, can't they?"

John seemed dazed, as if he had been struck. "You wouldn't. Christ, you wouldn't touch my son."

"Why wouldn't I?"

[313]

I heard the Queen gasp. "Oh, my God," she whispered. No one heard but me.

"Oh, William . . ." John could barely speak. His hand reached toward his brother. "And I loved you."

"No, you don't. You never did. You've never loved a living soul. Not Father, Richard, Eleanor, not even—" He broke off. My heart stopped. Was he going to say it? "No one, John; not even Isabelle."

"I do. She knows I do."

"She's here. Why don't you ask her?"

For a moment, John stood still. Then slowly, very slowly, he turned toward her. "Well?" was all he said.

She moved across the grass to where he stood. "I'll say it if you want me to." He nodded. "We have loved each other since the day we met; the day you walked into the garden. We have always been in love."

A cry came out of Longsword. "That's a lie!"

She looked at him. Her words were cold, like shards of ice. "You hate the King. You hate him so, you bastard, you'd do anything to hurt him."

"You love me."

She gasped. "God help you. You're insane."

My turn was coming then, I knew it. Longsword spun to me. "He knows, the monk knows, he won't lie." He started toward me. "Tell him, tell the King." His voice was ragged. "Tell him what we've done!"

I turned to John. "There's nothing. It is as the Queen said. There is nothing."

Had I done it well enough? Did John believe? He nodded. "Yes, I know the truth. I know my Queen." He took her hand and turned to Longsword. "See? I know. I know you, too, now, don't I?"

There was no mistaking what he meant. A silence came. I heard the wind whip through the grass, and noises from the beach below; French voices drifting up to us.

Then Longsword spoke. "One question, John. How long have I to live? A day? A week? When will it happen?"

"When?" John seemed to ponder it before he answered. "Why not now?"

They moved so quickly. There were daggers in their hands. They circled one another. Longsword towered over John, so much the stronger. I felt helpless, as if this were Fate and had to happen. There was nothing I could do but watch.

John's dagger flashed, then Longsword's. It was then the Marshal moved. He stepped between them.

"No," John growled. "Don't try to stop this."

"Stop you, either one?" The Marshal shook his head. "What for? I've served your family almost fifty years and that's enough. I've had enough of you Plantagenets. I haven't lived through all I have to stand and watch it end like this. May God have mercy on you both, for I have none."

He shook his head and started slowly off. The King and Longsword watched him for a moment. Neither moved. Then it was John who threw his dagger down. The brothers looked at one another, saying nothing. Longsword turned. Our horses were nearby. He mounted, never looking back, and rode away. The Marshal, who had not gone far, watched silently.

My knees felt weak. I heard the Queen sob as she ran to John. He put his arms around her and they kissed. I closed my eyes and thanked God it was over. It was then I heard the King say, "Christ, oh Christ . . . how could you do it to me?"

What was this? My eyes flew open. John was holding her, still holding, but his face was twisted, all askew. "Sweet Jesus, Isabelle, how could you?"

"Could I what?" Her eyes were huge. "What have I done?"

He shook his head from side to side. "Why William? Of all men, why him?"

"It never happened, John. I swear it. There was nothing. All he wanted was to hurt you. I have never known another man; nor wanted to. You heard Giraldus."

"Yes." John glanced at me. "I heard him."

"You believe him, don't you?"

"He's a fool; he loves me. Christ, why couldn't you have been a fool as well?"

[315]

He said the words with such despair, no hint of what was coming. Suddenly his hands moved toward her throat, he grasped her jerkin, ripped it, tore it from her. She was naked to the waist. He touched her breast, then struck her, hurled her to the ground. She lay there on her back. He threw himself upon her, straddling her and for an instant I thought, Jesus, no, he means to rape her.

"John!" I cried his name out. "John!" His hands were on her shoulders. Up they went and down. Her head, a loose thing, flew back on the grass. His voice seemed disembodied, not a part of him, as if it came from someone else.

"I'm going to put you in the tower, lady. That's where all the Queens go. Eleanor lived in the tower. Father put her there. He brought her out for holidays. I'll do as much for you. What tower would you like?" He started chuckling then. "Not Salisbury. It did for Mother, but not you. It's William's tower, he could come and have you every night." He started laughing. "Is he good? Is William good? How many times a night—"

The Marshal pulled him off of her, then helped her stand. She leaned against him, dazed. He took his cloak off, covered her, then carried her to where our horses stood. She held on somehow to the saddle till he mounted up behind. They moved off slowly down the slope.

I stayed there on the hilltop with the King. He either could not speak or did not choose to. Was he tired, would he like to rest? He nodded and I helped him settle on the grass. He lay there on his side and tucked his knees up.

I am writing in a little chamber in the abbot's house in Ramsgate. John lies on the bed, asleep. He will, I'm sure, feel better in the morning. For myself, I feel completely calm. Detached. As if the stool beneath me were not real. The hand that holds the pen that draws the ink across the page seems quite apart from me. I watch the marks it makes with mild interest; which way will it wriggle next?

Till next time, if God wills it.

At Ramsgate
The 23rd Day of May, A.D. 1216

The King is better, as I knew he would be. He has dressed himself
and speaks when spoken to. But as for leading an attack against
our enemies, he cannot possibly. Too much can turn upon the
outcome of a single battle; Hastings, for example, or Bovines. We
dare not risk it.

Thus, the Marshal has decided to withdraw.

Till next time, if God wills it.

At Minstead
The 28th Day of June, A.D. 1216

It is five weeks since the French invaded us, and not one day has
passed without some fresh defeat. Is there no end to it?

The King is not himself and from this rises our catastrophe. We
do the best we can, of course. We take the King from place to
place. Some days he will not leave his chamber. Other times he
does appear. He sits, holds audience; he listens but he cannot seem
to act. We issue orders in his name, write letters, put his seal on
documents. To no avail. We could not keep it secret, and too
many barons know they have no King.

And so the country runs to Louis, it embraces him. Our castles
do not fall: they kneel. John's friends, earl after earl, his lifelong
loyal friends have left us. All the south and east of England—
London, Sussex, Hampshire, Kent—all this is in French hands.

We are now on our way to Corfe. It is John's best and safest
place, his haven, and I thought it might restore him, being there
awhile. The Marshal fears that something terrible has happened to
his mind. It may be so. John seems beyond indifference, in despair
so deep and total that he has no wish to grasp at life at all.

Just yesterday, at Winchester, I went to him with something
which I felt he had to hear. The day was perfect, soft and cool; he

would have none of it. I found him in a corner of the council chamber, in the shadows, tucked up in a chair.

"My lord?" He looked at me, then looked away. "It's me, my lord."

"I know it's you."

The thing I had to say was this: Longsword had turned his back on us, betrayed us, joined the French. He stood with Louis now, dear God. And what is more, he has a public reason for his treachery, he gives it out to one and all. The King, he claims, has fornicated with his wife.

I stood there looking at the King and could not tell him, could not say the words. Instead, I said, "What would you like for supper, John?"

His answer came straight back, he knew exactly what he wanted. "Barley soup," he said.

Till next time, if God wills it.

Nota bene: The Queen, I should make note, is in the keep at Gloucester, under guard. No one may speak her name.

At Corfe
The 6th Day of July, A.D. 1216

The days are very much the same. He rises early, eats a little of his morning meal, retires to his chamber, sleeps awhile. He does not like to sleep at night. Then, toward the middle of the day, he rises and goes out.

He takes young Henry with him. They go walking in the woods or sit beneath the shade trees in the garden. John says nothing to the boy; nor does he take his hand nor look at him. I wonder, sometimes, if he even knows his son is there. Yet, he will not go out without him. It's bewildering for the boy, of course, and tedious; but he's a good boy and he goes along.

This afternoon, I saw them in the castle yard. The King was sitting on a piece of Purbeck marble. He was watching a stonemason as the fellow chiseled out a statue of some saint or other. Henry sat beside him on the ground, hands busy making little piles of marble chips.

It was so strange: I looked at John and scarcely knew him. He has grown so thin. His face, as if the mason had created it, was beautiful. Pure form, no flesh to hide the meaning of the bone. His hair and beard are white now, like the Marshal's.

The French have taken Winchester, and Windsor, I am told, is under siege. The Marshal writes from Chester: How is John? How do I answer him?

Till next time, if God wills it.

At Corfe
The 16th Day of July, A.D. 1216

This morning, I had brought the King some writs to sign. From time to time, his interest flickers and he asks what's on the page; not frequently, but now and then.

I handed him the pen, held out the ink. He was about to put his name down when he frowned and looked at me.

"Giraldus?"

"Yes, my lord?"

"What am I signing?"

It was to the Marshal, who was still in Chester with the Earl, and had to do with Longsword. I would have to tell him at some point. I did so now.

"My lord," I said, "it deals with Longsword and a meeting he has had with Louis."

John's frown deepened. "I don't understand."

"They are together now against you."

"What?" He sat back in his chair as if I'd struck him.

"He's gone over to the French. I'm sorry, John."

His voice was just a whisper. "When? When did it happen?"

"Weeks ago."

[319]

His head shook slowly, side to side. "You should have told me then, I should have known."

I looked away, I did not want to see his face. "I thought it best," I said.

"I know, I know . . ." I heard his chair move back. He stood and, with the pen still in his hand, he slowly left the room.

I did not see him, after that, till early evening. I was dozing in my chamber when the door flew open, banging back against the wall.

"Giraldus!"

He was in full voice and dressed for travel. "Yes, my lord?"

"We're off to Chester. Pack your things." And he was gone. Till next time, if God wills it.

At Chester
The 23rd Day of July, A.D. 1216

We reached here yesterday, late afternoon; through Eastgate, down the straight streets to the castle, just as we had done four years before when we had nothing but Llywelyn to contend with.

Chester the city looks the same. Chester the Earl is worn and gray; much changed. But it is only on the surface; for the man himself is hard and gruff as ever, and as loyal to his King. He met us in the castle yard, the Marshal at his side.

We went to work at once. There is a little chamber well up in the keep that looks out at the harbor, nothing in it but a table and some stools. We sat and listened to the Marshal's brief report about our situation. It is this: we have no money in our Treasury, no army left to speak of and the French have taken Norwich, Yarmouth, Ipswich, Colchester. His list went on and on, and at the end, as if it were an afterthought, he added that the King of Scotland had invaded from the north.

A silence followed. What was there to say? John looked up at the Marshal. Was he grinning? "Is that all?" he asked. The Marshal nodded. "Well . . ." John paused and cleared his throat.

"Well then, the first thing, as I see it, is to raise an army."

"Raise an army?" Chester sat there blinking. "How?"

"A little at a time," John answered. "Bit by bit."

And they will do it. They are all that's left of England, these three men. I felt so proud to be there. They intend to take the Kingdom back. It is impossible, of course, but I believe them. It will happen.

T.n.t.

At Leominster
The 15th Day of August, A.D. 1216

The King and I left Chester twenty days ago with nothing but a dozen knights as escort. We moved south along the edge of Wales. We stopped at hamlets, tiny villages; at Malpas, Whitchurch, Wem—at any place there was a castle or an abbey.

Time and time again, it was the same. The King would move among the people, talk to them, break bread and we would come away with men; not many and not all of them were soldiers, but they came. He offered nothing to them, no rewards; he warned them of the dangers they would face. No matter, nothing seemed to matter to them but their King.

And when we stopped at abbeys, we took treasure. Little chests of gold and jewels which John, throughout his life, had left behind him, hidden for safekeeping with the Church.

We grew. We stopped at larger towns, then cities: Shrewsbury, Hereford, Bristol. Men came flocking to their King. No mercenaries this time. These were Englishmen; fierce border knights and bowmen, townsfolk, farmers. There are thousands of us now, it is an army that we have.

I walked with John this evening through our camp, past wagons heavy with supplies and arms. He seemed inside himself, removed from me. At length we stopped, and turning back, looked at the field.

[321]

He shook his head and whispered, with a touch of wonder in his voice, "I did it, didn't I?"

We will reach Chester in a week. The Marshal and the Earl have been amassing arms and men. They should be waiting for us there. And then, together, we shall strike.

What John has done is not a miracle. It merely seems like one. Till next time, if God wills it.

At Chester
The 1st Day of September, A.D. 1216

Tonight, I sat around the table with the King, the Marshal and the Earl. There had been altogether too much wine, which may have prompted what I did. I turned to Chester, who was sitting next to me.

"My lord," I said, "I'm sorry."

"Why?" He paused to belch. "What for?"

"I took you for a bastard all these years and I was wrong. You are a prince."

He laughed, displaying all his teeth, and clapped me on the back.

My heart is pounding and I cannot sleep. The pieces are in place. All has been done that can be done. We march tomorrow. I feel like a boy of twenty.

God be with us.

T.n.t.

Near Macclesfield
The 6th Day of September, A.D. 1216

The news of our attack is spreading, we are flooded with reports. I cannot give them all nor separate the rumor from the fact, but cut it into half or quarter it and still it comes to this: events are shifting, tilting toward us.

No more do our castles fall. The French have hurled their best and they can hurl till Doomsday: we are holding. And as for Fitz-Walter and God's Army, they are of no use to Louis. They have yet to storm a single castle; they go plundering, they conquer villages.

As for the King—

He's calling for me, we are on the move again.

Till etc.

Near Leominster
The 12th Day of September, A.D. 1216

News reaches us from everywhere and all of it is good. De Vescy has been slain while fighting in the north. The French have fallen back from Dover, giving up their siege. And better still, earl after earl begs to return to us.

Some write to plead forgiveness, others come in person. John receives them all with open arms, he seems to bear no grudge. They kneel and vow their loyalty, he helps them rise and sends them off to battle. One among these was the Marshal's son, William the younger.

John takes everything in stride. He rides all day, then stays up half the night with letters, writs, decisions, plans. I help as best I can and then my head drops and I sleep, but he goes on.

Till next time, if God wills it.

At Windsor
The 18th Day of September, A.D. 1216

We have soared across the country like a flight of falcons, all the way to Windsor in six days. The French, who had been laying siege, threw down their arms and fled in front of us.

[323]

And there is more. Tonight I was at supper with the Marshal and the King before John's tent. A messenger came up to us, a captain, dank with sweat, still breathless from his ride. He served, he said, no less a man than William Longsword, Earl of Salisbury, and he handed John a letter. I have seen it, it is riddled with contrition, it implores John's mercy and it begs for his forgiveness.

John said nothing as he read it. When he finished, he was smiling. "Go and tell my brother this." His voice was low and soft. "Tell him my heart is filled with loving-kindness. I embrace him and it is in answer to my prayers that he comes back to me."

That was all. He said no more about it, then or later. But I know the King, I know what he intends. I said it to the Marshal as I left him by his tent.

"He'll use him now and kill him later, won't he? When the war is over."

"Wouldn't you?" the Marshal said.

Till next time, if God wills it.

Near Thetford
The 29th Day of September, A.D. 1216

The race goes on. From Windsor, we swooped north toward Cambridge, through the Gog Magog Hills, striking out in all directions, taking everything that stood before us.

Cambridge fell without a blow. The enemy, a mix of French and Scots and English rebels, staggered by the speed of our approach, broke camp and fled. The King pursues them, he will not relent. He is determined to destroy them utterly.

They are falling back toward Fenland and the Isle of Ely. When we catch them, when we finally engage them, they will get no mercy from us.

Till etc.

At Boston
The 3rd Day of October, A.D. 1216

They will not take a stand and fight, they keep retreating, scattering in front of us.

We have pursued them into Fenland now. It is a part of England I have never seen before. I find it strange; I do not like it here at all. The land is webbed with rivers flowing seaward toward the Wash. It is another world, a wilderness of swamps and marshes, paths known only to the local monks that lead to islands in the fens and secret places. There is higher ground, of course, on which grim villages and abbeys stand.

The people here live off the land; or off the marshes, I should say. On lampreys, eels, large water-wolves and pickerels, burbots and on water fowl. They tell me there are sturgeon, too, though I have yet to see one.

Our progress through the fens is slow. We stop while there is daylight, not because of John's exhaustion or his gout, which plagues him once again. He bounds about as ever in what has to be excruciating pain. I wonder, sometimes, if he even feels it.

No; we stop because we dare not move. Though we are inland, though the waters of the Wash are miles away, the tide slips in, the paths we follow dip and disappear, the evening mist rolls over us.

My sleep, when it does come, is poor. I close my eyes, and faces pass, like those that peer down from the corners of our churches. Gargoyles and grotesques, half-eaten men and things with bulging eyes. You cannot call it rest.

Till next time, if God wills it.

At Lynn
The 8th Day of October, A.D. 1216

The port of Lynn sits on the river Ouse, close to the Wash, that mighty tidal basin into which the North Sea pours its turbulence. The town is no more desolate than any we have seen, but I make note of it because, thank God, it is as far in Fenland as the King is going to go.

He told me over supper. Lampreys, which he loves and I do not. He got no pleasure from them, not tonight; he was too angry with himself. He was a fool, he said, for coming into Fenland to begin with. It was senseless, hunting for the rebels in the swamps while there were castles to be taken still and battles to be fought.

We leave here in the morning. I will sleep tonight, I think. Till next time, if God wills it.

At Lynn
The 10th Day of October, A.D. 1216

We go tomorrow, come what may. Our full train has caught up with us. The streets are lined with carts and wagons filled with food and arms, state documents and records, all the gold and jewels that constitute our Treasury, phylacteries and chapel relics, John's regalia and, of course, the books he never is without.

We would have left two days ago but for the fact that John and many of his officers are suffering from a sudden liquid of the bowel. I am exempt and, therefore, I suspect the lampreys which I did not eat. In any case, those stricken hover near the garde-robe pits, not knowing when the next attack will come, complaining of the cramp.

Except for John, who hovers but does not complain. His mood is foul, however; he is in such haste and he is angry with his body for the inconvenience.

It is late afternoon now, and the tide is surging in. Here, near the Wash, the water rises with such force that the lowlands disappear beneath it suddenly; it seems to take no time at all, and Lynn is like an island.

I cannot wait to leave this place.
Till next time, if God wills it.

Near Long Sutton
The 11th Day of October, A.D. 1216

The day dawned gray and stayed gray and the mist was late to rise. The King had passed a poor night; he was feverish, which, added to his gout, had drained him to the point that I suggested we delay. He would have none of it. We left Lynn early, making for the town of Wisbech, after which our route would take us north to Swineshead, where we meant to spend the night.

I must be very clear about these things for they explain what has occurred. These three towns, Lynn, Wisbech and Swineshead, form a triangle. Our path, though longer, is the quicker way for men on horse but not for carts and wagons, owing to the streams and marshes one must cross. Therefore, the balance of our force—foot soldiers, wagons, cattle—traveled the hypotenuse. This took them through the lowlands bordering the Wash.

Without the sun, it is impossible to be exact about the hour, but it was roughly midday when we stopped at Wisbech. John, like many of his officers, still could not eat. Instead, he paced and fretted back and forth; three days at Lynn for nothing, wasted, and his wagons moved so slowly. He decided he must urge them on.

We mounted, just the two of us, and started off. The way we chose was desolate. There was no path; the land is veined by rivulets and streams, some broadened and made deep by sluices which the peasants build. There was no way around these things; our horses had to swim. Then on through marshland, mud and sand that seemed to suck us down.

It took us longer than we'd thought, much longer. It was late afternoon before the land ahead of us began to rise. We pressed on harder, we were nearly there. Firm ground at last and we could gallop now. We reached the top, the highest hill.

I must be very clear again. Below us to the east, there lay the Wash. And to the south, the river Wellstream. We were on a point of land where we could see them both. The Wellstream's mouth, a full four miles across, is empty at low tide. There is a way across the sand. The monks here know it perfectly, and every day, I'm told, one sees them out there leading travelers across. They have long poles they use to prod the sand, for much of it is soft and treacherous.

Our train was out there now, dear God, where they should not have been. Our soldiers, wagons, treasure, everything. Midway across, an hour from the solid ground of either shore. Christ, how could they have ventured out? Without the sun, did they not know the time?

The tide, the tide was coming. We could see it, they could not. We cried in warning, shouting out, "The tide! The tide!" It comes in like a giant ram; it charges, head down, sweeping everything before it. We kept shouting, both of us, then we went plunging down the hillside, out onto the sand.

We waved, John stood up in his stirrups waving as we rushed across the riverbed. It made no sense to shout now, the sound was buried by the rising rumble of the sea. They heard it, too. They turned, we saw them turn. Then panic. Men began to run. Too late. The water reached us, churning, frothing white. We watched as horses reared, went plunging off in all directions, sinking to their chests in sand. Our wagons canted, tilted, tumbled, fell. Men screamed as they were swept away. A soldier floundered near me, close enough to touch; I could not hold his hand, I lost him. John's horse staggered, rose again. We made for shore.

How many men are dead? How much is lost to us? We have the night to live through first. I write this sitting on a hilltop, pocketed by mist. The fire near me does no good, the chill is in the bone. The King is standing next to me, arms folded, looking out at nothing. We are waiting for the dawn to come.

I am so cold.

At Swineshead
The 12th Day of October, A.D. 1216

The horses all were dead, of course. Lashed to their wagons, they could not escape and many of them lay half sunk beneath the sand. As for the men, we have no count; their bodies had been swept in all directions and we never found them all.

The wagons were more visible. They lay about, some half submerged, some on their sides, some capsized altogether. I went with the King as he inspected them. Their contents, for the most part, had been scattered by the flood. So many of the heavy chests in which all precious things were stored seemed to have disappeared. Beneath the mud or, possibly, in marshes far upstream. Not everything was lost, of course; we found some books, all ruined, and a scattering of clothes. A scarlet robe, in fact, and several furs.

What can I say? My heart broke. Everything was gone. Our records, all our documents and writs and scrolls; in short, the very government. And all the treasure we had with us: jewels and gold and silver goblets and the plate and flagons, basins, holy relics. And John's coronation robes and his great crown and golden wand. All this.

I sat down in the mud and wept. John settled next to me. "Not everything is lost," he said. "We have more jewels and gold than this; and holy relics, too."

I nodded. "Yes, my lord."

"We have your chronicle, as well. That's something, isn't it?"

I shrugged. It hasn't left my sight in months, not since those idiots had lost my ninety days. "It doesn't seem like much," I said.

"Perhaps not now; but later on, you'll see." He paused. And then: "Giraldus?"

"Yes?"

"You know these things. You tell me."

"If I can."

"What does God have in mind?"

I had no answer, then or now. I never will. In any case, we helped each other to our feet and went away.

The abbey here is very poor and I am quartered with the King. All evening long he lay in bed and talked of nothing but the need for pressing on, new battles, greater victories.

I told him, "Soon enough, my lord."

He sat up on the bed. "I have no time."

"You must feel better first."

"I'm better now," he snapped and then lay back. I rose and touched his forehead once again. It was extremely hot and very dry. I asked him if he cared for water.

"No," he said and turned his face away; some time after that, he fell asleep.

Till next time, if God wills it.

At Sleaford
The 14th Day of October, A.D. 1216

John rages or he shouts or glares, it is impossible to deal with him. We must have traveled thirty miles today at his insistence. It is lunatic. He burns with fever and his pain must be unspeakable. What is the need, I said to him this morning as I helped him dress. Why race to Newark? Why not rest? He cursed me.

Tonight, his body glistened as he lay in bed. He sweats now from his fever, it consumes him. I sat writing at a table near him. He sat up and hurled his blanket to the floor.

"The room is cold, my lord," I said.

"Must you write? Scratch, scratch, it's like a chicken yard. I cannot stand it."

"Yes, my lord." I put my pen down. "It can keep." I rose to get his blanket.

"Leave it where it is. What are you writing?"

"Nothing, Sire."

"Nothing?"

"Not that matters; it's a letter."

"Ah." It seemed to satisfy him for a moment. Then, "To whom?"

"To whom, my lord?"

"Is that too difficult a question for you? Too complex, for God's sake?"

"I was writing to the Marshal."

"Why? We've written him about the Wash. What else is there he needs to know?"

I shrugged. "He is a friend."

He looked at me with hot eyes. "I know you, you're telling him I'm dying. Well, I'm not." He lunged up from the bed and stood there naked. He has grown so thin. "Give me the letter." What was I to do? He took it. I had written that I feared for John, that he should come to us at once. John tore it up, then wavered on his feet. I helped him back to bed.

"Get me a barber-surgeon."

"Now, my lord?"

"No. Later, after Christmas, when I'm fifty."

I was back in minutes. John sat up and watched with interest as the fellow cut his vein. Then he lay back, eyes on the ceiling, as the blood came out.

I wrote the Marshal later, while he slept.

Till next time, if God wills it.

At Newark
The 16th Day of October, A.D. 1216

He could not sit his horse. He tried. God knows, he tried to. He clung on, he would not let us help him. Then, at midday when we stopped to rest, he could not mount again. We made a litter for him, saplings and a blanket, and we carried him the balance of the journey.

He seems to have no rage now. It is gone, burned out by all its fierceness, scourged away. And in its place there is such hopelessness. It goes beyond despair.

At least, the castle has some comforts. We are in a handsome chamber with a handsome bed. John lies there, utterly uncaring. Servants bring us food. He eats it if I put it in his mouth. There is a doctor, too; an abbot from the town of Croxden, which is noted for its fools. All doctors are, for all the good they do. He comes and then he goes.

John's mind is clear. He listens and he understands. It's only that he does not care.

The castle here belongs to Hugh of Lincoln, my old friend. I miss him; I could use a priest.

Till next time, if God wills it.

At Newark

The 17th Day of October, A.D. 1216

The King slept through the night and he was sleeping still this morning when I left his room to summon breakfast. I then settled on a stool outside his door to wait till it was brought. I closed my eyes and let my thoughts drift. Moments later, someone touched my shoulder. I looked up and saw the Marshal.

"Oh, thank God," I said.

"How is he?"

"Come and see."

The King was sitting up in bed. The change in him was something like a miracle. The night, whatever happened while he slept, had brought him back to us again. He ate, he smiled, he talked about the future, all the things that needed to be done. He asked about the conduct of the war. The Marshal told him; all the news was good.

He asked for his robe. We put it on him and helped him to the window. Down below, the waters of the Devon wandered across the sunlit valley, bright with autumn colors. He stood looking at it for a while. Then he said, "I had best write a will, you know."

I turned to him. "Today, my lord? But look at you."

He shrugged. "There's no harm done. Tomorrow, we can tear it up."

I brought my paper and my pen and what we wrote was this:

"Being overtaken by grievous sickness, and therefore incapable of making a detailed disposition of my goods, I commit the ordering and execution of my will to the fidelity and discretion of my faithful men whose names are given below, and without whose counsel, were they at hand, I would not, even in health, ordain anything. And I ratify and confirm whatsoever they shall faithfully ordain and determine concerning my goods, in making satisfaction to God and the Holy Church for the wrongs I have done them, in sending help to the Holy Land, in supporting my sons for the recovery and defense of their inheritance, rewarding those who have served us faithfully, and in distributing alms to the poor and to religious houses for the salvation of my soul."

There was more, a little, which we added later. He insisted. Such as where his body should be buried: at Saint Wulfstan's, Worcester. As to his executors, he named the Marshal, Chester and des Roches; and then, not knowing who might die before this war was ended, other men as well.

It wearied him, of course, and later on we helped him back to bed. He dozed and has been dozing ever since. From time to time, he wakes and speaks. He talks of many things: but not once has he said his brother's name. Nor does he mention Isabelle.

Till next time, if God wills it.

At Newark
The 18th Day of October, A.D. 1216

He is breathing, he is breathing. It is late. I sit here with the Marshal listening. In and out, we hear the air. My prayers are jumbled in my head, the words mean nothing to me any more. *Domine Deus, miserere nobis.*

He has had a peaceful day, a good day; beautiful, in fact. His mind was clear. He has no dread of death at all. He spoke to me of— I cannot; some other time. The room is bright now. I had asked that it be filled with torches and it is.

His face looks young, no lines at all; unmarked. And there is a translucence to the flesh of it; so clear that I can see his soul. I can. Dear God, I see the King. I love him. Please don't take him. Leave him with me, let him breathe.

He is still breathing.

At Newark
The 19th Day of October, A.D. 1216

Dead.

At Tewkesbury
The 23rd Day of October, A.D. 1216

I am a little overtired; nothing more. The fact that I have fallen once or twice has been exaggerated out of all proportion. Anyone can stumble. If the Marshal, who is in some pain himself these days, can weep or lose his train of thought and not be sent to bed, I am entitled to the same consideration.

We have buried John. Two days ago, or was it three? No matter. He is where he wished to be; at Worcester, by the altar, next to his beloved Saint Wulfstan. All the royal robes were lost and so we put him in a crimson cloak that was the Marshal's.

Tomorrow we shall be in Gloucester. All the barons loyal to us have been summoned. Isabelle will be there, too. What have I left to say to her? And young Prince Henry. We shall have a child to lead us now: a boy king. I have never seen a coronation. It is something to look forward to.

Till next time, if God wills it.

At Gloucester
The 28th Day of October, A.D. 1216

The boy is King. We had no crown to crown him with. We used, instead, a simple golden circlet of the Queen's which I have often seen her wear. It was des Roches who placed it on his head. The vows were sworn, the prayers were spoken. It was quickly over.

There was, of course, to be a feast. We left the church and, once outside, the King ran to his mother and he put his hand in hers. The Marshal stepped between them and he drew their hands apart. No words were said: he simply took the boy away from her.

I sat beside her at the feast. Captivity had left no marks on her that I could see. The changes are interior. She has no future here in England and she senses it; she knows. She will not get to be another Eleanor and rule the country through a son. Our barons do not like her much; and then, too, she is French. But more than that, the Marshal will not stand for it.

She sat there silent at the start, eyes down, hands in her lap. I was so sure I hated her; for she had killed my King, or so I thought. Not fever: it was Isabelle. And then, I could not help myself.

"My lady?"

"Yes?" She turned to me, I looked into those eyes.

"My lady, would you like to ask about him?"

"Would you tell me?"

And I did. I took her through the months since Pegwell Bay; the King's collapse, the days at Corfe, the glories of the last campaign, the nightmare that was Fenland and the end. She listened quietly till I was done. And then she asked her only question.

"Did he ever ask for me?"

I shook my head.

Her tears came later, when I took her to her room to say good night. She wept for John, I know; but in the main, I think the tears were for herself. In any case, I held her till she stopped.

Till next time, if God wills it.

At Gloucester
The 29th Day of October, A.D. 1216

The Marshal stood in the cathedral. He was taking on the burden of the state. Of England. Rector is the title they have given him; the barons here have put this on his back. At eighty-odd, he is to lead our armies on to triumph and to rule the Kingdom till the boy becomes a man.

He stood there like a Sherwood oak, ancient but indestructible. His voice, now fierce, now whispery, sent echoes through the church. Or were the echoes in my mind? I can't remember much of what he said, not well enough to put it down. Except for this:

"One King is taken from us and another given. I am nothing but the bridge between."

This the fourth king that the Marshal serves. They pass but he endures. Where does he find the strength? He is the greatest man I've ever known. I told him so tonight.

He smiled and shook his head. "It's age, Giraldus. I'm the oldest man alive, that's all it is."

Till next time, if God wills it.

At Gloucester
The 30th Day of October, A.D. 1216

Longsword arrived this afternoon, too late to see the ceremonies. He was well received; which ought to come as no surprise, since half the barons here went over to the French at some point. No one questions why he went; his story holds. For no one knows the truth, save the Marshal and the Queen and I, and we will never tell.

How Longsword lives with it, I do not know. He strides about, head up, back straight, all soldier. Were it not for him, we would have fought the French at Pegwell Bay and driven them into the sea. The King would be alive. I look at Longsword, God forgive me, and I wish him dead.

The Queen stays in her room. They have not seen each other yet. I must go down to supper. Will she be there?

T.n.t.

No, she was not. I watched him as we ate, his eyes continually darting toward the Great Hall doors. I knew what he would do. And so I waited through the evening, watching from a corner, listening to him talk about the war.

At last, when it was very late, he rose and left the Hall. I stayed a little longer, for I did not want to have him see me padding after him. When it was safe, I went.

I paused outside the doorway to the royal bedroom. They were free to have each other now, no King to stand between them.

[336]

Would I find them in each other's arms? As softly as I could, I opened up the door.

They stood there in the bedroom, well apart. The Queen was staring at him with a look beyond indifference, as if the man did not exist. I heard her say, "I never loved you." I believed her.

I have never felt such emptiness. There is some justice after all.

Till next time, if God wills it.

At Gloucester
The 31st Day of October, A.D. 1216

I found the Marshal packing. He is leaving soon, tomorrow or the next day, and I needed him to talk to. I have felt so lost of late.

He listened as I rambled on, all patience. He had better things to do, I knew, but it was hard for me to tell him what I'd come to say. That I was torn, uncertain what to do. My bargain with the King was done. That night at Corfe, four years ago, when I had asked how long I was to be his chronicler, his answer was, "Until the end, old man. Until you die, or I do." I was free to go. Not home to Lincoln yet, for it is still in rebel hands; but I could leave this war behind and do my work again.

At last, I got the words out. "What am I to do?" I asked.

He did not answer right away. And then, he said, "You miss the King?"

I nodded. "Very much."

He smiled. "It's easier for me. I've buried three, you've only buried one."

I looked at him. It was impossible to go. I could not leave this man. Then, too, I owe it to the King; it is his chronicle, I have to see it to the end.

He sat beside me and we talked for many hours then; but none of it can qualify as history.

Till next time, if God wills it.

At Windsor

The 24th Day of December, A.D 1216

It is a cold and quiet winter, there is little we can do until the frost and snows are gone.

I should make note that some five weeks ago, at Bristol, the Charter was reissued, this time in young Henry's name. There are some changes in it, the Committee of the Twenty-five is gone; and other things. This cuts the last ground from beneath the rebels' feet, I think, and spring will see the end of them.

It is a quiet Christmas Court this year. I seldom think about the past.

Till next time, if God wills it.

He would have been fifty today.

At Lincoln

The 21st Day of May, A.D. 1217

The Marshal has retaken Lincoln. Brilliantly, within a single afternoon. We have, in one encounter, captured half the rebel army. They are broken, utterly destroyed.

Last night, I sat beside the Marshal, celebrating. I have never heard such cheering. Peace; we are so near it now, so close.

I write this from my rooms. I'm home. I cannot bring myself to leave again. The last days of the war will have to do without me.

I must go and tell this to the Marshal. I shall miss him so. Till etc.

I've told him. He has promised to come back again and see me here. As for the rest of what we said, no matter . . .

At Lincoln
The 20th Day of September, A.D. 1217

I am not working very well. I cannot bring my mind to bear on my *Principia*. As for my chronicle, it sits inside a chest. I cannot, for some reason, look at it. At some point, I must open it and add another page.

We are at peace. A week ago, the document was signed. The Marshal signed it.

I have written him and told him come. Perhaps he will. I added, at the end, that Jean, my cook, is still alive and promises to do a pudding for him.

Till next time, if God wills it.

At Lincoln
The 27th Day of August, A.D. 1218

He writes me often but he cannot come. First it is one thing, then another. Now it is the Forest Laws, for they are drawing up another charter. It is called the Lesser one, his letter says, so that it will not be confused with the Great Charter, which is what they call the other now.

It seems remote to me. My thoughts turn more and more to John. I always meant to take my chronicle and turn it into something vast; a treatise on those times. Perhaps I will.

Till etc.

At Lincoln
The 27th Day of May, A.D. 1219

The day is ruined for me. Ruined. Damn the day to Hell. A letter from the Marshal came. The last one. There will never be another. It begins, "My dear Giraldus," and goes on to say he loves me.

He is dead. The words are at the bottom, different writing, I can't read the name, some son of his. He's dead, the Marshal's dead, they're all dead; Map and John and now the Marshal.

Christ.

At Lincoln

The 11th Day of April, A.D. 1220

I can begin, I think. Tomorrow or the next day, possibly; a little rest and I can start. For it is clear to me at last. The meaning of my years with John, the purpose of the pain, the form that lay within the chaos; I can see it all.

It has not been an easy time. There was much grief to purge, and rage and many veils to pull away. I am at peace now, I have come to terms. There is no moment left I fear to contemplate. The proper use of history truly is the elevation of mankind, and were John here, were he to ask as he once did, "What does God have in mind?" I could provide him with an answer now.

It is a thing to undertake, this piece of work. I cannot write the hours that I once could. My hand is less than steady, I admit it, and some days I look at what I wrote the day before and wonder what it is. My thoughts, like sheep, need shepherding; they have a tendency to stray.

But I will do it. It will be my monument. And his. Ah, my poor John. You came so close. I understand it all. If only you were here so I could tell you. You would find such comfort in it. And some peace as well, I think.

There is another point I wish to make. It is of great importance but I've lost it for the moment. I shall think of it, no doubt. But after dinner. Jean informs me we have fresh asparagus. I shan't be long. I have so much to do. Perhaps I ought to leave the candle burning. Thus, you see, when I return, I can resume where I

About the Author

JAMES GOLDMAN, whose prominence as an author began with his now famous drama and Oscar-winning screenplay *The Lion in Winter*, originally set out to be a musicologist. His postgraduate work was interrupted by military service, after which he turned his attention to the stage. His first play, *They Might Be Giants*, was directed in London by Joan Littlewood. His work as a librettist includes the award-winning *Follies* and *Evening Primrose* (both with Stephen Sondheim). Among his screenplays are *They Might Be Giants, Nicholas and Alexandra* and *Robin and Marian*. As a novelist, he has written *Waldorf* and *The Man from Greek and Roman*. Mr. Goldman lives in New York City.